No Other Time
Upon A Time
Book Three
By
Stella May

To my son George, my pride & joy, my true masterpiece.

CHAPTER ONE

T*ime was running out.*
     Abby wasn't sure why this thought was so troubling, or where the strong conviction of being on borrowed time came from. But that peculiar feeling filled her to the brim, and refused to dissipate. Time. She was intimately familiar with it, never feared it before. Never thought about it as anything but a kind force that brought her through the curtain of space to the only place where she belonged. The place where she found true happiness.

     A willing time-traveler, she jumped through the time portal last year with a reckless determination to follow her dream to become an artist.

     A mere girl of twenty, she arrived in the twenty-first century, confused, and a bit scared, but exhilarated. As her newly found freedom filled Abby to the brim, she plunged with an abandon into the midst of a modern society, so shockingly different from her own. She thrived in it. She had finally found her place, her time, and her family. Daisy, Alex, *Verochka*. They accepted her into the fold of the Morris family, and made her feel welcomed and cherished and loved. Except for Alex, that thorn in her behind. He made her feel confused. And bewildered. He made her yearn, and dream, and hope.

     Merde.

     Because of him, she stayed in California, and regretted it ever since.

     Time was running away.

Where did this thought come from? Why was it so disconcerting?

A ticking clock inside her head urged her to move, to do something.

But what?

Abby paced her bedroom, fully awake despite the late hour. She glanced at the clock on the nightstand. Almost morning.

God, why was she so restless? Her mind buzzed. Her nerves quivered.

Maybe if she snuggled under the covers? Maybe then that frightening urgency might go away.

The comfortable antique four poster bed beaconed with a promise of oblivion. She stretched out, rolled to her left, rolled to her right but her attempts to rest failed miserably. Sleep eluded her.

Abandoning all pretense of relaxation, she shoved the duvet aside, swung her legs to the carpet, and paced again while she brooded. Her decision to stay in California was a mistake, a folly Abby regretted enormously. Like a stubborn brat, she dug in her heels, and refused to see anything beyond her pique. Overwhelmed by her success, lost and indecisive, she turned to the only person she trusted more than herself: Alex. But instead of telling her what to do next, he stepped aside, and left her to her own devises.

That decision is yours, Princess.

To spite him, she grabbed the opportunity presented, and accepted the job in San Francisco. That'll teach him to perceive her like a little girl! She was a grown woman who made her own choices. Wasn't her audacious time jump the proof of that? The insufferable man! Who was he to treat Abigail Suzanne Coleman like a child?

Only he wasn't. At that time, her temper clouded her senses, but as soon as it cooled off, Abby realized her foolishness. Alex offered her freedom to decide for herself. He respected her enough to trust her own judgment.

Whatever you decide, I accept that, and always be there for you.

Too late. Why was she so blind? So stupid? So selfish? She acted like a little brat, and proved that she was indeed the infantile snob he accused her to be.

The Princess.

Oh, how she hated that blasted moniker! But she deserved it.

Alex was right. As always.

It grated on her, but truth was unyielding. And merciless.

She should have returned home with her family. She should have been there when Eli, that bossy brother she loved no matter what, and her best friend Daisy took their final leave to go back in time. She should have been stronger, and wiser, and more compassionate. But all of it was pointless now.

What can she accomplish by berating herself? Regrets were useless. One thing was clear as day: she must act. Now. Because time was running out.

Without hesitation, Abby stripped off her nightgown and snatched up the first thing she saw, blue shorts and a purple sweater. She grabbed her purse, then left the bedroom. The house was eerily silent. Star-kissed sky glimmered through the glass dome above. Her gaze skimmed over the Christmas tree with enough ornaments and lights to brighten a town square. It stood tall and majestic in the middle of the Great room. Only a few hours ago, the whole mansion was awash with lights, music, and laughter. The boisterous New Year's party was at full swing when Abby found herself close to tears. Silly as it was, she longed to be far away, in another place, with different people. With her family.

The mistake she made became even more apparent when everybody was exchanging their first New Year kisses. The only person she wished to kiss was half-a-country away. *Alex.* Bereft, Abby slinked behind the Christmas tree, away from the watchful eyes of her hosts. They were nice people, the Rostoffs, and treated her with kindness. But they were not family. The disturbing ticktock of the clock inside her head became incessant.

Time is running out.

In the semi-darkness of the quiet house, Abby crept down the marble staircase.

Everyone was fast asleep. Even the dogs. She let out a sigh of relief. Thank goodness the pair of huge Shepherds and tiny Maximilian, that peculiar Hairless Chinese Crested dog, was nowhere in sight. Otherwise, how to explain her sudden urge to leave in the middle of the night? She wasn't sure of the reason herself. But one thing she was certain of she must let the Rostoffs know of her decision, one way or another. She refused to sneak off like a thief.

Abby stopped, and rummaged through the stuff in her large purse. The sketchbook! Yes, that will work. With hands that shook, she grabbed her ever-present pencil and scribbled a few words. Then she teared the page from the book, placed it on the small antique table where they were sure to find it. As quiet as possible, Abby opened the oversized cedar doors, and stepped outside. Later she planned to call Kat and apologize properly, but right now she must hurry.

Time was running out.

CHAPTER TWO

Alex slammed the car door. Now what? Frustration that kept him up and running has ran its curse, replaced by brutal fear. Where was Abby? Where did she disappear to? And why so suddenly?

Last night, when he finally reached the Rostoff mansion, he was hit over the head with the shocking news that Abby had left.

The older Mrs. Rostoff, drawn and pale, showed him the note.

Sorry, but I must leave at once. Thank you for your hospitality and kindness.

Always yours,

Abigail

He was familiar with Abby's handwriting, so there was no doubt that the note was written by her. Alex's heart squeezed.

Dammit, she's run away.

But why? What prompted her to take such a drastic step?

Ushered inside, Alex found himself seated at the kitchen table, surrounded by bewildered and worried members of the Rostoff clan.

They all looked at him, like he was the answer to their prayers. Freaking out was not an option, but Alex was close. Very close. *Abby.* Alone. Somewhere. In the dark. God, was she scared? Hurt? Conjured out of fear, the pictures in his mind ran gamut from dread to terrifying horror. It was a nightmare. His hands shook. His heart ached. Alex gritted his teeth before he lost it.

Peter Rostoff was the only one who kept his cool during all this, making numerous phone calls. At last, he put his cell phone down and announced that there was no apparent reason for concern. Abby was not among the injured. Or worse. Thank God. So, that was the good news. The bad— she was nowhere to be found. Had she left under her own volition, or under duress? That was the million-dollar question. The head of the Rostoff's clan suggested a call to the police. After some deliberation, it was discarded. As Peter, the logical son, pointed out, they had no proof of foul play. Abby was of legal age, and she left a note. So, the unanimous decision was to wait.

Dammit all to hell and back.

His composure was frayed, his famous self-control all but shattered.

Holding onto his sanity by sheer stubbornness, Alex refused the offer to stay in Rostoff's mansion, and opted to head home. To lick his wounds in solitude, and wait. And hope beyond all hope that Abby was alive, and well, and will make contact soon.

Please, God, watch over her. Wherever she is.

At last, he was home. The flight and drive from the airport passed in a blur. Like an icy lining, a thick layer of dread coated his gut.

She was somewhere, alone, and vulnerable, and so out of her depth in this big tough world! His heart lurched, as the image of Abby, scared and helpless, floated though his mind. He was unable to do anything. Not a bloody thing.

Where are you, Abby? Why didn't you call me?

Alex swore, rubbed his head, then pressed both hands against his gritty eyes.

Please be safe, Princess. Please.

With fatigue weighing him down, Alex dragged his feet up the stairs. The door key was in his hand when the loud sound of laughter reached his ears.

What the hell?

Irritated, and in no mood for games, he scowled and cursed out loud. Damn that idiot JC, did he invite some chick over? This was not the time for socializing. But did his cousin care? Left to his own devises for just a couple of days, the pompous ass already managed to find some lady friend, and...

Alex froze.

Was it possible...?

With his heart lodged in his throat, he wrenched the door open. And here she was, in the middle of the kitchen, sitting at the table, and laughing with JC. Alex blinked, then saw red. He was unable to prevent the deep growl even if his life depended on it. The laughter died, as both heads turned in his direction. JC, the miserable skunk, recovered first.

"Well, well. Look who's wandered in."

The fool had the audacity to lift the mug in his hand in a mocking toast, and winked.

That does it.

Anger won out. Alex pounced, and hauled JC up from the chair.

"You goddamned imbecile, what do you think you're doing?"

Caught off guard, JC dropped his mug, sloshing its contents. He hissed, as the hot liquid splashed all over his shirt and pants.

"Why, having coffee with Abby, and—"

"I ought to pour that coffee over your head, you skunk!"

JC sputtered, trying to dislodge himself from Alex's grip.

"Hey, what the hell's gotten into you? I just offered our guest some drink—"

But Alex was beyond reasoning.

"She's not a guest, you moron. She lives here, and if you say another word, I swear—"

"Alex! Stop!" Abby slammed her palms onto the wooden tabletop. "What is wrong with you?"

Her hollering cut through the red haze of rage and switched his attention to her. What was wrong with *him*? Oh, the Princess had a gall, alright.

Alex dropped his hands from JC, and turned to glare at her.

"What's wrong with me? I'll tell you what's wrong with me. I just came from *Zolotoe Celo*, where—'

"You went to California? But...but why?"

"Take a guess, Princess."

"I...I..."

"Yeah, you. I flew back to knock some sense into that hard thing you call a head, and convince you to come home. Don't ask me why. I must've been delirious at the time." No point in a full disclosure. His plans to whisk her to Las Vegas for a quick wedding in some tacky chapel sounded ridiculous now.

"So, I arrived at Rostoff's doorsteps, and—surprise! You pulled a disappearing act." He waved his hand in the air like a magician presenting his world-famous trick. "Poof, into thin air. We all were going out of our collective minds, searching for a single reason—"

"But I left a note!"

"A note? Seriously? After all they've done for you, you left a *note?*"

"I was going to call them later."

"Later when? Today? Tomorrow? And how on earth did you manage to get here?"

"I hailed an off-duty taxicab, and it delivered me to the airport. There I secured the fair—ticket—to Fernandina. What's the big deal?"

An off-duty cab? In the middle of the night? Sonovabitch.

An acid residue of fear churned in his gut, but the anger prevailed. Choking on it, Alex plowed ahead.

"The big deal is, we were sick with worry. Peter was calling hospitals and morgues. Dmitry considered calling the police. Natasha cried. But do you care? Obviously not. Sitting here, drinking coffee, cool as you please."

"I left a note!"

"Yeah? And how were we supposed to know you did that on your own? How were we to know whether you just left, or were kidnapped?"

Abby opened her mouth to reply, but after a pause, clamped it shut.

"What? Nothing to say?"

"I admit, I didn't consider that possibility."

"No shit, Sherlock."

"I am sorry, I will call and apologize at once. It just...I had to leave."

"Why?"

"Because I...I can't explain. I just had to."

"That's right. *You* had to. It's all about you, isn't it? Did you ever think about *anyone* beside yourself?"

"That's not fair! Alex—"

"Don't you Alex me, Princess. As a matter of fact, don't talk to me at all."

Shaking, Alex balled his hands into fists. Damn, he was unraveling. Fast. Another moment, and he was afraid he might do something stupid. Or say something that he'll regret later. To eliminate that possibility, Alex kicked a chair out of the way, and stalked outside.

Must cool off, buddy. Take a deep breath.

God, he was ready to strangle her. And then kiss the hell out her. And then strangle her once again.

Cursing under his breath, Alex marched around the house, then plunged ahead toward the ocean. In his murderous state of mind, the only safe place for him was the beach. Thankfully, it was almost deserted. Only a couple of dog walkers at a good distance. He concentrated on putting one foot in front of another, trudging through wet sand. Minute by minute, the thought that Abby was unharmed and well, wormed its way inside, and squelched his rampaging fury.

The after-shakes still racked his body, but the fear slowly dissipated. Depleted, he sucked in the salty air and dragged his gaze toward the house. She came back. She hadn't run away, after all, but returned. Home. While he was on his way to California to convince her of the error of her choice and fetch her back, the Princess flew across the country, and came home.

The stubborn, willful, insufferable creature!

The most amazing woman in the whole wide world. *I'll be damned if I ever let her out of my sight again.*

Let *her? Are you crazy, pal?*

Yeah, well...If you put it that way, there was nothing he—or anyone else—was able to do if Abby didn't want it. Her brazen time-jumping escape was a testament to that. Or her resent travel from California to Florida.

I'll convince her.

Cajole, grovel, wheedle— whatever he must do. But convince her he will. Because Abby's place was right here, in Fernandina. With him. They belong together. Whether she realized it or not, they were destined. He just had to make her see the truth. Piece of cake, right?

You have your job cut out for you, pal.

Especially after the illustrious greeting he bestowed upon her a while ago. Damn.

They needed to clear the air. But first, he must apologize. To both, Abby and JC. His cousin had the misfortune to be in the wrong place at the wrong time.

Now, Abby? If you ask him, she deserved every angry word, and then some, for the hell she put him through. But still. He should've welcomed her before jumping down her throat. He shrugged. What's done was done. And now, for damage control.

He didn't need to be clairvoyant to foresee a lot of groveling in his immediate future. Braced, resigned, Alex executed a sharp U-turn toward the house.

CHAPTER THREE

JC was alone when Alex entered the house. He sent one furtive glance in Alex's direction, then tried to scurry to his room.

"Ah, JC, I'm sorry, man."

That stopped his cousin's retreat and earned him a mild curious stare.

"For?"

"For, you know, before."

JC pursed his lips, and made a production of mulling it through.

"Oh, you mean for manhandling me in front of Abby and calling me names?"

"Yeah, that."

"Okay. I guess. If you mean it."

"I do. Sorry, Cuz. I was just..."

"Out of control?" JC supplied with a knowing grin.

"Out of my fucking mind is more accurate," Alex conceded. Eating crow was not something he did often, but the moment seemed to call for it. His cousin pondered it for a moment.

"Personally, I thing you were scared shitless, but," JC shrugged, "whatever you say."

"Yeah, well. So, are we good?"

"I guess so." Emboldened by the apology, JC cleared his throat. "May I ask, why were you so hopping mad?"

"Scared shitless, as you succinctly put it."

"Because of Abby." A statement, not a question. Alex nodded.

"Yep. Flew all the way to San Francisco, only to find her gone. Can you imagine? Gone poof in the middle of the night, with no one having the foggiest where she might disappear to, or why."

"Well, I guess you have your answer: she came here, home. As to why, you must ask her."

"I will, after...well, after. By the way, where is she?"

"Locked herself in Nika's room. Said she has some calls to make."

"Oh, alright. That's okay, then. I'll talk to her when she's done."

"You may want to tell her truth, cousin of mine." JC cracked a smile.

"Truth?"

"Well, yeah. Just come straight, and say that you're fucking bonkers about her. I think that'll disarm her."

"Dis...disarm?"

"Uh-ha. She's revved enough to throttle you, buddy."

"I bet. Hell." Alex let out a breath with a whoosh, rubbed his bald head. After a moment, he squinted at JC.

"Bonkers?"

"Fucking bonkers, pal. Like certifiable."

"Shit. Am I that transparent?"

"Like clear glass."

"Dammit. Enjoying it, aren't you?"

"Immensely. Not every day you can see a strong man cut off at his knees. Smitten looks good on you."

"Bastard."

"I love you too, Cuz. But," JC switched his gaze to the direction of Nika's room, "I love my safety and comfort more, so I think I will take my leave before our Princess makes her entrance. Good luck. And Alex? She's one heck of a woman, so don't screw it up."

With JC's last words ringing in his ears, Alex braced himself. Bonkers, huh? Damn straight he was. Oh, well. He eyed the door to Nika's room, mentally preparing himself for the upcoming confrontation.

Abby didn't make him wait long. She swept into the room, all regal and magnificent, spared him a single glance.

"Back in one piece, I see."

Her announcement was articulated in that cool and snotty manner Alex adored.

Fucking bonkers indeed.

He cleared his throat.

"Abby, I want to apologize."

"Oh? Whatever for?"

"For yelling at you, and for—"

"No need, really." Her hand gesture was both dismissive and magnanimous. "And you didn't yell—you pointed at the facts in rather detestable manner." She shrugged, and feigned a smile. "Considering your state of mind at the time, I forgive you."

That irked. No, scratch that. That statement presented in such a royal-to-peasant manner bugged the hell out of him. Alex silently counted to five.

Oh, fuck that!

"And what state of mind might that be?"

"Why, irritated, of course. Ridiculously so."

"Irritated?" He barked something resembling a laughter. "Princess, I was way beyond irritation, and well into raging mad."

"Really? I didn't notice. Then again, I didn't pay much attention."

"You didn't pay attention." In two strides, Alex was in her face. His hands by volition of their own latched onto her forearms. "Are you paying attention now?" She winced. From his grip? From the hidden threat? He didn't care. "Are you, Princess?"

Without waiting for the answer, he jerked her to her toes. Caught off guard, Abby bumped into him. That sudden full body contact snapped his last restraint. Eye-to-eye, nose-to-nose, they glared at each other, both breathing hard.

Close. She was so close. He saw tiny speckles of silver in her dark irises. Her scent, something maddening and alluring, assaulted his system. Her hair, black as sin, long as a river, framed the face that disturbed his dreams. And that unholy mouth, naked and vulnerable, trembled slightly...

That tiny tremor was like a splash of cold water in his face.

What the hell are you doing, Alex?

Ashamed, he almost released her, but Abby lifted her chin.

Defiant.

Brazen.

Glorious.

"So, what if I am?" A gauntlet was thrown. Well, then.

The roar of blood in his ears drowned the whispers of any common sense.

Seething, Alex firmed his grip, dipped his head, and kissed her.

He meant to punish, to teach her a lesson. But he was lost the moment their lips met. An explosion of flavors. A banquet of textures.

Her helpless whimper thundered in his ears, and broke his heart. Swamped in tenderness, Alex gentled the kiss. Degree by torturous degree, his tongue coaxed her mouth open. And when she answered his silent persuasion, he delved in. A tiny ping of warning— *too fast, too much, too everything*—cut through the haze of his euphoria. Alex ignored it. Reckless, he drunk from her mouth like a man dying from thirst. Not enough. Not nearly enough.

Reluctant to end this sweet torture, but desperate for a gulp of air, he finally lifted his head. Her breathing was as fractured as his, which pleased him enormously.

Resting his forehead against hers, Alex closed his eyes, and just breathed her in.

A moment. He needed a moment to center himself. To find his bearings.

What just happened?

A shock of major proportions, that's what.

He always wondered what kissing Abby would be like. Now he knew. Earthshattering. Addictive. Like a potent drug, once tried, you were hooked up for life.

The moment stretched.

She felt so right in his arms. Alex wished they stayed like that forever. But the reality crept in. Abby stirred, then slowly lifted her head. When she blinked at him, her eyes were glazed. Fear? Confusion? With his throat suddenly dry, Alex held his breath. What was she thinking? Was she offended? Was she mad at him? Unable to bear the suspense any longer, he whispered, "Say something."

"W-what?"

"Anything."

"Is it... supposed to feel like that? Kissing, I mean."

"Like what?"

She scrunched her forehead and pondered for a moment. "Like you're soaring and burning at the same time?"

Relieved, almost dizzy, Alex let out a helpless chuckle.

"Oh, God, Abby, you'll be the end of me." He stroked his index finger along her cheek, then tucked a single lock behind her ear. She was so innocent that it scared the living lights out of him.

"Well? Is it?" She prompted.

"Only with someone special."

"Did you feel like that, too?"

"Yes." His gut was still ignited, while his head swam in lazy circles. Hell, yeah, he felt exactly like that.

"Does that mean that... I'm special to you?"

Alex wondered if she heard the sound of his poor heart hammering in his chest.

"You are most special and precious to me, Princess. I'm in love with you."

Her eyes widened. He had shocked her, but no more than he shocked himself. Was it always so hard to say it for the first time? Practice made perfect, they say. Well, then.

"I love you, Abigail Suzanne Coleman."

"Oh." Wide as two saucers, her eyes sought his. "Oh my..."

Alex held his breath.

Why wasn't she saying something? Anything?

But Abby kept silent. Alex curbed his growing impatience. She was inexperienced and innocent. Dear God, she was barely twenty-one! Never mind her *real* age.

And don't forget her upbringing, pal.

No matter how long Abby lived in the twenty-first century, she was still a product of her era. Alex racked his brain. What was the proper etiquette in her time? Courting before kissing, for sure. *The hell with it.* They butted heads for more than a year. Enough time for courting, if you asked him. But still. Was she ever going to put him out of his misery? Apparently not anytime soon. Alex let out a deep sigh.

"It's okay, Princess." He managed to split his face into a smile. "You don't have to—"

"I've always wondered what would it be like, when the man you love finally admits his feelings."

Alex's heart skipped. Did she just say '*the man you love?*' He searched her eyes, hoping, praying his hearing hadn't played a trick on him.

"But even in my wildest dreams I couldn't imagine..." Her voice trailed off.

"Couldn't imagine what?"

"That it would be so...right, and... splendid. Oh, Alex, what took you so long?"

"Abby." Wonder and plea, joy and hope. Just her name. "Abby."

She smiled, and cupped his face in both hands. "At first, I thought you didn't like me at all. I thought, we could be just friends. But deep in my heart, I knew that it wouldn't be enough. I even considered seducing you, but what do I know of an art of seduction? Then I've decided to become someone famous so you can be proud of me. But after my big success, you still didn't behave any differently. Even after I told you of my decision to stay in California, you stepped back and left me alone. Like it didn't matter. Like I didn't matter."

Is that what she thought? Horrified, he shook his head in denial.

"My God, Abby, *didn't matter*? I drank myself into stupor that night! I barely held myself from grabbing you, and taking you back home by force!"

"Why didn't you?"

"Because you *matter*. Because I love you, and want what's best for you."

"You are what's best for me."

His heart soared.

Thank you, God.

Undone, he lowered his brow to hers. "Say it, Abs. I need to hear it. Please say it."

"I love you, my dear Alex."

And now it was she who kissed him. Hard.

CHAPTER FOUR

A lex wasn't sure how long they were wrapped into each other's arms. Abby proved to be a talented pupil in the art of kissing. Eager and enthusiastic, she continued to kiss his brains out. He, on the other hand, was slowly going out of his mind. Did she have any idea what she was doing to him? What dark thoughts her avid mouth evoked? What erotic pictures exploded in his wild imagination? Probably not, or she might run screaming.

He must put a break on their passion, and soon, or he'll combust. But knowing it and acting on it were two different things. God, he was burning alive. Another moment...

The reprieve materialized in the form of his cousin. Or his discreet coughing.

Abby sprang away. Immediately bereft, Alex cursed under his breath. He still debated whether to kill JC or hug him for the interruption, when his cousin announced, "Sorry, sorry, guys. I don't know about you, but I'm famished. How about some dinner?"

"What? Dinner? Oh, yeah, dinner. I don't care."

What did he care? At the moment, food was very low on the totem pole of his needs. Or wants.

JC smirked. "Bet you don't. But the rest of us need some nourishment. Don't we, Abs?"

"Ah...I suppose so." A furious blush still tinted her cheeks, but Abby's voice once again turned to cool and snooty.

That's my girl.

A delighted grin split his face. My God, was it any wonder he was crazy about her? No, bonkers.

Fucking bonkers, according to his illustrious cousin.

As a testament of his joyful disposition, Alex decided to postpone strangling JC. Plus, he realized that he was starving. Surprise, surprise.

"Dinner it is, then," JC said as he opened the refrigerator. "Dang it, Cuz. You must do some shopping, and soon."

"I must?"

"Yeah, if you want to eat that is. Remember, there's two of us now. Sorry, three." He grinned over his shoulder at Abby. "So, a trip to the market, Alex."

And the skunk pointed a finger at him. Geez, was he giving him an order? Why, that pompous ass! If he wanted to eat, he better do his own marketing. But there was Abby to consider, too. Resigned, Alex grunted. Later. He'll shop for groceries later.

"As of right now," JC disappeared into the depth of their fridge once again, "we have some New Year's leftovers. Nika, bless her heart, cooked for an army."

And just like that, the good mood evaporated, replaced by gloom.

JC racked his hands through his hair, muttered something unintelligible, then closed the fridge with the loud bang. Alex cursed softly under his breath.

New Year's dinner.

Damn, was it only two days ago? Seemed like ages.

"Oh, I totally forgot." JC frowned. "While you were gone, a currier delivered the letters. For you and Abby."

"What letters?"

"From Nika."

Abby's sharp intake of breath echoed his own.

"Where are those letters?"

"There, on the counter." JC scoffed. "She didn't think to write one for her brother."

"And what did you expect? Did you think a few days could erase the years of neglect?"

"I didn't neglect her. Or you. I just—"

"Conveniently forgot about us."

"Yeah, well." At least his cousin had the decency to blush.

"Why don't you make yourself useful, JC, and put some dinner on the table, while Abby and I read our letters?"

"Sure, whatever you say, Master. We, lowly slaves, aim to please." JC stalked off in a huff.

Almost in unison, Alex and Abby tore the flaps of the legal envelopes.

A mixture of emotions warred inside of him while Alex read the letter.

Short, more of a message than a letter, it was clearcut, and to the point.

Nika bequeathed him everything: home, business, even her damned truck.

Alex swore, read the letter again, then swore some more.

What did you think you were writing, Brat? A business memo?

But the last sentence of the letter was different, and as personal as it could get.

> **You were always my rock, my best friend, my confidant. No matter where I am, I will always remember you. Be happy, Alex. You deserve it, and then some.**
>
> **Kick ass, Cousin.**
>
> **Love, Nika**

Something hot and scratchy pressed against his eyelids. So typical Nika! First, she irritated the hell out of him with her formal bequests, then she ripped his heart open, and left it bleeding. *Dammit.*

When Abby touched his hand, he grabbed it like it was an anchor. The silence was interrupted by the occasional clink of silverware, and JC's soft muttering.

"She loved you more than anybody, Alex. Half of my letter is about you."

"Yeah? Well, maybe I should read it, then."

"No, sorry. It's personal. But she asked me to look out for you." A wobbly smile played on her lips still puffy from their kissing. He grazed a fingertip along her bottom lip, a gentle caress, then with an effort pulled a smile of his own.

"Guess you'd better, then. Look out for me that is."

"Oh, I plan to." She sighed, then turned her misty eyes away. "And... she gifted me her Coco."

"God help us all." But his halfhearted attempt at humor failed. "Dammit, Abs. She gifted me every-fucking-thing. What am I supposed to do now?"

"And now, my dear Alex, we will eat these scrumptious leftovers, drink a glass of *Verochka's* excellent wine, and say a toast for Daisy and Eli's safe journey back to 1910."

She bit her lower lip. "Do you think they reached home by now?"

"Absolutely." Even though his smile was forced, Alex managed to keep his voice strong and convincing. "I'm sure everything went smoothly, and they are home, safe and sound, where they will live happily ever after."

He knew no such thing, of course, but hope sprang eternal.

Must think positive, or go stir crazy.

Abby gazed at him for a long pregnant moment, searching for truth.

"I want to believe you. More than anything, but..."

"But?"

"I have this strange feeling that something's...not right. *Time is running out.*"

All of a sudden, Abby's voice turned spooky and eerie; her eyes glazed over, wide and unblinking. Alex had an impression that she went to some faraway place in her mind. Was she in some kind of a trance? Suddenly, chills broke all over his body. Desperate to pull her back, Alex shook her, but received no reaction. Dammit.

"Abby? What are you talking about? What time?" Silence. She sat frozen, like a statue, staring into space. "Abs?"

"Dinner is served, Your Highnesses."

JC 's loud announcement shattered her reverie, and with a violent shudder, Abby came back to herself.

"Alex? Something's wrong. We need to go to the house. Now!"

CHAPTER FIVE

He didn't ask her what house, didn't have to. The Coleman house was the overriding thing in their lives. Overruling JC's protests, they jogged to the car, and instead of quiet dinner at home, sped up to the other side of the Amelia Island. Of course, his ass of a cousin tagged along. Short of clubbing him over the head, and leaving him unconscious in the middle of the kitchen, it was impossible to shake JC off. Tenacious bastard. Well, he was an attorney, wasn't he? On top of that, he was his father's son. Those damn New York Morrises were as relentless as they were self-serving. And stubborn. Alex didn't consider himself— or Nika for that matter—a true descendants of the same clan. They just shared a name and some blood, a misfortune of their birth. But in any other aspect? They were as different from them as day and night.

But JC was the chip from the old block, any way you slice it. Pompous ass. What were they going to do with him? And what if they find something— anything—inside the Coleman house? Clueless, JC still believed that Nika and Eli left to some godforsaken island in the middle of nowhere. To tell or not to tell him the truth? Well, hell. Alex decided to play it by ear. After all, what choice did he have?

Fueled by Abby's foreboding, he drove well over the speed limit. The city streets were half deserted, thank God, being the evening of January 2nd, where everybody shook off the last holiday cheer, and prepared to return to the normal swing of things. Come to think of it, he'd better go to the office tomorrow, just to see what's what. Granted, it'll be strange without Nika. And how on earth will he manage to run the business that was heavily invested into the renovations of historical houses? Hire another contractor? No way he'd be able to find one as good as Nika. Turn *Before & After, Inc.* into a traditional real estate firm? And how many of them did their favorite island boast? Hundreds? Just thinking about it gave him a headache.

So, don't think about it now.

Tomorrow was the day for business decisions. Right now? Alex cast his eyes sideways. Right now, they had another trouble brewing. Abby and her foreboding that time was running out.

Well, maybe not *trouble* per se, but something troubling for sure. Alex always trusted his instincts. And he trusted Abby. Is she was feeling some disquiet, he must pay attention.

"Is that why you ran away from California? Because time was running out?"

"Yes, but I can't explain it."

"You don't have to. We'll figure it out, Abs. I promise."

"I know."

After that, Abby kept quiet. JC, on the other hand, was complaining a mile a minute. As his stomach emanated some noises between growl and whimper, he pounced: "Hear that? If I die from malnourishment, it will be all your fault, Cuz."

"If you were so hungry, why didn't you stay at home?"

"And leave you two to traipse all around town?"

"We're not going to *traipse* anywhere. We're going to check on the empty house."

"What if something happens there?"

"Like what?"

"Like... I don't know. Something."

"Inside the vacant mansion? Seriously?"

"Well, stranger things happen."

"This is Fernandina, for goodness' sake, not New York city."

"So what? Fernandina or not, you might get in trouble, and need an attorney."

"Geez, you're crazy, cousin."

"Takes one to know one, pal of mine."

Between their bickering, Alex didn't notice they had reached their destination. And here it was, the house that stole Nika's breath, and later her heart.

Dazzling white, three stories' tall, with its soaring round tower, it stood apart from its counterparts, governing over a large corner of the old city. Now, restored to its former glory, the Coleman house was a true beauty, dignified and stately.

Nika referred to it as a Southern Gentleman. To Alex, it resembled a Dowager Queen, elegant and regal. Some referred to it as grandeur. But one thing was for sure, it made a statement.

The house was one of a kind. And the architecture, as much as it was unique, had nothing to do with it. It was alive, and it was waiting. And where did this bizarre observation come from? Alex stared at it, mesmerized.

"The Coleman house." JC's voice took on a reverent note.

"Home," Abby replied in a hushed voice.

"Oh, I forgot, it belongs to you now."

"Hmm."

With that noncommittal reply, she exited the car.

"Solid real estate." JC nodded. "The cost of the land must be up in the stratosphere. Nice investment, if you ask me."

"No one asked you," Alex countered, and strode to catch up with Abby.

"Are you okay?"

Paler than usual, she nodded. Then she reached into her purse, and took out the old-fashioned key.

"Home," she repeated in a mere whisper, and with an unsteady hand inserted the key into the keyhole.

Alex hated to admit that he was wary. Empty house, even humongous like this one, was still just an empty house.

He knew what was inside, the infamous grandfather clock that doubled as the portal between times. He'd never believed it, if he didn't have proof. He slid his gaze toward that unique proof: Abby. If not for that clock, she wouldn't be there today. He owed that damned grandfather clock a big one. And he hated it with passion, because it stole Nika. Well, not stole exactly. To be fair, it brought her and Eli together. In another time and dimension, but still.

How in blue blazes does that portal work, anyway?

Alex didn't have a desire to jump through time, thank God, but Nika and Abby were intimately familiar with the power hidden within that antique English masterpiece circa 1827. All it took was a single brass key to bring it to life. To open the time portal.

Alex shivered. Damn, it was spooky. And unbelievable. Crazy as all get out. Thank God that key was far, far away now, so he had nothing to worry about.

Or did he?

"Well? What are we looking for?" His annoying cousin strode along the foyer, then stopped in front of the grandfather clock. Thank God, JC wasn't privy to its secret, or he undoubtedly would run for cover.

No, first he'll commit us both to the asylum, and then run for cover.

"We are not looking for anything in particular, just..." Alex shrugged, but kept his eyes glued to Abby. Tense, she stood unmoving, her gaze taking a slow journey around the room. Was she remembering it from before? He wondered what did she see, what did she think. What did she feel. All of a sudden, the thought of losing her stole his breath. Where did it come from? Ridiculous.

Here she was, right here, standing nearby. And she loved him. She admitted it, kissed him senseless. So, what was this nonsense of losing her? To what? To the house? To time, that according to her, was running away? Alex rubbed his head, calling himself a thousand names for a fool. The key was back in 1910. Without it, the portal was sealed. The grandfather clock was just a clock, that's all.

So, shake it off, buddy.

But the effort to keep still as she come to stand in front of that damned clock, was enormous. His every instinct screamed at Alex to snatch Abby, and run for the hills. Instead, he came to stand beside her.

The golden face with its two ornate arms shone mysteriously, hinting at secrets.

Timeless miracle.

Alex held his breath. Then, mad at himself, he let it out with a loud whoosh and a soft curse.

Damn, getting fanciful in my advanced age.

To prove his folly, Alex reached out and touched the face of the clock. Immediate zing of electricity shot along his fingers. He snatched his hand away.

"What the hell?"

"It is a warning. You are not the one." Abby's murmur disturbed him more than he was willing to admit. Even to himself. Alex scowled.

"Not the one? A warning? What's that supposed to mean?"

"I don't know. But you are not the one."

"Abby, you're talking in riddles."

"I'm sorry. I just know what I feel. What it tells me."

"The clock? The clock tells you that I'm not the one?"

"Yes. Or, rather, that it's not your time yet."

"Fine, it's not my time. Whose time is it, then?"

JC materialized from somewhere behind Alex.

"Oh, hell yah, that's what I'm talking about!" He elbowed Alex aside. "I admired it from the first, back when Nika gave the tour to the Senator Lauder. The antique grandfather clock. What a beauty you are!" And with that, he placed both hands onto the clock's sides. "Geez, feels like a velvet. Whoever made it, was a genius."

Alex was struck mute. He was not the one, but JC was? What asinine shit was that?

In the meantime, his salivating cousin all but made love to the effing clock. Look at the idiot!

Positively orgasmic, the moron.

Dumbfounded, he gazed at JC as he touched the clock, caressing every square inch of it without much trouble. Oh, hell no. No way. Alex ground his teeth, and reached with his hand again.

This time the zing was so powerful, it reverberated through his arm all the way to his shoulder.

Dammit all to hell and back!

CHAPTER SIX

Abby watched him with an unreadable expression on her face. Then she turned to the clock, and placed her hand over its shiny face. As if in response, the clock emanated a single chime in a clear sonorous voice. Alex froze.

"No way, Abby. No way in hell!"

With force born out of fear and resentment, he dragged her away. Alex didn't stop until they were outside, and even then, he didn't let go of her. Baffled, scared, he stared at Abby. A thousand secrets reflected in her eyes. Or was it moonlight?

Why was she looking at him with sorrow? Like saying goodbye.

No way in hell!

Unaware of the turmoil, JC jogged after them, grinning like an idiot.

"Abby, if you ever decide to sell this clock, I'll snatch it in a New York minute. I'll pay you whatever you ask for it. Hell, I'll give you a pint of my blood, too."

"I will never sell this timepiece. I'm sorry, JC."

Even though she was talking to his cousin, Abby's eyes, sad and serious, were focused on Alex.

"Dang it, I knew it. Oh, well. You can't blame the guy for trying."

"Get in the car." Alex addressed JC, but his eyes were glued to Abby's face.

"I'd rather stay outside, and get some air, if it all the same to you."

"It's not. Get in the car, JC."

"But—"

"Get in the *damn* car!"

After one look at his face, JC capitulated. He grumbled all the way, and slammed the car door with unnecessary force, but he accepted defeat. Alex waited a bit to bring his jumping nerves and his voice under control. He failed.

"Abby? What in blue blazes happened?"

"I don't really know. But the clock...it rejected you."

"But accepted JC? Seriously?"

"And me. For some reason, it chose us. So, somewhere in time, we must be needed, the two of us."

It didn't bode well for his peace of mind. As a matter of fact, it infuriated the heck out of him, not to mention scared him shitless. A note of desperation crept into his voice. "You are not going anywhere. Especially with JC."

"I might not have a choice."

Her placid acceptance shot his panic into stratosphere.

"Bullshit. I'm not letting you out of my site. Ever. I'm not losing you!"

"Oh, my darling." Stepping closer, Abby lay her head on his chest. "I don't want to go anywhere. I want to be right here, by your side. Forever. But," she lifted her face, "I might have no choice."

Calm, almost serene, she gazed at him with something close to a regret in her eyes. Her features blurred around the edges, like she was slowly fading away. Nothing mysterious, just a play of the moonlight. But the effect was eerie and unsettling. Alex blinked, and brought her face back into a sharp focus. Now a cold dread replaced his panic.

"No. Not in a million years. And screw the choice. We always have a choice."

"Not always. But one thing I know for sure: this is not going to happen tonight. So, let's go home."

CHAPTER SEVEN

No, it was not going to happen tonight.

Tomorrow? The day after? Abby wasn't sure of the exact date, but one thing was for certain: soon, she must go away from here, because she was needed.

Somewhere. In some time and place. The reason wasn't clear to her. She just knew she must. She will. Because time was running away. Because something somewhere was wrong, and it was up to her to fix the problem. But what? Where? Not knowing was akin to illness. Not so much painful as maddening, until the source of the ailment was identified, and a proper cure applied. Until then, she must wait. Oh, how she hated the waiting!

Abby heaved a deep sigh, and looked around. Because JC was staying in the guestroom she usually occupied, Abby had no choice but to sleep in Daisy's bedroom, where everything still smelled like Daisy. Sadness washed over her in one huge sweep, as the memories of her dear friend and time-traveling companion played in her mind.

Where was Daisy now? Was she happy? Was she safe? And what of Eli?

Please Lord, keep them both unharmed.

Alex was so sure that everything went well with their time-jump. And she believed him. She trusted Alex more than she trusted herself.

Alex.

A wonderful feeling of contentment, joy, and happiness filled her to the brim. Wasn't it amazing that he loved her? In her heart of hearts, Abby knew that he was *the one* from the first. Even when he irritated the bejesus out of her, she knew. And knowing it, she yearned. And fretted, and feared. What if he didn't feel the same for her? What if he met another woman and fall deeply in love with her? What then?

Abby didn't know the answer to that. But miracles happened. She knew that for sure. Because what was it if not a miracle that Alex loved her right back? That he flew all the way to California to bring her home? He was such a darling man, handsome, smart, loyal. A true knight in shining armor.

Well, in shorts and a shirt, but what does it matter? He was beautiful, inside and out, and he was all hers. Abby hugged the knowledge to her heart. He was hers, as she was his. They belong together.

But for how long?

A nagging fear burst through her happiness.

When she goes away— and she will, of that Abby was certain— will he wait for her? What if her travel will take her away for months? Or even years?

Abby shook her head. No. She won't entertain such terrible thoughts. She won't abandon Alex. She can't. She'll go— wherever, whenever— if she must, but she was determined to return to him. Eventually. Because he was her other half. Her destiny.

Fatigue hit her hard. Abby almost swayed on her feet. She checked her watch. Goodness, she was going without sleep for twenty-four hours. No wonder she was so weary. Time to go to bed. Alone.

Abby huffed a breath, telling herself she was glad that Alex kissed her— demurely-like—on her forehead, and wished her sweet dreams.

Glad? Oh, who was she kidding? She preferred to sleep in his bed. Heat rushed up her neck.

What a scandalous notion!

So what? She lived in the twenty-first century now. People nowadays behaved freer, and were more tolerant of such things, weren't they?

Come to think of it, even in her own time, there was Eli and Daisy's example. They fell in love, and disregarded all the rules of that Edwardian society. So, why was it wrong for her? She was a grown woman, who loved and was loved in return. Why can't she enjoy it to the fullest?

She had no doubt Alex must be a wonderful lover. Gentle, kind, generous. He'll be the first man to touch her intimately. What bliss that would be! Anticipation mixed with anxiety fueled her imagination.

Her body tingled, her heart beat rapidly, her blood rushed in a violent flood. She yearned to discover all that wonderful experience she only knew from the books and movies. His kisses, as amazing as they were, weren't enough.

She needed, no, craved, more. She needed all of him.

For goodness' sake, her time was running out. Didn't he believe her?

Unable to stay still, Abby began to pace the room. He loved her. He must want her.

So, why didn't he act on his needs and wants? For men, she was told, it was even harder than for women.

Yes, she was inexperienced in the matters of passion, but she was a fast learner. And she was willing. Eager. Damnation, she was shaking on the inside.

Abby hugged herself tight to forestall her trembling. What to do? How to show a man she loved that she was ready? That she wanted his caresses?

You must seduce him.

Oh, Lord. She needed advice. Where was *Verochka* when she needed her? But her honorary grandmother was a world away, so Abby was on her own.

What did she know on the art of seduction? Abby pressed both hands to her temples in a futile attempt to juggle her memory, and came up blank. Cursing her strict Edwardian upbringing was no use.

Think, Abby, think.

From what she knew, the gentleman was supposed to make first moves. Abby scowled. What if the gentleman was too shy?

Alex, shy?

Laughable. He was the most bold and confident man on the planet. But what if the gentleman was too honorable and virtuous? That was a different matter altogether.

Abby considered her choices. Stay in her— Daisy's— room, or go knock on his door? What if he wouldn't invite her in? What if he turned her away?

Impossible! No one was turning Abigail Suzanne Coleman away! Not even Alex.

She ought to march into his room right this moment, and demand an explanation. Why had he left her alone tonight. Why didn't he take her to bed. Why—

"Abby?"

She yelped.

CHAPTER EIGHT

H e hadn't meant to startled her. But if her muffled scream was any indication, he managed just that, and then some. Lithe and agile like a gazelle, she whirled around, and kicked his unruly libido through the roof. Even in the dim light of the bedroom, he saw her eyes sparkle, and her beautiful body. And those legs! Dear God, they went on forever, shapely, fluid, gorgeous. Like the rest of her. Heat flared over Alex, creating a situation that soon would become obvious and embarrassing. He squirmed and tugged at his pockets to shift the flimsy material of his shorts that was tenting.

His unruly shaft hardened to the point of pain, pocking.

Down, boy.

"Sorry, I knocked a few times, but you didn't answer. So, I..."

Alex's words trailed off. Why was she looking at him like that? Was she embarrassed? But she was still fully dressed, so he didn't catch her in negligee.

So, why was Abby blushing? And she was, furiously so. Or was she scared?

"Abs? What is it?"

"Oh, nothing. I was just debating with myself."

"Must've been some debate, if you didn't hear my knocking."

"Yes, well, it was rather...intense."

"I see." He didn't. "Okay. I just wanted to make sure that you are comfortable, and..." *And still here.* "And don't need anything."

"As a matter of fact, I do need...something."

"What? Say it, and it's yours."

"Just like that?"

"Absolutely."

"What if I say that I need...someone?"

"Then, I'll...someone? Someone who?"

"You. I need you, Alex."

Alex sucked in a sharp breath. Geez, his knees were shacking. If anyone was capable to kick the legs from under him with a single word—or a single glance—it was Abby.

No question about it. Did she know what she does to him? What she was capable of doing? Probably not. And thank God for that.

"Well, I'm here. What is it you need, Princess?"

Alex congratulated himself on being in control of his vocal cords at least. Because inside he was quacking like jelly. His shorts had grown so tight they actually hurt him. He moved a bit, wiggled his butt to find some semblance of comfort to no avail. But his voice stayed clear and even. For just ten seconds. That's all it took, as she tilted her head, smiled, and sent his control to smithereens.

"I told you, I need you."

What was she doing? Was she unbuttoning her shirt? Sweet baby Jesus!

"Abby, what do you think you're doing?" Oh, it cost him dearly to ask, when all his instincts began to cheer and dance a merry jig.

"Why, undressing, of course."

"I can see that, but...why?"

Damn, man, and why do you care? Shut up, and be grateful.

"Are you dense? Don't you see I'm trying to seduce you?"

Oh, God, have mercy.

"Abs, you don't have to..."

"But I want to."

"Abby, you had a...trying day. Yes, that is, a very trying day. As a matter of fact, a couple of days, not just one. You...you must be exhausted."

He was babbling. Idiot. And if the heat scorching his ears was any indication, blushing like a virgin.

Virgin? Bad choice of words, buddy. Very bad.

If someone in this room was a virgin, it was her. Damn it. The picture of naked Abby, pliant, radiant and willing, flashed in his mind's eye.

Oh, hell.

Alex gritted his teeth. He needed to get out of here, as fast as possible. Or he wouldn't be able to keep his hands off her. She was tired, and stressed, and inexperienced. She was a virgin, for goodness' sake, and he'd be damned if her first time was anything but awesome. Mind-boggling spectacular. But the state he was in now? Awesome or spectacular wasn't even cutting it close. Alex was teetering on the brink, torn between his overwhelming need for her, and the last scruples of his decency. He was holding onto his sanity by the fingernails. The beast clawing inside of him demanded satisfaction.

Take. Feel. Burn.

Dark and forbidden images, erotic and savage needs.

He shook with it. No way he was taking her like a raging bull.

Alex fought his basic needs like a man possessed, but Abby wasn't making it easy. With her eyes on him, she continued her chaste striptease.

God, didn't she see the state he was in?

Isn't she afraid?

"Abby. Stop." With an enormous effort, Alex lifted both hands, palms up. "Please stop."

A mixture of bafflement and annoyance on her face quickly turned to shame. Like a splash of an icy water, it cooled off his rampaging glands.

"Princess..."

Her eyes welled, her voice hitched, but Abby didn't turn away.

"Why? Don't you want me?"

"Only more than I want to breathe."

She stared at him for a long moment. "Then, what's the problem?"

"The problem is, I want you too much. I won't be able to be careful with you. Not in the condition I am now." To demonstrate, he lifted his shaking hands.

"I didn't ask you to be careful with me. What am I, a tender flower?"

"No, but you are a virgin."

"Oh." She turned around, clutching her shirt with both hands. "So, you stopped me only because I am...never done this before?"

"Yes. Your first time supposed to be... pleasant, at the very least. And kind, and gentle. And yes, dammit, tender. It supposed to be a love-making, not mating. Not just sex. At the moment, I can't give you the romance you deserve. I won't be kind, or patient. I might hurt you."

"That's okay, I will forgive you."

"But I won't forgive myself."

She lowered her eyes but not before he saw a shadow of disappointment. Better disappointed, than disillusioned. Or, dammit all to hell and back, hurt.

"Please don't be mad at me, Abby."

She shrugged. "I'm not."

But she was. He knew her too well.

"I'm sorry."

"Whatever for?" She shrugged again, lowered her eyes. "And it was entirely my fault. I threw myself at you like a wanton woman, you said no. End of story."

"You didn't...I didn't...Damn." Alex rubbed his bald crown hard enough to skin a layer or two.

Leave it, buddy. You won't win this argument.

He heaved a breath, swore. "We'll talk tomorrow. Better try to rest now."

Two steps to the door, just two steps, and...

"Will you be able to rest?" Abby's question stopped his progress.

"Not likely."

"Good."

Despite everything, Alex chuckled. "Sweet dreams, my vengeful Princess."

The smile she bestowed upon him was sharp and quick and all teeth.

"Go to hell, my cowardly knight."

For some unbelievably crazy reason, Alex felt much better. With his spirits flying high, he grinned, shook his head.

God, what a woman!

Was it any wonder he was crazy about her? He was crazy, period.

How else to explain his deliberate choice of a sleepless night after a long, cold shower as oppose to a night of passion?

At the threshold, he stopped, and turned to look at her over his shoulder.

"Abby?"

"Changed your mind already? Pity. Now, I'm not in the mood. Go away."

One hell of a woman.

And she was all his.

"When I take you to bed, Princess—"

"If I allow it. And that is a big *if.*"

He ignored her snooty remark, and her blazing glare.

"*When* it happens, you'll understand why I stopped tonight. What it cost me to stop. And you thank me."

Abby's snort was loud and derisive. "In your dreams."

"Oh, if only you knew my dreams, Abby." Best that she didn't. "But I promise you one thing, you will be in the mood. One hell of a mood. You have my word on it."

With this part warning, part pledge still shimmering in the air, Alex left the room.

CHAPTER NINE

As predicted, he spent a miserable night, torn between the erotic dreams and sleepless brooding. At 5:15, Alex decided to stop pretending to rest, and get an early jump on his day. This Monday morning, for the first time since the holidays, *Before & After, Inc.,* was going back to business. Alex was revved and eager.

He missed the busy atmosphere of the office, the noise and chaos and occasional mayhem. For Alex, it was like a game, where he was the lead player at the controls, supervising, guiding, nudging. But the main point was having fun. He fucking loved it.

He wasn't sure who was surprised more, him or Nika, when they first started their business all those years back, and Alex discovered his true strength. A follower, an affable guy, and a people's person, he seemed such an unlikely candidate for the position of power and leadership. But he proved everybody wrong, himself included.

He thrived on the stress of juggling several projects at the same time, dealing with realtors and clients, and fixing problems. He loved what he did, was darn good at it, and made a decent living. Every freaking penny in his bank account was earned. He might be a descendant of the New York rich and famous Morrises, but he didn't need the family fortune to survive, thank God. Together with Nika, they chose to make their own mark. And they'd made it, all the way from the few hundred dollars they had between them nine years ago, to the multi-million-dollar enterprise their company was today.

His company now. As in solo. Damn. *Time to face the music, pal.*

Alex swung his legs over the bed, rubbed his face. He needed a shower, a shave, and some coffee. And a whole new perspective on how to run the business without Nika. Not an easy task, but he'd manage. He must, because otherwise he'd let his cousin down, and all what she poured into the company will have turned to dust.

Over my dead body.

No way would that happen. Alex was determined to work, sweat, and fight tooth and nail to avoid failure. In the next year or two, he swore to bring the company to a new level. For Nika, yes, but also for himself. And for Abby.

How on earth he planned to accomplish that was still vague in his mind, but he had no doubt his plan will come true. It will require all his creativity, but he'd think of new venues to make it work. *Before & After, Inc.* would more than survive. It would shine under his leadership.

Right now, though, he needed to think of some excuse to the staff as to why he was the only Morris at the helm of the company. What did Eli say? *Thunderation.*

Cursing every step of the way, Alex dragged himself to the shower, where he spent twice as much time as usual. He chalked up his weariness to the unsettling effects of the last few days events. First, Nika and Eli's departure, then his flight to California, and scare about Abby's disappearance, and then her sudden reappearance here.

But the bigger shock he still was recovering from came later: Abby loved him!

She had blown him away. Blindsided him and brought him to his knees.

And then she kissed him.

Okay, he kissed her first, but she responded. Boy, did she ever! Her taste still bloomed in his mouth, sweet, and hot, and potent as sin. Her breathless whimpers still thundered in his ears. And her little striptease the night before? Who would've known that Abby's attempt at seduction, so innocent, so clumsy, turned him on more than any porn flick he watched in his misspent youth?

At the mere memory of that scene, his little friend swelled to a dangerous proportion. Alex winced. Damn, it was almost painful.

"Easy for you, pal."

He scowled, and decided it was high time to put an end to his self-inflicted water torture.

Stepping out, he wrapped the towel around his hips. And just stood there for a moment, listening to the quiet.

Time is running away.

Alex cursed. He hated to admit that Abby's odd prophecy had spooked him.

He shouldn't have driven her to the Coleman house last night. That was a mistake. But, as resourceful as Princess proved to be, he had no doubts that she'll find a way to get there by herself.

How can he stop her? The house was legally hers. She might even decide to move there. And then what? And what about the zapping he got from the infamous grandfather clock? Must admit, it bugged the hell out of him that his dick of a cousin got a different treatment, and according to Abby, was 'accepted' by the clock, whereas Alex was rejected.

"Rejected, my ass. We'll see about that."

In the meantime, no way Abby was getting within an inch of that stupid clock. Not without him. That, at least, was in his power. If Alex was unable to prevent her trips to the house, he will join her, rejected or not. And the next time, he'd wear electrician gloves, and by God, he'd touch that fucking clock no matter what.

Note to himself: buy high voltage protection gloves.

Pacified by his decision, Alex looked around. Why was he standing naked in the middle of his room? And what time was it, anyway? He slanted a glance at his iPhone. Shy of six in the morning. No wonder it was still dark. But what the heck? He decided to hit the road early. Alex dressed in his usual office attire of casual pants and a polo shirt. A glimpse in the mirror proved that he forgot to shave. Annoyed, he pulled his shirt off, and detoured to the bathroom. The ragged pirate look might suit him the best, but as a businessman, he must project a clean professional image. Thank goodness he didn't have to deal with his hair every day. A few minutes later, Alex admired his handiwork. Pleased, he nodded at his reflection in the mirror, patting his bald crown and face with a towel.

"Smooth as baby's bottom."

Presentation aside, Alex was unwilling to commit a crime of putting whisker burns on Abby's delicate skin when he kissed her next time.

I applaud your eternal optimism, buddy.

After last night, he'd be lucky if she talked to him. Or let him within an arm-length of her. Damn, he hurt her feelings, embarrassed her. Never mind that he acted in her best interests, because under the layer of her false bravado, she was innocent. Untouched. Pure. As much as he wanted her— make that craved her— he couldn't touch her. The timing was wrong. Everything was wrong.

And who are you kidding, pal? Admit it, you were scared, plain and simple.

And who could blame him? She was a virgin. He'll be her first.

Hell yeah, he was scared shitless. And excited to the point of dizziness. A cold sweat trickled at the base of his spine. Damn. Was he man enough to be worthy of that honor? The gift was priceless. And horrifying. And enormous.

Delirious and petrified at the same time, Alex cursed. Panicking was not an option. Nor was standing in the middle of the room, obsessing.

Get moving, pal.

Go to the office, spin a fib about Nika, check current listings, make some calls, and...

And buy a ring, Cuz.

Alex jumped, turned around. Where did that come from? Did he really hear Nika's whisper? Or was he losing his mind? *A ring.* Then Alex banged his fist against his forehead. Of course! He was such a moron.

"Thanks, Nik. Thanks a lot!"

Revved, Alex grabbed his keys, and all but ran outside.

If he wanted to marry Abby, and he did, he has to propose first. He must have a ring, something elegant and regal, something shiny and classy. Like her.

A diamond. Abby was born to wear diamonds. The closest Tiffany store was in Jacksonville. A long hike, but not over the top, especially at this early hour.

With the almost nonexistent traffic, Alex calculated the round trip to just around two and a half hours tops.

He'd make it back on time for sure, but just to be on a safe side, he quickly texted his office manager, Sue.

Please open the office. Be back later.

Despite the hour, his longtime secretary answered immediately with a thumb's up emoji. Grinning, Alex jumped in the car, pushed the start button, and speed off in a flash. The A1A was almost deserted, so his trip to Tiffany's wouldn't take long. And he didn't need much time in the store either, because he knew exactly which ring he wanted.

A princess cut diamond in a platinum setting. Yes, that was perfect.

A princess for the Princess. Abby might get pissed. But he knew how to pacify her Highness: kiss her senseless. Damn, was he good, or what? Delighted with the prospect, and with life in general, Alex chuckled. He slanted a glance through the car window at the morning sky. The blending colors were spectacular: shy pink, tender lilac, deep violet. The beauty of it stole his breath away and reminded him of Abby's paintings. Overjoyed, Alex slid all four windows open. Light breeze caressed his face as the salty fragrance of the ocean teased his nostrils.

Drawing a full chest of fresh air, Alex let it out in a whoosh, then laughed like a loon. So, what if he behaved like a silly boy? He was the luckiest man alive, and he was bursting at the seams from joy and happiness. At that moment, even the unsettling event in the Coleman house yesterday lost its significance. He'd deal with it. Later. For now, he had more pressing and important issues at hand, such as buying a ring, and proposing to the woman he loved. Oh, and flowers. Lots of flowers were an absolute must. Okay, a detour to the florist on the way back. What kind of flowers? After a short deliberation, he settled on roses. Yes, definitely roses. Two, no three dozen of long-stemmed buds tied with an elaborate bow.

Pink or red? Or maybe yellow? Alex shrugged. A dozen of each, to be on a safe side. Visualizing Abby's surprise, he smiled. The plan was beautiful: to shake her composure with flowers, then whisk her to the deck, and, finally, propose.

And don't forget to kneel, pal.

The lady was all about class and tradition, so he added a bended knee to complete the picture. A good plan, if he said so himself. Solid, simple, straightforward.

What if Abby says no?

Out of the question. He flat refused to entertain that possibility. She loved him, so she most definitely will say yes. No ifs or buts about it. And after she agreed to marry him, they will pop the champagne. A nice, chilled *Dom Perignon* that she preferred.

Okay, and how will he manage to chill the bottle while zipping around? JC! But can he be relied upon to do the deed? Alex has no choice. Might let him in on the secret, but hey, the guy was his cousin, even if he was a dick. He won't betray Alex's confidence, will he?

No, Alex didn't think so. JC was so eager to get in Alex's good graces, he'll keep his mouth zipped. Thinking of JC, his mind circled back to yesterday.

Why did that stupid clock accept him, but not me?

Alex frowned, then shrugged. Ridiculous to get so worked up about it.

But still. Abby and JC both touched the grandfather clock without any problem. But he almost got electrocuted. Alex shuddered at recollection. Why?

He didn't want to think about it, but the fact remained. He was rejected. How did Abby put it? *It's not your time yet.* And when might *his* time arise?

And time for what?

The whole situation was driving him crazy. He understood Abby's 'acceptance' by the clock, as insane as that sounded. She was a direct descendant of the Coleman clan; she owned the house, and everything in it. Including that infamous grandfather clock. But what about JC? He was a Morris.

He was Nika's older brother.

No, not Nika's— Daisy's. Daisy Coleman. A possible connection?

Alex mulled that for a moment. No, he didn't think so.

JC wasn't even privy to the real story. He had no clue about who Eli really was, or where he took Nika. And he had not the foggiest idea about the portal.

Alex preferred to keep it that way. The less his cousin knew, the better it was for everybody. First, he won't believe it. Not for a million years. Or he might become curious, which was even worse. His cousin, for all his faults, was a smart and shrewd man. He was already enamored with the grandfather clock, even wanted to buy it from Abby. What if he suspected about the portal? What if he decides to open it? Absurd. The portal was sealed.

Without the original key, located in another time, albeit at the same house, the danger of opening the portal was as good as nonexistent. Alex drummed his fingers on the steering wheel. His mood plummeted as another troubling thought flashed inside his brain: can the key somehow materialize in this time?

What if Eli or Nika put it in its hiding place on the back of that clock? Possible, he supposed, but for what reason? The key served its purpose. Nika and Eli were reunited, and Abby was here. End of the story, period.

Shake it off, buddy. You're making a big deal out of nothing. And driving yourself crazy in the process

Alex blew out a noisy breath, and ordered himself to stop being an idiot. He turned on his blinkers, preparing to ease onto the interstate 295, as a tiny two-seater zipped in front of him. His breaks squealed in protest, but he managed to stop the car and avoid rear-ending that ridiculous thing camouflaging for a vehicle.

Alex swore out loud. *Damn, that was close.*

Up ahead, that fucking two-seater kept zig-zagging between the other vehicles. In his opinion, those irritating Roadsters should be outlawed, or at least banned from driving on highways. The other drivers seemed to agree with him, if the loud angry honking disturbing the air, was any indication.

"Stupid moron will break his stupid neck." Oh, well. Not his problem.

With a couple of deep calming breaths, Alex pressed on the gas pedal, and once again, eased his car onto the road. For some silly reason, the episode unsettled him.

A moment in time, a second, that's all it took to change things. Irrevocably.

One tiny mistake can cause a tragedy, like a single snowflake can produce an avalanche. Timing was everything. Fate, that fickle bitch, chose that morning to remind him of that. And time *was* running away. Abby's warning rang in his ears, as Alex dropped a glance at his in-dash clock. Almost 6:45. He better hurry if he planned to accomplish anything today.

CHAPTER TEN

As Alex took the next Exit to the Town Center Parkway, he locked away all his unsettling thoughts about fate, timing, and stupid jerks in tiny cars, and concentrated instead on his to-do list. The words 'ring, work, flowers, champagne' looped in his mind. The first three were no problem. But with the last one he needed some help. And that reminded him to tag JC. Without taking his hands off the wheel, Alex engaged Siri on his iPhone, and sent a voice text to his cousin,

> Put the bottle of Dom on ice. Don't tell Abby. Will explain letter. ATA around 4ish.

Two minutes, three, four. No reply. Alex swore out loud.

"JC, you jerk, are you still sleeping?"

He supposed 6:45 was early for some people. But, dammit, by lazing in bed JC wouldn't accomplish anything, not for the career he planned to start anew, and definitely, not for Alex. He was about to dial and give JC a wake-up call, when the single ping announced the arrival of a text. Finally. He slanted his eyes to look at the phone's screen. A thumb-up emoji and a kissy face. Stupid jerk.

He smothered his chuckle. "Up yours, cousin of mine."

Now everything was in place. Well, almost. First, he must buy a ring.

The Jacksonville Town Center, a sprawling kingdom of superstores, boutiques and restaurants, was almost deserted at this hour. But soon it will be bustling with life, full of motions and colors and sounds. Alex loved this special place, with the Apple and Tesla stores among his favorite spots. Not so long ago he was toying with the idea of buying a condo at the Oasis, the complex in the middle of this city within a city. The deal didn't jell, which was for the best. He was not a big-city boy, and the life in quaint Amelia Island suited him.

To admire the bustle and hustle from afar was one thing, but to live in the middle of it? He would go nuts. And what would he do without the ocean, the beach, the cries of seagulls? Lost in thought, Alex was pulled from his reverie when the GPS's modulated voice announced his arrival at desired destination. The familiar teal-colored doors and golden logo Tiffany & Company above the entrance met his gaze. Alex parked the car, shut off the engine. He arrived early. The store was closed, almost two hours until the opening time. No biggie, he'll wait. Listen to music, or log-in to the MLS system to check some new listings.

After a moment's deliberation, he stepped outside. The weather was nice, even if a bit chilly. Grabbing his sport jacket from the passenger seat, Alex shrugged it on. A little walk, some fresh air, before the store opened. No problem.

He palmed his cell phone to do some work, but soon realized that his heart was not on the business matters. Instead, he sent a quick text to his grandmother *Verochka*.

Call me when you can. Have terrific news.

Wherever on the globe she might be, *Verochka* ought to be the first one to hear about his and Abby's engagement. She'd be ecstatic. And maybe— just maybe— she'll decide to cut her travels short, and return. Alex missed her. He hoped that the news of his and Abby's engagement might be the ticket to bring her back.

Hope springs eternal.

Just before Nika and Eli's ultimate departure, his grandmother left for some godforsaken island in the middle of nowhere. And shocked them all. Especially Nika. As much as it upset him, Alex understood *Verochka's* reasoning. She loved Nika more than anybody. Losing her was hard for his illustrious grandmother. Even harder than for Alex.

So, *Verochka* removed herself from the scene altogether, and stayed incommunicado ever since. Alex received just a single text, saying that she was okay. That's it. She ignored his calls, and his messages. She all but vanished from the face of the earth. The truth was, *Verochka* was grieving. And his grandmother preferred to do it in private. She hated tears, and any display of emotional distress.

According to her, a weakness of any kind was an unworthy and undignified behavior. That went double for herself. Hence, the trip to a remote island. Alex got it, but damn it, he missed his grandmother. He needed her.

She was the only family he had left. Despite the hordes of Morrises, Nika and his grandmother were the only people he considered family. Now Nika was gone, so there was only *Verochka*. And okay, JC, too, but the jury was still out on him.

As to his parents and sisters? Alex shrugged. They were complete strangers to him. Didn't matter. He stopped hurting about this sad state of affairs long ago. Sometimes he wished things were different, but...Alex was smart enough to understand that not every family was close. Or loving.

He was lucky to have Nika and *Verochka* in his life. And now there was Abby. And somewhere in time, there was Eli Coleman, his honorary brother, his best friend. A small smile tugged at Alex's lips. He was glad that he admitted the truth to Eli, and got his blessing. Of course, he'd marry Abby no matter what, and that's exactly what he told Eli. But to be accepted and blessed by the man he respected and admired? It meant a lot. A helluva lot.

Alex fingered the old-fashioned watch in his pocket. A priceless Coleman heirloom Eli left him as a gift. From the moment Alex found it under the Christmas tree on that memorable January 1st morning, he never parted with it. Even at home, he always had it on him. As a link, as a reminder. As a memory of the best man he had the privilege to know, even for a short period of time. When his son was old enough, he will pass it onto him. After all, as Eli had mentioned in his note to Alex, 'he'll be a Coleman too, even if in part.' Yes, Alex will pass on the Coleman heirloom and Eli's note to his son. And tell him about his uncle, and his amazing time-traveling aunt, Nika-Daisy.

One day, he'd take his son to the Bosque Bello cemetery and show him two graves. One day...

Alex shook himself from his musings when the Tiffany's doors swung open. What do you know, the two hours passed in a blink.

An impeccably dressed store manager stepped outside, and nodded a greeting to Alex. To skip or not to skip? Better not. To indulge in such an undignified behavior was unseemly, and plain childish. Alex bored down on his impatience, and made an effort to shorten his gait to a simple walk. And almost succeeded.

So, pal of mine, this is it. The rest of your happy-ever-after starts today.

He could hardly wait.

CHAPTER ELEVEN

Abby paced the room. She was alone in the house, and despite its sheer size, the walls started to close in on her. JC left her a note that he went to the market, and Alex was off to the office. So, she was by herself.

Thunderation.

No way Abby was scared. Just...annoyed, she supposed. And impatient. And testy. The foreboding that prompted her haste departure from the Rostoff's estate two days ago was mounting with every passing minute.

Time was running away.

That merciless ticking of the invisible clock inside of her head was getting louder.

Time. Her best friend, and now her enemy.

Time brought her here, to this incredible century, and gave her Alex, and *Verochka*. Time gave her family and friends, and taught her a lot about herself. But now it was pushing and pulling at her, driving her insane with worry. Something was wrong. She was needed somewhere. She felt it deep inside her.

But where?

Maybe, it was just a byproduct of her excitement about Alex? But no, this strange feeling started long before she found out that he loved her.

Way before he kissed her, and set her blood on fire. Abby was torn in so many different directions, it was pure wonder she still managed to stand upright and function.

Think, Abigail, think.

But no matter how hard she tried to rack her brain, the result was the same. She had no idea where this troubling thought came from, or what was at the root of it.

So, alone, agitated, she paced the house, from one corner to the other, brooding.

They left her alone, JC and Alex. And just when she needed them most! Selfish feeling, and silly at that. They all were grown people with duties and obligations. She had no right to expect to be entertained by them. Or be the center of their attention.

But, oh, God, how she wished to have someone around to talk to, to share her fears. Not just someone—*Verochka*. Abby swallowed the lump in her throat. She missed her, her wisdom, her quirky humor, and her confidence. Why did she leave so unexpectedly? And why did she have to travel to that silly island, with no phone connection, or Internet?

"Grandmother, I need you something fierce."

Tears, unwelcomed and hot, misted her vision. Abby allowed herself a moment of weakness, before whipping them away. *Verochka* hated tears. So, Abby will not cry. Even if she wanted nothing else but to curl in a ball, and sob her heart out.

Abigail Suzanne Coleman was not a weakling. She was a strong, independent woman. But even strong women needed help sometimes. Abby was not ashamed to admit that. If only Alex was here! No matter how cross she was with him still, she needed his presence. When he was around, she felt like nothing bad could befall her. She grew to depend on him. Well, maybe *depend* was a wrong word. Abby mulled that for a moment. Having him in her life was a more accurate description. He was like a single stalwart, reassuring, everlasting constant in her life, bigger than ocean, calmer than sky. She loved him so much it should be illegal. Abby pressed both hands to her thumping heart. Joy and hurt, delirium and pain.

Was it supposed to be like that? Like she was rejoicing and dying at the same time? That love was so huge, so fierce, she was all but bursting from within.

Abby didn't know whether she'd survive if Alex hadn't returned her feelings.

Her body? Probably. But her heart, her soul? Not likely.

She needed him on the most primal level. In order to breath, to think, to live.

Should she be scared to need someone that much? Possibly. Probably.

But what about Daisy and her brother?

They both overcame such an impossible obstacle like time to find each other, to be together. She must borrow their example, and be brave. Like Daisy.

The thought of her dear friend brought another flood of tears, and a touch of sadness. Where was Daisy now? Did she think of Abby even if in passing? God, she hoped so.

"Be well, my darling sister. I miss you so much."

Unable to stand a moment longer in the stifling room, she whirled around, and stepped onto the deck. Oh, the glory of the ocean! Immeasurable, infinite. The view managed to calm her jumping nerves like nothing else. Pacified, Abby closed her eyes, and inhaled the salty air. Was it silly that gazing at the vast opulence of the water she felt less alone? The cry of seagulls was strangely reassuring, as was the hum of the waves up ahead. She loved this island. How did she ever think she could live in California? Foolish girl. Amelia was her home, plain and simple. The first constant in her life before Alex. Abby smiled. Now she has them both, her home, and her beloved. And wasn't she the luckiest woman alive? She threw her hands up, and laughed out loud. She was so happy! She wished to shout her happiness to the whole wide world. The pull of the scenery was too strong to resist.

Without a second thought, Abby slid her feet into the flip-flops, grabbed her sketch book, and ran outside.

CHAPTER TWELVE

T hat's where Alex found her when he returned home earlier than planned.

Three hours at the office passed before he admitted his heart was not on business. His thoughts circled to the beach house, and the woman in it.

What was she doing? Was she still mad at him? Will she like the ring?

He was driving himself crazy with all those questions. Daydreaming was not something he was prone to, but today seemed to be the day for it. When he lost the thread of conversation with a potential buyer, Alex decided to call it quits.

The heck with it. To be distracted was one thing, but to be totally and unapologetically impatient with the client was unprofessional and rude. *Before & After, Inc.* has the highest standards. He was determined not to ruin the reputation of his company by acting like a jerk.

The ring burned a hole in his pocket. Anxious to put it on Abby's finger, he left the office in Sue's more than capable hands, and drove away. In his haste to get home, Alex almost forgot to stop by the florist. He cursed, called himself a few unfavorable names, then cursed some more.

Stop being a moron, and keep still.

But his body refused to obey his brain's command. While waiting for his floral arrangement, Alex fidgeted like a schoolboy on his first date. His fingers shook so badly, he dropped the credit card. Damn, he was in bad shape.

The bouquet was huge. He had no choice but to place it in the back seat. Then he worried all the way home if the tender roses might weather the trip.

Alex forgot everything when he pulled into the driveway. He ran up the staircase, then remembered the flowers, and, cursing, reversed his steps.

After he collected the damn thing, he all but flew up the stairs. The door was unlocked. That gave him pause. Why did JC leave the door open? The silence greeted him as soon as he burst inside. He called Abby's name, then JC's, but no one answered. The thought Abby persuaded his cousin to go to the Coleman house without him stopped him cold.

Did she dare? Of course. The infuriating, stubborn creature!

And what might she accomplish by going into the house? Nothing. She cannot unlock the stupid portal. Or...can she?

Alex dropped the flowers in the middle of the floor, and was about to run to his car, when something in his peripheral vision caught his attention. He turned to the window, squinted, and focused on the lone figure sitting on the sand dune up ahead. Abby. Thank God.

Almost dizzy with relief, Alex took a few calming breaths. She was here. She hadn't left. She only went to the beach. Weak as two noodles, his legs refused to carry him. Alex dropped into the chair. Then he rubbed his head. Now what?

And now, buddy, you may proceed with your plan. Just slight change in the scenery. Instead of the deck, you will be kneeling on the sand. Don't forget the bouquet.

Alex looked at the flowers laying on the floor. Thank God they weathered his unceremonious handling, and were no worse for wear. He hefted the roses, then patted his pocket that held the ring.

Time to face the music.

CHAPTER THIRTEEN

Abby sensed his presence long before he dropped beside her on the sand. Was it small of her not to acknowledge his presence? Yes, but so what? She was still cross with him. And the fact that she was more embarrassed by her own wanton behavior than his strict conduct, didn't mean diddly squat. He left her when she all but threw herself at him. Scandalous.

"Abs? What are you doing?"

"What does it look like?"

"Looks like you about to drill a hole on that page with your pencil."

"Huh. A lot do you know about drawing."

"Maybe not a lot, but I know fury when I see it. That poor page doesn't deserve the treatment you're giving it."

"Maybe it doesn't, but it's safer to mangle the page than do what I really want."

"And what might that be?"

"Oh, for goodness..." That was as far as she managed, before she turned to face Alex. He was the only person on this side of grass that managed to make her speechless.

Abby's jaw dropped as she stared at the flowers that almost covered his person. Gazillions of roses, in all shades of the rainbow, swaddled in gossamer and tied with a huge red bow. Abby's breath caught. She had never seen anything so beautiful in her life.

"What...what is it?"

"What does it look like?" He repeated her earlier question.

"Like a marvelous bouquet."

"Right." And with that, he deposited the flowers onto her lap. Abby all but sagged under their weight.

"Alex? What is it?"

"I thought we established it already. Flowers. Roses, to be precise."

"I...can see that. Are these for me?"

"For someone smart, you're asking a really stupid question, Princess."

"Oh." Helpless, she focused on the fragrant bounty, then burrowed her nose in it.

The sweet scent was intoxicating. How else to explain the haze in her brain and mist in her eyes? And the music, something fragile and mesmerizing, that started to play in her ears. Pure magic. Enchanted, Abby looked from the flowers to the face of the man who made that magic possible.

"Alex."

She smiled.

"So, I figure you like it."

"Like it?" She laughed. "I love it! Thank you, thank you so very much! But what is the occasion?"

"I realized that I never gave you flowers before."

Was it her imagination, or Alex was nervous? Abby had a distinct impression that he was evading the true issue.

"Not true. You sent me a bouquet when I was at the hospital."

"That doesn't count. Those were get-well flowers. This..."

He looked away, rubbed his bald head with both hands. No, she was not wrong, Alex was nervous about something. But what?

"And this?" She prodded when the silence stretched.

"And this is...Dammit, I wanted to do it differently. Properly. On the deck, where I..." He rubbed his head again, cursed softly under his breath. As if seeking an inspiration from nature, Alex looked at the ocean, then lifted his gaze toward the sky. Abby watched him in silence, holding her breath. The suspense became unbearable.

"You...what?"

"Kneel in front of you."

"Kneel? Like a knight?"

He was confusing her. Abby frowned, but kept her eyes on his face.

"No, dammit, not like a knight. Like...oh, hell."

Alex jumped to his feet, paced a moment, then turned to her.

"Like this," and with that he dropped to one knee. Then he fingered a small teal box from his pocket, held it in his palm.

Her heart drummed in her chest. Her vision blurred. Through the web of mist in her eyes, Abby focused on his hand with the little box. Unsteady. Shaky. Like his voice. She heard the words, but it took her a moment to realize their meaning.

"Abigail Suzanne Coleman, I love you. Loved you from the first moment I lay my eyes on you, will love you 'till my last breath. Only you. I want to have a future with you. Family, kids, dogs, cats. Hell, we can have a parrot, or a damn monkey, if that's what you wish." Cursing under his breath, Alex took an unsteady breath. "Will you please do me an honor of becoming my wife?"

And just like that, Abby's world tilted, then spun off its axis.

He flipped the small box open. An icy blue fire shot upward the moment the diamond caught the sunrays. A gorgeous, square cut gem in a platinum setting. The ring was both simple and elegant, and stole her breath away. Abby gazed at it as if mesmerized.

Future together. Family with Alex. Children. There was nothing she desired more.

"Well, Princess? What do you say? Will you marry me?"

"Oh, Alex."

"That's all you have to say? 'Oh, Alex?'"

"I wish I could say yes. Thousand times yes."

"What's the problem?" He came a step closer, squinting at her. "Just say it."

"I cannot."

"Why? Do you love me?"

"More than I can say."

"Then, what's the problem?"

"The time. The time is wrong."

Abby couldn't explain why or how she knew that.

"Please, Alex. I love you. I do. So much that it hurts. I do want to live with you, create a family. But not now. I can't accept your proposal, I am sorry."

"Because?"

"I told you. The time is wrong."

"Why? What's wrong with it?"

"I honestly don't know. I just know that I can't marry you now, even if I want it more than anything."

"Bullshit. You either want to marry me, or not. Simple as that. So, which is it?"

"I want to marry you, Alex. But, please, be patient, and ask me some other time."

"What other time? In a month? In a year? Or maybe, in the next century?"

"I...don't know."

"Oh, that's rich, Princess. Even for you. I never figured you for a tease. But live and learn. Well." He flipped the box shut. The sound of it reverberated like a gunshot. Abby winced.

"I am sorry, Alex. Please believe me."

"Yeah, me too." He raised to his feet then looked at her like never before. Reserved, detached. Aloof.

She recognized a cold disdain when it stared at her.

Damning her.

A mere two feet lay between them, but at this moment they were so far away from each other, like they were two centuries apart.

Suddenly cold, unbearably sad, Abby gazed up at him, already grieving.

"You know what, Princess? There will be no other time. When you're ready, you can ask me. But I'm done hitting my head against your whimsy."

With that, Alex turned around and left her sitting in the sand. The enormous bouquet of roses on her lap now seemed like a funeral arrangement. Its sweet aroma turned cloying, nauseating. Abby closed her eyes.

He didn't believe her. And not a wonder. She had a hard time believing herself.

Should she run after him, and accept his proposal? Her heart shouted yes, while her mind said no. She had no right. The time was running away, and she must leave soon. Where? When? She'd give anything right now to know the answer.

But the Universe guarded its secrets. They came in bits and pieces, like a whisper in the wind. She was needed somewhere. Because somewhere something was wrong, and it was for Abby to fix it. She felt it deep in her soul. But Alex didn't believe her. He thought she was playing coy, teasing him. Damn his proud hide!

How to prove him wrong?

You can't. Only time will.

Only time.

CHAPTER FOURTEEN

I f Alex was more infuriated in his life, he'd yet to recall that day. No, not just infuriated, but humiliated on top of it. So, that was her revenge? And for what? For treating her like a lady? Alex wondered how many guys were capable of walking away from a willing, beautiful female when she all but offered herself on a damn platter. Not many. If it was just sex, he'd jump on the opportunity, and think later. If the woman was anyone but Abby, he'd say hell yeah, and sing hallelujah.

But it was not just sex. She was not anyone. She was Abby.

Abigail Suzanne her Snobby Highness Coleman. Damn it all to hell and back.

Sizzling, mad at himself and her, Alex stomped inside the house. And who greeted him with a wicked grin if not his ass of a cousin. Alex swore. He needed a witness to his humiliation like he needed an ulcer. At the moment, an ulcer was preferable. Still grinning, JC pointed at the bottle of champagne chilling in a silver bucket.

"Got your message, Cuz. Congratulations and all the best wishes. Where is the blushing bride?"

Already at the boiling point, Alex's temper fueled by irritation exploded. He let out a long string of very inventive curses, caught his breath, then hollered. "On the fucking beach."

Unfazed, JC tilted his head, as his smile spread even wider.

Son of a bitch.

"What's she doing there?"

"Blushing."

"Okay." JC scrounged his forehead, rubbed his chin. "So, are we popping a bubbly, or not?"

"Not." Alex's irritation shot all the way up into the stratosphere. "On the other hand, why the hell not?" He grabbed the champagne.

Wrap a towel, pal.

The thought flashed a second too late. Wet and cold, the bottle slipped from his fingers, and exploded in the thousand shards, spewing an excellent French wine across the parquet floor. As a coup de grâce, Alex managed to cut himself. Blood spurted from the deep gash in his palm, infuriating him even further.

"Fuck! Fucking fuck!"

He clutched a kitchen towel, and pressed it to his wound.

"Listen, it looks bad, Cuz. Let me drive you to the hospital."

"Fuck the hospital."

"Okay, but let me wrap it properly, and put some Neosporin on it. Although, stiches might be better."

Alex gritted his teeth. Damn, that stupid cut hurt like a mother.

"Don't need any stiches. Just get the First Aid kit."

"On it. Go wash it under cold water then I'll take another look."

Wincing, Alex stuck his hand under the water. The wound was deep and ugly. The hell with it. No way was he letting someone poke a needle in it. A Band-Aid and a painkiller, that's all he needed. JC returned with Nika's box of medical supplies. He took Alex's hand gently and examined it. After a short moment of consideration, he let out a heavy breath.

"Not so bad. Deep, but not bad. You're a lucky bastard."

Alex averted his eyes as JC dealt with the gash. He was not afraid of blood, but neither did he draw pleasure looking at it. He winced, but managed to prevent a yelp, as JC poured a generous portion of peroxide over the cut.

"Want me to blow on it?"

"I'll tell you what you can blow. Ouch!"

"Don't be a baby, man." JC's tone was deceptively humorous, while his eyes were glued to Alex's hand. He deftly applied antiseptic, then wrapped the hand in gauze. "There, all done. Such a brave boy. Want a lollipop?"

"Up yours."

"The patient will live." JC cracked a smile. "Want to tell me what happened on the beach?"

"No."

"Okay, I can connect the dots by myself. Your pocket is bulging with a small box. Ring, I suppose? Some stray rose petals on the floor. You texted me to chill the champagne. Smart man that I am, I came to the only possible conclusion: you chose this beautiful day to propose. And, seeing like you came back with a murderous expression on your pretty face, and Abby is still on the beach, blushing—"

"Bastard."

"Thank you. So, my conclusion is the lady refused."

"So, what?"

"So, nothing. Are you going to pursue the issue?"

"No fucking way."

"Okay, then I guess it's only fair to inform you of my intentions to make a play at her. You're not interested. I'm very interested, so—"

"The fuck you are!"

And before JC had a chance to blink, Alex pounced.

His fist connected hard with JC's chin. Because it was his injured hand, Alex yelped with pain. Cradling his abused hand, shaking, he faced his opponent. JC worked his jaw gingerly, but didn't step away. The bastard! Millions of bright stars dotted Alex's vision, but his outrage fueled his resolve.

Make a play at Abby? Very interested, is he?

What irritated him further, JC didn't break a sweat, while Alex was breathing like an overloaded freight truck. Then the indolent moron lifted a brow, and had the audacity to laugh.

"Just what I figured. Feel better?"

Alex saw red. "I'll show you—"

"Relax, Cuz. I was baiting you. On purpose. You idiot, she loves you. Even a blind man can see that."

"Yeah? If she loves me that much, why did she say no?"

"That's all she said? Just no? Without explanation?"

"There was a bullshit explanation about time's being wrong."

JC shrugged. "So, the time must be wrong, then."

"What's wrong with it?"

"No clue, but why don't you ask Abby?"

"I did. What do you think I am, an idiot?"

"Well, the jury's still out on that one. But back to my previous question. You asked her, and...?"

"And she said she didn't know."

"Then, there's your answer."

"You think you're funny, JC?"

"No. Smart, shrewd, selfish, yes. Funny? A definite no."

"Oh, the hell with it."

This absurd conversation was getting nowhere.

Deflated, Alex took a deep breath, rubbed his head with his good hand. Not JC's fault, any of it. But, boy, that man hit all the wrong buttons.

He needed solitude, a few moments of blessed oblivion to brood and decide on his next course of action. Because no matter what he said earlier, he will pursue the issue. Abby will marry him; she'll say yes. Maybe not today, or tomorrow, but she will. Alex was a patient man. He'd wait. If she needed some time, he'd give it to her. Even if it killed him.

"Tell you what, cousin of mine." JC's cheerful voice cut into his musings. "How about we go to that famous historical bar, The Palace Saloon? Since you destroyed the excellent champagne I had the craving for all day, let's go and have a drink. My treat."

Alex was probably in worse shape than he thought, if JC decided to play babysitter. He squinted at his cousin.

"Are you by any chance feeling sorry for me?"

"Sorry? For you? Why would you think that?"

"Just like a fucking lawyer, always answering a question with a question."

"My dear Alex, I am a fucking lawyer. So, what do you say? Guys night on the town?"

That was the last thing he wanted. His reply—"Why the hell not"—both surprised and annoyed Alex. What was wrong with him?

"I'm driving." And before Alex had a chance to object, JC snatched the keys, and was by the door. "Coming?"

"Shit."

Too late to retaliate. Dammit, he didn't want to drink, or go out with his dick of a cousin. He wanted to be left the fuck alone. His hand throbbed like a rotten tooth. His head pounded.

Why did you agree?

Because the prospect of spending the evening in a close proximity to Abby was daunting. Cursing all the way, Alex followed JC.

After a short drive they entered the famous bar, guarded outside by a huge sculpture of a pirate. JC made a beeline toward the table at the farthest corner. Alex had no choice but trail in his footsteps. A tall waitress followed in their wake.

Against Alex's better judgment, JC ordered straight whiskey, no rocks. Alex preferred vodka, but JC appointed himself host of this impromptu pity party, and took the lead. Whatever. Frankly, Alex didn't care. He didn't feel like drinking at all. He decided to indulge JC, who seemed to take his role seriously.

Shmuck.

"So, Alex, tell your older cousin everything." And JC clicked his glass with Alex's. "Cheers."

The Palace Saloon, was the playground for the rich and famous in its hey-day. Carnegies, Rockefellers, Yulees, and his brother-in-law, Eli Coleman, were all frequent patrons of that fine establishment in the early 1900s. When he visited it a few weeks ago, Eli was surprised and pleased that the ambience stayed exactly the same, but for a small change. *Eli.*

Damn. Alex mood plummeted as he remembered his friend.

Shouldn't come here. Too late now.

"Cuz?" JC's voice pulled him out of his reverie.

"What do you want me to say?"

So, what if he sounded like a petulant child? He was tired, and on the last leg of his endurance. His head ached. His hand throbbed. He was a mess.

Damn, should've stayed home.

"Truth, all the truth, and nothing but the truth."

As humor went, that was a good one. Probably.

Shrugging, Alex parried with his own. "You can't handle the truth."

JC burst out laughing. "Checkmate. Still, why don't you try me?"

"Try you? Okay." The hell with it. Too tired to think, or weight through the wisdom of his decision, Alex shrugged.

JC wanted the truth? Well, let him get a load of it. The beckoning of a full glass of whiskey became irresistible. Why not? Alex upended it in one long gulp. His abused gut screamed in protest, but the burning sensation was just what the doctor ordered. JC raised his brow, but didn't comment. Instead, he signaled for another round with his left hand.

"So, you were saying?" He prompted when the order was delivered. As soon as the whiskey was in front of him, Alex snatched it then brought it to his lips. After he emptied half a glass, he squinted at his cousin. Damn, the Counselor was insistent.

He asked for it.

CHAPTER FIFTEEN

"**T**he truth, then." Alex nodded. "Last year, Nika, my cousin and your sister, was transported through time, to the year of 1909. There she met Elijah Coleman, the original owner of the house she was hired to restore. They fell in love. Then Nika decided to come home, to say goodbye to me and *Verochka*, but lost the key that opens the damn portal. And she was stuck in this time. Oh, and she brought Eli's sister with her. Abby." At the mention of her, Alex stopped, cursed, then gulped the remaining whiskey. "As soon as I saw her, I was lost. Just lost, man. I knew she was the one. But she's so young, barely no longer a girl, and from another era. Edwardian lady. Can you beat that?" He looked at the passing waiter, and raised his empty glass in silent order for a refill. "But nothing mattered. I love her, and I will marry her." He patted his breast pocket. "Got a ring. It's a beaut. Wanna see it?"

"Maybe later. Go on."

"Couldn't work. Bought flowers. Roses. Came home early, saw her on the beach. She took my breath away. As always. Go to the beach, give her the fucking bunch of roses. Kneel on the fucking sand. And what did she say?" Disgusted, half-way wasted already, Alex grabbed a fresh glass.

"What did she say?" JC prodded.

Alex gazed at him, trying to gauge his reaction. But JC's face was blank, devoid of any expression. Weird. For some reason that eluded Alex at the moment, he was pleased. His thoughts became jumbled, and he had trouble holding onto the thread of the conversation. Okay, where was he? Oh, yeah.

"She said the time's not right. She loves me, mind you, but can't accept my marriage proposal yet, because the fucking time's not right. Can you believe this shit? What time, I ask you? When two people are in love with each other, what does time have to do with anything?"

"You asking me?"

"Do you see anyone else here, Counselor?"

"Hmm." JC lowered his eyes. "I'd say, under the circumstances, time should be the last thing on her mind, but—"

"Exactly!" Warming up, Alex gulped more whiskey. Once again, he raised a hand for another round. "Time. I started to hate it, you know. Especially after Nika."

"Speaking of which. What happened next? After Nika came here, I mean."

"Oh, yeah. She came, brought Abby. Did I tell you that? Guess I did. Okay. When she realized she was stuck here, she almost died. Restored that stupid house in record time. But couldn't open the portal without a key. Then, more than a year later, Eli popped here, and after a while, he and Nika went back in time. That's all. End of story."

"And Abby stayed here."

"Yes."

"And now she...what? Wants to come back?"

"No." Alex frowned. She didn't, or did she? "Just made some weird statement about something, somewhere is wrong. And time's running away."

JC mulled that in silence for a long moment.

"And the portal? Is it in the Coleman house?"

"Yeah, that stupid grandfather clock you became orgasmic over the other night."

"Figured. And it could be open with the key?"

"Not just a key, but the original key. The one and only."

"And that key is presently...where?"

"In 1909. In the original house."

"That's how Nika and Eli got back in time?"

"Exactomundo."

"And now you are afraid that Abby might open the portal?"

"Yes." *Afraid?* He was terrified.

"Without a key?"

"Oh, she's a resourceful sort. She'll find a way if she wants to. Wouldn't surprise me if she said some abracadabra and opened it just like that." He snapped his fingers under JC's nose.

"Then, cousin of mine, what are you waiting for?"

"Huh?"

"Alex, pay attention." Now it was JC who snapped his fingers under Alex's nose. "The grandfather clock is the portal, right? No portal, no problem. Simple as that."

"W-what?"

He must be drunker than he thought. For the life of him, he failed to grasp the significance of his cousin's statement.

"Cuz, the solution is simple. We must destroy that clock."

"We must?"

"Abso-fucking-lutely, as our Nika says. Well," JC's enthusiastic back thump almost sent Alex face first into the table. "Let's do it."

CHAPTER SIXTEEN

Almost midnight. Abby glanced at the clock for the umpteenth time. Where were they? Where did Alex and JC go? Alex's car was missing, so they must have driven somewhere together. But where? She was worried about Alex. He took her rejection badly. She didn't reject him exactly, just postponed the acceptance of his proposal.

And why did you do it, you imbecile?

Should have said yes, and accept the ring, and worry about everything else later. Oh, well. Beating herself over her stupidity was both unwise and unproductive.

No crying over spilled milk, Abigail.

And it won't change anything, except giving her anxiety. And shame. And guilt. And...

"Oh, for crying out loud!"

Abby swept the room with her eyes. She cleared the mess from the broken bottle earlier, removed all the shards, and mopped the floor. The roses she carried into the house were now in water. There was so many of them, she used every last available vase, and still was forced to use a few empty bottles. The living room now resembled a garden and smelled like ambrosia.

Why did she hate it?

Because it reminds you of your folly.

No, she refused to cry or fret about *what ifs*. What's done was done. Now, she must think. But her mind was blank like a clear page from her sketch book. What should he do now? And where were those two imbeciles? Driving in the dark like two rowdy teenagers after a few sips of beer. Fernandina Beach was not a dangerous city, and crime was a rare occurrence. But what if they were in an accident, injured? Oh, God. Should she call Alex? Or JC? Abby grabbed her phone, then decided against it. If they wanted her to know where they were, they would have called.

"At least they could've left me a note."

But no, they just disappeared without a word, the blasted morons. She was more cross with JC than Alex. How could he do that to her? Alex's motivation was obvious. Insulted and humiliated, he didn't want to be under the same roof with her.

But JC? Didn't he understand how worried she might be? Did he even care?

With a deep sigh, Abby relented.

No matter how friendly and kind to her JC was, his first allegiance lay with his cousin. As it should be. Well, at least, Alex wasn't alone. He needed the presence of another man right now. He was cross with her, unsettled, and probably sad.

But what about me?

She too was sad, and unsettled. And, God, so scared! She desperately needed someone to talk to. No, not someone, but another woman.

"Oh, *Verochka*! I need you so much."

But *Verochka* was God knows where, and unable to console her.

Abby squared her shoulders, straightened her spine, and inhaled deep. Abigail Suzanne Coleman was made of sterner stuff. She'll manage.

What choice do I have?

She'd be strong and brave like Daisy, and wise like *Verochka*. And if she made a mess of her relationship with Alex, she'd fix it.

As soon as he returned home, the stubborn scamp. Fortified with her decision, Abby looked at the clock again. Midnight. A familiar sonorous chiming filled the room.

The Coleman grandfather clock.

Loud and insistent, that *bong-bong* reverberated through the house, making the vases on the table shake. Abby froze, then whirled around. Did the clock somehow materialize here? But no, of course not. Why, then, did she hear it so clear like it was behind her?

Bong, bong, bong.

Gaining strength, the chiming was almost deafening. Ominous.

Her heart leaped into her throat. Something was wrong. Trouble was brewing. With Alex? But no, in her heart she knew that he was unharmed. What, then?

A strong, almost painful pull from deep within her was impossible to ignore.

Time has run out...

The knowledge cut through. She must go to the Coleman house. At once.

She was needed.

There was no time to lose.

Without a second thought, Abby grabbed the key from the car Nika so generously gifted her, and ran to the garage. She jumped inside the red Corvette, bore down on her uneasiness, and started the engine. The low humming of the powerful motor gave her a minute of apprehension. She hadn't driven for a long time, and she was afraid she forgot all the lessons. She had a strong resolve and vowed to do what she must.

Taking a deep breath, Abby patted the dashboard. Daisy always talked to the car. Unsure of the wisdom of it, but desperate enough to try anything at this point, Abby cleared her throat. "Okay, Coco. It's me, Abby. I'd really appreciate your help now."

The motor purred like a kitten, quiet and steady. A good omen.

Still nervous, Abby allowed herself a moment to settle, then shook her head.

What was she waiting for? Time's awasting.

With the unsteady hands she gripped the steering wheel and pressed the gas pedal.

CHAPTER SEVENTEEN

He was drunk as a skunk. Disgusted, Alex tried to orient himself. Leather, dashboard, seatbelt. So, he was in a car. A moving car. Huh. What car? He squinted at a jiggling trinket hanging from the rearview mirror. A four-leaf clover and a grinning leprechaun. A lucky charm. *His* lucky charm, the one Nika gave him when he bought his Porsche. Alex cracked a smile. *Nika.* Then his muddled brain had a sudden moment of clarity. Why was he slumped on the passenger seat of his own damn car? He slanted a sideways glance and grimaced. If he had any moisture left in his mouth, he'd have spit and cursed.

JC, his pain in the ass older cousin, was at the wheel, happy as a clam.

The bastard.

No one was allowed to touch his Baby, never mind drive it! Even inebriated, Alex remembered that sacred rule. With what was left of his strength, he tried to sit up. But weak as a newborn, his body refused to oblige. Damn. Strong liquor always did that to him. Rendered to the state of a overcooked noodle, his limbs lay limp, almost useless. On top of everything, his throat was parched, and his head pounded with a steady rhythm of a Nazi march. Not to mention his wounded hand, that throbbed like a rotten tooth. In short, he felt like shit.

With an enormous effort, Alex gathered the last crumbs of his willpower.

"Y-you're... drivin' m-my car."

Geez, he was slurring. Humiliating.

"Yes, I am." Unperturbed, JC kept his eyes glued to the road.

"W-why?"

"Because you're wasted. Like totally."

He supposed that make sense. He was wasted. Alex squinted at his cousin.

"And y-you're n-not?"

"Nope. Barely had a couple of sips."

"Huh. Why?"

"Because someone had to keep a clear head. And drive."

"T-there's Uber."

"Yes, but I'd've lose all the fun driving your excellent car."

"N-no one's all'wed to d-drive my B-baby."

JC dared to smirk.

"I know." And patted Alex's knee. The jerk.

"Ash-shole."

"Yep, that's me. Among other things."

"Enjoying you'self, a-are you?"

"Enormously."

"You'll so p-pay for it, Junior."

JC shrugged his shoulders. "Still be worth it."

Cursing, Alex pulled himself all the way up in a seat. Shit, his head was about to explode. He was ready to give his right nut for an aspirin. Why was it always right nut? Why not the left? *And why do you care?* Stupid. He was stupid. The situation was stupid. Everything was fucking stupid. Shouldn't drink whiskey. Shouldn't drink, period. Why did he? Oh, yeah. Abby, and his botched marriage proposal. Caved under pressure because his ego didn't handle rejection. But she didn't refuse. She said...what did she say? Something about time wasn't right. Didn't take his ring. Didn't even look at it. Stubborn, insufferable creature. Didn't she understand that his pride was on the line?

Dammit, what pride?

Alex no longer had a drop of that precious commodity left. Today at the beach, embarrassed and discouraged, he was ready to beg.

And wouldn't that be the ultimate humiliation?

Ask her again later? No way in hell. She can do all the asking from now on.

His head was killing him. The attempt to clear it by a vigorous shaking was a huge mistake. A helpless moan added more indignity to his current predicament.

The hell with it. Alex concentrated on the view through the window. Another mistake. His abused head started to swim and churning nausea scorched his gut. Bile charged up his throat.

Damned if I throw up in my own car. Out of the question.

Alex clamped his jaw in defense and closed his eyes. After a long charged moment, the burning sensation passed, and he breathed easier.

JC executed a sharp right turn, and the unexpected maneuver sent Alex smack against the door. He cursed. Like he needed a bruised shoulder on top of everything! Another turn of the car, then another. Damn, where was that jerk driving?

"W-where are we g-going?"

"To the Coleman house. Where else?"

Poleaxed, Alex forgot about his discomfort.

"Why?"

"Why? He's asking why." JC glanced at Alex and rolled his eyes. "Because, Cuz, that's where the infamous grandfather clock is."

"S-so?"

"You really don't remember?"

"Remember... what?"

"Our conversation. Or, rather, your monologue." JC dropped an amused gaze at him. "About time-travel, and portal, and your fears that Abby might jump back in time."

More curious than angry, Alex gazed at JC. "Did I tell you all that?"

"And then some."

Frowning, Alex mulled that for a moment. Did he really reveal the truth to JC? What on earth possessed him?

On one hand, he was glad that everything was up in the open, on the other...

JC seemed to take his crazy confession in stride, if his calm demeanor was any indication. Then again, he was a lawyer. A poker face was his tool in trade.

He slanted a wary glance at his cousin. "And you believed me?"

"Let's just say, I didn't disbelieve you. I always thought there was something about Eli..." He shrugged again, as his voice trailed into silence. "And Nika and Eli's disappearing act on the New Year's Eve made me curious. Then, there's our Abby."

"*Our* Abby?"

The nerve of the bastard! A sudden fury burst free.

Riding on it, Alex jerked at the seatbelt. Instead of releasing the stupid device, he managed to open the cut on his palm.

A hot searing pain and oozing blood onto the gauze added to his rage. Incensed, Alex pivoted, and struck out with his left hand. And failed. His intended jab to JC's jaw grazed his shoulder instead. Barely.

A string of crude and colorful curses stole his breath, but didn't squelch his fury.

"She's my Abby, you lousy jerk! Mine! Got it?"

"Don't get so worked up, buddy." Without effort, JC brushed Alex's hand from his shoulder to his knee. To add insult to injury, he patted it. "I just meant, she's family now. Our family."

Still sizzling, Alex flung his cousin hand away. "She's my future wife, so don't get any ideas."

"None whatsoever, Cuz. Just stating the facts." And the bastard smirked.

Oh, to wipe that slimy leer from his face! Later.

Unaware of his impending fate, JC returned his laughing eyes to the road.

"As I was saying before being so rudely interrupted, some things just didn't add up. I wondered, and when I wonder, I tend to become suspicious. And when I become suspicious, there's no stopping me from getting the answers."

JC braked, turned off the ignition. "And we are here. Do you happened to have the keys?"

"What do you think?"

"I'll take it as a no. Terrific. Well, breaking and entering, then. Aren't you lucky to have a lawyer at your disposal?"

"In case its s-slipped your mind, Counselor, if we're c-caught, you'll get arrested, too."

"We'll see about that." JC sent him a wicked grin. "First, they need to catch me. But fear not, cousin of mine. I'll post your bail." And with that cheerful statement, JC opened the car door. "Coming?"

The nagging feeling in Alex's gut became persistent.

Why did JC bring them here?

Something fluttered in the back of his mind. A blurry thought about time, and Abby, and...Damn, why can't he concentrate?

Because you're drunk.

"JC, wait."

Alex almost fell off the car, cursed, and managed to drag himself upright by gripping the car door and roof. "W-why are we here?"

"To destroy the stupid clock, of course."

The throbbing in his head intensified. Was he drunker than he thought or was JC demented? Destroy the prized Coleman grandfather clock? That doesn't make any sense.

"Remind me again, why do we want to destroy that clock?"

"Sure thing, Cuz. According to you, that blasted thing is a portal. Correct?"

"Y-yes."

"And you're afraid that Abby might open it somehow, and disappear?"

"Yes."

"Well, then, the only way to ensure that it won't happen, is to close the portal. Ergo, destroy the most marvelous antic timepiece I've ever seen in my life. But, what's an object d'art compared to family?"

Alex rubbed his aching head. "And you're willing to do it?"

"Willing and able, buddy. But we'll need some tools. Do you happen to have anything in the trunk?"

This situation was ridiculous. Like a scene from a bad and cheesy sitcom. Befuddled, he looked at JC.

"Like...what?"

"Like a crowbar, or a baseball bat."

"A ...crowbar? Geez, Junior. What do you take me for?"

Unperturbed, his cousin nodded. "Didn't think so."

JC went around Alex, popped the trunk up, and rummaged around. "No worries, we'll manage. Somehow."

After a moment, JC exclaimed "Eureka!" and lifted a portable jack.

Flabbergasted, Alex watched as his cousin slammed the trunk close, and hefted the small but heavy tool in both hands. "Better than nothing."

"You're crazy, you know that?"

"Maybe. It's in the blood, I guess. Well," and JC nudged Alex with his hip, "what are we waiting for? Time's awasting."

Abby's voice cut into his subconsciousness: *Time is running away.*

As Alex turned, his gaze collided with the imposing structure up ahead.

The Coleman house. Eli and Abby's home. The magnificent building his cousin so painstakingly restored. Illuminated by the wan moonlight, its tall looming tower seemed eerie. Ominous. Breathtaking.

In a blink of an eye, the picture in front of him shifted, and shimmered.

Something dark and shapeless slithered from the windows of the building.

Obscene. Vile.

The acrid smell clogged his throat, and stung his eyes. His eardrums popped from the pressure. Alex froze, unable to tear his eyes from it. Then, just as suddenly, the horrific images flashed away, and the picture snapped back into sharp focus.

All the fine hair on his body raised to painful points. What the hell was it? His imagination? A trick of moonlight? But no matter what, the impression was sinister. Chilled to the bone, Alex shivered. Nika always claimed the house was alive. And he laughed at her.

Guess I am a moron.

He had no doubt about it. The Coleman house was alive, and it just issued Alex the warning to stay away.

He glared at it, still spooked, but unrelenting.

The hell I will!

The day when a pile of bricks scared him away would be long coming. Like never. One the plus side, the freaky spectacle helped to clear his fuzzy brain and chase his headache away. Steady and almost completely sober, Alex took a deep breath. Now what? The most sensible course of action was to turn around, get in a car, and go home. To think, and reevaluate. And return later, but in daylight, and with the keys.

And alone.

JC! Damn, he forgot about his cousin. Where was that idiot? Alex looked over his shoulder, and froze. JC was at the gates, about to scale it.

Adrenalin pumped into his bloodstream and Alex started to run.

"JC! Wait! Wait, dammit. We can't."

Already perched atop of the wall, his cousin spared him a withering glance.

"Of course, we can. What, getting cold feet all of a sudden?"

"No, just finally reclaiming some common sense. Get down. I'm serious. It's Abby's property. Her home. We can't just get inside and demolish her things."

"Not things, Cuz, just a single thing—the grandfather clock."

"I don't care. Get back down, JC. I changed my mind."

"Chicken."

A screech of tires caught their attention. Still astride, with the jack in his hands, JC pivoted his head at the sound.

"Uh-oh. We're so busted."

Dammit, a police cruiser was all they needed at the moment.

Cursing under his breath, Alex turned and lost his breath.

Magnificent in her wrath, with her eyes shooting fire, Abby glared at them in turn.

Fury, thy name is woman.

"What the hell do you think you're doing?"

CHAPTER EIGHTEEN

The ensued silence was deafening. Alex wondered if she heard his drumming heart. At long last, he untangled his tongue.

"Abby, why are you here?"

"Why am I here? This is my property, in case you forgot. But," she gave him one smoldering glance, before lifting her eyes to JC, "what are you two imbeciles doing here? And at this ungodly hour?"

"Abs, we were just..." Obviously at a loss for words, JC shrugged. His grin did nothing to pacify Abby's anger. Even though her head was thrown back, she somehow managed to look at JC down her nose.

God, what a woman!

Try as he might, Alex failed to swallow his chuckle. That earned him another disgusted glare. Clearly irate, the Princess crisscrossed her arms over her chest, and lifted her spectacular boobs higher. Alex groaned. Damn, she was killing him.

Abby ignored him, and addressed JC, "Just what? Visiting? And what is that thing doing on top of my gates?"

"You mean, JC, or the jack?"

Alex's attempt to humor fell on flat ears. Unimpressed, Abby aimed her fumigating glare at him, and all but scorched his skin.

"If you think you're funny, I beg to differ," she said through clenched teeth.

"Hey, don't blame Alex. It was my idea." Limber as a goat, JC jumped down from the gate to stand near him. The damned jack rested under his arm.

"Your idea? And what that idea might be, if you don't mind my asking?"

"To...to..." JC stammered, then looked at Alex for help.

"To...what?" Abby prompted in an icy voice.

Okay, the poor jerk was over his head. Time to interfere.

After all, it was Alex's fault. If not for his drunken confession, JC would never have attempt anything so crazy.

"To see the grandfather clock again," he blurted.

Two pairs of eyes turned in unison to stare at him. Alex plunged ahead. "JC fell in love with that stupid thing, remember? So, he wanted... to see it again."

If he ever heard an explanation lamer, he had no recollection of it.

Stupid, Alex. So stupid.

Abby's expression changed from incredulous to disgusted.

"And you couldn't wait until morning to see it? Or had a sagacity to ask for the key?"

"Sweet baby Jesus, *sagacity*!" JC's delighted grin split his face. "I love how you talk, Abs."

Far from amused, Abby tilted her head, and aimed an insolent glare at his cousin.

Uh-oh. If eyes could kill, JC would be suffering from the mortal wounds by now.

Better you than me, buddy.

"That's Abigail to you, you rascal. And don't change the subject!"

JC winced, and lowered his gaze. "Wouldn't dream of it, Your Highness."

"And you," she wrinkled her nose in apparent distaste, as she turned to address Alex, "you're drunk, sir. Drunk like a sailor! And dirty on top of it. The stench of you can flatten the rock! And what on earth did you do to your hand? Got in a drunken brawl?

Scandalous." Abby huffed in disgust. "Good thing your grandmother can't see it. Well, what do you have to say for yourself, sir?"

"I don't know." Alex swallowed his laughter, and tagged at his earlobe. "Sorry?"

His mock apology phrased like a question earned him another glare, and a sneer.

"Sorry? Huh! We'll talk later about your abhorrent behavior."

Probably not smart to enjoy himself so much, but damned if he was able to do anything about it. She was so adorable, flushed and disheveled, with her hair coming undone from her tidy bun, and her brows knitted.

And calling him 'sir' in that snooty voice.

Grinning like a fool, Alex couldn't tear his eyes away from her.

"And you," she turned to JC, pointing at the jack under his arm. "Remove this thing at once, and—"

Whatever Abby was going to tell froze on her lips, as an explosion of brilliant light illuminated the estate from within. The thunderous earsplitting *boom* shook the ground. Before his brain processed it, Alex sprinted toward the gates. The sounds of running footsteps behind him made him stop. He pivoted in time to catch Abby, who all but flew into his arms.

"Give me the keys."

"What? Why?"

"The keys, Abs. Quickly. And stay here."

"Oh, no! No possible way!"

"Way." He accompanied his words by grabbing her arm, and thrusting her at his cousin. Stupid jerk still had the jack in his hands. "Lose the fucking thing, will you, and hold her. Don't let her get inside. Got it?"

"Yes." Without breaking a stride, JC dropped the tool, and enfolded Abby in tight embrace. Shocked at first, she soon came to her senses, and started to fight.

"Let me go, you stupid imbecile! Remove your hands from me at once!"

She wiggled, stomped her feet, and butted JC with her head. Wincing, his cousin gritted his teeth, but didn't move an inch.

"I mean it, JC. Whatever you must do, do it, but don't let her get inside that house."

"I hear you." JC grunted as Abby's head connected with his jaw again. "Don't worry, Alex. Go, go already!"

He didn't need another encouragement. Snatching the keys from Abby hands, Alex run toward the gates. The alcoholic fumes in his brain seemed to evaporate on cue. Almost sober, he navigated the path toward the house with a surefooted sprint. An inventive string of her angry curses increased his speed.

JC was strong, but Abby was determined. Just a matter of time before she broke loose and joined in pursuit. He must get to the house first. Whatever was happening inside the estate was unnatural. It was for him to deal with it. No way Abby was stepping a foot inside that house. No freaking way.

As soon as he opened the gates, the wave of an invisible force all but threw Alex backward.

The stupid bastard.

Undeterred, he gritted his teeth, and plunged forward. It was like walking though churning water. Every step was an effort. Every breath an agony. By the time Alex reached the massive doors of the house, he was drenched in cold sweat and shaking. The tremor in his hands was so bad, he dropped the keys. After three attempts, he managed to insert the key into the slot.

The blasted doors groaned like a living creature, and fought his entrance.

Cursing a blue streak, Alex threw all his weight, and finally managed to flung it open. The first thing that caught his eye was the grandfather clock at the end of the hallway. Tall and imposing, it seemed to pulse and vibrate. Fireworks of radiant beams flew in every direction in short, angry bursts, while the clock chimed the hour in its clear sonorous voice.

Fire and ice.

Rage and calmness.

The contrast was daunting. Despite being awash in a brilliant golden glow, the scene was ominous.

A macabre dance of light.

Disoriented, half blind from that unholy glare, Alex stood frozen to the spot.

He was unable to move a single muscle. Trapped. He was trapped in a nightmare, rendered deaf, blind, and mute. Useless, helpless.

The hell I am!

Gathering all his resolve, fighting against the invisible force, Alex moved forward. One step, then another, and another.

By God, he would get to that blasted clock, and break it with his bare hands. Alex stumbled, as his foot encounter some obstacle on the floor.

By a pure miracle he managed to stay on his feet. What was that thing?

Alex squinted down, then let out a broken oath, as he realized what he was looking at. A body. Someone has broken in. But how? The door was intact, the lock untouched. And nevertheless, someone had found the way inside, and was even now sprawled on the floor. An accident? A murder? Dammit all to hell and back!

Thank God he left Abby outside. His scattered thoughts raced around his brain. Call 911.Where was his phone? In the pocket. Get it out, and call the cops.

Okay, stay focused, Alex. Don't panic.

Don't panic? Really?

Fighting his bubbling hysteria, Alex reached his right hand to grab the phone. He yelped as pain shot through him. Damn, that was his injured hand. But the pain was welcomed. It reminded him that he was alive and well, blinding lights and eerie chiming notwithstanding, while this stranger on the floor...

The moan was tiny and fragile, and sent his drumming heart into overdrive.

Alive, thank God.

Whoever was laying on the floor was alive. Probably injured, but alive. He dropped his phone into a back pocket, then bent over the moaning stranger. As soon as his fingers brushed over the warm flesh, the insistent chiming ceased, and all the lights died. He was plunged into a total darkness.

Disoriented, blindsided, Alex froze. That abrupt stillness was more disconcerting than the spooky light show just moments ago. But at least, the incessant chiming stopped. His brain has cleared enough to send orders to his limbs.

Get moving. Get to the person on the floor. Get help.

Alex shook off the last remnants of his shock, and groped his way to a light switch.

As far as he remembered, it was on the wall, somewhere on his left.

But someone beat him to it. Alex blinked, as the bright lights poured in. Abby, her hand still on the switch, faced him across the room. JC, breathing hard, entered on a limping run.

"Sorry, Cuz, but she fights dirty. I couldn't hold her any longer."

Before Alex formed a reply, Abby sucked on a sharp breath, and sagged against the wall.

"Oh, no, no. No!"

Then she jolted, and ran the short distance to the prone figure on the floor. Too late to stop her, Alex turned and followed. First thing that registered in his mind was the stranger was female. Long skirt, dainty shoes, small hands. Kneeling in front of her, Abby tried to gather the unmoving body into her embrace, all the while wailing 'no, no, no.' Then she looked over her shoulder at Alex. Her terrified face was drawn, her eyes glazed with shock and sorrow.

"I'm too late! Oh, God, this is all my fault!"

"What? No, no, Abby. Whoever it is, she was moaning—"

"Whoever it is?" She sat on her hunches, and allowed him the first unobscured view of the woman on the floor. "This is Daisy! Can't you see? She returned!"

Who the hell is Daisy, and why did she return?

And then his scattered brain connected the dots, and Alex's world dimmed.

Narrowed to tunnel vision, with bright sparks licking at the edges, his eyes refused to accept the truth. Impossible. Unthinkable. Un-fucking-believable.

There, in the middle of the floor, was his Nika, dressed in an old-fashioned long skirt, and high-necked blouse. Her sunny curls fanned around her head like a golden halo. In stark contrast, her face was ashen, paler than virgin snow.

But the real shock came a moment later. Stunned, Alex stared at Nika's large protruding stomach. Were his eyes deceiving him, or his cousin was really pregnant? She wasn't when she and Eli embarked on their final journey. Now, five short days later, she was sporting a baby bump larger than a watermelon. He blinked a couple of times. Was he still under the influence? He shut his eyes, opened them again. The picture in front of his eyes remained the same. Nika. Pregnant. Unconscious.

Alex shook his head. Denial and shock rendered him speechless.

"She's... pregnant."

"No shit, Sherlock." JC, still limping, elbowed him aside. Then he kneeled in front of Nika. "Your observation skill is terrifying."

"But...but..."

"But nothing." He snapped. After a warning glare at Alex, he turned to tend his sister. Still unresponsive, she lay on the floor, so small, helpless, and fragile, it broke Alex's heart. He missed her. Just five short days, but it seemed like centuries. Why did she return? What happened? Only a disaster of major proportions was able to force her to risk her pregnancy. And where was Eli? Why did he let her jump through that damned portal alone? Something was wrong. Very wrong.

Alex watched as JC took Nika's wrist, held it for a long moment, then let out a huge breath of relief.

"She's okay. Her pulse is a bit scattered, but strong." He touched Nika's head, gently raking his fingers through her hair. "No bumps on her head, or any visible scars. That's good. Let's move her to a bed."

JC took control. Intense, cool and composed, he barely resembled the fool with a jack under his arm. Alex swallowed his bubbling resentment. He was enormously grateful for his cousin's presence, and his willingness to assume the command of the situation.

God knew, Alex was in no position to take reins in his own hands.

Too shocked, too stupefied. Too fucking scared.

This bizarre night was taking its toll on him. He needed a little time to center himself, to gather his thoughts, and get rid of that paralyzing gnawing fear.

Nika has returned. Because she needed help. Whose help?

But deep in his heart he already knew the answer: Abby's.

A ripple of terror sliced through his gut. Cold sweat slithered down his back.

He was willing to do anything—risk anything—for Nika, but not that. Not Abby.

Please, God, please don't let me chose between the two women I love.

But the choice was not his. If Abby was needed, she'd go without a second thought. He knew that too.

Alex stood glued to the spot, and watched the scene in front of him. Like from a great distance, he heard JC's voice calling Abby. When she failed to reply, his cousin grabbed her shoulders, and gave her a mighty shake. Alex saw red. He ought to break JC's arms for handling Abby like that! But his helpless stupor kept him immobilized. While his mind screamed at him to move, his frozen body refused to obey.

Snap out of it, Alex!

Captive to his own terror, he was unable to move a single muscle.

"Abigail. Look at me. Listen. Are you listening?" JC administered another rough shake, and finally captured Abby's attention.

"Y-yes."

Through the ringing in his ears, the voices came out soft and distorted.

"Good, that's good." JC nodded, and removed his hands from Abby's shoulders. "Nika is okay, just winded. We need to lay her on a bed. Okay?"

"Yes, yes, of course. A bed." In unison, they both jumped to their feet.

"Upstairs. My bedroom. Please be careful."

"Oh, I am, Princess. Trust me."

Princess? Did the miserable skunk just call my *Abby* Princess?

And his rage smashed the wall of his stupor. Roaring, Alex sprang forward.

"Get away from her!"

The force of Alex's push sent JC skidding on the floor. He landed on all four, cursed, then scrambled to his feet. Looking more befuddled than angry, he blinked. "What's up with you?"

"Nothing." Bending over, Alex gathered Nika into his arms then gently cradled her head against his shoulder. "And don't you dare call Abby Princess. Got it?"

Nika's arms, boneless, lifeless, hung like two ropes. Dislodged by the movement, the fingers of her right hand unclenched, and something clattered to the floor. Almost on autopilot, JC bent to pick up it up, but his eyes never wavered from Alex's face.

"You've lost your marbles, cousin of mine. Must be all that whiskey."

"At least I had some marbles to lose, Counselor."

With an angry scowl, JC lifted his fists.

"I'll carry Nika. She's my sister, you idiot!"

The small object fallen from Nika's fingers was still clutched in his right hand. A thin leather cord attached to it dangled like a metronome.

Mindful of the baby bump, Alex carefully adjusted Nika in his arms.

"She's mine. My best friend and family. I'll take care of her."

Brandishing clenched fists, his face distorted in an ugly grimace, JC lunged forward. Alex would have welcomed the confrontation, if not for the precious cargo in his arms. But nothing prevented him from tripping his obnoxious cousin. With that in mind, he stuck his right foot, already anticipating JC's humiliation.

"Are you two out of your freaking minds?"

Wide eyed, pale and shaking, Abby planted herself between them.

"Daisy is unwell, she needs help, and you two morons are arguing about who's closer to her? Shame on you! Shame on you both!" She spat the last words, glaring at them in turn.

"You," she stabbed her index finger at Alex's shoulder, "carry Daisy to my room at once. And you," JC's chest received the similar treatment, "shut the hell up, and proceed after me. And not a word out of your mouths, or else!"

With her head held high, Abby marched toward the staircase with a purposeful stride of a general herding the troops.

CHAPTER NINETEEN

As much as it irritated him to be chastised in front of his cousin, Alex deserved it.

Following Abby, he placed his steps carefully, and ignored the sound of stomping feet behind him. Let that skunk steam all he wanted. Better to be humiliated than let Nika out of his arms. A quick glance at her face stole his breath. Oh, God, she was so pale, so tiny. So vulnerable. Nika would hate being like this.

Come on, baby, snap out of it. Open your eyes. You can do it, Nik.

But his silent encouragements went unanswered. Colder than ice and whiter than porcelain, she lay in his arms as still as a statue. Aside from that first quiet moan, she hadn't made another sound.

Nika didn't stir when he lay her on the bed, then covered her with a thick quilt.

Why wasn't she waking up? Dammit, was she hurt? How badly?

Call an ambulance, or hazard a trip to a hospital?

But how to explain her old-fashioned clothes? Or her pregnancy? Many doctors and nurses in that hospital knew them well since Abby's bout with COVID last year. Damn.

Okay, worry about it later. Now, concentrate on Nika. God, why wasn't she waking up?

"We need to call 911. She needs medical attention."

Even though JC just voiced his own thoughts, Alex bristled.

"What she needs is rest. And her family."

Bravo, you idiot. Now what?

"Dammit, Alex, can't you see she's out cold? Unmoving? What if she's bleeding internally? Or in a coma? The baby—"

"Is fine." Abby's grim voice interrupted their bickering before it had a chance to explode into a full-fledged argument. With both hand on Nika's stomach, she gently caressed the protruding mound. "It's moving, even kicking, the little rascal." A fleeting smile curved her lips. "Daisy is in a deep swoon. But she'll come around. Let's postpone calling the doctor just yet."

"But—"

"JC, trust me. I've seen Daisy in a faint before. Alex, make yourself useful, and open the window. JC, please stop pacing. You're making matters worse by your senseless fussing. We need to stay calm."

"Calm? Easy for you to say, Princess." JC's snide reply set Alex's temper on fire.

The stupid moron just didn't know when to stop!

"I told you not to call her Princess!"

"Oh, put a muzzle on it, will you?" JC shot him a smoldering glare. "Don't you think your juvenile jealousy is ridiculous under the circumstances?"

"Juvenile jealousy? Why, you miserable scumbag, I'll—"

"If you don't stop right this minute, I'll throw the pair of you out of my house, you stinking pricks!"

Alex didn't know what shocked him more, her foul mouth, or the expression on Abby's face. She never cursed. The extent of her exasperation was the mutter of *merde*.

And even on those rare occasions, she didn't resemble a formidable Amazon, outraged, indignant, and ready to pounce.

"Abs—"

"Abigail—"

"Hush! Both of you." She stepped in between them. "Your behavior is simply atrocious. I'm so disappointed in both of you! What would *Verochka* say?"

Crossing her arms, Abby glared at them in turn.

In the following silence a fragile moan struck like thunder. Nika's eyelids fluttered, as another moan slipped from her bloodless lips.

"She's coming around." Abby hurried to the bed, sat, then took one of Nika's hands in both of hers. "Open your eyes, dear heart. Please, Daisy, please wake up."

After a moment that seemed like an eternity, Nika finally moved her head.

"That's right, little one. Open your beautiful eyes. All the way up now."

Under Abby's murmured encouragements, Nika finally resurfaced. Pale and disoriented, she murmured something under her breath. Her hands shifted, as she struggled to dislodge the quilt from her body. Then she slowly lifted herself up, but immediately dropped against the headboard.

"W-where...am I?"

Pleased that the color started to seep into her face, Alex let out a heavy breath. Thank God. Nika was back. Confused and weak, but no worse for wear.

"W-where...?" She pivoted her head side to side, as her agitation grew. "Eli."

Glazed with fear, her eyes circled the room, then stopped on Alex.

"Where am I?" She repeated in a barest of whispers.

Say something, you idiot!

But a lump in his throat made talking impossible. Abby, bless her, quickly took matters into her hands.

"You are home, Daisy." A tremulous smile hovered on Abby's lips, as she tucked a stray curl behind Nika's ear. "You are well, safe and sound."

"H-home..."

Nika bolted upright. Stark terror bleached her face of all color. In contrast with her milky-white skin, the twin dark smudges under her eyes were like two ugly bruises. With the brutal precision of a laser, her eyes locked on Alex.

"Where is Eli?"

Good question.

Where was his cousin-in-law, and why did he let Nika out of his sight long enough to repeat her time-traveling journey, but alone this time?

Fuming, Alex kept Nika's horrified gaze, when the picture in front of his eyes started to shimmer. A familiar sense of de-ja-vu gripped his gut in a steel fist. Like curtains in a theater, the distorted images began to slide upward, and then dissolved completely. Astonished, Alex found himself in a dark dingy place barely large enough to hold one dirty coat, and a wooden table with a broken leg. A filthy barred window near the ceiling allowed a feeble slice of moonlight. The awful stench of sweat, desperation and sorrow took his breath away.

Where am I?

Alex blinked, too stunned to be afraid.

My God, it's a holding cell!

How on earth did he know he was in a jail? And not any jail, but the one in Fernandina Beach circa 1910. Something scurried on the floor. Disgusted, he took a step back. The sound of his own breathing thundered in his ears. But, wait, was there another noise? Like a sigh. Deep, quiet, desperate.

And suddenly Alex realized he wasn't alone.

Uneasy now, he shifted his eyes to the lone figure sitting on a narrow coat.

He, definitely a male, was large with a mane of unkept black hair. The prisoner's face was hidden behind his hands. Something stirred in Alex's memory. The shape of those hands, strong but elegant, was acutely familiar. The image of those long fingers caressing Nika's hair, or gripping the steering wheel of his car, or holding the frozen turkey by the dangling thread...

Oh, my God! Eli!

As if hearing his silent exclamation, the prisoner dropped his hands, and jerked his head toward Alex. His face was reflected in Eli's shocked wide eyes. It was like looking in a mirror. Alex blinked and everything went black.

Once again, he stood in the brightly lit bedroom, where three pair of eyes stared at him with expressions of anxiety and apprehension.

"Alex? What happened?" Abby took a tentative step in his direction. "For a while it seemed like you were far away."

I was. So far away it isn't even funny.

"Eli is fine."

There was no time to marvel at, or question his crazy experience. Alex was just grateful that his voice sounded strong and clear. Shaky and baffled, he bore down on his emotions, and tucked his shock away for later. His composure was hard won, but Alex managed to arrange his face into what he hopped was a calm expression.

"He's fine, Nika," he repeated firmly. "Scared, dirty, but otherwise unharmed."

She made a sound close to a whimper, and pressed both hands against her lips.

Strange, but Nika didn't ask the obvious question, and accepted his statement with a terse nod. Abby, though, wasn't satisfied. Figures. Her sharp intake of breath arrowed through his ears.

Wide-eyed, she looked at him, her expression suspicious and curious at the same time.

"How do you know that?"

Instead of inventing some fib, Alex opted for the untarnished truth.

"Because I saw him."

"Saw him? But...but how? Where?"

"In a holding cell. In jail. As to how, your guess is as good as mine."

A pounding headache was as sudden as it was vicious. Alex rubbed his temples in the attempt to keep his head from bursting while his drumming heart was doing its best to break free from his ribcage.

My God, did I really travel in time? Or was it just a figment of my imagination?

But, no. The smell, the dirty cell with its miserable barred window, was real. And so was Eli's stunned expression when he sensed his presence. No, not *sensed*.

He saw me. But how?

Thank God the shocking news switched Abby's attention to Eli's fate.

"In jail? Eli is in... jail?"

Recoiling like she was slapped in the face, she turned to Nika.

"Daisy! What happened? Is Eli really in jail?"

"Yes." Warily, Nika closed her eyes.

"But why? Whatever for?"

"Eli was arrested yesterday. Allegedly for murder. Your murder."

Nika's voice was strained and scratchy, as if every word cost her enormous effort. Alex's heart squeezed.

"W-what? What kind of nonsense is that?"

Thin and brittle, Nika's laughter scraped along his nerve endings.

"Utter nonsense for sure." She lifted her drawn face to Abby "But the almighty Carnegies didn't believe that you chose to leave instead of marrying one of their offspring. They decided that in a heated argument, Eli killed you, and hid the body, and then pretended that you left. The police were alerted. They came yesterday with the warrant, searched the house top to bottom, and dug in the backyard. It was horrible. But worst of all, they took Eli." Her composure crumbled, and a lone tear streaked down her face. "They took him away...in handcuffs."

"Are they out of their collective minds?" Abby's outrage, hot and brilliant, lashed out like a bolt of lightning. "Kill, and hid the body? That's insane! Eli never raised his hand to me, or his voice. Why, Eli would never strike a fly, never mind another human being. Especially a woman. Especially if that woman is his sister."

"Preaching to a choir, Abs. But Carnegies beg to differ."

"Well, then, we must prove them wrong." Indignant, she drew to her full height and balled her fists. "We must put them to shame, the lot of them!"

"That's exactly why I came here." Nika's pleading eyes locked onto Abby's face. "I need your help."

"Anything, Daisy."

Alex's gut revolted. Sour bile rose to his throat.

Oh, God, please, no!

But his prayers were shattered when he heard Nika's urgent request.

"I need you to come back with me. I know it's too much to ask, but there's no other way. They need to see you alive and well, and clear Eli's name. As soon as he's home, you can come back. Please, Abby."

"You don't have to ask twice, Daisy. I'm ready. Let's go. Time is running away."

Understanding finally dawned, brutal and clear. Unmerciful.

Her brother's time was running out. Abby felt it from the beginning. Didn't she insist that something was wrong and she was needed somewhere? Well, she was right. She was needed back in time, in 1910. To save her brother.

CHAPTER TWENTY

D*ammit to hell and back.*
      A mute horror filled Alex to the brim. Even though he figured from the get-go the reason why Nika had returned, he still harbored a sliver of hope.

Now his hope was smashed to smithereens and his worst nightmare was about to spring to life. He watched Abby as she balanced of the balls of her feet, all but shaking from restless energy. Sizzling with angry sparks, her indignation was almost palpable.

Now he understood why she refused his proposal of marriage. Because the timing was wrong. Because she was sure she must travel far away, she wasn't sure if she might ever return.

The hell she will not!

"You are not going anywhere." Even though his statement was meant for both of them, Alex's eyes were glued to Abby. A sharp intake of breath accompanied by her mutinous glare was nothing less than he expected. "At least, not tonight."

Smarter to backpedal. For now.

"It's not for you to decide. It's my choice. Mine! I say we're going. Now." With an arrogant tilt of her head, she dared him to contradict. Undeterred, Alex held her gaze. "No, you are not."

Damn if he let the pair of them skedaddle back a century.

Must buy some time. Then we'll see.

With an effort, he tore his eyes from Abby, and looked at Nika. Ultimatums never worked with his stubborn as a mule cousin. He must appeal to her common sense. One look at Nika's belligerent expression made him wince.

Are you kidding? What common sense? She's ready to rip your heart out.

Eli was in danger. That's all that mattered to her. Come hell or high water, she would follow through with her plan, and the consequences be damned.

Thunderation, as his favorite cousin-in-law loved to say.

There was another trump card in his sleeve, and he was about to use it.

"You are a smart woman, Nika. Be reasonable. For goodness' sake, you're still not hundred percent, and you know it. The repeat trip in a such a short timeframe will be dangerous. Certainly for you, but even more so for the baby."

And bullseye. His arrow reached its mark. Mentally patting himself on the back, Alex cracked a half smile as the string of his cousin's curses exploded in the air.

More inventive than angry, they loosened a steel fist around his heart, and reminded him of his old Nika. Not Daisy, the lady of Coleman manor, but the mischievous feisty little mischief-maker he had known all his life.

A couple of broken sniffs later, Nika capitulated. "Dammit, I hate it when you're right."

In a soothing motion, she rubbed her belly with both hands. This gesture, so typical of expecting mothers, grabbed him by the throat and misted his eyes. Damn. Was there anything more beautiful than a pregnant woman?

When she lifted her face all the mysteries of the Universe shone back at him from her tired, violet eyes.

"Okay. We'll stay for the night, but leave tomorrow morning. Early." She glared at Alex. In lieu of an answer, he brought both palms up to demonstrated his surrender.

Surrender, my ass.

He just needed to buy time to think of something.

Like what?

Like any fucking thing to prevent Abby and Nika from going back.

What about Eli? He's in grave danger, locked in that stinking hellhole like a criminal. Without Abby's reappearance, he'll be tried and accused of murder. Probably executed. How would you live with that?

His conscience screamed in his head as the images of Eli, dirty, defeated, and desperate, swam in front of his eyes. With a herculean effort of will, Alex bored down. Eli would understand. He'd do the same thing—sacrifice anything—to save his wife and unborn child. And his sister. Yes, Eli would understand, and approve. But Nika will never forgive him. And neither will Abby.

Dammit all to hell and back!

The unwelcome thought that at the root of his decision was pure selfishness, filled Alex with shame. He ruthlessly shoved it from his mind. Nonsense. He was concerned about them, first and foremost. And that's why he easily justified disposing of the damn key. Once he found the blasted thing.

Betrayal cannot be justified. Not even by love.

Where did that come from?

Like a punch, the quiet murmur left a stinging imprint on his conscience. Alex cursed under his breath and rubbed his bald crown. What the hell was he supposed to do? No matter what, he must find that key. It was imperative.

Where was it? Fallen somewhere?

He vaguely remembered a tinny sound, like something hitting the floor when he carried Nika upstairs. The key? Possible. He decided to go back and search if he didn't find it sooner. What about the bed? Maybe it was stuck somewhere between the sheets.

As unobtrusive as possible, Alex approached the antic fourposter, scanned it with his eyes. Nothing visible. He needed a more thorough search. Later.

One way or another, he must find it. But what if Nika put it in her pocket? More difficult, but doable. He just has to check her clothes while she slept.

Pervert! Traitor! Forget about it while it's not too late! Snap out of it, Alex!

Once again, his conscience reared up. Ashamed, torn, but undeterred, Alex ignored it. Too late for remorse.

His eyes locked on Abby. She met his gaze and held it.

As if sensing his torment, she approached him, touched his arm. "I will be back. I promise."

Damn, can she read my mind?

"When?"

"As soon as Eli's out of jail. I swear it, Alex."

"It could be weeks, or months. Or even years."

She didn't argue, just continued to stare at him with eyes as dark as storm clouds.

Time moved differently in two dimensions, and they both were aware of that.

If nothing else, Nika's advanced pregnancy was a stark reminder of that phenomena. Flat as a board when she left on New Year's Eve, now, just five days later, she was sporting a huge belly ripe with a child.

"No matter how long—days, weeks, or years—I will return to you. You have my word."

She meant it. But not everything depended on her will or determination.

They both were aware of that, too.

The stupid portal might not work, or, God forbid, throw her a few years back, or forward. Or even the wrong location. She might be lost in time, alone, helpless and vulnerable.

No way in hell.

Even as fear slipped through, his resolve strengthened. No, he was not willing to risk it. He must do everything in his power to prevent that catastrophe. And if he must commit a betrayal, so be it.

Afraid that Abby may be able to read his treacherous thoughts, Alex lowered his gaze.

Suddenly Nika jolted. She cursed, tugged at her long skirt, all but tearing it apart. Raw panic was written over her face as she continued to pound the bedding with both hands. Frantic and incoherent, her muttering gained in volume until it caught on a shrilling note.

"The key! Oh, God, where is the key?"

CHAPTER TWENTY-ONE

T he key!
  Did she lose it again?

Alex's heart beat so fast he was afraid it might explode.

That'll be the answer to all his prayers. Before his hope had a chance to sprout, a loud *ahem* cut the charged silence. Jerked from his reverie, Alex turned his head. JC! Shit, he forgot about his obnoxious cousin. Again.

"What the hell are you doing here?" Nika's shocked gasp shattered the bubble of their collective stupor.

If he wasn't so thrown off balance, he'd laugh.

Like a reigning emperor, his cousin sat in the highbacked leather chair, with one knee negligently crossed over the other, and surveyed the room with a smirk on his face. Alex barely had a chance to process it before Nika rounded on him. Hopping mad, her glare raked him with scorching fire. Damned if she didn't manage to scrape a layer or two of his skin.

"For crying out loud, Alex, what is he doing here?"

Alex winced. Hard to miss an accusation when it was staring at you straight on.

"Ah, Nik, he—"

"Can speak for himself, in case you're wondering." JC butted in. His drawling voice high on negligence.

"Fine." Nika streaked her molting eyes toward her brother. "Speak."

"Well, thank you, sister dear. Don't mind if I do." All indolence, JC lazily re-crossed his legs. The careless half-smile he aimed at Nika was a breath short of insulting. The bastard. Fuming, Alex visualized a few different ways, all of them employing violence, to wipe that irritating smirk off JC's mouth.

"Since y'all completely forgot about me, I decided to sit here, watch and listen. And let me tell you, it was enlightening, not to mention highly entertaining."

"Entertained enough?"

Nika's question lashed out like a whip. Undeterred, JC just nodded his head.

"Yes, I think so, Mrs. Coleman."

"Then get the hell out of here. This matter doesn't concern you."

"Oh, I beg to disagree, Midget. Whatever concerns you, concerns me."

"Since when?"

"Since our cousin revealed your little secret." In an instant, JC's face and manners underwent a complete one-eighty. All pretense gone, he watched her out of troubled eyes. "I know, Nika. I know everything."

Nika froze. Her jaw worked, but not a sound came through. For the first time in Alex's memory, his fearless, brazen cousin seemed at a loss for words.

"But...but..." She looked at Alex, then at Abby, and finally returned her shocked and heavy with skepticism gaze to JC. "And you...believed?"

"Hard not to, seeing your bulging kinder surprise. Gave me a pause, I must admit. But, as Alex told me, time moves differently, here and there."

"Y-yes, it does."

"Excellent. Okay, ladies and gentleman, let me summarize what I gathered while sitting here, listening and watching." JC pursed his lips, tapped a finger against his chin. "Let's see, your friends Carnegies, accused Eli of alleged murder. Your murder." He nodded toward Abby. "He's been arrested, because, hey, we're talking Carnegies here, and nobody contradicts the almighty. So, Eli's in jail, as our dear cousin Alex confirmed via his short but informative side trip through time." He stopped, and focused his shrewd eyes at Alex. "By the way, that was highly impressive, pal of mine. Shocking as hell, too. But," he looked again at Nika, "back to the matter at hand. Eli's arrested, and falsely accused. To prove his innocence, you must provide the cops with hard evidence, i.e., Abby, alive and well. Am I correct so far?"

Nika shut her eyes and shook her head. "Damn you, JC."

"I'll take is as a yes. So, in order to carry out your crazy, risky as all get out plan, you jumped through time to fetch Abby."

"I had no choice, I—"

"There's always a choice. Yours was to jeopardize your baby— congratulations by the way— to save your husband. Understandable, even admirable, but unwise."

"Oh, go to hell, Counselor."

"Thanks, but as much as it's tempting, I'll restrain myself. But back to our little dilemma."

"We don't have any dilemma. Abby's agreed. We'll go back and save Eli, and then she'll return. "

"Just like that?"

"Exactly like that."

"Hmm. "

"What's that supposed to mean?"

"Only that in every situation there's some unpredictable circumstances. And whatever seems cut, dry, and easy, usually ends up in a major cluster fuck, pardon my French."

"You're just skeptical by nature."

"And by trade. So, being a skeptical sort, I can't help but wonder—"

"Oh, shove it, JC. We're going. And you may wonder all you want."

"Okay. I wonder... how will you be going without this."

JC lifted his right hand. A long leather cord was dangling from his fingers like a metronome, small solid object attached. Alex squinted.

What the hell was that?

Unable to tear his gaze from the hypnotic movement, he followed it with his eyes. Nika's sudden cry of indignation knifed the air.

"My key!"

Alex swore under his breath. The shape, the size. The key from the portal.

Damn. That's what JC picked up from the floor earlier. The bastard.

Well, then, he had to get it from JC first, before Nika had a chance.

A definite challenge. Alex barely avoided being mowed down, when like a human missile Nika lunged herself at her brother.

"Dammit, JC, hand it over! Or else."

"Or else what?"

Oozing with sarcasm, JC's reply set Alex temper on boil.

The stinking moron, the condescending, miserable dick! How dare he mock Nika, when she was frantic with worry! But cool as a cucumber, his cousin continued to sit, dangling the key like a proverbial carrot.

A low growl erupted from Alex's throat. He was ready to kill JC for that alone. But Nika beat him to it. She planted herself in front of her brother, and brought the heal of her shoe down onto his foot. Hard. JC howled with pain.

"You little hell-cat! That hurts!"

"Oh, I hope so, brother dear. If you won't give me that key immediately, I'll show you where it really hurts." And grabbing her long skirt, she lifted her foot again.

Give him hell, baby.

"I'll give it back, I promise, but tomorrow. First, you need to rest. Second, I don't trust you not to change your mind, and try to go back tonight." Saying so, JC looped the cord with the key around his neck, and dropped it beneath his shirt. "Tomorrow," he repeated.

Alex's hands itched to ring the slimy weasel's neck. Later, he promised himself. He would deal with his obnoxious cousin later.

"Are we bunking here for the night?"

JC's question drew Abby's attention. She frowned, then nodded. "Yes, it would be most logical thing to do."

"*Wunderbar*. Where can I sleep?"

"Ah, I suppose in any of the guestrooms. Just chose one you like."

Still frowning, Abby switched her gaze to Alex.

"You can take Daisy to her and Eli's bedroom—"

"No. I can't." Nika shook her head. "I can't go there. Eli..." Her fight with tears was valiant, but lost before it barely started. "I just can't. I'll stay here."

"That's alright, *ma petite*. That's perfectly fine." Gentle, like she was talking to a frightened child, Abby lowered her voice to a murmur. After a long moment, she straightened then turned around. Face set, shoulders stiff, she surveyed the room before announcing in a clear loud voice, "Okay, gentlemen. Daisy will stay in my bedroom. Alex? You can take any other room on this floor. There's plenty of space. We all must rest tonight. Tomorrow will be a trying day."

"I have to have my key, JC. Not tomorrow—now!"

"No way, Midget."

With her teeth bared in an ugly grimace, Nika whirled around, then fatigue overruled her indignation. Swaying, she almost fell, if not for Alex's quick reflexes. As it was, he managed to catch her in the nick of time, picked her up.

"Dammit, Nik."

"Let go of me! I'm going to kick his ass!"

Pale and weak as a newborn kitten, she made a feeble attempt to fight, and disengage herself.

"And I'm going to hold your coat, but not right now. For god's sake, Cuz, don't you see you're whipped?"

"I need that key! Please, Alex."

"You'll have it. But not tonight. You need to rest."

"But—"

"Trust me, Nika."

"I do. With my life. With my baby's life. And with Eli's."

Alex stomach knotted. What would it do to Nika when he betrayed her trust?

Because as sure as day was long, he was going to remove that key from his bastard cousin's sticky hands. Correction: his stinking neck. But he had no intention of handing it to her.

Who's the bastard now?

Cringing inside, Alex assured himself that it was for the best. Nika was pregnant. She needed medical attention. And Abby...Well, she was happy here, with her paintings and her family. He'll make it up to her. To them both. Somehow.

But what about Eli?

Leaden guilt coated his gut. The Coleman heirloom watch that Eli gave him as a farewell present lay heavily against his heart, in his breast pocket. Just for a split moment, his mind took him back to that dingy filthy cell.

Eli's gaze, full of sorrow and shock, swam in front of his eyes.

Dammit all to hell and back.

Unaware of his inner battle, Nika finally quieted in his arms. With a broken sigh, she lay her head on his shoulder. Trust. Absolute, unquestionable.

Torn to pieces, Alex averted his eyes, then shut them tight. A light touch on his arm brought him around. Abby.

She'll never forgive you.

He wasn't surprised to hear this tiny voice in his head anymore.

His conscience? Universe? Does it matter?

And the truth, brutal and vicious, slammed between his eyes.

You'll lose her either way.

He might lose her whether he got rid of that key, or not.

The difference was, if he let her go, he's got a slim chance of seeing her again. Tomorrow, or in a few months, or years.

And what were the few months or years? A ripple in time.

Like a tiny butterfly, hope stirred, and fluttered its fragile wings. Love added strength, and spread them wider. Faith nudged it up, and rejoiced. And that tender butterfly unfurled its wings, and soared. High and true and strong.

In that moment, while he stared into Abby's expressive eyes, a blindfold was ripped from Alex's heart. And left a scar. Tender, it throbbed painfully.

But the pain was sure to go away, and the scar had to heal. In days, or months, or years.

As soon as Abby was back.

Unable to tear his gaze from her, Alex accepted the inevitable.

Fly, my little butterfly, my precious Princess. But please come back to me. Please.

As if sensing his turmoil, Abby squeezed his arm. Reassurance, promise. Commitment.

With her eyes on his face, she addressed his cousin, "JC, why don't we give Daisy and Alex some privacy?"

Held in his arms, Nika stirred, opened her eyes. "Abby, take the key from him. Hurt him if you must, but get the key. Please."

"I will, Daisy, don't worry."

"Swear it."

"I swear, *ma petite*."

With that promise hanging in the air, Abby unceremoniously ushered JC out.

JC was not pleased, if his mutinous expression was any indication. Good. Serves him right. Alex fumed at him for being a sarcastic jerk to Nika. And for pocketing that key. Will he hand it over as promised?

Sure, he will. Otherwise, he'll be sporting a broken arm, and twisted neck, curtesy of yours truly.

Satisfied by the prospect, Alex shoved the matter away. Nika needed him now.

He looked down at the precious cargo locked in his arms. Thin and pale, with a riot of dark golden curls, she was quiet, with both arms curved around her protruding stomach. Her breathing became even, her eyes fluttered shut. Had she fallen asleep? Looks like. The little fearless warrior. She always fought tooth and nail for those she loved. For her baby, for her family. Fight dirty, to the last drop of blood, risking her life. Like today. JC said she *chose* to jeopardize her baby for her husband's sake. He was wrong. For Nika, there was no choice. Eli was her life, her love, her everything. Without him she was as good as dead. Who if not Alex can attest to that? His breath hitched. Something hot pressed behind his eyelids.

Love hurt as much as it healed. But without it, life lose all meaning. Eli's farewell message flashed in his memory:

...love *per se* does not make any sense, but it infuses everything else in the world with it.

You are so right, brother.

Nika stirred, moaned, and opened her eyes. Disoriented, she looked at him with confusion. Then she blinked, and her eyes cleared.

"Alex..."

"One and only."

"I'm...sorry. So sorry."

"For what, Brat?"

"For everything. For coming back, for needing help."

"Hey, even a wonder woman needs help now and then."

"Yeah, I guess so." She shifted, grimaced. "Put me down already. Even a superman has limits to his strength."

"You're light as a feather, Brat. So, no worries. I like carting you around. Makes me feel kinda like Rhett Butler." But Alex sat on the bed, still cradling Nika in his arms. With a long sigh, she snuggled closer.

"Guess that makes me kinda like Scarlett O'Hare?"

"No way, no how. Not even 'kinda'. You are nothing like that sly, selfish bitch."

"Well, I sure hope not." Nika's deep sigh lifted her bust almost to his eye level. Heat spread in his face, as he tried to get rid of the mental picture imprinted on his brain.

Good luck, brother.

Unaware of his discomfort, Nika took another deep breath. Damn.

"I'm sorry, Cuz. I wish I could avoid this, but I really can't. Eli..."

When her voice broke, Alex gathered her close.

"Shh, baby. I know."

Nika hiccupped. "JC disapproves."

"What do you care?"

"But I do. He's my brother, my family. It's just...he doesn't understand."

"And how could he? The bastard never loved anyone. The very concept is totally alien to him."

"But it's not alien to us, is it, Alex?" She stared at him, long and hard. "Have you told Abby?"

Now it was his turn to take a deep breath.

"Hell, I did more than that. I proposed to her."

"You did not!" Nika pivoted in his embrace, squinted at him. "Oh my God, you did!"

"And a lot of good it did to me."

"Don't tell me she refused, because I won't believe it. Abby's crazy about you."

"Yeah? She sure has a funny way of showing it." Then he remembered their kiss, and the unbridled passion of her response, her avid hungry mouth, her helpless throaty moans...

"And I'm being unfair. It's just..." What? Upsetting? Embarrassing? Maddening? He supposed he was overreacting, but for God's sake, he was just a guy who offered the girl his heart on a damn platter, and she turned him away.

And what did you do when she offered herself to you?

That familiar little voice in his head popped back.

That was different. More of a sacrifice than anything else.

But the result was the same. She was upset, and embarrassed, and mad as hell.

Now he was arguing with his inner self. And losing.

"Well, what happened?" Nika pinched his arm, and brought Alex around.

"Huh?"

"What did she say?"

"Who?"

"Abby, you moron. Or did you propose to someone else?"

"There's no one else. She's the one and only."

"Okay, and...?"

"She said she loves me," Nika gave out a short Yippee, and punched him in the shoulder, "but cannot accept a marriage proposal, because, and I quote "Time is not right". Unquote."

Nika frowned, more curious than concerned. "I wonder why."

"Because she knew that something, somewhere was wrong. Told me that she might need to go away, but wasn't sure when, or why. Now she does. We all do."

"Yes, and I'm really—"

"Brat, if you say 'sorry' one more time, I might hurt you."

"But you won't." Nika patted his cheek, then kissed it.

"Wanna bet?"

"Make it a big one, Cuz. I'll win anyway. Because you'd never hurt a pregnant woman, and you know it."

"Hell, you play dirty, Brat." His brittle chuckle lacked any humor.

"Always." Nika flashed him a cheeky smile, then kissed him again. "Miss you."

The sudden lump in his throat was huge as a fist. "Miss you more. I even smelled you on the deck and heard your voice in my mind. Can you beat it?"

When the silence grew, Alex realized Nika had drifted to sleep.

Careful not to wake her, he kissed her forehead, and lay her on the bed. She didn't move a muscle even when Alex tugged the quilt from under her, and covered her with it. She was out to the count. Finally. His little cousin had exhausted herself to the full extend. Alex listened for her slow breathing for a long time. The memory of the previous year intruded. Many a time, he sat quietly by her bed, catching each shallow intake of breath, praying, fretting, raging.

The two graves he discovered at *Bosque Bello* cemetery then showed to Nika meted a turning point of her survival. She bounced back to life, full of energy and hope.

Now, as he sat by her bed, Alex was too tapped out to fret or pray, never mind rage. The only thing that was left to him was hope multiplied by love. So, hope he chose. And love.

But dammit if he would just sit and wait.

CHAPTER TWENTY-TWO

Abby stalled as long as she was able to endure. Patience was not one of her strengths, but today it was stretched thin like a worn-out rubber band, and about to snap. She paced one of the guestrooms by blind chance rather than design, all the while lecturing herself that *talk* was the last thing Alex required right now. What he needed was rest, peace and quiet—not conversation, or, God forbid, an argument. Because all their communications usually ended in a quarrel. And why was that? Why was it that two people who truly loved each other can rarely see eye to eye?

Love.

Still tender and precious, it trembled in her chest like a little bird.

She loved and was loved back. And wasn't that the most wondrous thing?

Alex. Her protector, her knight, her best friend. He was the most amazing man, loyal, fearless, steady as a rock. Gentle and strong, fair and funny. And proper.

"Too darn proper." Abby let out an irritated breath.

Shame heated her cheeks as she recalled her wanton behavior the other night. Offered herself like a damn pastry. Curse it. And what did he do? Nothing, that's what. Patted her on a head, and kissed her goodnight, chaste and innocent. Like you might get kissed by a favorite brother.

Brother, my butt.

If she has anything to say about it, this *brother* will soon become her lover.

Like tonight. Because she hadn't much time left. Tomorrow she'll stumble backward in time, and even though she had every intention of returning, Abby wasn't sure when it might be. Time was a peculiar thing. It stretched on one side, and ran faster on the other. And what side will it flow slower? Her century, or the previous one?

Surprised, she realized she thought of 21st century as her own. How or when did that happened?

"And what does it matter, Abigail?"

But everything aside, she wasn't sure when she'd be able to make that trip back. Or forward. She prayed soon, as soon as possible, after she presented herself to the authorities, and freed her brother. Oh, those Carnegies! How dare they accuse Eli of something as dastardly as murder? Didn't they know his character? Weren't they friends for a long time? And what of her uncle, David Yulee? He was as influential a man as Thomas Carnegie, respected by all and sundry. Couldn't he do something? Anything?

Too late to dwell on it. Tomorrow she'll be back in 1910, and take the matter in her own two hands. The first thing Abby was determined to do was go to that horrible jail and free her brother. Then, she'll spend time with their dear housekeeper, Mrs. Smith, and at midnight, after she said her final goodbyes, she will return. She prayed their heirloom grandfather clock will bring her back to the same point in time from where she came.

Dear God, what if it not?

What if she comes in a year, or ten years from today? Will Alex wait for her? Or, upset and discouraged, seek solace in another woman's arms?

The hell he will, the cad!

Fuming, Abby continued to wear a hole in the priceless Oriental rug.

Said he loved her, didn't he? Said he wanted to marry her, the rascal. How dare he even so much as look at other women? Not if she had something to say about it, and Abby had plenty to say. Better yet, she has to demonstrate. She will seduce him.

Seduce? Like you did the first time?

That time didn't count, because...well, just because. She must be more persistent this time around, and leave him no choice. How hard was it, anyway? Removing the clothes, then...Abby drew blank. Searching for inspiration, she looked around the room. A little shepherdess figurine on the fireplace mantel, albeit half-naked and smiling mischievously, failed to produce any help. Abby averted her gaze.

The troubling thought that she was as unexperienced in the matters of passion as a newborn popped into her head, but was shrugged aside. She was a quick learner, if she said so herself. Just play it by ear, and improvise.

You have a lot of improvisation to perform, my girl.

So what? And, by Jove, how hard could it be, if her actions were guided by love?

Bolstered by her pep talk, Abby squared her shoulders, raised her head high, and marched out of the room.

CHAPTER TWENTY-THREE

Grateful for solitude, Alex rubbed his head, closed his scratchy eyes, and took a deep breath. His decision might be outrageous, even crazy, but it was the only one that felt right. That was justified, and made sense. To him. The ladies may disagree. But by the time they realized his intentions...

Sorry girls, too late.

If he can't prevent the two women he loved from jumping through time, Alex had no choice but to join the party. And if they thought he would let them traipse through time on their own, both of them were in for a helluva surprise.

Alex frowned, when a sudden dull ache began in his right hand. What on earth?

The wrapped gauze around his palm bloomed with red splotches. Blood?

Shit. He forgot all about his earlier injury. Must've opened the cut while carrying Nika. Born out of reflex rather than anger, his muttered curse lacked its usual creativity. Then he shrugged. Doesn't matter. Not anymore.

No point to dwell on the *before.* Tomorrow everything will slide into past.

His drunken marathon, and JC's outrageous suggestion to destroy the grandfather clock, even his botched proposal to Abby—all of it will be a distant memory.

Because everything changed in a matter of hours.

During this phantasmagorical night, his perspective—along with his slant on reality—had shifted. He hadn't decided yet whether he liked it. And that eerie trip through time...Impossible. Un-fucking-believable. And still.

Alex cast a quick look at sleeping Nika. What would she feel if she saw Eli in that cell? Devastated. Good thing it was him, and not her, zipping through the layers of time.

Son of a bitch.

And how on earth did he manage it?

The images were so vivid, so...real. He still smelled the horrible stench, and saw Eli's stunned face.

Dammit, had he developed a freaking brain tumor? Or some mysterious talent that lay dormant until now? Yeah, right. Alex the Clairvoyant. He let out a quiet humorless laugh. What next? Telepathy? Flying on a freaking broom?

And why the hell not?

After everything that happened tonight, he believed in little green people, too. Maybe he ought to schedule a cat scan for his head, just in case. Or an appointment with a shrink. Or start yoga like his grandmother nudged him to do all along. *Verochka* claimed that meditation did wonders. Yeah, right.

And the day Alex sat for hours, meditating his ass off, will be the day the little piglets sprouted wings.

What he needed was six hours of uninterrupted sleep. Eight would be ideal.

But exhausted to the bone, Alex knew sleep was out of the question. His body was heavy with fatigue, but his brain worked like a Swiss timepiece. Or that infamous grandfather clock.

Speaking of which, will the bastard accept him now, or blast him with a jolt of electricity again?

Only one way to find out.

But not right now. Better rest for a while, because tomorrow promised to be a doozy. He needed a few hours until the big show-time.

Need to find a room, preferably with a bed. But not far away from Nika.

Shower wouldn't hurt either. God knew when he'll be able to take another one.

With the last look at his sleeping cousin, Alex tiptoed out of the room.

CHAPTER TWENTY-FOUR

Abby's resolve carried her as far as the hallway, before she realized she had no idea about Alex's whereabouts. One of the guestrooms, but which one?

"Damn, how could you be so stupid, Abigail?"

Now what? Accept the defeat, and go back to her room? *Never!*

Tonight. Now. Time was not on her side. It must be now, or never.

"Well, Abigail, no better time than now." She glanced to her left then to her right.

Okay, which room? JC occupied the farthest one on the left, Daisy was in Abby's old bedroom. Which one did Alex choose?

Think, Abigail, think.

Not Eli's, that's for sure. That left three more guestrooms, not counting the one she just came from. Okay, three wasn't so bad. She'll knock on each door.

Eventually, I'll find him.

She approached the closest one on the left. As she lifted her hand to knock, the door flung open. Abby's shriek froze in her throat. Her heart stopped, then plunged all the way to her stomach. Brows raised, jaw slacked, Alex was gaping at her like he'd never seen her before. The silence grew, uncomfortable and awkward, as they stared at each other.

He was naked. Well, almost. His trousers rode low on his hips, but his torso and feet were bare. Sweet Lord in heaven! All her nerve endings sprang to life. The fine hair on her neck sprouted as goose-bumps danced all over her skin.

Abby shivered.

Alex recovered first. A deep frown marred his forehead, as he glared at her.

"What are you doing here?"

Although quiet, his voice sounded graver than usual. Was he angry?

When was the last time she was so embarrassed? Or so fascinated. Fascination won. She guided her eyes on a slow journey over his body.

My, oh my.

Now her shivers had nothing to do with temperature.

As an artist, she was familiar with the anatomy of a male body. But Alex's took her breath away. Pure shock slammed its fist into her middle, rendering her mute. But not blind. For the life of her, Abby was unable to tear her eyes away. He was beautiful.

The sculpture of Michelangelo's David paled in comparison.

Wide and straight, his shoulders blocked the entrance. Well-proportioned forearms were roped with muscle. A thin line of dark hair circled his areolas and snaked to his navel button. And lower still. Abby swallowed. Hard. Her eyes slid lower.

Safer to concentrate on his feet.

His bare feet. They were large but narrow, with long sculpted to perfection toes. She didn't know that men's feet were so enticing, or so riveting.

Okay, not safer. Not even a little bit.

She dragged her gaze upward again.

Magnifique!

Dressed, Alex projected the image of a business executive, smooth, classy and civilized. Unclothed, he epitomized the wild strength. Raw and primitive.

Like a strong fragrance, it permitted the air, and clogged her suddenly parched throat.

And he is all mine!

Or he will be, as soon as she managed to unglue her tongue, and...

"I repeat, what are you doing here?"

Like a splash of icy water, his question jolted her back to reality. Somehow Abby managed to gather her wandering thoughts. Or so she hopped.

"If you allow me to recover for another moment, I'll...ah... remember."

If he caught a hidden meaning, he didn't let it show. Instead, his frown deepened, and his stance turned combative. Crossing his arms over his chest, Alex stared at her. Abby almost salivated at the sight. Something hot and fluid churned in her middle, then gushed lover. As liquid pooled between her thighs, she recognized it for what it was. Although innocent, Abby lived in this progressive century long enough, read many romance novels to understand that what was happening to her had a name: desire. Can he see it in her eyes? Is that why he paled even so slightly? And why was he looking at her like that? Eyes wide, face drawn, mouth arranged into a thin line. When Alex swallowed, and let out a little helpless oath, she rejoiced.

By God, he was afraid!

Pleased by his reaction, Abby curved her mouth in a knowing smile.

Oh, yes, her magnificent knight was trembling inside his trousers like a leaf in the breeze. Deliberately she took her eyes on another journey, trailing them from the crown of his bald head to his adorable bare toes.

Yum.

By volition on its own, her tongue flickered over her lips.

Delicious.

"Damn." Alex sucked on a sharp breath, muttered something almost crude.

Like a music to her ears, that little oath bolstered her resolve.

As a true sign of his acute discomfort, Alex rubbed his head with both hands. Feeling brazen, Abby took a step forward. He stepped back.

Delighted. Emboldened. She repeated the process. Another step later, and she was inside the room.

Covered under a ferocious frown, panic all but danced in his eyes.

"You shouldn't be here, Princess. Go to your own room. Or to Nika's. And for God's sake, stay there."

Raw and desperate fear in his voice was hard to misinterpret. She wanted to laugh. Her heart drummed in her chest.

Triumphant.

Victorious.

The heady feeling of exhilaration filled her to the brim.

Absolutely marvelous!

Still smiling, she lifted one brow in a deliberate arrogant manner. Call her Princess, does he? Well, she was not afraid to act like one.

I'll show you what this *Princess is made of.*

Giddy, she raised her hand, and removed the clip holding her hair. "Where I should or shouldn't be, my dear sir, is for me to decide." Shaking her head, Abby let her hair cascade down her waist.

He swallowed, hard. She rejoiced.

"Or where should I stay." With her backside, she bumped the door closed. A quiet click thundered in her ears.

No way back now.

For either of them.

"And I've decided I'm staying with you tonight."

Shameless, fearless, flying on the tender wings of her newly awakened power, she kept her eyes on Alex.

A heartbeat. That's all it took. The change in his features was almost surreal.

Color drained from his face. His eyes darkened from violet to deep purple.

Danger!

He didn't allow her time to react. With a low, guttural sound trembling in his throat, Alex lunged forward.

Like a predator, he pounced, grabbed, and hauled her into his arms. With a loud *whoosh* Abby collided with his chest.

His bare chest.

Smashed against his torso, her breast twinged. Her hands flew upward. To push away? To grab purchase? A sudden panic paralyzed her.

Hard. He was hard all over. Something hot and rigid pressed against her stomach.

My Lord...

She was no match for his strength. No match for his burning passion.

No match at all!

What were you thinking, Abigail?

Surprised, Abby pushed against his chest, all the while loving the feel of his hard muscles against her palms. She glanced up. The tumultuous expression on his face stole her breath.

"By God, I'm tired of fighting you. Fighting this. You want to stay? Alright, but don't tell me I didn't warn you."

His mouth swooped down, found hers. And Abby ceased thinking altogether.

Madness, dark, savage.

Need, overwhelming, scorching.

Insanity, blind, raging.

Straining, squirming, she had no choice but to take, and take, and take.

His hands were everywhere all at once, brutal, ruthless. They possessed and demanded, controlled and enthralled.

Lost, bewitched, stripped of all her defenses, she could only feel. And feel, and feel...

Too much. Not enough. Please, God...!

CHAPTER TWENTY-FIVE

D oomed. He was doomed for all the eternity, and didn't give a damn.

She was everything he imagined. And so much more.

Madness.

Insanity.

Paradise.

Alex tore his mouth away, gulped a lungful of air. Oh, God, he was so angry, he shook with it. All her fault. Everything was her fault.

Who else was able to snap his control like a brittle bone?

Only her.

Only Abby.

The woman turned him into a raving, raging lunatic. Her eyes were closed, but her mouth, that luscious mouth...Swollen, wet.

Sweet baby Jesus!

Blind and hungry, guided by instinct and need, Alex found her mouth again.

Teeth nipped.

Lips pressed.

Tongue delved.

Punishment.

Revenge.

Unmindful of the helpless little sounds she made, he deepened the kiss.

Don't stop, don't stop. Don't...

An incessant chant in his mind spurred him on. He can't stop. Didn't want to. Greedy for the feel of flesh, he grabbed her blouse, gave one tug, and the thin material ripped apart. The tiny buttons flew across the room.

His hands roamed over her silky skin until he found her breast, cupped it.

His thumb and forefinger plucked at her nipple through her lacy bra.

Not enough. Not nearly enough.

More.

With a deep growl, he unclasped the fragile barrier.

High and rounded, with the twin conical peaks, her breasts all but spilled into his hands. Just for a moment, he let his eyes roam. Perfect.

Pale as porcelain, soft as rose petals. Tender as a cloud.

And you're handling her with all the panache of a Mac truck.

Not now. The last thing he needed right now was that tiny censoring voice in his mind. Alex shook his head to get rid of it. But that persistent voice carried on.

She is innocent, a virgin. Have you no shame?

Even as his brain buzzed a warning, his overwhelming need to poses, to take, to have, overruled everything.

And taking one of the rosy peaks in his mouth, Alex sucked.

A feast of flavors, a banquet of textures.

Like a starving man, he devoured hungry, greedy, gorging himself. His hand molded her breast, as his knee separated her legs. His bulging shaft strained against his pants. The cut in his palm opened, pulsing in rhythm with his blood.

Pain, bright and sharp. Hunger, cold and brutal.

And underneath it all, the need, overwhelming, incredible. Unquenching.

Abby's fragile moan knifed into the haze of his insanity like blade into flesh.

What are you doing? For fucksake, man, what the hell are you doing?

"What am I doing?!"

Horrified, Alex lifted his eyes and looked at Abby. Clothes in tatters, breasts bare, lips swollen. A parade of faint bruises bloomed on her tender flesh.

You did it. Bastard.

He never felt any lower or more miserable at any point in his life. Hurting all over, he almost folded with pain.

A small price to pay for what you've done.

Abby didn't move, didn't utter a single sound. Still like a statue, her eyes shut tight, she stood against the door, with her hands above her head imprisoned in his fist. Alex cursed, released her hands, shut his eyes.

More than anything, he wished to erase this image of her—violated, vulnerable— from his memory. But it burned behind his eyelids, etched into his brain.

Nothing less than you deserve, you animal.

In his head, he was cursing, screaming the expletives on the top of his lungs.

But when he opened his mouth, the only thing that came out was her name.

"Abby..." A whisper. An apology. A plea.

She opened her eyes, dazed and unfocused. Slowly, her gaze cleared, sharpened, and zeroed on him.

He expected tears, and shock, revulsion, and rage. Not the blazing inferno that scorched his skin. Molten, her eyes swirled with silver fire.

Passion. Desire.

Was it possible...?

Holding his breath, Alex peered into her face.

"Abby?"

"Why did you stop?" A whiplash of an accusation paired with a menacing glare was hard to misinterpret.

Astonishing. Amazing. Unbelievable. And hallelujah.

Alex barely had a chance to take a relieved breath, as she wound her arms around his neck, and slammed her mouth against his with a brutal force.

Thank you, God.

CHAPTER TWENTY-SIX

Her flavor, rich and sweet and potent, stole the last drops of his sanity.

She smelled of meadows and clouds and heaven.

Paradise.

Languid, as if in a dream, he was suspended in another dimension where every sound was music, and every action magic. She was his personal miracle, his most desired and sacred dream come true. She owned his heart, his soul, his life.

She owned him.

Abby.

She almost destroyed him, then dragged him away from the abyss of madness.

His destiny, his salvation.

Undone, Alex tore his mouth from hers, and smiled at her murmur of protest. Tenderness, deep and overflowing, filled his heart to the brim, as his churning need swirled and snarled. He bore down. Greed and hunger cast aside, he reached deep into his soul for patience, for gentleness. For romance. There was so much he wanted—needed—to show her, to give her.

Unwilling to rush and cheat both of them of something precious, Alex took his lips on a slow journey over her face. Unhurried, his hands glided up, sunk into her hair. How many times he imagined doing just that, just ran his fingers through all that glory. Soft as a sigh, long as a river, black as a summer night.

Joy, quiet and kind and gentle, shook him to the core. Overwhelmed, Alex lifted his face, and looked at her. For as long as he lived, he'd never forget this moment. His breath hitched. His heart shattered into a million tiny pieces. Love grabbed him by the throat, sweet and sharp and staggering.

"Abby." Her name, just her name. Wonder. Revelation. Miracle.

She opened her eyes. Slumberous, heavy as rain clouds, they glimmered with the promise of a storm.

"If you stop now, I swear, I'm never going to marry you."

For the life of him, Alex couldn't prevent his quick laugh. Trust Abby to make him laugh at the moment like this.

"What's so funny?"

"You are. My God, I'm crazy about you, Princess."

"Good, because I'm crazy about you enough to overlook that Princess crap."

Now his laughter was full and loud and unrestrained. "Language, Abs, language."

"And what's wrong with my language?" Her brows winged up, two perfect arcs of royal indignation.

"Not a thing." Alex tried to keep the smile from his voice. "There is nothing wrong with any precious inch of you."

"Wonderful." She stepped back, held out her hand to him. "Then, take me to bed, and show me."

Invitation and demand, request and order. Only Abby was able to master it. Only Abby can—and did—bring him to his knees, and at the same time, made him feel bigger than life.

"Yes, my Queen." Alex accepted her hand, curled his fingers around it.

Point of no return.

Doomed.

Blessed.

Exhilarated.

Almost naked, her blouse in tatters, Abby drew to her full high, and regally inclined her head. And damned if she didn't look like royalty. He'd laugh if he wasn't so scared. Anticipation clawed at his gut, his blood churned in his veins. The passion he suppressed for so long was threatening to break free.

His loins pulsed with desire border lining on pain.

Close to losing his self-control, Alex swore to keep the inner beast chained for as long as was humanly possible.

Must be careful with her. Gentle and easy. She is a virgin, for goodness' sake.

Was he good enough for her? Did he deserve this honor?

"Abs, are you sure?"

Cocking her head, she snaked her designer jeans down her legs. In a deliberate reckless gesture, she sent them flying over her shoulder. Mesmerized, Alex watched as she shrugged off her blouse and bra, all the while holding his eyes. Shameless, brazen, Abby squared her shoulders, tilted her head.

A dare, was it? Well, he was more than up to the challenge. Or so he hoped.

But when she hooked her hands to the waistband of her panties, he almost lost it. Damn. Chaste, almost demure, that white cotton triangle struck him as most alluring and erotic piece of a lingerie he'd ever seen. His little friend hardened to the point of pain, ready to explode. Another moment, and it will be all over for him.

No way in hell.

"No! Wait. Just wait." Alex shifted his stance, praying for control.

"Why?"

Sweet baby Jesus! Because I'm about to embarrass myself.

He almost laughed and cringed at the same time.

Think fast, pal.

"Allow me that privilege."

Privilege, my boot. But not so bad, considering.

"Oh," she took a moment to process that, then nodded. "Alright."

But when she looked over her shoulder at the bed, a first sign of uncertainty flickered in her eyes. Gloriously naked, except that little triangle of her panties, she frowned, and shifted her gaze at him. "What do you want me to do?"

Alex swallowed his groan. Oh, he could name a few things, alright. Instead of verbalizing them, and sending her running in panic, he chose a safer approach.

"Let's just take a moment." He tagged her by hand. Side by side, they perched onto the corner of the bed. She slid her hand away from his hold, folded it on her knees. Her other hand crept upward, covered her chest in a belated attempt at modesty. That typical female gesture sobered him like a splash of icy water.

Instantly contrite, Alex called himself a few bad names in his mind. Dammit, what did he know about virgins? Not a heck of a lot. Zero, to be precise. Now what?

And now, pal, you must calm her down. Talk, for crying out loud!

Okay. Alright. I can do that. I think.

Shaking like a damn virgin himself, Alex prayed for inspiration to strike. What to say? What to ask? Touch, or stay apart? At the end, he went with his heart.

"Scared?"

"No." She blushed and lowered her eyes to the floor. "Yes. A little."

"Don't be scared, Princess. I'll do my damnedest not to hurt you."

"I know. I trust you." She cast a quick glance at him. "Don't you want to..."

"What?"

"To unclose. Your... trousers."

"I will. Later."

"Oh, okay." A little sigh escaped her lips. "Well? What's next?"

"For starters, let's make you comfortable." Alex climbed onto the bed, patted the place beside him. Strange, but all his nerves had finally settled. Calm and in control of all his faculties, Alex mentally patted himself on a back. Relaxed, he perched on his elbow, as he waited for Abby's next move.

Patience, Alex. Keep it slow and easy.

After a moment hesitation, she followed his suit. All reassurance, he smiled down at her. "Here you go, Princess. And now—"

And all his good intentions to take it easy flew out of the proverbial window, as she reared up, pulled him on top of her, and fused her mouth to his.

Damn. Losing it, Alex.

A warning bell rang in his mind. Struggling, he tried to wrench his mouth free, but she was having none of it. With more fervor than finesse, Abby hooked both legs around his hips, all the while kissing the life out of him.

He was unable to control his passion any more than he could will the sun to stop rising. Not when her mouth, hot and moist, moved with unrestrained hunger under his lips. Not when her legs, long and supple, imprisoned him with the force of a bolt chain. Not when she bowed her body, fluid and long, and pressed her core to his center.

Innocent and wanton, shy and bold, naïve and sophisticated, Abby was a kaleidoscope of contrasts. She was killing him.

Unraveled, Alex pressed his lips to the long pale column of her throat, inhaled the fragrance of her skin. Seductive, enchanting. Maddening.

Scrape of her fingernails over his back wrenched a deep growl from his throat. More, more, more.

Her hands sneaked lover, past the waistband of his pants and boxers. When she squeezed his butt, Alex all but exploded.

Now, now, now!

A roar of blood in his ears was deafening. Unable to endure this torture any longer, he reared up. In a blink of an eye, he shed his remaining clothes, then ripped apart her panties. A musky scent of her arousal hit him like a fist, sent him reeling.

Finally.

Abby's shocked gasp echoed his own choked cry.

Revved, trembling from head to toe, Alex had enough willpower to not plunge in there and then. He cupped her in his hand. Burned from the liquid heat, his palm tingled. She was wet, and hot, and ready.

Yes! Dammit all to hell and back, yes!

Panting, writhing, Abby let out a litany of short strangled gasps. His name. "Alex...Alex..."

Through the heavy thunder of his heartbeat, her chanting pulsed in his ears.

He pressed his hand harder, urging her forward.

"Let go, baby. Just let go."

Abby squirmed, strained against his palm, then all but flew off the mattress.

"Alex!"

And the hungry beast sprang free.

Powerless to withstand its demand a second longer, with a part curse and part plea on his lips, Alex surged forward, and in a single stroke sheathed himself to the hilt.

A fragile barrier of her innocence was no match for the brutal invasion. Attune to her body, he all but heard that tiny tearing sound in his head. Abby cried out.

He froze, then cursed, when she began to buckle like a tempestuous filly in a frenzy to dislodge a rider. Grinding his teeth, Alex used all his strength to stay on top. The hardest thing was to keep still, when the instinct older than time screamed at him to move. He bit his lip, tasted blood. And prayed.

Time stretched. Seconds turned into eternity. When he was about to lose all hope, Abby stopped her mad thrashing. Boneless, her arms and legs glided away, leaving him oddly bereft.

Son of a bitch.

He hurt her. Damn that physiology to hell and back. And damn him for tearing into her tender flesh with all the finesse of a fucking sledgehammer.

Was she in pain? Was it unbearable?

Alex held his breath, strained his ears. In the charged silence of the room, her shallow breathing was barely audible. She lay motionless, violated, defeated.

Son of a fucking bitch.

Gutted with remorse, swimming in guilt, he was afraid to look at her. What now? Panic swept over him in a brutal wave of cold sweat.

What do I do now?

Quiet, she was so quiet. Dammit, why didn't she say something? Anything?

A single sound of protest from her, and he swore to stop. Even if it killed him.

No if *about it.*

Mastering the last drops of willpower, Alex lifted himself higher on his elbows.

"Abby?"

After a long moment she stirred, opened her eyes. And stole his breath away along with the last drops of his sanity. Fierce, almost savage, her glare scorched a couple of layers of skin. But instead of pain, expected and justified, her eyes transmitted an acute disappointment.

Dammit, was she pouting? Or were his eyes playing a trick on him? Baffled, dumbfounded, he peered into her face.

"Princess?"

"That's all there is to it?" An accusation?

Damn if she didn't make him laugh. Again. Shaking with it, swamped with tenderness, Alex lowered his brow to hers.

"Oh, God, Abby, you'll be the end of me."

"Laughing at me again, are you?"

She made a production of pushing at his chest with both hands. "Fine. Laugh all you want, you cad. If you're finished with me, I'd like to get up now."

"Not on your life. You're not going anywhere."

"Says who?"

"Your future husband." He smiled down at her, smoothed away a lock of hair fallen into her face. Odd, but Abby furious expression managed to evaporate all his tension. "Forgot that you agreed to marry me?"

"I did not!"

"Did too."

"I said I was never going to marry you if you stopped."

"True. But I didn't, so you are marrying me, Princess."

She bristled, opened her mouth to contradict. He stopped her with a quick, but passionate kiss.

"As to your question— there is much more to it than that."

"Really?" Curiosity mixed with a heavy dose of disbelief was written all over her face.

"Yes, really." He smoothed another lock of hair from her face. "Much, much more."

"Well? What are you waiting for?" All eagerness, she hooked again those sky-scrapers legs of hers around his waist. "Show me. Time's awasting, you know."

Alex hooted with laughter as her little wiggle plunged him deeper into her glorious body. She was wet, tight, and hot as a furnace. His shaft swelled, his gut clutched. But his heart melted. On the verge of an abyss, straining against sweet agony, Alex smiled into her face.

"I simply adore you, Princess."

"You have a very peculiar way of showing it, sir."

"Peculiar, is it?"

He rocked forward. Abby gasped, clutched at his shoulders.

"Pain or pleasure?"

"I...don't know." She tightened her legs, drew him even closer, deeper. Now it was his turn to gasp. A slow wicked smile played over her lips.

"Why don't you do it again? So I can be sure."

"With my absolute pleasure."

CHAPTER TWENTY-SEVEN

Poleaxed. Wrung dry. Maybe even dead. Alex wasn't sure at that point.

His release left him all but comatose. Release, my ass. It was a nuclear explosion followed by fireworks. The drumbeat of his heart was so brutal, his ribcage felt bruised. He had sex before, plenty of it, but all of that vast experience paled in comparison with what happened tonight. Because he never was in love before, never made *love* before.

He liked women, never lacked female companionship. Some of them as friends, some as lovers. He even had a couple of semi-serious relationships during his thirty years. Sex was always a pleasure, a gift to cherish and enjoy. And enjoy it he did. But, God almighty, had he known the true difference between having sex and making love, he'd probably have abstained until tonight. Until Abby.

Breathless, awestruck, he struggled to reclaim his sanity. Not to mention the feeling in his limbs. Sprawled on top, he was probably suffocating her. *Must move.* In another year or so. Maybe.

Move, Alex. You're squashing her.

That tiny voice in his head irritated the hell out of him.

You can do it, pal.

I applaud your infinite confidence in my ability.

Move, you bastard!

Okay, alright, jeez.

He tried his arms first, then his legs. Even though weak as a freaking noodle, his extremities appeared to be in working order. In a stark contrast with them, his shaft stayed awake and alert, on the ready for the next round. *Down, boy.* Of course, the little bastard refused to obey, nestled inside, all warm and cozy.

Mildly embarrassed, Alex tried to withdrew, but Abby objected. Her murmur of protest was barely audible, but the feel of her teeth on his shoulder meant business. Ouch. Brazen wench.

Wench? Really, Alex? What are you, practicing old fashioned slang for the upcoming trip?

The subject of the big event was unwelcomed and sobering.

His mood plummeted, as his euphoria dimmed. Like a shadow, tomorrow loomed ahead, dark and menacing. No, not tomorrow, but already today. Still dark. What time was it? Alex squinted at the clock. On the opposite wall the old-fashioned antic timepiece Nika found at an estate sale last year, glowed like a warning. Four-thirty. Dawn was another couple of hours away. Still time to bask in the glow of stolen paradise. As if echoing his thoughts, Abby sighed. Alex smiled, hugged her closer, and rolled to his back with his prize in his arms. She tucked her nose into the hollow of his throat, then hummed in contentment.

"Now I definitely must marry you." Muffled against his skin, her slurry statement was barely audible. Afraid that his hearing was playing a nasty trick on him, Alex grabbed a fistful of her hair, and gently lifted her head.

"What did you just say?"

"Thunderation." A smack at his arm, accompanied by a little grimace, stung quite smartly. Alex ignored it.

"No, that's not what you said."

"For the love of God, Alex, if you don't let go of my hair—"

"Abs, please say it again." He let go of her silky hair, then framed her face with his palms. "Please."

Begging was a new experience for him. Then again, everything about tonight was new and amazing. Exciting. Frightening.

Humbling. Like a blind man, he navigated this uncharted territory, guided by heart alone.

"I said, I must marry you." Her smile shimmered with wicked humor. "How else can I make an honest man out of you?"

"Okay. Alright." Unmindful of his nakedness, Alex jumped from the bed.

"What...where are you going?"

"Wait, just wait. Dammit, where is it?"

He turned his head, zeroed in on the heap of clothes on the floor. Grabbing his pants, Alex routed in the pockets.

Hallelujah.

"Here." With shaking hands he managed to open the small Tiffany box on the second try. "Give me your hand, Princess."

And for the second time that day, Alex kneeled before her.

CHAPTER TWENTY-EIGHT

A bby eyed the ring with a mixed expression of longing and regret. For a split second her outstretched hand hovered above it.

"Oh, Alex. It's gorgeous! But—" She closed her fingers, moved her hand away.

A sparkle of disappointment ignited his temper. "No buts. You proposed, I agreed. Now take the damn ring, and let's make it official."

Dammit, stay cool, Alex.

"I want to, more than anything. But I can't. Not now."

"Why the hell not?"

"Because..." Abby heaved a breath, shook her head. "I'm leaving soon."

"So?"

"So, maybe you should hold on to it, until I come back. Then we'll make it official."

An icy drop of fear trickled through, dampening his anger.

"Are you by any chance planning to stay there?"

"No! God, no. Just long enough to free Eli."

"Then, what's the problem?" Inspiration struck. "If you're worried about your brother's approval, he gave me his blessing."

"He did? When?"

"Just before he left."

"Did you ask for my hand in marriage?"

"Not exactly. I told him that I love you, and going to marry you, and he—"

"Without asking me first?"

Uh-oh. Trouble.

Trust Princess to find a single weak spot, and pounce on it. Two perfect arches of raised brows transmitted the beginning of a major argument.

Naked, flushed from head to toe, Abby sat straight as an arrow amidst the wrinkled sheets that still carried a heady perfume of their lovemaking. Her accusing glare was hard to misinterpret. Disapproval mixed with indolence rolled from her in a tidal wave. Damn if she didn't remind him of royalty. A totally pissed off royalty.

Familiar with her moods, Alex had no trouble translating her emotions. Or predicting her next move. Been over that road many a time, mastered the art of avoiding the obstacles. But, God, the frustration of it! No one tried his patience like Abby. Her stubborn streak fascinated as much as it irritated the hell out of him.

Thunderation.

Now for the damage control. With a fortifying breath, Alex plunged ahead. "You were in San Francisco at the time. I didn't know how long your funk was going to last—"

"My *what*?"

Geez, sinking fast, buddy.

"I'm sorry, Abs, I meant to say, your..." *What? Think, Alex. Fast.* "Ah...your decision to stay in California. To, you know, teach the kids, and all that."

So lame. His explanation earned him another smoldering glare. Alex rubbed his head, cursed under his breath. The fact that he was still kneeling, and naked to boot, added another layer to his discomfort. Embarrassing. Ridiculous. Raising to his feet, he snatched the sheet from the bed, covered his essentials, and started to pace.

"Yes, I should've asked you first, I guess."

"You guess?"

"Dammit, Abby, what do you want me to say? I'm sorry, okay?"

Abby didn't move. Did not utter a single word.

Patience was never a problem for him, but God, she managed to strip him off of that commodity in a flash. Stubborn, impossible, maddening creature!

Well, if logic can't sway her, the only other thing was repentance. *Grovel, buddy.*

Alex stopped his pacing, sat on the corner of the bed, and looked straight into her insulted, defiant eyes.

"Abby, I am an idiot. My only excuse is, I was afraid."

"Afraid? Of what?" Disbelief rang true and clear in her voice. But at least she was talking to him. Good.

And now, pal, for the full disclosure. Don't hold anything back.

Caution was a double-edged sword. As half-truths, or doubts. What was the point? Guarding his heart? It already belonged to her. Hiding his vulnerability? Pointless. He was stripped of any and all defenses where Abby was concerned.

Deliberately, Alex smashed the last shield of his resistance, and bared his soul.

"Afraid that you're too young, too beautiful, too talented. Too everything. Afraid that you looked at me as a brother. Or a friend. It would destroy me. Call me a coward, but not knowing the truth gave me a small hope."

Was it his imagination, or were her eyes misted? No, he was not mistaken. With his fingertip, Alex caught the single tear that trickled down her cheek.

"I was afraid to confess, because I love you, Abigail Suzanne Coleman. So much, it's impossible to breathe. Forgive me?"

"Oh, Alex." She all but jumped into his arms, pressed her tear-stained face into his shoulder. "There is nothing to forgive. I love you too, my dear. So much, it hurts. I thought I was not enough for you. Not pretty enough, not sophisticated enough. Not enough woman."

"Are you kidding me? Abs, if you were more of a woman, you'd kill me."

"Honestly?" A soft red blush spread over her cheekbones, as she gazed at him.

Her innocence pierced his heart, turned it over in his chest. An ache, sweet and tender, spread all over, bringing him to his knees. If he wasn't sitting, he'd have slid down into a puddle at her feet. He managed a wobbly smile.

"Cross my heart and hope to die."

Like a blind person, he gently traced a fingertip over her face, committing her features to his memory. Dear Lord, she was so beautiful. For the life of him he couldn't tear his gaze from her face.

Remember, Alex. Remember this moment in time. For all eternity.

Cold all over, he sucked in a breath. Where did that come from?

The thought he might never see her again punched its brutal fist into his gut.

No way in hell.

Before his brain registered his intention, his hands shot up, and framed her face with more force that he intended to. Abby jolted.

"Alex? What is it?"

"No way in hell I'm losing you."

"What? What are you talking about?"

He scared her. Scared himself even more. With an effort, he gentled his hold.

"I can't lose you, Princess. Not even for Nika's sake."

"Why should you lose me? I told you, I'm coming back. I'm giving you a solemn oath."

Oath or not, she was coming back, because he'll be there, too. With her. No matter what or when, he vowed to bring them both back. If that damn clock cooperated. Or they both were lost between the centuries. But they'd be together.

Tell her about your decision. Just tell her, for goodness' sake.

Not now.

When?

Some other time.

There's no other time, Alex.

I'll make time.

To shut up his annoying conscience, he bent his head, then kissed her with every ounce of love in his soul.

Abby murmured something against his lips. In protest? In agreement? He didn't care. Alex continued his assault on her mouth until, pliant and eager, she opened up to him, and returned his passion beat for fiery beat.

His blood sang, his heart drummed, his loins ached.

You're going to hurt her. Another round of lovemaking is too soon.

Even as his brain shouted the warning, his arms imprisoned her, held tight.

Together, heart to heart, they lowered to the bed. Suddenly, Abby wrenched her mouth free.

"Give me the ring."

Befuddled, he looked down into her glowing face.

"The...what?"

"Ring, Alex. Give me my ring."

"W-why?"

"Because I changed my mind." She waggled her fingers under his nose.

Geez, only Abby! With the blood dancing a jig in his veins, Alex disengaged himself from her embrace long enough to find the turquoise box laying on the floor. With unsteady hands he picked it up.

"Put it on. Hurry, for goodness' sake!"

Laughing, cursing, he managed to retrieve the ring, then slid it onto her finger. Free of its protective folds, the magnificent gem shot a burst of white fire. The air shimmered, pulsed like a living breathing thing. Mesmerizing. Mysterious. Magical.

And what woman wouldn't take a moment to admire a gorgeous four carat diamond on her finger? Only Abby.

Without a pause, she reached for him. Caught off guard, Alex fell on top of her.

"Now we are officially engaged. You may kiss your bride, sir."

Sweet baby Jesus.

She made him laugh, even at the moment like this, when he hurt all over from the arousal, and burned from within. Straining, laughing, he ducked his head, found her breast. Abby gasped as he pressed his lips over her heart. Strong and fast and true, in beat in unison with his own. Destined. Pledged to each other at last.

Swamped in gentleness, steeped in kindness, he took his lips on an leisurely journey. There was so much to enjoy, so much to worship and cherish. Shoulders, elegant and white as alabaster, the valley between the mounds of her breasts, soft and silky, the perfect round innie of her navel. Fascinating.

Then his tonged slipped lover, tracing a long-wet line along her tender thigh. So much to nibble on, to taste, to relish. A gourmet feast, a delicacy meant to sample and appreciate. Exquisite.

A symphony of Abby's moans shattered the predawn silence of the room. The music of passion, it stirred his hunger simmering on a slow burner. The flames flew. The roar of blood in his ears became defeating. Engorged, his shaft all but screamed in pain and frustration. With an enormous effort of will, he ignored it, and continued his slow, sweet explorations, as much for her pleasure as his.

Greed scraped along his nerve-endings, but he fought it off. The overwhelming need for tenderness swept over him. Who said that men didn't need romance?

He cheated them both off it before. Not now. Not ever.

Like a rosebud, kindness unfurled its tender petals, saturated his soul.

Enchanted. Bewitched. Spellbound.

Undone by the quiet wonder of the moment, Alex looked up at her and smiled.

His own image reflected in the mirror of her silver eyes. He wished to stay like that forever, just gazing at her, drowning in her.

"Please."

Soft and quiet, her plea washed over him like a gentle breeze.

Slow and careful, he slipped inside her. Now it was his turn to moan.

Gloriously tight, drenched in liquid fire, she clamped her legs around him like a velvet vise.

And still, he kept himself in check, unwilling to spoil the magic of the moment.

Steeped in it, unraveled by it, Alex entwined their fingers.

Meshed, body, and soul.

United for all eternity.

Fated by the Universe.

Gentle, unhurried, he rocked them both toward blissful delirium.

Just for a heartbeat, they hovered at the edge of the precipice. Eyes locked, they smiled at each other, and together took that final leap.

CHAPTER TWENTY-NINE

She was soaring, high and free and joyful. Another moment, and she might dissolve into a million tiny pieces. Bliss. Overflowing, astonishing. Magical.

Content, happy, Abby smiled. Her nose, tucked into the hollow of Alex's throat, tickled.

Alex.

Her own miracle, her destiny. Her love. Ever considerate, he reversed their positions, so now she was sprawled on top of his large, muscular frame.

Like an anchor, his arm lay across the small of her back, preventing her from any movement. If not for that protection, Abby was sure she'd fly up and away, boneless, weightless, ethereal. The ring on her finger pulsed in unison with her heart. Pledged. Not a singular person anymore, but part of a union.

A half of the whole.

Glorious.

The sense of belonging, deep and powerful and overwhelming, swept over her.

Elated, humbled, overjoyed. Cocooned into the folds of happiness.

Oh, to stay like that forever!

But time was ticking away. Abby squinted at the clock on the wall. Eight o'clock. Time to get up. She must get dressed, and find Daisy. Together they will wake JC, and take the key he promised to release in the morning. It was up to Daisy to deal with the scoundrel.

Abby still felt a bit apprehensive about him. Even though he was more than kind and courteous to her, his previous behavior toward his family was questionable at best. Trust was a precious commodity that must be earned. And, as Daisy was fond of saying, the jury was still out where JC was concerned. Abby frowned, then sighed, as the sound of Alex's breathing reached her ears. Deep asleep, he didn't stir when she started to slide from the bed.

Sleep, my love. Please sleep a while longer.

She wasn't sure if she was strong enough to say good-bye to him. Better not.

Careful not to wake him, holding her breath, Abby continued her slow progress. Her plans, however, were busted to smithereens, when Alex's arm snaked over, and stopped her in mid-motion.

"Going somewhere?"

Merde. Fate was not on her side this morning.

"Sorry, I didn't want to wake you. I must be going."

With both hands, Alex grabbed, tagged, and brought her back on top of him.

"Where?"

Heavy, slumberous, his violet eyes stopped her heart along with her breath.

God, he was beautiful! It should be outlawed for a man to look so amazing in the morning. Or at any time of day or night.

"To, ah... Daisy's room. I n-need to check on her. And... JC t-too. I'm not sure what time... she wants...ah, to...to go." Babbling, almost stumbling on every word, Abby lowered her gaze. Suddenly self-conscious, she tried to look anywhere but him. She failed.

"Okay." His eyes cleared, focused. "Give me a moment to dress."

"Oh, but you don't have to. As a matter of fact, it would be much easier if you stay here, and not see us...away."

"Easier?" His brow shot up, as he peered into her face. "For who?"

"For me. And I'm sure, for Daisy, too. Alex..." Abby swallowed, as she drew in his unique fragrance. Potent. Strong. Unquestioningly male. Damn if he didn't make her head swim. Miserable, she gazed at him, already mourning.

"I can't bear to say farewell to you."

"You don't have to, since I'm going with you." He smiled at her, dropped a quick kiss onto her lips.

Abby jolted. "What do you mean, you're going with me?"

Her abrupt body movement wrangled a hiss and a helpless oath out of him. Too late she realized that she pressed both elbows into his stomach.

"Ouch, Princess. Mind the family jewels." Alex moved a couple of inches away to safety. "As to your question, I'm coming along for the ride. With you and Nika."

"But you can't! You mustn't!"

"Why?"

"Because it's too dangerous."

"Oh, so it's too dangerous for me, but not for you two?"

Merde. Think, Abigail. You must discourage him. Think good and fast.

"Alex, be reasonable. Daisy and I already made such a trip before, so we're used to it. But you—"

"What am I, a weak sister?"

Thunderation. Now she managed to insult him.

"No, you're nobody's sister, for sure." Heat burned her cheeks, as Abby remembered the events of last night. Now, in broad daylight, the memories of what they'd done together made her uncomfortable. She darted a look at his loins, quickly averted her eyes. Naked, and unconcerned of it, Alex lay in all his splendid glory. His lower parts, nestled in a thick thatch of dark hair, looked all soft and tender and vulnerable. A deception of nature.

The astonishing difference between their bodies hit her anew. Fascinating.

Do you honestly think it's a good time to be curious about physiology? Idiot.

Embarrassed, Abby masked her mortification by clearing her throat. A smile that split his face was positively wicked. Then he winked at her.

"Bashful all of a sudden, Princess? You saw all of this already."

The gall of the cad!

With an effort, Abby pulled on a mask of schoolmistress. Prim and prudish.

"Well, be that as it may, sir, I would greatly appreciate if you covered your...essential parts at least."

Amused, Alex let out a short bark of a laughter, but finally draped a sheet over his lap.

"Better, Your Highness?" His inquiry was delivered in a formal way, but his eyes danced with mirth. Borrowing the page from his book, Abby mastered a curt nod.

"Yes. Thank you."

"What about you?"

"What about me?"

"In case you forgot, my lady, you are naked too. Not that I'm complaining."

Now his smile was that of a pirate.

"*Merde.*"

Abby snatched a quilt in a belated attempt to cover her nakedness.

Alex sighed.

"Pity. But cannot be helped, I guess. Now, where were we...?"

Sweet Lord, she forgot all about his insane notion to accompany her and Daisy though time. Cursing under her breath, Abby decided to reason with him in a calm manner. She took a couple of deep breaths.

"Alex, listen. You cannot go with us. Besides being dangerous, the clock rejected you. Remember? It didn't tolerate a single touch from you. How on earth would you embark on a time traveling, if you cannot approach the portal?"

He shrugged. "I'll think of something." And with that, Alex swung his legs off the bed. Now what?

"Alex—"

All merriment left his features when he whirled to glare at her.

"Now you listen to me, Abs. And listen good. I wouldn't let any woman to traipse through time alone. Not to mention my bride and my cousin. Come hell or high water, I'm going with you. Period. And that stupid grandfather clock be damned!"

He stopped, drew a couple of deep breaths and rubbed his head. When he looked at her again, his face was set in that stubborn way Abby was too familiar with.

Alex had made up his mind, curse it. Will she be able to change it? Not likely.

"It was me in that stinking cell with Eli. Why, or how, I'm not sure. But I was there. I saw him with my own eyes. Miserable, humiliated, degraded. It tore me apart, Abby. Do you honestly think I would sit and wait, and do nothing? Dammit, he's like a brother to me!"

Alex was a protector by nature, a trait she always admired. She should've predicted his reaction. Stay away when someone he loved was in trouble? Impossible.

Thunderation.

"Alex, if something happened to you, I won't survive."

He came closer to her, tucked a hair behind her ear. "Same goes, Princess."

"Please, be reasonable. This time travel is not only dangerous, it's unnatural. The balance of time is fraught with peril. What if we disturb the flow of things enough to cause some disaster?"

He chuckled and tapped her nose with a fingertip.

"But we won't. We'll jump, free Eli, and will be on our merry way back in a matter of hours. Okay, a day at the most. Your flow of things wouldn't know what hit it. I promise."

Seething, frightened, she swapped at his annoying finger.

"Damnation, it's not that easy!"

"I know, Princess. And that's why I'm coming with you."

Maddening. The man was nothing short of maddening, damn his delicious hide.

Short of tearing her hair out, she was out of options. Abby closed her eyes, took a deep breath. *What can she appeal to? What can stop Alex from this insanity?*

And then it dawned at her: *Verochka.* Only her honorary grandmother might talk sense into Alex. She must reach out to *Verochka* right away.

Where is my phone? Abby whirled around to search for it, as she remembered *Verochka* was on the other end of the world, on some tiny island in the middle of nowhere!

Abby's only option was to send a text, and wait for a reply. How long? One day? Two?

Several?

Merde.

Discouraged, Abby all but abandoned that idea, as inspiration struck. Would Alex abandon *Verochka*? She'd be left all alone, unaware of the family crisis. Even though feisty and independent, she was elderly. Not counting JC, Alex was all the family she had left. And he loved his grandmother. Okay, this might actually work. Fortified, Abby opened her mouth to deliver her most weighty argument, as the door flew open.

"He's gone!"

Pale, breathless, Daisy all but stumbled inside. Jiminy, she looked a fright.

Matted and dull, her curls clung to her head like a dirty yellow cloud. Withered beyond recognition, her old-fashioned clothes hung onto her slender frame like a curtain. But her amethysts eyes shone with an dazzling light.

Shaking, Daisy brandished her hands balled in two fists.

"The son of a bitch is gone!"

Her protruding stomach made her pacing difficult, but she waddled around the room, cursing a blue streak. What on earth?

One thing was clear: Daisy was horribly distraught, all but falling apart. Only once before had Abby witnessed her in such a pitiful state and that was when they first arrived in this century, and discovered that the key to the portal was lost.

"Daisy, what is it, *ma petite*? Who's gone?"

But God help her, Abby already knew the answer.

The key. JC refused to hand it over yesterday. He promised to do so today, before the trip. Did he lie? Did he run away with it? But why, and to what purpose?

The snake! The filthy traitor! The lying sack of *merde*!

God help her, if he escaped with it, Abby vowed to hunt him down like a rabid dog, and strangle him with her bare hands. But her first concern now was Daisy.

Shakes that rocked her small body all but rattled the delicate bones. Vibrating from the force of it, Daisy resembled a live electric wire. Another moment, and she might burst into flames. Unmindful of her state of undress, swaddled in the bulky quilt, Abby hurried to her sister-in law. Her heart was breaking. For Daisy, and her poor brother Eli. If he wasn't in jail, Daisy would never have had to time travel alone in her condition. But that was neither here nor there. And since Eli was accused of *her* murder, Abby's guilt multiplied tenfold. Even though it was not her fault, she was culpable all the same. Abby came closer, but when she tried to hug Daisy, she wrenched from the embrace. Her eyes, wide and horrified, shot sparks in all directions.

Worried in earnest, helpless, Abby watched her best friend.

Do something, Abby! Don't just sit like a feeble damsel.

Daisy's struggles subsided, then stopped altogether. She all but folded into herself like a house of cards. Fluid, she slid to the floor in a boneless heap. Abby dropped to her knees beside her, anxious to comfort, but still afraid to touch. In a harsh broken whisper Daisy validated Abby's suspicions.

"JC. He's gone. With the key. Oh, God, Abby, what am I going to do?"

Spent, she dropped her head onto Abby's shoulder. Small tremors continued to rake her body, sending ripples through her rounded belly.

Cradling both mother and a child, Abby murmured sweet nothings in feeble hope to bring consolation. When a hand lightly touched her bare shoulder, she froze, then tilted her head. Misty from the unshed tears, her eyes landed on Alex. Sweet Lord, she forgot all about him! Alex stepped closer, kneeled on the other side of his cousin. Daisy jolted.

"Don't be afraid, Nik. It's me."

"Oh, God, Alex? You... but..." As realization dawned, she closed her eyes. "Dammit, I didn't know that you two...Sorry, sorry. Should've knock first."

"Never mind that. So, the jerk has disappeared?"

"Yes. The baby woke me. The little stinker was kicking up a storm, hungry. At first, I didn't know where I was, and then I remembered. Everything was so quiet, like I was alone in the house. So, I went to check. His room...I knew it was his room, because the bed was unmade, and his tie was on the chair. The freaking Hermes tie. Then I checked the bathroom. I even went outside, but except for Coco, there was—"

"Wait, wait a second. Coco? What about my Baby?"

"No, just the Corvette sitting on the driveway."

"The jerk took my car? My Baby? I'm going to kill him!"

Enraged, Alex jumped to his feet. In the process, the sheet tucked around his hips slipped away. Naked as the day he was born, Alex stood there, in a bright daylight, shaking, cursing. Abby sucked in her breath. Lord, he was gorgeous.

And all mine.

Even as her blood began to hum, a tide of heat flooded her cheeks.

Sweet baby Jesus.

The situation could not be more obvious. Now Daisy will know that she slept with her beloved cousin. Although *slept* was a loose term to be applied to their nocturnal activities. Scandalous.

Daisy turned to Alex and let out a strangled sound of outrage.

"Geez, Cuz. We are in the middle of a major disaster here, and all you worry about is your precious car? Really?" She threw her hands up, then settled them onto her hips. "Unbelievable! By the way, in case it slipped your mind, you're in your birthday suit."

"So? You've seen me in it before."

"Yeah, when we were three, if memory serves. Let me enlighten you, pal, you looked a little different then."

Alex snatched a fallen sheet from the floor, and wrapped it around himself.

"Okay, your modesty is preserved. Now, I'd like to know—"

But his sentence was interrupted by a loud clearing of the throat.

"What's all this? An orgy? And no one invited me?"

CHAPTER THIRTY

The mute scene that followed JC's surprise appearance was worthy of vaudeville. A cheap and tacky one.

All three of them turned their heads toward the newcomer. The expression on Daisy and Alex's face were that of a shocked bafflement. Abby didn't have to look in the mirror to affirm her own emoticon. The moment stretched while they surveyed JC who held the paper sacks in one hand with unmistakable golden arches imprinted on them. In his other hand was a caddy with four paper cups. Daisy found her voice first.

"Where...where the hell were you?"

Brows arched, he gazed at his sister with acute puzzlement.

"Why, at McDonald's, getting some food. I don't know about you guys, but I'm used to having my morning coffee and some breakfast. Of course, it ain't Ritz's continental spread, but beggars can't be choosers. What? No thank you, JC for your consideration?"

"Damn you, JC."

"I take it you're not hungry, Midget. Okay, I'll eat your portion."

"Touch it, and die." Daisy made an attempt to stand, but sunk back onto her knees. Sitting on the floor, she wiggled the fingers of one hand at her brother. "Gimme."

"Nope. Not until you thank me properly."

"I'll thank you," Alex marched toward his cousin, and delivered a smart smack on the back of his head. "That proper enough for you?"

"Ouch. What gives?"

"What gives? You jerk! You scared Nika half to death, not to mention, took my car."

"Well, as I had the keys you gave me yourself, by the way, I decided to drive your Porsche. A dream of a car. I'm thinking of buying one."

"Think later, moron." With that, Alex snatched the sacks and a caddy from his cousin's hands, and returned to the spot where Daisy sat.

JC let out a long-suffering breath, then followed Alex. He plopped on the floor near their small group.

As the aroma of food permeated the air, Abby realized she was famished. The loud growling sound that emanated from her stomach was quite embarrassing. But since everybody had a similar reaction, no one was paying any attention to her. Alex delved into one of the paper pouches, and handled Daisy a wrapped egg muffin. She smiled her thanks, tore at the wrapper, and sunk her teeth into the greasy delight. Abby's turn was next. As soon as she bit into the warm sandwich, her hum of pleasure burst free. Marvelous. She had never tasted anything more scrumptious in her lifetime.

Alex, more in control of his emotions, chomped his own muffin in silence.

After a long moment, JC chuckled. "You are welcome. All three of you."

"Thank you, JC. This is delicious." Ashamed of her own behavior, Abby managed a wobbly smile.

"You are welcome, Abby. And, by way, congratulations. That ring is a doozy."

A sudden dose of reality hit like a splash of icy water in the face.

She was all but naked, sitting in the middle of the blasted floor, sporting a glamorous engagement ring. Damn, how could she act in such a blasé manner?

JC must have figured by now that Alex and she spent the night together. As to what transpired here... Abby cast a furtive glance at the bed. God have mercy! It resembled a battlefield. Only a blind, or totally demented person, wouldn't come to the apparent conclusion. Mortified, Abby blanched, shut her eyes. One thing for Daisy to figure out the truth, but JC?

Scandalous, Abigail. You must look like a harlot.

Burning from shame, she tucked the ends of the quit around herself tighter. She'd pray for the earth to open and swallow her alive, if she had any rational thought left in her mind. Alex chose that moment to scoot closer, and then draped his arm around her shoulders. Dropping a kiss on her forehead, he smiled at his cousins.

"You may as well congratulate us both. Lady and gentleman, meet my future wife, Abigail Suzanne Coleman, soon to be Morris."

Daisy, too busy devouring her food, just grunted.

"Well, my children," JC saluted with his paper cup, "to the newly engaged couple. May your life together be as cloudless as that diamond. Lots of love, luck, and patience."

After one quizzical glance at his cousin, Alex replied, "Thanks. I think."

Still uncomfortable, without lifting her eyes, Abby just nodded.

When Daisy swallowed the last bit of her food, she squinted at her brother.

"Is there any more?"

"But of course. I ordered breakfast for five. One for the baby."

With that clarification, he dropped his hand into the sack, and handled her another small bundle with a flourish. "Figured you have to eat for two, Midget. Darn it, you're pale enough to see through." He muttered before flicking away one of her curls. In lieu of thanks, Daisy snatched the coveted egg and sausage muffin, and barely unwrapped a corner before she bit into it.

"Damn, I forgot how tasty these little suckers are."

JC smiled, and handled her a paper cup.

"What's that? Coffee?"

"A vanilla latte."

Daisy made a small grimace. "That's not coffee. It's a sissy drink. I want a real coffee. Black and strong."

"Well, you're not getting it. Black and strong is not good for the baby."

Her lip curled into a sneer. "What are you, a prenatal care specialist?"

"Just a smart guy who uses a common knowledge. So, take you sissy drink, and be grateful."

Grumbling, Daisy sipped from the cup. "It's not even hot!"

"Can't be helped, sorry. And hot beverages aren't good for you anyway."

"Damn."

She returned to her food, chewing ravenously. After Daisy swallowed the last morsel, she looked around like a lioness on the hunt. "Still hungry. I can eat a dozen of those eggs McMuffins."

"Yeah, well, I wouldn't recommend that." All reason, JC cast a quick glance at her.

"You can get sick before our trip, and—"

"Whoa, wait a minute." The cup she was about to sip from tilted precariously in her hand. "Just a damn minute. What do you mean 'our' trip?"

"That's exactly what I mean, Nika. I'm coming with you."

"You too?" Abby's exclamation sent three heads in her direction.

"What's that supposed to mean?" Daisy's scorching glare was hot enough to scrape a layer off her. Abby winced.

"Only that I'm coming with you," Alex answered before she uttered a sound. Unperturbed by a string of curses coming from Daisy, he pointed a finger at her. "Don't even try, Cuz. You need me."

"The hell I am!"

"The hell you don't!"

"Okay, kids. Chill out. We're all coming." After JC made a production of wiping his hands with a napkin, he smiled at his sister. "The more the merrier, I say."

"You don't say, you moron! It's not up to you to say anything!"

"But it is. Forgot that I have the key? If you refuse, I won't release it to your anxious little hands."

"Blackmail, Junior?"

"You bet your pregnant ass."

Frustrated, Daisy grabbed two fistfuls of her hair.

"Dammit, that's not funny!"

"Who said it was?" JC shrugged, pursed his lips.

"Alex, say something."

"Okay. It's not funny. And you, cousin dear," Alex turned to stare at JC, "are not coming."

"Who's going to stop me?"

"Well, let's see." In a mocking gesture Alex tapped his lips with his fingertips, as if debating this little dilemma. "How about yours truly?"

"Not happening. You see, I'm wearing the key, so if you—"

In a lightning-fast move, Alex grabbed his cousin by the collar of his shirt. With his other hand, he reached inside, took hold of the cord around his neck, and yanked. With a brittle sound the leather broke in two.

"Not anymore. So, you were saying?"

"Dammit, Alex." JC rubbed the abused skin on his neck. "Have you thought that Eli might need a lawyer?"

"I highly doubt it. All he needs is for Abby to show up, alive and well. But, just for the sake of the argument, let's say he needs an attorney. A criminal one, you dum-dum, not a numbers cruncher like you."

"Before I became a number-cruncher, as you so indelicately put it, I was training at the offices of Kline & Stromberg, the best criminal attorneys in New York."

"Good for you. So?"

"So, I am familiar with the system, and quite proficient in that part of law."

"Be it as it may, you are proficient in the twenty-first century criminal law. See a difference?"

"Not much of a difference between now and then, not at all. And showing Abby, alive and well, is fine, but the presence of a lawyer from New York might offer some weight in swaying the officials."

"And how on earth do you propose to explain your presence? Where did you come from? Who the hell are you?"

"I am JC Morris, Daisy's brother from New York who accompanied Miss Abby on her journey from up North. The lady of her status cannot travel alone, can she? But with the member of her family—"

"She can travel with her fiancé, thank you all the same."

A shrilling whistle interrupted their bickering. Abby's ears were still ringing, as Daisy removed two pinkies from her mouth.

"Enough." Raising to her feet, she glowered at both men. "What a childish squabble! You two should be ashamed of yourselves. Now, give me that."

Before Alex realized her intention, Daisy snatched the leather cord with the attached key from his hand.

"Damn, Nika."

To ensure its safety, she dropped it inside of the pocket of her voluptuous skirt, then patted it.

"That's that. Abby? Get dressed, and let's move. Time's awasting."

Calmer now, Daisy moved to the door. With the last fumigating glare at the men, she made her exit.

"Shit. Now what?" Alex rubbed his head.

"And now, Cuz, we must hurry. Because our Midget is quite determined to proceed with her mission without us." JC jumped to his feet. "Coming?"

"Yeah. But you're still not tagging along."

"We'll see. By the way, did anyone mentioned to you that you're stark naked?"

"A time or two."

"Okay, just wondering." JC managed a crooked smirk. "Planning to go in the nude, and shock the bejesus out of all the Victorian people?"

"That's Edwardian, you idiot."

"Whatever."

With an exasperated sound, Alex began to pick up his scattered clothes. "Go and try to stall her."

"She won't go without Abby, so you have time to make yourself decent. But skip the shower, Cuz. Even though you're ripe after all the amorous activities of last night."

"Kiss my ass."

"No, thank you. I'd rather—"

"JC, do you mind stepping outside?" Still sitting on the floor, Abby interrupted the verbal sparring between two cousins. "I am in a need of some privacy."

A swift blush unfurled over JC's cheekbones.

"Sorry, Abby, sorry." Already at the door, he stopped, and looked over his shoulder. "Please don't be too long, both of you. Nika's all but chomping at the bit, and I wouldn't be surprised if she decides to go ahead without any of us."

"No, she won't. She needs me. Eli needs me."

With a curt node, JC hurried out. Silence ensued. Abby held her breath. They've got a few minutes alone. She must find the right words to convince Alex. But what can she say?

Think, Abigail, think. Just a few precious moments left.

A rustle sounded behind her back. She turned to see Alex dressing in a hasty manner. She must get up, and do the same, but for the life of her, Abby was unable to move a muscle. The looming disaster paralyzed her limbs.

"Alex?"

"Humm?"

"Please reconsider."

"Not even for you, Princess."

"What can I say to dissuade you?"

"Nothing. Absolutely nothing."

"Have you thought of *Verochka*?"

"What about her?"

"She'll be left all alone, without a notion of where you disappeared to."

"She won't even know that we're gone. She's on the other side of the globe. By the time she decides to come home, we'll be back."

"What if we don't?"

That stopped him in his tracks. "What do you mean?"

"What if the grandfather clock refused to bring us back?"

"All the more reason for me to accompany you."

"Alex—"

Suddenly he was beside her. A hard, impatient tug at her arm brought her all the way up. Pressed to each other, they were so close that his heartbeat reverberated against her breast.

Why then did she feel like they were miles apart?

Gentle and soft as baby breath, his fingertips grazed her cheek. But in contrast, his eyes were serious, and hard as diamonds.

"I don't care if that stupid clock refused the back passage for us. As long as I'm with you, I can live anywhere. Even in a cave. Don't you know that?"

"Oh, Alex. It is the same for me. But what about the people left behind? *Verochka,* your parents, your business associates?"

"My parents won't care, one way or another. My business associates will function without me. *Verochka...*" he took a deep breath, released it on a long whooshing sound, "she'll understand."

"But how will she know?"

"I'll send her a text."

"But—"

"No buts, Princess." With a quick firm kiss on her lips, and a swat at her bottom, Alex closed the subject. "Now, dress up, and let's get this show on the road."

CHAPTER THIRTY-ONE

D *ress up?*
Abby eyed her torn blouse and shredded panties. And how did he propose for her to do that? The scoundrel. His own clothes were in perfect order, if wrinkled a bit. But hers? She didn't have any to speak of. Her jeans were in one piece, thank God, but that was about the only item that survived his marauding hands.

Merde.

Now what? Abby pulled her pants on, grimacing as the denim brushed her tender private parts. Not to mention shameful, it was quite uncomfortable without a barrier of her hipsters. Oh, well, must bear the consequences. Her bra was a lost cause, too. That presented a bigger problem.

Abby let out an exasperated oath. How on earth will she manage to conceal her breasts? Even when she tied her ruined blouse in the middle, her bust all but spilled over. Cursing under her breath, Abby managed to tuck them inside the flimsy material. Barely. Now, keeping them in place? A challenge for sure. Can't be helped. She just had to hold one hand in front of herself at all time. And anyway, as soon as she arrived home, she planned to change into her old-fashioned clothes. Long skirt, high-collared shirtwaist, and laced shoes.

My God, how will she be able to wear them after being spoiled with comfortable wardrobe of this century? Abby sneaked a quick glance at her feet. Clad in Manolo Blahnik sandals, her toes sported a pedicure in cheeky peach. Memories of the first time she noticed

Daisy's painted toenails flashed in her mind. Then, shocked and intrigued, Abby couldn't even dream of such a frivolity. Look at her now. She wiggled her toes. Pretty. But unseemly for the century she was heading off to. *And how do you propose to hide them, Abigail?*

Thunderation. I'll think of something.

"Ready?"

Alex's question put a stop to her inner debate. With the last fortifying breath, Abby turned to him, nodded. "As I ever will be."

Unmindful of her curt response, Alex grinned, then ushered her out. When she hesitated, he pulled her by the hand, all but dislodging it in his hurry.

"Alex, wait. What's the rush?"

"Time's ticking away."

And so it was. Eli had been in that cell long enough. They must act quickly to stop all that nonsense. And his sufferings.

Poor Eli.

Now it was her who urged Alex forward. On the run, they hit the staircase together, jumping two steps at a time. Both breathless, they reached the first floor in a flash, then turned in the direction of Daisy's angry voice.

Oh-uh. Something's going on. Abby sprinted down the hallway followed closely by Alex. On a screeching halt, she stopped and surveyed the picture in front of her.

Brother and sister, both red in the face, glared at each other in front of the grandfather clock. They were wrestling for the cord attached to the key. JC, being the strongest of them, was winning the scuffle. A shrilling scream from Daisy put Valkyrie's war cry to shame. Enraged, she tugged at the cord with all her might to no avail. A sound of Alex's angry bellow all but burst her eardrums. He plowed into the middle of the melee.

"JC! Have you lost your mind?"

Pushed out of the way, JC stumbled, but managed to stay on his feet.

"Fuck. Pardon my French, Abby."

"Are you nuts?" With both hands, Alex administered another mighty push against his cousin's chest. "She's pregnant, for crying out loud!"

"I didn't mean to hurt her, just take the key."

"And do what with it, you imbecile? The clock won't let you insert the key into the slot, much less turn it. It's only for Nika to do."

"Says who?"

"Says me. That grandfather clock accepts only her touch. And Eli's."

"Shit, now you're telling me. Hell, Alex, she refused to take me with her."

"She's right. You're staying put, cousin."

"Yeah? What about you?"

Alex opened his mouth to reply, but Daisy beat him to it. Her unarguable verdict put a stop to their argument.

"You both are staying. Period." Holding her prize in both hands, she glared at them. "You're not going anywhere. So, help me God, if either one of you approach this clock, I'll deck you. See if I don't."

Without turning her head, in a voice that bore no argument, Daisy commanded, "Abby? Come here. We're leaving. You two! Back off. All the way. And when the portal opens, run for the hills. I promise you, it ain't for the fainthearted."

"Who do you call fainthearted?" JC made an attempt to step closer, only to be kicked out of the way, curtesy of Daisy's fast little foot.

"Ouch! What the hell, Midget?"

"I told you to back off, Junior."

With a frustrated oath, Alex racked both hands over his head.

"Nika—"

"Alex." She turned her attention to him. "Please listen to me. I'm not kidding. You two must remove yourself from here. Better go to the second floor, and stay there. And don't try to interfere no matter what."

"No matter what? Dammit, Nik, if it is that dangerous, you and Abby—"

"I don't care! Don't you understand? Eli is jailed! They put him in handcuffs like a criminal. Even now, he sits in that cell, desperate, humiliated. Scared."

"No, he's not. He's...concentrating."

Alex's voice became hushed, as an eerie stillness came over him.

Pale, he held his breath, as his eyes, glassy and unblinking, stared at something beyond the realm of the present.

In an icy wave, chills washed down Abby's back.

Mesmerized, she stared at Alex's face. Was he really seeing through the curtain of time?

How was it even possible?

Daisy quietly stepped closer, as if afraid to shutter his trance. "Eli...what is he doing?"

After a long pause, Alex shivered, and came out of his reverie. Disoriented, he blinked a few times, sucked on a sharp breath. His eyes, cleared of that spooky luster, were burning with violet fire.

"He is writing a letter."

"A l-letter?"

"Yes. To you, and his unborn child."

A farewell letter.

Even though he didn't say that, the implied meaning was loud and clear.

Tears sprung to Daisy's eyes. A violent shudder ran though her body. As a sound of despair emanated from her throat, she fisted both hands. A light from within, her blazing glare was a sight to behold.

"Writing a letter, is he? The bastard! Well, we'll see about that."

She straightened her shoulders, whipped the moisture from her face. And the little fearless Valkyrie was back. Stretching her hand to Abby, Daisy declared, "We must go. Now."

"Wait, Nika. Just wait a damn minute." Grabbing her arm, Alex halted her progress in mid step. "What's happening to me? Any idea? It's the second time I have..." Struggling to put his experience into words, Alex swallowed, "I've seen Eli. Like I was there."

"You were, sweetheart." Daisy cradled his face with the palm of her hand. "You were all the way there."

"But...how?"

"Ask *Verochka*. She'll be delighted that you finally came to your gift."

"Gift? What are you talking about? What gift?"

But Daisy was already moving toward the clock. She repeated over her shoulder, "Ask *Verochka*. And tell her that I love her."

"Where are you...Nika, stop!"

Too late. She was in front of the clock. A look of utter concentration came over her face, as she inserted the key into the slot.

"Abby? Hold my hand. Don't let go."

When Abby complied, Daisy whispered, "They will try to come closer. After I turn the key, we must push them out of the way. As hard as we can. Understood?"

"Yes."

Abby was about to place her hand on Daisy's shoulder, when the reality dawned on her. This might be the last time. She might never see Alex again.

No!

Turning, Abby ran to him. Fueled by desperation, she hugged him hard, and tugging his head down, pour everything into the kiss.

"I love you. More than life itself. I'll be back. I promise."

He kissed her hard, then sent her a cheeky wink.

"Of course, you will, Princess, because I'll make sure of it."

Wrenching out of his hands was the hardest thing she'd ever done.

"Abby? Hurry!"

Daisy's cry reached her ears through the sudden loud chiming of the old grandfather clock.

Bong.

Alex was a few steps behind her, with JC trying to wrestle him out of the way.

"Alex, no!"

But he just smiled at her. All of a sudden, a horrible grimace split his face.

As he tried to step closer, an invisible force sent him flying backwards.

Alex crashed with a terrible thudding sound. Abby's cry struck in her throat.

When she tried to move, a sharp pain gutted her middle. Her ears began to ring, then popped like from a great pressure.

Everything around her dimmed, even as the brilliant light burst free from the face of the clock. Blind from the horrible agony, she struggled to keep upright. Breathing became unbearable. Everything swirled and turned in a maddening speed, sucking her body into the whirlpool. Oh, Lord, she was dying.

Alex!

Her hand clamped in Daisy's turned numb. Abby squinted at her. What was she doing? Didn't she feel that terrible pain? Didn't she see that Alex was hurt? But Daisy paid no attention, as she concentrated on the key.

"Remember: push Alex as hard as you can. If you love him, push him away!"

Push?

Didn't she see he was already pushed far back? With an enormous effort of will, Abby turned her head. Eyes closed, unmoving, Alex was lying near the landing of a staircase. Fainted? Dead?

No, God, please no!

Mad from shock, trembling from the invisible torture inflicted on her body, Abby tried to wrangle her hand free. She must go to Alex. He was hurt. Oh, God, what was happening? JC! Where was JC? Why wasn't he tending to Alex?

"JC! Help! Please help him!" Inside of her head she was screaming on top of her lungs. But only a garbled babble came out, as her vocal cords refused to function.

Through the macabre, horrendous chiming of the clock, she heard Daisy's desperate command. "On the count of three, Abs. One, two…"

Bong. Bong. Bong.

Deafening noise.

Blinding lights.

"Alex!"

And the world went black.

CHAPTER THIRTY-TWO

P ain. Terrible. Unbounded. Brutal.
Yanked out of the dense fog of his oblivion, Alex gasped for
breath, choked on it. He hurt everywhere. Unbearably. Tethering on
the sharp point of that savage pain, he prayed for this torture to end.
Darkness, calm and welcoming, beaconed with a promise of a relief.
Oh, God yes. Alex reached for it, almost touched it, as a flash of
searing agony wrenched him away.

No... please...

A low moan...helpless...pitiful...

A moan? Who was moaning?

He tried to open his eyes, but the sharp hot needles of pain
pierced his eyelids shut.

Bone dry, his mouth was devoid of a single drop of saliva. An
attempt to move his tongue was like plodding though sunbaked
sand. A bitter bile abraded his throat. Gagging, soaking wet from an
ice-cold sweat, Alex almost passed out.

Another tiny sound. Inhuman. Gut wrenching. Like an animal
in pain.

They didn't have any pets. Or did they?

Hazy, wrapped in a thick layer of fog, Alex's brain struggled to
focus.

A sudden pressure of his vocal cords... And that moaning again...

Oh, God, that pathetic sound was coming from his throat!

He hurt like hell. Broken to pieces. Dammit, what happened?

Must remember. Must get up.

But the pain was so excruciating, every attempt to move ended in blinding agony. Better to lay still, and wait.

For what? For oblivion? For death?

The irritating little voice in his head buzzed on like a nagging pest.

Shut up and leave me alone.

Get up, Alex! Time's awasting!

An instant alarm. Time. What about it? He struggled to focus. Dammit, what was it about time? Dense fog all but obliterated his memory, but the desperate urgency cut through his trance.

Time.

Alex ground his teeth, clamped his jaw, and tried to sit up. But his limbs, numb and useless, refused to move. Was he paralyzed? Mind numbing fear spurred him into action. Fighting the waves of blinding pain, he managed to prop himself on his elbows. He blinked, squinted. Everything swirled in a slow dizzying circle. Hideous nausea sucker punched him with brutal force.

Shit. Puking his guts out was all he needed at the moment. As dry heaves scorched his abused throat, Alex bore down with every ounce of willpower. After a long moment, that macabre swirling became almost barrable. He drew a shallow breath. Okay, he was able to open his eyes without passing out. A victory.

What was that noise? Ringing?

Yes, definitely ringing, like... chimes. Nika loved to hang them around the house. Alex smiled. His little cousin was crazy about those contraptions. Dream catchers she called them. But the pealing clear noise he remembered was somehow different now. Persistent. Loud. Irritating.

That ringing drove him crazy. Where the hell this was coming from? Oh, God, his ears! They were ringing like a effing campanile. A vicious headache threatened to pound its way clear through his skull.

Swimming in pain, all but drowning in it, Alex struggled to think.

Where was he? And what was so urgent about time? Dammit, why can't he remember?

Concentrate. Must concentrate.

The blurry images behind his closed eyes slowly began to crystalize.

Faces. Familiar. Nika, pregnant. Eli, in jail. Geez, what a weird dream.

Dream? But if he was dreaming, why the pain? Dammit, he hurt all over like never before in his life.

My God, was I in an accident?

That must be it. With an effort, Alex dragged his eyelids half-open, squinted at the fuzzy picture before his eyes. White ornate ceiling, a massive chandelier.

Where was he? A hospital? No, doesn't look like it. Doesn't smell like any hospital. And the surface under his back was too hard for any bed, even ER cot.

Dammit, where was he? A house? Was he showing a property to a prospective client? Which one? But he didn't have any listings, and, besides, a client wouldn't leave him incapacitated on the floor. Unless it was an attempt to mug him, which, unfortunately, was not unheard of in his line of business.

Alex contemplated that scenario for a moment before rejecting it. Impossible.

They vetted their clients thoroughly. Plus, he didn't have anything of value on his person.

Eli's watch!

Hastily, he pressed one hand against his breast pocket. Thank God.

The shape of the Coleman heirloom under his palm was familiar. Comforting.

Okay, no mugging. What, then? Through the wave of searing pain, Alex managed to turn his head, glanced around. He was in a room. A huge one. Hard floors, high ceiling, arched windows. Something nagged at his memory.

An eerie sensation of déjà vu washed over him. He was here before. He was sure of it. Unsettling, spooky. Goosebumps broke over his skin.

Alex strained his ears for any sound. Nothing. So, he was alone. Or was he?

The air all but sizzled, saturated with uncanny power. Still cracking, a ripple of current danced in the atmosphere. The room *smelled* of energy.

Potent. Unreal. Sinister.

What a silly thought.

Must have hit my head harder than I thought.

With herculean effort, hanging onto the staircase banister, Alex dragged himself to a sitting position. His head revolted along with his abused gut, but he managed to stay upright.

Okay, Alex. Think. Look around, and think.

"Easy for you to say." Shocked by the scratchy, feeble sound of his own voice, he muttered a curse.

So, he was not in a hospital, and he was alone, whenever he was, but where—

A sudden sonorous peal shattered his musings. His ears again?

Bong. Bong...

No, not his ears. It was coming from somewhere on his right. Cold all over, with every hair on his body standing on high alert, Alex shifted his eyes toward that sound. He knew that chime.

The infamous grandfather clock.

His worst nightmare. His enemy.

Mystery solved. He was in the Coleman house.

As that blasted clock continued to count time, the events of the last day came crushing back. Flattened by the enormous weight of it, Alex hunched his shoulders, shut his eyes. But there was no defense against the flood of memories.

Nika's sudden reappearance. The news of Eli's arrest. JC's crazy notion to travel through time. And Abby, who played the instrumental role in saving her brother.

Abby, who agreed to return to 1910 with Nika.

Abby, his fiancé. His love. His everything.

Sweet Lord, Abby!

Where was she? Where was everybody? He was supposed to go with them!

No way in hell will he allow Nika and Abby to return to the last century alone. He remembered Nika started to turn the key, then Abby ran back to him, hugged him. And her feverish whisper, *"I love you. More than life itself. I will be back. I promise."*

He remembered the terrible sound of chiming, horrifying, insistent, swirling all around. He was about to grab Abby's hand, as an invisible, impenetrable wall sprung between them. Cold as ice, hard as granite, that unholy barrier refused his mad attempts to breakthrough. He remembered his fear, before a ferocious blow to his chest sent him airborne. And then nothing. Until he woke up, writhing in pain, on the floor.

"Abby! Nika! JC!"

Alex bellowed their names as loud as his dry throat allowed. But deep in his heart, he already knew. They're gone. All three of them. While he was unconscious, they stepped through the portal, and disappeared beyond the curtain of time.

No! No way!

Incensed, he hauled himself up. His legs almost buckled under his weight. Cringing, cursing, Alex dragged himself to stand in front of that blasted grandfather clock and glared at it.

Six feet tall, polished to a mirror gloss, that XIX century English masterpiece ticked the time away, calm and indifferent. A brilliant golden light shimmered around its intricately laid face and arms. Alive. No, it was not just a figment of his imagination. The bastard was alive, mocking him. Smirking.

Infuriated, Alex clenched his hand into a fist. He was about to deliver a crashing punch, when a familiar electric blast went through his arm, and turned it completely numb. So, he was still a pariah.

We'll see about that!

"You stinking shit. You miserable fuckwit! Take me back. Open that goddamned portal, and take me back!"

And how insane it was, cursing an inanimate object, demanding an action from it?

Alex shoved that thought aside. Inanimate object, my ass. That clock was his nemesis, and he hated it with every damned fiber of his being. Riding on fear and rage, beyond any common sense, he tried to hit the clock again.

This time, the force of the current slammed into him, front and center. Paralyzed from it, breathless, Alex stumbled back. He'd sacrifice everything for the pleasure of kicking the old junker until it was nothing more than a pile of broken wood!

If you break the clock, you'll destroy the portal. And never see Abby again.

He hated that little voice of reason almost as much as that cursed clock.

But it was right, dammit. If he wanted to see Abby again, he must separate his emotions from logic, and take control over his rage. Even if it killed him.

With enormous willpower, Alex turned away. But damn if he let the bastard have the last word.

"Live, you miserable piece of crap. For now. I swear, as soon as Abby's back, I will break every single inch of you."

Bong. Bong. Bong.

"That's right, jackass. Go ahead, and bong all you please. Because your own time is ticking away."

As consolations go, this was not much of one. But at least he got his say.

Alex was a patient man. He'll bide his time, and then unleash all his pent-up frustration on that blasted clock. And seal the portal for good. But only after Abby was back.

Abby, please be safe. Please.

As if hearing his silent plea, his mind conjured her beloved face. His heart lurched, stopped, then jumped into overdrive, bruising his ribcage.

Alex ignored the pain, and concentrated on her image.

Abby.

He felt her presence, smelled her, like she was standing right in front of him.

A cruel illusion. Hot mist blurred his vision, as he sagged with grief.

She was coming back. She promised.

She must.

To think of the alternative was unimaginable. Impossible. Inconceivable.

Patience, Alex, patience.

Unlike Nika, he was never short of it, but now it turned to a precious commodity, rare as the Hope diamond.

The diamond he put on Abby's finger last night flashed in his mind.

A princess for the Princess.

Despair, black as a southern starless night, covered him in a dense blanket. Sorrow, deep as the ocean, surged upward in a crushing wave. Alex doubled over, clutched his chest. The pain knifed through his heart, hot and brutal.

Unable to stand, struggling to catch his breath, he dropped to his knees.

I will be back. I promise.

Abby's voice washed over him like a cool gentle breeze. Slowly, the pain in his chest melted away. Hope, tender as caress, untied the knot in his gut. Love, infinite like the Universe, chased away his doubts.

She'll be back.

Alex drew a deep breath, let it out. Lightheaded with relief, like he was granted a sudden pardon from an execution, he smiled, as the shadow of Abby's image flickered, then dissolved into air.

"Come back to me, Princess. I'll be waiting. For as long as needed."

Something on the floor caught his attention. Alex blinked, brought the object to focus. Dark, and long, it was almost hidden under the clock. What on earth? Puzzled, he picked it up, squinted at it. And then it hit him. The cord!

The leather cord that Nika and JC were wrestling for. The key it was attached to was gone, but the broken cord remained, old and withered, still warm from their hands. Carefully, like he was handling a fragile flower, he cradled it in both hands.

An anchor. A tangible connection. A precious link between times.

Gently, he tucked it into his pocket, near Eli's watch. Another priceless gift.

After a long moment, Alex rose to his feet. Strange, but all the pain was gone. He was still sore where his body hit the unyielding floor, but that was all.

Even his headache receded to a mild throb. A couple of aspirin was sure to take care of it. And a hot shower. But not here. Home. He wanted to go home as soon as possible, because everything inside this mausoleum reminded him of Abby, and Nika, and JC. And his eerie vision of Eli in jail.

A vision, or—

Alex shook his head in an attempt to chase that thought away. Whatever it was—dream, vision, or out of body experience—he'd yet to gather his courage to deal with it. Later. When he was calmer and more centered. When he got home.

Later, when he drank a gallon of coffee, and put something in his stomach.

But first, he needed to text *Verochka*. His illustrious grandmother was about to cut her island adventure short, if he had anything to say about it. And he had plenty to say, and a great deal more to ask.

Ask Verochka. She'll be delighted that you finally came to your gift.

Gift? Alex grunted. More like a curse.

Flipping a middle finger at the grandfather clock was probably childish, but satisfying. With a last look at it, Alex stumbled to the entrance.

Through the closed door of the Coleman house, a resonant *bong* reached his ears. A warning? A sneer?

The hell with that.

"We'll see who has the last laugh, you bastard."

CHAPTER THIRTY-THREE

"**O**h, Miss Abby! I can't believe you're finally home!"

Still reeling from their time jumping journey, Abby half listened to Mrs. Smith's exuberant voice. Excited and teary-eyed, their old housekeeper was all but bursting at the seams, running in circles around Abby. She wasn't the only one. Belle, their sweet mutt, pranced back and force, sharing her adoration between Abby and Daisy. Unoffended by Mrs. Smith shooing motions, the colossal shaggy creature administered her licks with abandon, shaking from excitement.

Absently, Abby patted the dog's head, scratched between her ears, all the while trying to pay attention to their housekeeper's excited oration.

"...and just in time, too. Poor Master Eli, he will never be able to prove his innocence otherwise."

That resonant voice set her teeth on edge. To prevent herself from acting in a rash manner, Abby clutched the delicate China cup in both hands. Her knuckles went white with strain. Presently, Daisy and she sat the dining room table. Like a mother hen with her chicks, Mrs. Smith bustled around, flapping her pudgy hands like wings. Wishing to be anywhere else but here, Abby forced herself to sit still.

Not even Daisy was brave enough to contradict the formidable woman who ran the Coleman household for longer than Abby was alive. As much as she and Daisy bristled with impatience, they were compelled to sit and endure the commotion.

God, how much longer?

Abby forced a smile and nodded at something Mrs. Smith was saying, even though she hadn't heard a word.

Pay attention, Abigail.

Her unexpected arrival created a great shock.

Poor old dear, Mrs. Smith almost fainted at the first glimpse of Abby. Thankfully, she was already changed in her old clothes, and was able to spare Mrs. Smith the shock of her state of dress.

Or rather undress.

This time, their time travel caused no ill effects, thank God. Both Abby and Daisy were clearheaded, if a bit nauseated, but firm on their feet. There was no pain or dizziness that accompanied her previous journey. But Daisy's brother was in a bad shape. He landed with a heavy thud, and was out of his senses ever since. Accompanied by Daisy's colorful curses, they managed to drag his unconscious body to the library, and laid him onto the sofa. There he stayed, sprawled in a helpless heap, comatose. Instead of calling for a doctor, as Abby suggested, Daisy cursed, and propelled her out of the room.

"He'll be fine, the jerk. But you must hurry and change, before anyone sees us. Go, go!" And her sister-in-law quite forcefully pushed her away.

Spurred to action, Abby sprinted into her old bedroom, downed her old-fashioned dress, and hurried back. As all the members of the household were already afoot, her return created an excitement of major proportions. Tears, shouts of joy, hugs, and more tears. Chaos ruled for about five minutes before Mrs. Smith took up the reigns. Per her orders, someone was dispatched to fetch a doctor for JC, the cook ordered to prepare food, and maids sent to air the rooms. Without a qualm, Daisy bowed to the older woman's command. Abby followed her lead. Because in the Coleman household Mrs. Smith's word was *the* law. Unarguable and unquestionable. Even for the mistress of the house.

The only one who dared to dispute her authority was Eli. And only occasionally.

"Here are your favorite scones with peach jam, Miss Abby. And your coffee with cream. Eat, eat. You must be famished from the long journey."

Eat?

Abby pressed her palm against her stomach. The notion of putting food inside herself made her queasy. She struggled to keep her lips curved in what she hoped resembled a smile. Her face was about to split from strain.

Merde.

How long will she be able to endure this torture? When are they going to the jail? Every moment in a cell was agony for Eli.

Why was Daisy delaying their trip? She shot a glare in her sister-in-law's direction. Pale, but composed, Daisy seemed to be lost in thought. Both of her hands lay protectively over her stomach, as if she was shielding the babe.

Momentarily contrite, Abby averted her gaze. If it was so hard for her, how horrible it must be for Daisy. And now she had to worry about JC, too.

The big help he proved to be, the rascal. How on earth did he manage to come through? Probably clamped his hand on her or Daisy's arm at the last moment.

For the life of her, Abby failed to remember. Then again, she hadn't paid attention to anything except Alex. After he flew through the air, and dropped with a sickening noise near the staircase, horror took a hold of all her senses. If not for Daisy's firm clasp on her arm, she would have broken free, and run toward him.

My God, Alex! Was he okay? Did he suffer broken bones, or... worse?

No, she refused to think of that. Or she might go crazy.

Eli. Must think of Eli only. She was here on a mission. The whole purpose of this trip was to save her brother. So, save him she will then travel back home.

To Alex. As soon as humanly possible.

Impatient, Abby sent an absent-minded nod to Mrs. Smith, then forced herself to listen. What was she talking about? With all the attention piled onto her, Abby was about to scream from bubbling frustration.

With an enormous effort, she focused on their old housekeeper. Did she ask something? Is that why she was peering at Abby expectantly?

"I'm sorry, Mrs. Smith. What was that again?"

"I said, how on earth did you learn about your brother's fate? I wanted to send you a missive, but no one knew your whereabouts."

"Daisy knew." *Yes, Daisy knew exactly where to find me.* "She...ah, managed to dispatch a message. And here I am."

"Oh?" Mrs. Smith switched her focus to her young mistress. Stern frown arranged her eyebrows into a disapproving line. "You knew, and didn't think of telling me?" The accusation in her voice was hard to miss. Abby winced, but Daisy just shrugged, seemingly unoffended.

"I'm sorry, Mrs. Smith. With the baby, and Eli's arrest, it completely slipped my mind." She sent a tired smile to the older woman. "Please don't be mad at me."

Harrumph.

The loud sound burst from Mrs. Smith. Her frown melted to an almost gentle expression. One that was of a loving mother. She patted Daisy's hand, then turned her gaze back to Abby.

"Thank the good Lord, you managed to travel so fast. And with Miss Daisy's brother in tow. An attorney from New York, no less. It's a pity he fell ill during the journey. Let's hope it is nothing serious. Damnation, where is that doctor when you need him?" She shot a worrying glance in the direction of the library. "And such a shame about the lost luggage." A disapproving tsk-tsk later, she shook her head. "Oh, the times! Oh, the customs! By the by, I didn't know you had a brother."

Daisy was subjected to another frown and a shrewd glance.

Uh-oh.

"I have two of them. And I told you I have a family in New York. You probably forgot."

"Forgot? I'm old, young lady, not demented. I never forget anything. Especially something of importance."

"I'm sure you don't. I must've mentioned it in passing, that's all."

Mrs. Smith uttered another *harrumph*, and crossed her arms over her ample chest.

Familiar with the gesture, Abby held her breath. Poor Daisy. The least she needed right now was a brewing argument.

Merde.

Quiet, full of regret, her voice broke the charged silence. "You see, my family and I... we are not close."

"And why is that? A family is a family. It's unseemly to forget your roots."

"I've never forgotten!" Daisy's sudden shout seemed to take Mrs. Smith aback. "I just learned to live without them. So, sue me."

Both women glared at each other. This time, it was Mrs. Smith who relented first.

"Well, I guess you put new roots here. And mighty fine they are."

Daisy nodded, hugged her belly, and briefly closed her eyes. Abby's heart went out to her sister-in-law. Pregnant, crazy with worry about Eli, and now JC, Daisy barely held herself upright. But she was a fighter. Despite her size, a force of a hurricane lived in that tiny body. Even wrung dry from fatigue and fear, Daisy would jump in the middle of any battle to save those she loved. She'll risk anything for her family, her own life included. Like she jumped through time to bring Abby here, and save Eli. Like she saved Mrs. Smith last year.

The relationship between their old housekeeper and her sister-in-law was always tricky. At first, Mrs. Smith acted in an openly unfriendly manner toward Daisy. Of course, then she was pretending to be the boy Nick, homeless and lost. Openly suspicious toward the 'street urchin', Mrs. Smith taken on a notion of hiding their family silverware. But one day, when the older woman suddenly collapsed, it was that 'boy' who saved her life by injecting the strange medicine into her body. Thank God for the EpiPen, a modern cure for an allergy attack, that Daisy managed to sneak out through the portal. Otherwise, their revered housekeeper would be long dead.

Since that dramatic episode, Mrs. Smith's demeanor toward Daisy took on a drastic turn. Finicky and stern as ever, she never verbally acknowledged Daisy's role in saving her life. Instead, she became her most stalwart champion.

And when Eli announced their betrothal, it was Mrs. Smith who first shed the happy tears, and welcomed Daisy to the family.

"Well, I guess all's well that ends well." Mrs. Smith's voice cut through Abby's reminiscence. "Your brother, such a considerate soul, dropped everything, and accompanied Miss Abby home, for which my gratitude has no bounds. And such an important man he is! A criminal attorney from the big firm. It is my duty, and honor, to make his stay with us as pleasant as possible."

Abby chocked on a sip of coffee. Even as it went the wrong way, she masked her laughter with coughing. JC was many things, but considerate was not one of them. Then again, he clearly was concerned about his sister's fate. Stayed through the night, refused to give her the key before she rested properly. Even brought food before their journey. Then, the insufferable, self-serving jerk, inserted himself in the middle, and despite Daisy's wishes, came through the portal with them.

Merde.

Attorney was also questionable, since, banished from his father's place of business, JC was currently without any position. An *important* man, indeed.

But Mrs. Smith, bless her heart, was unaware of any of this. She saw the handsome man, unconscious, pale and disheveled, and assumed he was suffering from some malady caught on the trip. They weren't about to disabuse her of that belief.

And the lost luggage? Abby came up with that brilliant fib on the spur of the moment. How else to explain their lack of any bags?

Oh, Lord, what were they supposed to do with JC? Like they have no worry in the world, but only his needs to cater to. Well, Mrs. Smith can deal with the rascal for now. A commotion in the hallway announced the arrival of a doctor. The old housekeeper retreated from the dining room, leaving Daisy and Abby alone.

At last.

"Daisy, why are we waiting? Let's go to the jail, and free Eli. Time's awasting!"

"Do you think I want to procrastinate? But it's late in the afternoon, Abby, so no one of the authority will be present at this time. As much as it galls me, we have to go tomorrow morning. And maybe my idiot brother will be stable enough to accompany us."

"*Merde.*"

"My sentiments exactly."

Belle chose that moment to but her head against Abby's hand, asking for a rub. She complied in an absent manner, all the while occupied by her troubling thoughts.

"Do you think Alex is okay?"

"Why wouldn't he be?" Daisy's brows arched in question.

"You didn't see it, being busy opening the portal, but he was flung away from the clock in a horrible manner. I still see him, laying on that floor, unmoving. My God, what if he—"

"Don't even think that, Abs. He'll be fine. What's one hard knock? Alex is made of a sterner stuff. No one I know is as strong as he." But she averted her eyes, clearly disturbed.

"Strong is unquestionable, Daisy. But he's as vulnerable to bodily injury as any other man. Why does the grandfather clock hate him so?" Despair clutched her heart in a mighty fist. Hot tears pressed against her eyelids.

"Abby, that clock is just a *thing*. An object. It can't hate, or love."

Daisy's hand on her arm prevented Abby from jumping up from the chair. Pacing the room was not the answer, but at least she'd be able to move. An attempt to dislodge Daisy's hand ended in failure, as her sister-in-law pressed down onto Abby's shoulder.

"Sit, for goodness' sake, and stop fidgeting."

Chastised, exhausted, Abby relented. She shut her eyes, slumped into the chair.

"I'm telling you, Daisy, that clock hates Alex. It rejected him!"

"Rejected? That's silly."

"Silly or not, it did just that! Oh, that stupid clock, I wish I was—"

Daisy interrupted her in a harsh whisper, "What do you mean, rejected? Tell me."

"One day we went to the Coleman house. I was...distraught, kept hearing that blasted chime in my ears. So I asked Alex to take me there, and..."

In a slow dizzying motion, the pictures from that day floated before her eyes. An impatient shaking administered by Daisy broke Abby's trance.

"What happened? Abs?"

"Alex... he pulled me from the clock, tried to touch it, but got electrocuted. Painfully. That clock all but pushed him away."

"Huh. What about JC?"

"He seems to have no problems whatsoever. Touching the clock that is. More like pawing it. Even asked me to sell it. He didn't know about the portal then. And today..." Abby swallowed the heavy lump lodged in her throat. "Today JC was allowed through, while Alex was knocked back. Dammit, it's not fair!"

"That's one way to put it. Strange as all get out, I'd say."

Frowning, Daisy tapped her lips with her fingertips. "Alex, rejected by the stupid grandfather clock. I wonder why."

"Well, I don't! And I don't care *why*. Don't you understand, I want to return as soon as possible. If Alex suffered, I won't be able to forgive myself!"

Daisy's eyes pleaded with Abby to stop her childish tantrum. Ashamed, Abby slumped her shoulders, hugged herself in a feeble attempt to prevent from breaking into pieces.

"Oh, Abs. I'm so sorry, but Eli..."

"You don't have to be sorry, Daisy. Eli is my brother. I'll do anything for him."

"I know, but I'm sorry anyway. To drag you away, and on the day of your engagement, too."

"Engagement? And what engagement that might be, pray tell?"

Unnoticed by them, Mrs. Smith stepped into the room in time to hear Daisy's last words. She frowned, and if the gleam in her eyes was any indication, the old dear was on the verge of losing her temper. Abby sighed. God, she needed another confrontation like she needed an ulcer. Irritated, fresh out of patience, she opened her mouth to deliver a rebuke. But Daisy beat her to it.

"We wanted to tell this news to everybody at once, but since you already overheard us..." Daisy shot one of her most brilliant smiles. "Mrs. Smith, as our Abby's too shy to do it herself, I will let you know that as of yesterday, she became engaged to Alexander Morris, my cousin."

"Cousin? By Jove, girl! In the matter of a single day, I met your brother, and learned about your cousin. Mindboggling."

"Aren't you glad you did?"

The woman looked perplexed with her hands fluttering like two humming birds and at a loss for words.

"Well, I—" She managed weakly.

"What, no congratulations?" Daisy interrupted with fake astonishment, then chuckled at the old housekeeper's befuddled expression.

"Oh, Lord, of course. Pardon me, Miss Abby. Just took me a moment to comprehend." Mrs. Smith curved her lips into a warm smile. "I'm very happy to learn about your upcoming nuptials. When will we have the honor to meet your betrothed? And why, pray tell, did he let you travel alone?"

Abby gritted her teeth.

Let her?

No one *let her* do anything nowadays. She was her own woman, free and independent, and decided her own fate. But, of course, Mrs. Smith was a product of her own time, and as such, the notion of female independence was not only unfamiliar, it was quite scandalous.

With an effort, Abby reigned in her irritation.

Remember where you are, Abigail. And why. Eli's safety is more important than your beliefs.

She bore down on her temper, realizing it was natural for Mrs. Smith, the woman who raised her, to be curious about the man she was engaged to. But, Lord, what to say?

"My betrothed is a very busy man, Mrs. Smith. He has a business to run, a large company that deals in..." God, what was the term for Real Estate here? "...marketing and sales of a real property." She hoped she found the right verbiage.

Since Mrs. Smith was not frowning, or acting peculiar, she managed to pull it off.

Thank God. Emboldened, Abby hurried ahead, "You see, he was unable to drop everything at a moment's notice and accompany me on this journey. But, as you understand, it was impossible for me to delay my trip, because Eli's fate is in danger. Luckily, Mr. JC Morris, was available, so Alex entrusted my wellbeing to his very capable hands. And my brother needs an attorney more than a real property entrepreneur. So..."

"Oh, sure, sure. You are absolutely right, Miss Abby. But, good Lord, it's such a shock to me. To see you, so mature and beautiful, after all these months, and betrothed on top of it. Oh, my heart is about to jump out of my chest!"

A loud sniff broke free before their formidable housekeeper pulled herself together. Her eyes glistened with tears, and her smile wobbled helplessly on her comely wide face. Unable to stay cross with her any longer, Abby got up and ran toward the older woman.

"Here, here, Mrs. Smith. Don't despair. I'm sorry I didn't tell you my news sooner. But I'm so worried about Eli, I—"

"Do not be sorry, my sweet *Papillon*. It is I who should be sorry for losing my temper and peppering you with all those silly questions. Tell me just one thing," she framed Abby's face with both hands. "Are you happy, girl?"

Abby didn't have to think twice. The truth poured out of her in a rushing stream. "Oh, deliriously! I love him so much, I could dance on clouds! Sometimes it hurt. Here." Abby pressed her hand to her chest, where her heart thumped heavily.

"My Alex..." Her throat squeezed painfully, robbing Abby of speech.

Alex. Dear God, please keep him safe. Please.

Mrs. Smith enveloped Abby into her comforting embrace, patted her on the back.

"Is he nice looking, your Alex?"

"Oh, he's so handsome, Mrs. Smith. Tall, and strong, and beautiful. He took my breath away as soon as I laid my eyes upon him."

"Well, I gauge that on my own after I see him. When is he coming?"

Merde. Now what?

"Oh…oh, well, you see—"

"He'll come as soon as he's able to arrange some urgent business matters."

Thank God for Daisy's quick wit. Otherwise, Abby might have made matters worse by mumbling something asinine. And what to say? The truth was unthinkable.

You see, Mrs. Smith, Alex wasn't coming at all, because he is stuck on the other side of the portal, unable to breach the curtain of time.

Yes, a disaster for sure. A sudden laughter tickled her throat. She recognized it for what it was: bubbling hysteria. Abby bit hard on her lip.

Must stay calm. Must control my impulses. Snap out of it, Abigail!

On the verge of a major meltdown, she pulled free of Mrs. Smith's arms. Her tears, however, gave the older woman the wrong impression.

"Hush, little one. I know you must be missing your beloved, but I'm sure you'll be reunited soon. And then, we can throw a real party to celebrate your betrothal."

Oh, Lord. Helpless, Abby cast a quick glance at her sister-in-law. But no help came from that direction. Daisy shrugged, seemingly unperturbed by the prospect of an engagement party. Her placid demeanor irritated Abby to no end. Doesn't she understand the implications? That celebration was doomed, because it was never coming. What to say? How to react?

Unaware of her torment, Mrs. Smith beamed like the sun, gazing at Abby with pride and adoration.

"Let me see your ring."

Befuddled, Abby lifted her left hand.

"Oh, what a beauty! A ring worthy of true royalty. Your groom is a man of fine taste, and a generous nature, my dear."

"Yes," Abby hiccupped, "he is all that, and so much more."

A sensation of being watched turned her blood to ice. All fine hair on her body rose up to painful points. What on earth...? Uneasy, Abby closed her eyes, and concentrated on that eerie feeling inside of her. Dear God, what was it?

You are just tired, and overwrought. That's all. Nothing to be concerned about.

But that cold foreboding refused to recede. Almost tangible, it seemed to reach out, grazing her hair. Shivers of exquisite pleasure rushed all over her body, even as she revolted from the embarrassment. Scandalous. Indecent.

Belle chose that moment to raise herself to her feet. Lifting her nose, she sniffed the air, tilted her head, and emitted a loud bark.

Abby.

She jerked, turned her head, and froze.

Alex stood just a few steps from her.

Alive, thank God.

Alive and well, and oh, so handsome! Afraid to take a single breath, Abby gazed at him in shocked wonder. How was it even possible? Were her eyes playing tricks on her? But then his dear voice caressed her ears, *Come back to me, Princess. Come back soon.*

And his beloved image shimmered, and dissolved into a thin air.

Lightheaded, Abby swayed, and all but fell into Mrs. Smith's waiting hands. Long and pitiful, Belle's moan filled the room, and sent chills down Abby's back. Was she losing her mind? Because for a moment, she saw Alex right before her. Smelled him. Heard him. A low sob wrenched from the depth of her soul.

"I will be back, my darling. As soon as I can. I promise."

She must have said it out loud, because Mrs. Smith's face creased into a concerned expression.

"Miss Abby? Who are you talking to? Are you well, child?"

"She's just speaking to Alex in her mind, Mrs. Smith. Nothing to worry about. You know how it is with lovebirds."

Daisy's answer, light and humorous, pacified the older woman. Daisy waddled closer, and gripped Abby's arm with brutal force, all the while smiling at their housekeeper. "It is endearing, really. Don't you think?"

That pain brought Abby back to reality in no time.

"I'm alright, Mrs. Smith," she managed in a weak voice. "Just like Daisy said, I was talking to my betrothed in my mind. Silly me."

"Oh, miss Abby, that's not silly at all. It's sweet and lovely. But maybe we should ask the doctor to take a look at you, too? Just to be safe."

"Oh, no, no, Mrs. Smith. I do not need any doctor."

Only Alex.

"I'm truly alright, and in command of all my faculties. I just miss him so much." Caught in a pitiful whimper, her voice broke.

Belle snapped to attention. She uttered a low growl deep in her throat, as her fur stood up. Their usually docile dog now resembled a monster, huge, hairy, menacing. What on earth? Abby turned her head to the door, and blanched.

Swaying on his feet, pale and bedraggled, JC gazed upon them with something close to horror on his face. Close behind him, was the stout figure of their old family doctor. He lifted his hands in defeat, shook his head, and glared disapprovingly upon his patient.

Wide-eyed, JC looked around. "Nika? Abby? Where are we?"

As his stare landed on Mrs. Smith, he sucked on a sharp breath, then stumbled backward.

"Oh, fuck me. We made it!"

And he collapsed, hitting the floor with a sickening thump.

CHAPTER THIRTY-FOUR

Time crawled like a sloth. The two hours since Alex had stumbled inside his home seemed like an eternity. Shower took all of five minutes, his record to a day. Scruffy and scratchy, his face begged for a shave, but Alex had no inclination to oblige. The hell with it. On the spur of a moment, he decided to skip shaving altogether until Abby's return. And if he will be covered with a long beard by that time, so be it.

She'll be back.

Must believe that. One day, she'll pop out of that blasted portal. Or else, he'll find a way to break through it. See if he won't.

With his prized Coleman pocket watch clutched in his fist, Alex paced the living room. How much longer? Dammit, two hours and twenty minutes. Fucking forever. A loud grumbling sound erupted from his stomach. Food. He needed food in order to survive, to move forward. To wait.

Okay, grab some cereal, or better, a bagel.

Alex checked the cupboards, then rummaged through the refrigerator. As Murphy's law would have it, they were out of bagels. Or chips, or cereal for that matter. After slamming the fridge door, he stood, motionless, and contemplated his choices. Cook? Unthinkable. Even making a sandwich was beyond his capabilities right now. Okay, there was always a delivery. Pizza? The mere thought of a hot pie oozing with gooey cheese was revolting. Sushi? He never was a fan of a raw fish rolled in rice. The hell with it. Opening the fridge again, he grabbed a wedge of sharp gouda cheese and an apple. A perfect alternative to a healthy dinner. One bite later he gaged, then spit it into the garbage disposal. His favorite cheese tasted like a cake of soap, and the perfect Granny Smith suddenly lost its appeal. With a helpless little oath, Alex shoved both items back into fridge.

Now what? He looked around, as if seeking an inspiration. In his peripheral vision he caught a faint flicker, like a burning candle. A candle? He didn't light any candles.

Alex swiveled his head, and froze.

A bright glimmer pulsed like a heart in a middle of the room. With a mix of shock and fascination, he watched a gossamer gauze in palest hues unfurl like a sail. The living room began to ripple and shimmer. The walls, the furniture—every object slowly disintegrated, melting like ice. An earie glow infused the space, until everything around him was awash with that otherworldly light.

Mesmerized, he followed that uncanny illumination with his eyes.

A sensation of floating. Narrow tunnel vision. Swirling shadows.

Weird, but familiar.

No longer spooked by it, giddy from anticipation, Alex braced himself.

Abruptly, the slow spinning stopped, and the picture snapped into a sharp focus.

Alex sucked on his breath.

A dining room. The Coleman house. Not the renovated one, but the original.

Three people, and an enormous shaggy dog.

Nika at the table, her hands on her pregnant belly. The older woman beside her, stern and unsmiling, clad in a shapeless dark dress. As if alerted, the dog lifted its huge head, sniffed the air. Its liquid eyes stared at Alex in mild surprise.

Can the dog sense his presence?

The furry giant cocked its head, then gave one mighty bark. Detached and weightless, Alex glanced at the dog. So, it not only sensed him—it saw him, too. But even though its hackles were raised, and a low growl trembled in its throat, the dog cowered in fear. Poor beast. After a moment, Alex ignored it. His eyes zeroed in on the third woman in the room.

Abby.

He would recognize her anywhere, even in that dull long skirt and high collared blouse. Her hair, that magnificent river of black, was pinned up in a loose bun, with a few tendrils dancing around her heartbreaking face.

In his mind, Alex reached out, and tucked one lock behind her ear, then trailed a fingertip along her jawline. Abby shivered. Oh, God, can she feel him? See him?

Alex's heart squeezed. Holding his breath, he whispered her name, "Abby."

She jolted, turned her head, and looked straight at him. All the color drained from her beautiful face. Motionless, she stared back in mute shock. Oh, yes, she saw him, heard him. Boundless joy filled his heart to the brim. Something warm pressed against his eyelids. The lump in his throat turned his voice into a hoarse whisper.

"Come back to me, Princess. Come back soon."

A moment later, her sob burst though.

"I will be back, my darling. As soon as I can. I promise."

Abby's features began to blur and fade.

No! Please, God, a moment longer.

But the picture before his eyes tilted, revolved, then disintegrated into a million pieces. Still reeling, Alex swayed. If not for the marble counter he grabbed with both hands, he'd be down on all fours. His ears popped, his vision cleared. No longer floating, he was back in his kitchen, shaken to the marrow.

Dammit, what's happening to me?

What just happened? Did he really travel through time? Again?

A sharp knock on the front door sent his heart hammering. He didn't expect anyone. Who might that be? A delivery? Dammit, did he order something and forgot? Wouldn't be surprised. Still shaken and bewildered, Alex watched the door. Probably a neighbor. Or mail.

The hell with it.

The smartest thing to do was to play opossum. He was no fit for any company right now. Whoever was at the door, will get the drift, and get lost, sooner or later.

But no such luck. Another knock, more insistent now. Crap. Just go away.

What if it was Abby? What if she returned already?

Oh, God, please let it be her!

Hope spurred him into action. He sprinted, but his wobbly legs protested the sudden action. The short distance from the kitchen to the main door turned into an obstacle course. Stumbling, cursing, Alex managed to stay on his feet. Finally he reached the door then flung it open.

"Ta-da!"

Alex froze. Gorgeous and fresh as a dewy rose, impeccably put together, his grandmother greeted him with a high-voltage smile. As usual, *Verochka* projected an image of a wealthy socialite ready for the most anticipated Broadway premier. A whiff of her trademark Chloe teased his olfactory sense.

Familiar. Dear. Unforgettable.

A sharp stab of love almost brought him to his knees.

Verochka.

His grandmother. His family.

The first woman he loved, deeply, truly, unconditionally. She returned his feelings with a reckless abandon, and forever held his heart on the palms of her small elegant hands. *Verochka* was the only one who understood him completely, accepted his quirks and shortcoming, and never tried to change him. Besides Nika, she was the ultimate constant in his life.

How did he manage without her those last few weeks was a mystery. Happy to see her beloved face, but sad, she was not the one he yearned for, Alex gaped at his grandmother in silence. An acute disappointment and ridiculous relief fought the battle inside of him. That inner turmoil was hard to disguise. *Verochka's* smile slowly fell, as a deep frown puckered her forehead. All jubilation forgotten. She stared at him with a mix of worry and panic on her aristocratic face.

"Alex? What is it, darling?"

"Oh, Gorgeous." His helpless sob would embarrass him if it were anyone but *Verochka*. Alex almost fell into her waiting arms. Her slender body accepted his weight, anchored him.

"There, there, my baby. Come here, sit, and tell me everything."

Verochka took the matter into her hands. She closed the door, ushered him into the room, and pushed him onto a sofa. Alex collapsed, immensely grateful to pass on all the immediate decisions to his grandmother.

She sat, enfolded Alex into her tight embrace, and made him feel like a child again. Undone, he tucked his head under *Verochka's* chin, and inhaled her familiar fragrance. Peace. Kindness. Tranquility.

He closed his eyes, cocooned in her warmth, and allowed himself a moment of weakness. After a short while, his pain and confusion receded, as if absorbed by a sponge. Steady and centered at last, Alex gently pulled out of her arms.

"Okay, darling, talk to me."

"God, *Verochka*, I'm so fucked up."

A spark of disapproval flashed in her violet eyes before she sighed.

"I will overlook your bad language, because I can clearly see you're upset."

"Upset? I'm beyond upset, Gorgeous. I'm spitting mad. And scared. I'm afraid I'm losing my marbles."

"For the love of God, Alex! I'm going to lose *my* fucking mind if you don't tell me what's going on. Your text hinted on something happy and wonderful, but that's not the case, is it?"

"My text?" Puzzled, Alex blinked a few times. What was she talking about?

Dammit. He remembered that he intended to tag his grandmother. Right after he left the Coleman house. But as soon as he stumbled home, sick and hurting and bewildered, he forgot everything and everyone except Abby.

And after his astonishing mind travel to the last century? Wouldn't be surprised if he forgot his own name.

"I didn't text you, *Verochka*." Or did he? Damn, why can't he remember?

"Alex, you sent me a message yesterday."

Verochka fished inside her stylish bag, and produced her cell phone. After a couple of taps, she turned it around for Alex to see.

Call me when you can. Have terrific news.

Oh, God, of course! Yesterday morning, in front of Tiffany. Exhilarated, almost giddy with happiness, he sent that text to *Verochka*.

Was it just yesterday? Feels like lightyears ago.

"I completely forgot."

"Forgot?" *Verochka's* eyebrows shot up, forming two perfect arches. Reproach in her squinting violet eyes was hard to miss. "You texted me *that*, and you forgot?"

She didn't have to raise her voice to make him squirm. His grandmother honed the skill of chastising with her eloquent eyes alone to perfection.

"Geez, Gorgeous, if only you knew what happened between yesterday and today."

"So, why don't you enlighten me? I think I deserve that, after I cut my vacation short, chartered the plane, and rushed back here from another part of the world."

"I'm sorry, *Verochka*. But I'm so damn glad you're here, you have no idea."

"Aww." That cooing little noise was adorable, and so *Verochka*. Her smile teased two tiny dimples on her cheeks. "Thank you, darling. And I'm so glad to be home." She patted his face, a gesture that melted his heart. "Shouldn't have gone to that godforsaken island in a first place, but..."

Verochka's famous shrugs spoke volumes. She always managed to communicate with her shoulders better than words. Now, that typical Gaelic motion reflected a mixture of regret and sorrow.

"You realize why I did it, don't you?"

"Hard not to. Nika."

"Yes. Nika." Her eyes misted. A deep sigh later, *Verochka* curved her lips into a sad wobbly smile. "Well, our Nika is where she supposed to be, happy and content. Now, what about you, baby?"

"I was happy and content when I texted you that message." Alex rubbed his head and drew in a deep breath. "Okay, a short version. Two days ago, Abby came back home from California."

"Wonderful! If you ask me, she shouldn't have stayed there in the first place. But that girl is so stubborn, bless her heart. Well, thank God, she came to her senses at last. Thank you for texting me. A terrific news indeed."

"That's not why I texted you."

"No? *Mon Dieu*, Alex, why else? Don't keep me guessing."

"You see, I proposed to Abby."

"*Merveilleux!*" Brimming with exuberance, *Verochka* clapped her hands. "I'm so, so happy for both of you! Oh, congratulations, my darling! I'm so excited!"

Alex grinned despite his mood. So contagious was *Verochka's* elation, that for a moment he lost the track of reality. But that ugly bitch was not easily forgotten.

A helpless oath broke from his mouth.

"Abby refused."

"What?" *Verochka* recoiled like from a slap in a face, gasped in outrage. "*Mon Dieu,* had she lost her mind? That girl was in love with you from the first! *Merde!* So help me God, when I see her, I'll—"

"Hold your horses, Gorgeous. She refused at first. But last night..."

Images of Abby—naked, writhing—flashed before his eyes.

The feel of her skin, the taste of her mouth, the flavor of passion.

Broken sighs, moans of ecstasy. And the ultimate twin screams of fulfillment.

Alex shut his eyes, as memories of last night assaulted all his senses. Low and wanton, the sound of his groan reached his ears. Dammit.

Maybe *Verochka* missed it. His hope was shattered as soon as he glanced at her grinning face.

Fat chance, buddy.

"Oh-uh." Positively wicked, the gleam in his grandmother's eyes completed an impression of a smug satisfaction. She all but licked her lips, the shameless minx. Alex doubted he was ever more embarrassed in his thirty years.

Unperturbed, *Verochka* patted his face. "I like that sound. And the sight of your blushing face. It is so endearing." A personification of mischief, she raised her brows, wiggled them. "So, what happened? Tell me everything. And please, don't get stingy on the details."

Still mortified, Alex gave a bark of helpless laughter. "Oh, Lord, Verochka, only you."

"Don't get sidetracked, boy. Well? What happened last night?"

"I think you can guess it on your own, you brazen coquette."

"Party pooper." With a mocked sigh, *Verochka* relented, and shrugged. "Well then, I shall use my rich imagination."

"God help us all."

"Okay, aside of your erotic activities, what happened?"

"She accepted my ring."

"Of course she did! Hope you didn't embarrass little old *moi*, and bought a spectacular one?" A faint whisper of French accent in her voice was adorable, and somehow naughty.

"The best that Tiffany had to offer. A four carat flowless diamond, princess cut, in a platinum setting."

"A princess for the Princess? You are a clever boy, my darling. I'm proud of you. So, when is a big day?"

"Whenever she's back."

"Oh, don't tell me she returned to San Francisco, Alex!"

"No."

"Oh, good. Good. But...but where did she go, then?" The first notes of unease crept into her voice, as she squinted at him. "Alex? Where is Abby? And why did you let her travel alone?"

Let her? Alex cursed. If only it was up to him, dammit.

"She's not alone." He opted to answer the first part of the question. "She's with JC."

"Like you can trust that boy. Honestly, Alex—"

"And Nika."

"Nika? Our Nika? But...but..." *Verochka's* eyes clouded with puzzlement. True meaning of his words slowly penetrated her confusion. At first, her perplexity turned to a denial, and then transformed into a pure, unguarded shock.

A lava of curses worthy of any seasoned pirate erupted from his grandmother's aristocratic lips. Because he understood most of those extremely colorful and rowdy words, he winced. *Verochka*, bless her heart, always cussed in Russian, the habit she passed onto him. But if he'd ever dare to repeat the words exploding out of her mouth now, she would kill him first, and kick his lifeless body later.

Finally, *Verochka* ran out of her vast repertoire of profanity. Her chic classic bob turned into a messy disarray after she racked both hands through the silky stands.

"*Merde.*"

"*Verochka*—" He began, only to be cut short.

"*Le silence!*"

After lifting herself from the sofa, she went directly to the bar. Without contemplating her choices, *Verochka* grabbed the first bottle closest to hand, and filled the crystal glass to the brim. Alex watched in mute fascination as his grandmother upended the liquor in one gulp. The level of *Verochka's* current state of bewilderment was obvious, because she used a round cognac ball for tequila.

She would be horrified to learn that. Alex wiped the smirk from his face. As a smart man, he'd rather cut his arm that to enlighten his grandmother. Especially when he was at the root of her shocking daze.

After a long moment, *Verochka* managed to pull herself together. Turning to him, she crossed her arms over her chest.

"Okay, Alexander Zachariah Morris. Start from the beginning."

He didn't have a prayer when his grandmother used his full name. Stern and somber, her tone of voice brooked no argument. What choice did he have? Cringing inside, Alex held her gaze, and complied.

CHAPTER THIRTY-FIVE

The ride to the Nassau County jail took forever. No great wonder, since they were traveling by carriage. Abby swallowed some rude cuss words, and reminded herself where she was. Oh, the possibility to drive her fast as the wind Corvette! Any sacrifices were worth it.

Curb your imagination, Abigail. You are not in the twenty-first century anymore.

Restless, she fidgeted as the two bay horses trudged forward. They were beautiful animals, strong and clever, but oh, Lord, so slow! Or was it her impatience at play? Should've harness Sultan instead. Better yet, should've forgone the carriage, and rode the stallion.

Abby sighed. She was being selfish. There were two other people to consider beside herself. Daisy was a mediocre equestrian at best, her current condition notwithstanding. No way should she be allowed on horseback. She already endangered the babe by jumping through time not once, but twice. And in a matter of a day, no less. And JC? He claimed to be a great rider, but somehow Abby doubted it. Mrs. Smith, enamored with the rascal for no reason Abby comprehended, forbade him to preform anything more strenuous than lifting a cup of tea. After his swooning episode yesterday, the old dear all but covered JC in a blanket, and kept him abed. Horseback riding? Mrs. Smith would bodily prevent it. So, the unanimous decision was cast. Travel in a carriage driven by the two docile geldings.

Merde.

With a deep sigh of resignation, Abby settled into her seat, all the while silently urging the horses to go faster. To add to her discomfort, the cumbersome clothes she was forced to wear restricted her movements, and made her uncomfortably hot. Sticky sweat covered her from head to toe the moment she stepped outside. Even though mild by Florida standards, April temperatures soared to upper the 80s.

Unrelenting sun shone brilliantly from the cloudless sky. Squinting, squirming, Abby wished for her sunshades. And her shorts, and sandals, and sleeveless blouse.

How did she endure it before? Spoiled by the modern fashion, Abby got used to the comfortable attire of cropped pants and light shirts. Dragging the hem of a long heavy skirt was unbearable. Her only consolation was that she won't suffer for long. Today, or tomorrow at the latest, she'll return home. To Alex.

Please, God, keep him safe until then.

Despite her anxiety, the pleasure of seeing her old family was overwhelming.

She was surprised at how much she missed everyone, but most of all the animals.

At the crack of dawn, unable to settle down, Abby gave up on sleep, and ran to the stables. The familiar smell of hay and horses brought great joy to her heart. Even as a child, she sought her solace here, often lost for hours. One time she even spent the night in a stall, lulled to sleep by the quiet neighing and fragrance of horses. How old was she? Too young to understand the danger of curling on the floor by the mighty body of a stallion. When Eli finally found her, she was forbidden to leave the house for days. Abby smiled. Oh, the precious memories.

This morning, disturbed by her presence, the horses poked their heads through their stalls, at first eyed her curiously. Luna, her own Camarillo filly, greeted Abby with great exuberance. Sultan, Eli's magnificent stallion, went mad with jubilation at the sight of her. Nuzzling like a kitten, he caressed her face, and peered at her with unconcealed adoration. Their happy reunion, however, was spoiled by none other than Daisy's annoying brother. JC bounced back to his old irritating self, and with great enthusiasm started to enjoy his adventure. The jerk. Without a care in the world, he strolled about the mansion, poking his head into every nook and cranny. The stables, apparently, were not to his liking as JC scrounged his nose in a distasteful manner. Instead of leaving, however, he approached Abby and grinned. His mischievous wink set her teeth on edge. The gall of a rascal!

Upset at being interrupted, cross with JC, Abby totally forgot about Sultan's prickly nature. Stepping close to the stallion, JC reached with his hand to pet him. And almost lost his fingers. Infuriated to the dangerous point, the great black beast all but broke free from his stall. Wild and enraged, he shook his huge head, and snapped his teeth ferociously.

Abby's attempt to pacify Sultan earned her a fumigating glare and a mighty push.

The stallion refused to be mollified, kicking and neighing for all he was worth.

Even after she dragged JC out of the barn, Abby heard the angry sounds of Sultan's outrage. Guilt prevented her from enjoying JC's misadventure. After all, it was her fault. If she'd been a little quicker to react...

Berating herself, Abby accompanied the hapless fool to the house, and delivered him into the waiting hands of Mrs. Smith. But no matter how scared he was by his earlier encounter with Sultan, JC refused to stay home. The jerk, the incorrigible idiot. The fool. She cast a quick glance at JC. Abby must admit, the rascal looked rather dapper in his freshly cleaned suit, and Eli's borrowed shirt. The high collar brushed his chin, the intricately tied cravat added a note of sophistication, and the top hat completed the image of a highly successful debonair. If only JC refrained from running his mouth, and pepper his vocabulary with modern slang, they had a chance of pulling this charade off.

Please God, help us all.

Not too soon they pulled up to the red brick building of a jailhouse. Located on South 3rd Street, the property was considered to be modern by design. Her uncle David Yulee, a former senator, signed the deed for this property in late 1800. Familiar with the history of Amelia Island, Abby was aware of the expansions to the jail that will take place much later. Somewhere in the 1930s, a second story will be added to its masonry frame, along with the plumbing and improved cells. And later yet, a jail marker will be placed in front of the building, where it stood proudly ever since. In the future, the building will house the Museum of History where Abby was a frequent visitor. Often, she went there with Alex.

Oh, God, Alex!

Don't go there, Abigail.

Easier said than done. Abby squinted at the structure, and try as she might, was unable to prevent a shudder. Hostile. Grim.

Strange, but it never seemed forbidding to her in the twenty-first century.

The museum was welcoming, dignified, and friendly. The jailhouse was anything but. Thank God she never had a need to visit it in its original situ before today.

Abby swallowed hard. God, she'd give everything to turn around and leave this forbidding, cold place. But Eli was inside, and she was the only one who able to end his horrible suffering. Dallying right now was inexcusable.

Get a grip, Abigail. Time's awasting.

She shook off her unease, and was about to jump down from the carriage, when the proper etiquette intruded.

Remember where you are.

With an effort, she sat back, and turned her eyes to JC. Daisy, too, glared at her brother, who was gaping at the jailhouse like it was the eighth wonder of the world. An expression of utter befuddlement on his face spoiled the impression of an important man of the law. Thunderation, he looked like a simpleton. What on earth were they going to do?

"And?" Tired of waiting, Daisy poked her brother with her elbow. "What are you waiting for?"

"Huh?" JC blinked a couple of times before turning to Daisy. "What?"

"Snap out of it, you moron. As a gentleman, you supposed to exit first, and then assist the ladies from the carriage."

"Oh, yeah, yeah, of course. Sorry." Quickly he unfolded his legs, and hurried to comply. "How silly of me, Mrs. Coleman," he added in a mocked aloof manner, and inclined his head toward Daisy. Unbalanced by his movement, the top hat slid sideways, and hung precariously on his ear.

With a deep sigh Daisy reached over to straighten it.

"Stop clowning, you idiot." Her voice was more annoyed than angry. "We're here on serious business, in case you forgot."

"I know, sorry. I just can't help myself." He flashed the lopsided grin to his sister, before offering his hand to Abby. "Miss Coleman."

"Oh, stuff it, Junior."

She didn't know who was more surprised by her reply, JC or her. She never called him by that moniker before, or allowed herself to use the blatant profanity. Shrugging mentally, Abby chalked it up to her current state of extreme anxiety.

After a charged moment, JC guffawed, then quickly muffled his mirth. "You are a continuing surprise to me, Abs."

"That's Miss Abigail to you."

"Got it. Okay, ladies. Let's get this show on the road, shall we?"

Fast as the god Mercury, JC pulled the indolent mask onto his face. The overall picture was spoiled by the devil dancing in his eyes. He was enjoying himself, the obnoxious imbecile. Fuming, Abby accepted his hand, and stepped down from the carriage. She was ready to strangle the jerk! But it had to wait. Later, she promised herself. First, they must accomplish the deed of freeing Eli.

Bending his elbows in invitation, JC switched his waiting gaze between her and Daisy. They had no choice but to hook their arms with him. As they started toward the building, her sister-in-law instructed JC in a quiet, stern voice, "Don't say anything after introducing herself as Eli's attorney. Got it?"

"Got it. But don't you think I need a cane? You know, for the full effect. One of those heavy sticks with a silver handle. I think—"

"I'll get you a stick later, and shove it up your—"

"Okay, okay. Shish. Just wanted to make sure I look the part, that's all."

"JC!"

"Right. No stick. Got it. But—"

"Cut the bullshit. Just shut your mouth, pretend you're mute, and concentrate on looking important."

"Sure, sis, sorry, Mrs. Coleman. No worries. I just introduce myself, then stand as a prop, and act important."

Daisy took a deep breath. With the last look at her brother, she hissed the warning out of the corner of her mouth, "Don't screw it, JC."

"No way. After all, important is my middle name."

"Your middle name is asshole, but we'd better not enlighten the sheriff."

"Oh, you're so mean to me." His mocking reply earned him a jab of Daisy's elbow.

"I can be meaner. So, help me God, JC, if only you—"

"Relax, Midget. I won't do anything stupid. I promise." Even though his voice carried a note of sincerity, his demeanor lacked the seriousness the moment required.

"Why am I not convinced?" Barely audible, Daisy's mutter reached Abby's ears.

Finally, they reached the door to the jailhouse, and the siblings stopped their bickering. With a flourish, JC opened the door, and bowing slightly, let Daisy and Abby precede him inside. A bit bored and with a snobbish expression he pulled over his face, he transmitted a perfect image for an extremely busy, expensive attorney.

His bearing screamed important with a capital *I*. Either JC used to be a really a big shot back in New York, or else he missed his calling as an actor. Abby had no time nor inclination to ponder on it. She was just glad for his presence, since her gut began to churn and her knees threatened to buckle. Dear Lord, inside of this place was even more dismal than outside. Glum, unwelcoming. Cold.

The foyer was empty this early in the morning, safe for a thirty-something skinny man in uniform. He barely spared them an indifferent glance. Bleak and faded, his eyes matched his surroundings. Without standing from his position at the rickety desk, he drawled, "And what can I do for you, ladies and gentleman?"

Abby's anxiety soared. From his bored expression and indolent tone of voice, it was clear that he was as interested in hearing their inquiry as acquiring an indigestion. Abby wondered if his abhorrent manners were due to his character, or the dreary place where he was employed. Probably both.

"You can unglue your ass from that chair, and greet properly Mrs. and Miss Coleman, young man." With an arrogant tilt of his head, Daisy's brother glared at the uniformed man. His loud voice lashed out like a crop, brutal and sharp.

So much for keeping his mouth shut.

Unimpressed, the guard nevertheless dragged his puny body out of the chair.

"Sorry." His demeanor, however, contradicted his apology. Frowning, clearly displeased at being dressed down, he glared at JC. "What can I do for you?"

"You can—"

Daisy stepped forward. Nudging JC aside, she addressed the guard.

"I am Mrs. Elijah Coleman. We are here to present evidence of my husband's innocence."

"And what evidence might that be?" Squinting, the young man looked at Daisy. His lazy drawl was irritating and mildly insulting.

"Enough." Sweeping motion of JC's hand slashed the air, cutting off Daisy's reply. "We refuse to communicate with you any longer. Your lack of manners is despicable, and simply unacceptable. I will talk to your superior about it. Please call your...commander at once."

Abby winced. Had the young man caught the barely perceptible pause in JC's tirade?

Merde.

Blinking, obviously thrown off balance, the skinny guard stared at JC.

"Sheriff Johnson is not on the premises, sir, so you either have to go to the station, or relay your inquiry to me." The first notes of doubts crept into his response. He clearly didn't know what to make of JC. Unsure, but reluctant to let go of his position of power, the guard arranged his face into a mask of feigned insolence.

"The hell I will!" Drawing to his full impressive height, JC speared the guard with an angry stare. "I request to see the sheriff immediately!"

"Well, as I told you, he's currently not—"

"Send for him, then. Because we are not traveling to the station." Without waiting for a reply, JC turned on his heels, and propelled

Daisy and Abby to the two chairs adorning the glum foyer. "We'll wait. But don't keep us waiting for long."

Silent *or else* hovered in the air.

"Yes, sir. I'll telephone him at once, and relay your request."

"That's better. Tell the sheriff that JC Morris, Esquire from New York, and Mrs. and Miss Coleman demand an immediate audience."

"Demand? An immediate audience? Are you nuts?" After dropping heavily into a chair, Daisy turned her angry face to her brother. "Who talks like that?"

"What, should I say 'politely request his presence'?"

"Why didn't you just shup up and let me deal with it?"

"Yeah, and a very fine job you did too, Mrs. Coleman. *Present evidence of my husband's innocence.*"

Daisy hissed through her teeth. "You don't *demand* to see the sheriff, you arrogant dolt."

"Sure, I do." He patted her hand, and shot a glance at the younger man, who was busily talking over the old-fashioned telephone. "The more arrogant the better. Trust me."

"I swear, JC, if you fuck it up, I'm going to kill you."

"And I'll hold your coat." Abby muttered out of the corner of her mouth.

As proper protocol dictated, they should've gone to the sheriff station first, and request an audience with Sheriff Johnson, present him with the evidence—Abby—and wait for his decision. But impatient and worried about Eli's current condition, they decided to come straight to the jailhouse where he was detained.

Now the foolishness of their decision dawned on Abby. No matter how important a man Eli Coleman was, he was accused of murder, and simply ambushing the jailhouse was not the answer. *Merde.*

Holding her breath, Abby watched the guard talking over the telephone. She expected to hear the sheriff's flat refusal to come from the station to the impromptu audience at the jail any moment, but after putting down the receiver, the rude man kept busy, and ignored their presence.

What was going on? Why didn't he relay the sheriff's response to them?

Abby fidgeted in her seat, then cast a quick glance at her sister-in-law. Poor Daisy. If it was so unbearable for her, what must she feel? With her chin set at a stubborn angle, and the mutinous expression on her bloodless face, Daisy sat, straight as a board, and kept her eyes on the door. Her whole demeanor was that of a willful determination. One thing was clear to Abby, her fearless sister-in-law will not budge from this spot until she talked to the sheriff and freed Eli. The force of a hurricane was not strong enough to change her mindset. Tiny, seemingly fragile, and heavily pregnant, Daisy was stubborn like a thousand mules, and tough as proverbial nails. Raising admiration for her sister-in-law warmed Abby's heart.

If she ever found herself in a dire predicament, there was no one she wished to have by her side. No one save Alex.

Soon, my love. I'll be home soon.

And so, they waited in a hushed charged silence interrupted by the sounds of the awakening jailhouse. More guards shuffled in and out, carrying on with their duties. The young rude man that greeted them earlier soon left, sparing them the indolent glance on his way out. Another one dressed in a similar uniform took his place at the desk, and still they waited. JC began pacing the small foyer, muttering something under his breath.

And finally, after what seemed like ages, the main door flung opened. All three of them turned their heads in unison.

CHAPTER THIRTY-SIX

The tall figure of Sheriff Johnson filled the room. Abby remembered him well. Sworn to the office last year, he was a frequent guest at their house. Sheriff hadn't changed much. An imposing figure despite his lean built, he carried his years with military precision and dignity. The only telltale sign of his age was streaks of silver in his dark gleaming hair.

Eli regarded the new sheriff as a man of honor and integrity. Abby heavily counted on this to be true.

Now, unsmiling and somber, he stopped, and arrowed his shrewd eyes on Daisy. Totally ignoring JC and Abby, the older man towered over her pregnant sister-in-law. Was he trying to intimidate Daisy? Abby almost snorted. Although shorter by a good foot, her miniscule sister-in-law managed to glare at the sheriff down her nose. Even in a sitting position.

After the initial words of greeting, the Sheriff addressed Daisy, "Mrs. Coleman, I'm sorry to keep you waiting. But you really should've come to my station instead of here."

"Sheriff." Daisy refrained from inclining her head, and continued to stare at the older man in a mutinous disgust. "With all due respect, what I should or should have done is irrelevant. My husband is in this jail. You took him in restrains, and dumped him in this place despite the lack of any evidence against him. As I see it, it is your duty now to personally set him free." Her stern voice matched the icy glare in her eyes. "And apologize."

If the sheriff was a more sensitive man, he'd feel all those daggers piercing his skin.

Abby studied the sheriff's face as his jaws clenched. Apparently, his training took

hold and stopped him from snapping back.

"I will be more than happy to do just that, but the evidence—"

"What evidence? The written slander?" Daisy slowly rose from her chair. "I, on the other hand, have ironclad evidence of my husband's innocence."

"Ironclad, is it? Well, let's hear it."

"Better yet, let's see it." With that, Daisy pointed her right index finger at Abby without removing eye contact with her opponent. As soon as Sherriff Johnson turned his face toward her direction, he blanched.

"Miss Abby!" All color drained from his face, then rushed back in a furious scarlet. "But...but..."

Afraid to be a cause of an apoplexy, Abby jumped from her chair. "Hello, Sheriff."

"But...Miss Abby, is it truly you? But how...where..."

"Yes, it is truly me. As to where, I'm sure my brother and sister-in-law informed you of my travels up north. You chose to ignore them. So, summoned up, I returned back home to present myself as evidence of my brother's innocence."

Abby managed to pull a fake smile onto her face. The sheriff stared at her for a long moment in uncomfortable silence. She almost heard the wheels turning in his head, while his jaw worked hard from going slack with shock.

"Well?" Unable to endure this scrutiny any longer, Abby tilted her head.

Sheriff Johnson swallowed a couple of times before answering, "Well...what?"

"When are you going to release Eli from that horrible cell? Immediately, I trust?"

As if coming to his senses, the sheriff puffed his chest, and pulled himself together. He contemplated her question for a few moments.

"As to your request, I'm afraid—"

"This is not a request, Sheriff, but a demand." Forgotten by everybody, JC chose that moment to make his presence known. "What else do you need to release my client, who was falsely accused of murder, no less, than bulletproof evidence? Here is the alleged victim of his alleged crime, alive and well."

"And who are you?" Still befuddled, the sheriff turned to the man who interrupted him in such a rude manner. He squinted at JC, displeased and suspicious. JC didn't blink an eye.

"JC Morris, Esquire, at your service. I am Mr. Coleman's attorney."

"Attorney, are you? Huh. I didn't know that Mr. Coleman had one."

"That's rather irrelevant, isn't it?" A picture of an incurable arrogance, JC shrugged his shoulders negligently. "Now, I left New York in a lurch to come here by the request of my sister and Miss Coleman, and—"

"Your sister? Mrs. Coleman is your sister?"

"That is correct."

"But—"

JC rolled over the older man like a runaway steam train over rail tracks. "My time is very valuable, Sheriff. I trust you won't waste any more of it. And my family ties to Mrs. Coleman are rather beside the point. I'm licensed to practice law in several states, yours included."

Abby held her breath. As far as she was aware, the rascal didn't have a license in Florida. He didn't have any licenses in this time, period. My Lord, did the attorneys even needed a license in 1910? She didn't remember. And what if the sheriff demanded the proof?

Merde.

Suave as silk, with a haughty half smile on his face, JC cocked his head, and continued to spin his tale, "If you need my credentials, Sheriff, you only have to contact the firm of Morris & Morris in New York. Well?"

He arched one brow. Abby wondered how he managed to seems so polite and insulting at the same time. Must be a true gift.

For a moment both men, one smirking, another frowning, stared at each other like two duelists. The contest of wills ended with the victory for JC, as the sheriff lowered his eyes.

"No need, Mr. Morris. No need at all." He hefted a mighty sigh. Then, still frowning, he turned to Daisy. "Out of respect for you, ma'am, I will give an order to release the prisoner immediately. But you and your husband, and you, Miss Abby, will have to come to the station later today, to sign some paperwork."

"Marvelous." Riding on his victory, JC barely inclined his head. "We'll visit with you tomorrow." The smile he bestowed upon the older man was all teeth. "I trust tomorrow is convenient for you, Sheriff? Say, at ten in the morning? That'll give you plenty of time to finish said paperwork."

"Fine. Tomorrow's fine." Surrendering, Sheriff Johnson executed a curt nod. His stiff posture and irritated manner of speech contradicted his statement. No doubt, he was quite tired of the pompous young attorney.

Without missing a hitch, and pleased with himself, JC sent the sheriff one of his most dazzling wide grins.

"Splendid."

Abby barely swallowed her groan.

JC sent a mischievous wink in her direction that set her teeth on edge. Does the rascal know when to stop? Thank goodness, the sheriff was busy issuing orders, and didn't notice this highly unprofessional prank. She glanced at Daisy. But her sister-in-law didn't pay any attention. With her eyes glued to the narrow door that separated the room from the prisoner's cells, she all but vibrated from palpable energy. This time their wait wasn't long. Soon, that narrow door opened, and Eli, pale, dirty, but unharmed, emerged accompanied by a guard. He wasn't wearing restrains on his hands, nor was he shackled. Probably Sheriff Johnson's orders, thank goodness. Abby wasn't sure how Daisy would have reacted otherwise.

With a broken helpless whimper, Daisy ran toward her husband. Even from a distance Abby smelled an unpleasant odor of something foul wafting from Eli. Unwashed for several days, her brother was sweaty and stinking like a boar. But unmindful of his soiled clothes and pungent stench, Daisy enfolded him in her arms, and burrowed her face into his chest.

"Eli, my God, Eli..." Shaking uncontrollably, she held on to her husband for dear life.

Her brother was not the one to display his emotions, especially in public. But now his face creased, and he grabbed his wife in a bear hug. Resting his forehead on the crown of her head, Eli closed his eyes. Unguarded, his outcry seemed to burst free from the depth of his soul, "Daisy, my Daisy..."

Drained, but elated, Abby sniffed. Thank you, God! Her tears ran freely down her face, but she didn't care. Eli was free at last. Her mission was accomplished.

Now everything will be fine, and she can return home.

JC, too, seemed to be overwhelmed by the spousal reunion. Swallowing audibly, he kept his glistening eyes on the pair locked into a tight embrace.

A sound of discreet coughing brought everybody back to the moment.

Unwillingly, Eli released Daisy, and raised his eyes toward the sheriff.

"Are you taking me to stand before the judge, Sheriff?" Hollow, resigned, his voice lacked its usual rich overtones.

"No."

Eli nodded. "Am I being transferred to another jailhouse?"

"No. Mr. Coleman, you are free to go. On behalf of the sheriff's department, and me personally, I apologize for the regrettable, unfortunate mishap."

Disbelief on Eli's face slowly faded to confusion. A deep crease on his forehead cleared, replaced by two dark arches of raised brows. Still unconvinced, he stared at the sheriff.

"And what mishap might that be?"

"Your arrest, sir."

Hushed silence filled the void. After a moment, Eli frowned.

"Did the Carnegies finally come to their senses, and revoked their accusations?"

"No, Mr. Coleman, they did not."

Clearly uncomfortable, Sheriff Johnson averted his eyes, cleared his throat again. "However, earlier today I was presented with the ironclad proof of your innocence."

"What proof?"

"Why, your sister, of course."

Eli's head snapped, as his eyes zeroed in on Abby. A myriad of emotions—puzzlement, confusion, shock—played over his face. His jaw tensed, then slacked, and almost hit the floor. As if mesmerized, he opened his mouth to speak, but no sound came through safe for the little helpless croak.

Uh-oh. Do something, Abigail.

She aimed a wide-eyed stare at her brother, wiggled her brows, and hoped that her desperate mimicking didn't look like she was having a seizure. The sheriff, who stood with his back to Abby, didn't see her grimacing, thank God. Still in the grip of his stupor, Eli gazed at Abby like she suddenly sprouted wings. Or horns. Or both.

She hurried to add hands gestures to her facial exercises, but to no avail. Dumbfounded, Eli had yet to find his voice, or his normal demeanor.

Merde.

But even that was nothing compared to his expression when his eyes landed on JC.

Horrified, as if seeing a ghost, Eli slowly shook his head. But his denial was futile. JC, all six lanky feet of him, stood proudly erect, grinning mischievously.

Eli made an attempt to move forward, but his legs buckled. If not for the sturdy guard, he'd probably have collapsed. Either the sheriff was unconcerned about his former prisoner's strange behavior, or else he attributed it to the sudden turn of the traumatic events. Whatever the cause, he didn't let it show. Instead, he frowned, and addressed Eli, "You should've told me beforehand that you have engaged an attorney." He nodded at JC.

Unperturbed, the rascal sent Eli an engaging smile, and inclined his head. Eli's eyes all but jumped out of their sockets.

"At-t-torney..." A horrible gurgling sound, akin to a helpless oath, flew from his bloodless lips.

Time to interfere.

Abby jumped forward, and tugged on the sheriff's sleeve in an effort to draw his attention from Eli. "You see, Sheriff, it was Mrs. Coleman who hired Mr. Morris in his legal capacity. My brother didn't know about it. That's why he's so surprised."

Poleaxed was a far more accurate description. Abby held her breath. But after a moment of pondering, the sheriff nodded. "I see."

Then he pulled his watch from his breast pocket and consulted the time. Abby surmised the older man was getting weary of their presence. Hallelujah.

She struggled to keep her features schooled in a polite but aloof expression, while inside she was vibrating from panic.

Please, God, let us get out of this place before Eli blurts out something inappropriate!

As if her desperate plea had reached his ears, the sheriff pocketed the watch.

"Well, don't let me hold you any longer, ladies and gentlemen. Mr. Coleman, again, please accept my sincere apology." Sheriff Johnson inclined his head stiffly, as if the words burned his tongue. But the remorse in his eyes was hard to miss. Sheriff Johnson was the man of law and order. In Eli's case, he was tricked into abusing his position of power, and it clearly didn't sit well with him. Abby almost felt sorry for him. Then again, Carnegies or not, the sheriff should've believed the pure and unmerited speculation regarding one of the most upstanding citizens of his town. Abby shook off her sympathy toward the older man.

Serves him right.

"Don't forget I expect to see all of you tomorrow at the station," the sheriff added gruffly.

"Sure thing." Suddenly in a hurry, JC started to herd all of them out of the room. "We'll be there." Out of the corner of his mouth he muttered to Eli, "Move it, man. Let's get the hell out of here before the good old sheriff changes his mind."

As soon as they were out of earshot, her brother finally broke free from the restrains of his stupor. Seething, he wrenched his arm from JC's hold, and turned his accusing glare at his wife.

"Thunderation, Daisy, what have you done?"

CHAPTER THIRTY-SEVEN

After Alex finished recanting the events of the last few days, *Verochka*, who kept quiet during all that time, slowly rose from the sofa. But instead of going to the bar for another drink as he expected, she strolled to the Palladian window. Pensive, seemingly lost in thought, his grandmother stared outside.

Bet my last nickel she's not seeing the ocean.

Holding his breath, Alex watched her. What was on her mind? Did she believe him?

Alex must admit, after spelling it out loud, his tale sounded bizarre even though he had lived it.

Bizarre? Don't flatter yourself, pal. It's fucking insane.

If he hadn't been an eyewitness to the whole mindboggling affair, he doubted he would believe it himself. Hell, probably not. But he *was* there. He saw everything, and watched his two cousins and his fiancée poof into thin air.

Frankly, he didn't see that part, as he was sprawled unconscious on the floor, compliments of that bastard, the grandfather clock. Fueled by the memories, his impotent rage ignited anew, burning hot.

Alex balled his hands into tight fists. His right palm began to throb in rhythm with his heart. What on earth? He cast a quick glance at it. The once white bandage rode unevenly around his right hand, sporting a few drops of blood. Oh, yes. Cut himself on the shards of a champagne bottle after his botched proposal yesterday. Dammit, was it just yesterday? He shook his head, rubbed it with his left hand. Seemed like an infinity had passed between then and now. In reality, mere hours separated those two events.

Oh, Lord, how long after Abby disappeared through that portal?

He glanced at his wristwatch. Almost four hours. An eternity.

Shit, how much longer? A day? A week? A month? About to explode, Alex pressed both thumbs against his eye sockets. How will he make it?

You will. You must. Because you promised Abby to wait for as long as it takes.

"So, Abby went back to help her brother."

Verochka's clear voice cut into his silent, desperate debate. Heaving a deep breath, Alex turned to her. "Yes."

"And Nika is six months pregnant."

"Yes."

"And JC went after them."

What was wrong with her? Hadn't she heard the whole nine yards? Must she recount every freaking point?

"Yes." Grinding his teeth, Alex tried to curb his irritation, but he was unable to force more than a single syllable past his tight lips.

"There is hope for that boy yet." *Verochka's* quiet reply was like a splash of gasoline to the dying embers. Incensed, Alex jumped to his feet.

"Hope? I'll tell you what is there for that *boy*. As soon as I have a chance, I'll—"

"Calm down, Alex. Do you truly believe that JC acted out of pure selfishness when he jumped through the portal into the unknown? And a possibly very dangerous situation?"

"I don't know what was on that warped mind of his."

"Yes, you do." With a deep sigh, his grandmother turned from the window, and aimed her direct gaze on him. "Despite our turbulent family history, JC is a Morris too. He was concerned for his sister, and Abby. It would be prudent to acknowledge the fact."

"Prudent? You said *prudent*?"

"You heard me."

"I can't believe it!" Turning in a tight circle, Alex almost tripped on his feet. "I can't fucking believe it!"

"Admit it, Alexander, your anger has nothing to do with JC per se, but the fact that *he* was allowed through the portal, whereas you were rejected."

She was right, dammit. A thousand times over. His short fuse, however, burned hot, and declined to be squelched. Maybe it was small of him, but funneling his anger at his cousin prevented Alex from concentrating on the chilling fear clawing at his gut.

Verochka watched his struggles like a surgeon about to perform a life-saving operation. Direct, almost brutal, her violet eyes held his gaze without an ounce of sympathy. Her beautiful face mirrored her inner resolve. Alex squirmed, and braced himself. *Verochka* was about to deliver a verdict. Or a mortal blow.

"Now, you have two choices, my boy. First, you can stay pissed off and wallow in your misery. Second, you can calm down, and start to use that sharp brain of yours. As much as the first choice is simpler, it's also quite demeaning. You were never a coward, or a poor loser, Alex. The second choice is fraught with pain and disillusionment, but at least you'll be at the helm." She paused, then added in gentler voice, "You are a protector, *mon ami*. Always were, always will be. You are the one of the strongest and smartest people I know. And one of the kindest." She stepped closer, laid both hands on Alex's face, and aimed her laser-beam glare square on his eyes. "So, don't you dare to disappoint me now, Alexander."

Only his grandmother was capable of praising and unmanning him simultaneously. Spent, shaky, Alex covered her hands with his own, then simply folded. He was tired. And ashamed. And, dear God, so frightened. Closing his eyes, he pressed his forehead to

Verochka's, and enfolded her in his arms. "I will do my damnedest, Gorgeous. I promise."

The moment stretched.

Her familiar fragrance settled his nerves, her strong embrace seemed to channel her own determination and resolve into his soul. Gradually, Alex relaxed. He needed that. A slap in a face—or kick in the butt.

God knew, no one was able to deliver it more efficiently than his elegant, classy grandmother. But most of all, he needed her indestructible faith in him.

"I'll do my best."

"See that you do." *Verochka's* stern reply accompanied by the light pat on his back shattered the moment.

Slowly Alex withdrew from the embrace. To lighten the moment, he sent her a crooked little smile. If not completely calm, he felt more in control, and less anxious. Still not hundred percent, but sliding toward it. That'll do for now.

With a deep breath, Alex shook himself like a wet dog shaking off water. "Okay, my pity party is officially over."

"Glad to hear it. Now, let's get something to eat, and brainstorm. There is nothing like a piping hot pizza to jump start your brain. And a decadent chocolate pastry to prompt it to work."

With that declaration, Verochka grabbed her cell phone. In a matter of thirty-five minutes, the pizza from their favorite place, Moon River Pizza, sat on the kitchen table, tickling his olfactory glands. Surprised, Alex realized that he was ravenous. By the time *Verochka* finished her single slice, he plowed through three helpings, and was currently devouring his fourth. As always, his grandmother was right. There was nothing better than a hot meal to energize the mind. Alex swore he heard the humming sounds of his now fully engaged brain, ready for action.

Almost human again. Almost.

A chime of the doorbell announced a special delivery.

"I swear, I can live on those tiny delights alone." With greedy hands, *Verochka* untied the ribbon on the glitzy box containing Ritz's signature chocolate pastries. Miniscule, with a thumb sized raspberry on top, those round cakes oozed Belgium chocolate sprinkled with real edible gold. Without waiting for coffee, Verochka plopped one into her mouth.

Her orgasmic purrs of pleasure were one of the most erotic sounds he'd ever heard. Despite his mood, Alex chuckled.

"Come on, Gorgeous, you're making me blush."

"And it looks good on you, *mon ami*."

Carrying two mugs of coffee, *Verochka* sat, and placed one before him.

After they crammed down half of the box, Alex pushed the food away. He was stuffed, energized, and bristling with impatience.

Time for brainstorming.

Verochka mirrored his action. Blotting her lips, she folded her napkin.

"Okay, pal of mine. Let's sum it up." She laced her elegant fingers, and looked up.

"Nika returned for Abby. Two of them, plus JC, jumped through the portal to save Eli. You, despite all your valor, were denied—quite violently—access to the blasted thing. Abby and you got engaged. Anything else I missed?"

"Yes. My traveling to Eli's jail cell. Twice. And to the original Coleman house today. That's about it." For some stupid reason, that statement embarrassed him more than anything. To cover his reaction, he averted his eyes. "Go ahead, tell me I made it all up."

In a matter-of-fact tone of voice, *Verochka* delivered her bombshell,

"I won't, because you really saw Eli in his cell, and Abby in her house, in 1910. That's your gift, my boy."

"What?" Alex wondered if his ears played a nasty trick. Did she say *gift?* He blinked, and tried to pick up his jaw from the floor. Dammit, trust *Verochka* to knock him on his butt without moving her pinky. Currently, his grandmother's face sported a huge satisfied smile. Absently, he noticed her naked mouth. Without its usual layer of Rouge Coco red, *Verochka's* face seemed much younger, more vulnerable.

But, strangely, even more impressive.

This was a face of the woman who overcame everything life threw at her, Alex knew it was plenty, and came up the victor. With a capital V.

His heart squeezed. Wasn't he the most fortunate man alive to be related to a such an incredible woman? But sometimes she confused the hell out of him.

Like right now. He finally worked his jaw, and found his voice. "A... *gift?*"

Okay, so it sounded more like a croak, but what the hell? Her revelation knocked him flat, and sent him scrambling. With a effort, Alex cleared his throat. "What are you talking about?"

"A Violet Eyes Gift. Welcome to the club, Grandson." *Verochka's* smile was smug and a little arrogant. "It's about time, too."

His head began to reel.

The Violet Eyes Gift? Welcome to the club? Was she kidding?

No, doesn't look like it. If anything, his grandmother looked pleased and proud like a mother whose child suddenly exhibited genius tendencies. Opting for a joke, Alex sent her a wobbly smile. "If you are the member of that club, Gorgeous, sign me in."

"I am, and so was your great-grandfather." She winked at him. "And so is our Nika." She let it sink in, before chirping, "Surprised?"

Surprised? More like poleaxed. But, hey, what else was new? Since yesterday, it had become his usual state of mind. Alex shrugged, feigning nonchalance. "Why would I be? Nothing surprises me anymore."

But you managed to shock the socks off me.

Grappling with the implications of her words, Alex kept his focus on *Verochka*. Like two pools of calm lakes, her violet eyes, like his and Nika's, didn't waver from his scrutiny. She was the most sane and stable person he had the honor to know.

Yes, sometimes she was showing some signs of unusual intuition, and she believed in past lives, reincarnation, and all that jazz. But...

My God, was it possible?

"Of course it is."

Did he voice his last question aloud? Obviously. Well, then.

"So, the great-grandfather...?"

"Had the same unusual shade of eyes. He claimed he inherited it from his grandmother. And before you asked, my *Pere* was clairvoyant. Since I passed those violet eyes to you and Nika, I always knew you both carried that special gene."

"Thanks a bunch, Gorgeous."

"Don't mention it."

He must admit, he was curious. Not altogether convinced, though, but curious.

"And our Nika...is she clairvoyant like your father, or intuitive like you?"

"Precognitive, pal of mine. I call it precognitive." *Verochka* executed her trade-mark shoulder move he considered the magnum opus of shrugs. Only a true Parisian could pull it off. His grandmother excelled in the skill. "Same thing, but has more... panache to it, don't you think?"

Panache was the last thing he was concerned about. But if she wanted to put it that way... "Whatever you say, Gorgeous."

"But back to Nika. Her gift it truly unique: she manipulates time."

"Huh?" Alex blanched. Nika? The time manipulator? Oh, that was rich.

Dammit, what's next?

Animated, *Verochka* leaned closer. "Think about it. The time moves differently in two centuries. Why?"

"Why?" He sounded like a damned parrot.

"Because of Nika. Whenever she is, it slows down. Like tenfold. Haven't we puzzled that she spent three months in 1909, and here it accounted for three days? Or, when Eli was back in fourteen days as he thought, and here it spanned into fourteen months?" She sat back, and pointed an elegant and manicured finger at him.

"You said she was hugely pregnant, when only five days ago she was flat as a washboard. Right?"

He still failed to wrap his brain around *that*, but...

"What has it to do with Nika?"

"Everything, my boy! Everything! When she's excited, happy or overly upset, she tends to slow time down. You probably don't know, but just last week the car almost ran down Eli, and your attorney's dog in downtown. Nika, shocked and horrified, stopped the time, or rather slowed it enough for both of them to avoid the barreling SUV, and come back unharmed."

"I wasn't aware of that."

"Of course, you weren't, because I was the only one she confessed to. I had my suspicions before, but that episode just confirmed my hypothesis."

"She...I mean, Nika knows about the Violet Eyes Gift?"

"She does now."

"And I...I can do... what? Fly in between two dimensions? In my mind?"

"In a nutshell, yes. But again, it has more scientific and elegant term: OBE. Or out of body experience. It's a phenomenon, really, and a very rare at that. You are so lucky, Alex."

Amazing.

"Yeah, well, I'd rather be less lucky, thanks all the same." Absently he rubbed his suddenly pounding head. He even pinched himself to make sure that he was not dreaming. Nope. No such luck.

"You don't mean that." The light censure in *Verochka's* voice was unmistakable.

"It's just too new an experience for you, that's all."

That's all? Really?

"Too new?" Alex threw both hands up. "It's fucking mindboggling, that what it is!"

"Or that," dead-pan, *Verochka* patted his arm. "Tell me, sweetie, I'm so curious, how does it feel?"

Alex allowed himself a moment to reflect. How did it feel?

Surreal. Shocking. Unbelievable. And, dear God, so horrifyingly real!

"Fucking mindboggling," he repeated after a long pause.

"That's what I thought." Disturbed by her vigorous nod, a single lock of hair came loose from her sleek chin-length bob, and fell into her face. Impatiently, she blew at it.

Just like Nika.

Alex's heart squeezed.

"As I said, lucky you, my boy."

Lucky? Alex shook his head. Lucky was the last thing he felt. Lost, and confused. And unsettled.

"Seriously, *Verochka,* it was spooky as hell. Not only did I *see*, I could *smell* too. The sweat in Eli's cell, or coffee in the dining room of the Coleman house. And what's more, both Eli and Abby saw me. I think Abby heard me."

"Oh, that's extraordinary!" She clapped her hands, delighted like a child with a new toy. Alex wished he could share her enthusiasm.

"But why? Why did it happen at all? Yesterday evening I was standing in the room, talking to Nika, and— smack— I was in a dim, dingy jailcell. Or today. I was in the kitchen, then bam! Lights, the clock chiming, and in a blink of an eye I was there, at the Coleman house circa 1910."

"But on both those occasions you *were* excited, right?"

"Yeah, you might say that again. Seeing Nika, pregnant, sprawled on the floor...For a second I thought she was dead."

In slow motion, that scary scene unfolded in his mind's eye. Even hours later, a shudder of pure horror shot through him like an arrow. Alex closed his eyes and swallowed the knot in his throat. When he opened them again, *Verochka* nodded, silently prodding him to continue.

"After I came home today, I was beside myself with worry about Abby, and..." And just like that, the realization dawned. "My God! When I was scared for Nika, I saw Eli; when I was getting crazy about Abby, and...and here she was. I'll be damned!"

"Yep. See the pattern? When you're overly emotional, you get to see the people you are worrying about. Because you were born a protector, my boy."

"Protector, my butt. And I did such a great job, protecting the woman I love."

"Not your fault, Alex. The Universe intervened. Or that infamous grandfather clock."

"But...why I cannot control this...thing, whatever it is?"

A brief frown later, *Verochka* shrugged, dismissing the problem. "A downside for sure, but I bet with more time and experience, you'll get the hang of it."

"The *hang of it*? Really?" Alex let loose a short bark of laughter. "Damn, you are something else, Gorgeous."

"True, oh so true." All demure, his grandmother folded her fluid ballerina's hands, cast her gaze downward. Damn, she was good. There was not a single shy bone in her body, but if he didn't know better, he would buy that utterly fake humble expression, too.

"Save that false modesty, *Verochka*. It won't work with me."

"Well, since you ask so nicely." With a typical Gaelic shrug, his grandmother recrossed her skyscraper legs, and assumed her normal demeanor. "Okay, Alex. Besides your lack of control over OBE, what else is on your mind?"

"A single question. Why that freaking grandfather clock didn't allow me to pass through?"

"Maybe because you didn't need it." *Verochka* tilted her head, as if pondering her own reply. Her puckered brows formed a deep V between her bewitching eyes.

"Come again?"

"Think about it, Alex. You can navigate between times on your own. So, you don't need a portal."

"Gorgeous, in case you've missed it, I can travel back and forth in my mind only."

"Does it really matter?"

"Hell yeah!" Agitated, Alex jumped to his feet, paced the room. "I'd rather be in my physical body than out of it while cruising in between two centuries."

"Maybe, one day you will, my boy. Maybe you will."

Uneasy, Alex stopped, then turned to his grandmother.

Why did her statement strike him as ominous?

Lost in thought, her gaze distant, *Verochka* stared at something beyond the realm of the present.

What did she see?

Her breath became shallow, as color slowly drained from her face. Unmoving, unblinking, frozen, she sat a mere few feet from him, but seemed so far away he barely squelched the need to touch her, just to make sure that she was still here. Was she experiencing that effing OBE too? Did her mind travel beyond the curtain of time, while her body was stuck here, in their kitchen?

Damn if she didn't freak him out. Spooked, Alex shuddered. Goose bumps the size of Texas covered his skin like armor. All the fine hairs on his body sprung up to painful points. The silence grew, oppressive, menacing. Dark foreboding hung around the room like a wet, rainy cloud.

Come on, Gorgeous, snap out of it!

As if hearing his urgent plea, *Verochka* jerked her head, gulped some air, and turned to him. The dark shadows under her eyes stood out like two ugly bruises.

In the hollow voice devout of her usual warmth, she repeated, "Maybe you will."

CHAPTER THIRTY-EIGHT

"What have *I* done?" Nika almost chocked. The gall of the man! "I saved your sorry ungrateful ass, and freed you from jail, that's what!"

"How? By dragging Abby and your brother here from another time?"

"I would have dragged the demon from Hades if needed!"

Yelling in front of the jailhouse was probably not the smartest thing to do, but Nika was too incensed to care. The pompous jerk, the obstinate imbecile! Instead of rejoicing and thanking her for the rescue, he glowered at her. Steam was all but bellowing from her ears when Nika decided enough was enough. Ignoring her husband, she climbed into the carriage without help from the fidgeting driver.

The poor man was visibly uncomfortable by their altercation. Even though he kept his expression emotionless, his cheeks flamed with acute embarrassment. And after the phrase 'from another time,' his ears all but perked up like Belle's when she was curious.

Damn Eli for forgetting they had an audience, and blurting those words in front of the stable hand. How on earth were they supposed to explain that?

Later. I'll think of it later. As of right now...

She turned to her brother and Abby. Hovering nearby, visibly uncomfortable, they both wore the identical frowns of disapproval. JC watched Eli like he was a bomb about to detonate, while her sister-in-law worried her lower lip with her teeth hard enough to draw blood.

"Well? How long will you stand here like a bunch of morons?"

Familiar with her temper, Abby and JC immediately scrambled up the single step of the carriage, and seated themselves. Eli, his hands perched at his hips, was still standing on the sidewalk, glaring at her. Damn his stubborn aristocratic hide.

Well then. *Two can play the game, mister.*

More than willing to oblige, Nika glared back.

"Mr. Coleman? Will you grace us with an honor of your presence? Or have you changed your mind, and decided to go back to your cell? I'm sure the accommodations were on par with your status, considering the current state of your dress, and bodily aroma." To emphasize, she made a production of wrinkling her nose in distaste. "So, maybe you'd like to continue your tenure as a guest of the state's finest establishment?" Sarcasm dripped from her tongue like drops of venom.

You should be ashamed, Nika-Daisy. After all, he was just concerned for his sister and your brother.

That tiny voice of her inner I piped in, poking Nika's consciousness.

Yeah? What about me? Not so concerned about his wife, *jumping back and forth between two centuries. And what about his child?*

But her inner bitch decided to retreat after stating her mind.

Fine. Leave me alone.

Fuming, Nika concentrated on keeping her head high, and her spine straight. Hot tears pressed against her eyelids, but she'd be damned if she cried. No way was she letting the insufferable jerk know how much he hurt her. And after everything she'd been through! Nika balled her shaking hands. Let him stew all he wants. She's not going to explain her actions to anyone, Eli included. The dolt. The idiot. The overbearing fool!

But inside she was cringing. Dammit, didn't he understand? Wouldn't he do the same if their positions were reversed? Of course, he would.

So, what's his problem?

After a long moment of charged silence, Eli clambered aboard. Taking a sit across from her, he growled, "We'll talk more at home."

Bet your ass, we will.

Seething, Nika ignored him. Without another word, Eli nodded to the driver, who jumped up, and prompted the geldings forward.

To say that the ride back home was uncomfortable, was an understatement of two centuries combined. Gloom hung around the open cabin like a suffocating blanket.

The dark expression on Eli's face forbade any conversation. Beside her, Abby pressed herself into the cushion as hard as was humanly possible. Her obvious attempt to make herself invisible was futile. JC, unperturbed, and pleased with himself, sat near Eli with a smug little smile on his face. The stupid baboon enjoyed every moment of his so-called grand adventure. Just look at him! Top hat, cravat, shiny as mirror shoes. The only thing that was missing, according to the idiot, was the cane with a heavy knob. Nika itched to administer a couple of mighty whacks with that imaginary cane over his stupid head. She asked him to keep quiet. But did he comply? No way. The ignorant jerk jumped right in from the get go, turning their encounter with the sheriff into a comedy worthy of the academy award. Damn his running mouth.

The very important attorney from New York, my ass.

But as much as she hated to admit it, without JC they probably wouldn't manage to free Eli so quickly.

I'd sooner cut my right arm off than acknowledge it aloud.

JC was too full of himself as it was without her stroking his gargantuan ego.

Shame on you, girl. Your brother risked a lot, coming here.

Nobody asked him to risk his stupid neck.

Maybe not, but he did it anyway. Because he's family.

She always hated being mollified by her own inner *I*. But, as usual, that bitch was right. Despite her vocal protests, JC shouldered his way in, jumping after her and Abby through the portal. Because he was concerned about them, or because of other, more selfish reasons? Probably. Possibly. Did it really matter?

Yes, he bounced back from the ill effects of the journey rather quickly, and began to enjoy himself, but so what?

He was here, and, as much as it galled her, he saved the day.

So, don't be a bitch, Nika-Daisy.

With a deep sigh, Nika relented. "JC, thanks."

"Anytime, Mrs. Coleman." A cheeky grin split his face. "Anytime at all."

Her brother still hadn't mastered the skill of wearing a top hat, and at every turn of his head that object slid askew, making him look like a clown. Like right now. Despite her mood, Nika chuckled, and leaning forward, straightened his headwear.

"I mean it, JC. Thank you."

"You are very welcome, Midget."

That familiar childhood nickname brought a flood of memories. Not all of them were happy, but every one of them defined her as the person she was today. Something warm unfurled inside of her chest. Gratitude? Tenderness? Love? Swamped in it, Nika smiled through the sheen of tears at her older brother. Moron or not, he was family, and whether she wanted it or not, she *was* responsible for him being here. So, it was her job to keep him safe, until his trip back—or forward—home. Suddenly sad at the prospect to say good-bye to JC, Nika shifted her gaze away. But the sooner both JC and Abby take their leave, all the better. Not only was it abnormal for them both to stick in this time, it was fraught with repercussions. Fiddling with nature was both dangerous, and unwise. The Universe was hard to forgive or forget. If something happened to either one of them, it would solely be her fault. And how will she live with that guilt?

Fear gripped her by the throat. Cold sweat pooled in rivulets down her back. The air became hot and oppressive. Her ears started to ring with the unmistakable chiming of the grandfather clock. A premonition of a disaster loomed above, like a heavy, dense curtain. Her vision began to grey, narrowing to a tunnel.

On the verge of passing out, Nika gritted her teeth. Please, God, not now!

At that moment, the baby inside of her stirred, and started kicking for all she was worth. Nika jolted. Saved by the bell. Or by the baby.

Thank you, Button.

Wrenched from her near-fainting episode, still shaky and nauseated, she drew in a gulp of air. Damn, that was close. Too close. Cradling her stomach, Nika rubbed it in a soothing motion with both hands as much for baby's sake, as her own.

They both will return home today. I'll make sure of it.

With a deep, calming breath, Nika sat back, rested her head against the cushion. Yes, she *will* make sure both Abby and JC return immediately. As soon as they are back inside the Coleman house, she'll get them that blasted key and usher them to the grandfather clock. If needed, she'll turn that key herself, and bodily push them through the portal.

But in that case, the key will be lost to you forever.

She didn't care. The main point was for JC and Abby to return home, safe and sound. Everything else compared to that was insignificant.

Nika had no idea why she was so disturbed by that fleeting episode, but all her instincts still screamed in warning. She never disregarded, or questioned her intuition. Saved by it more time that she cared to count, Nika learned to always heed its message. Now that urging message was clear as a baby's tear. JC and Abby must go back. *Or forward.* Semantics aside, they must leave as soon as possible, or the repercussions may be dire.

Nika cast a brief glance at Eli. Had he noticed anything? Did he feel the same unease that plagued her? But her husband sat ramrod erect, with his face drawn in disapproval, and ignored his companions.

The stubborn fool.

The adrenaline that surfed through her body suddenly ebbed. And all pesky discomforts associated with her pregnancy sprung back to life.

Shit.

There was nothing she hated more than the demands of her gestating body.

Swollen ankles, as unseemly as they were, presented just a small portion of her problem. The major part was her overacting bladder. Dammit, she needed to pee. Like right this minute! Nika glanced at the street they were currently passing. Where were they? How much longer will they trudge before they arrived home? Her bladder was about to burst. She shifted her legs in a futile attempt to get some relief. No such luck. Cursing under her breath, Nika readjusted her position.

As if sensing her predicament, Abby placed a hand on Nika's arm.

"Just a couple of streets farther, *ma petite.* Not long at all. Just hang in there."

With her teeth clamped tight, Nika managed a tight nod to the girl.

"What's wrong with you?"

More cross than attentive, the deep baritone of Eli's voice rubbed her the wrong way.

Hallelujah! Her husband finally decided to descend from his funk, and bestow his invaluable attention upon his wife. The obnoxious dick.

What's wrong with you? Really?

"I'll tell you what's wrong with me, mister." If Nika wasn't so uncomfortable, she would jump straight ahead, and then strangle him with her own two hands. "Besides being married to the insufferable ingrate, I'm six months pregnant, and need to pee right now more than I need to breathe!"

Without a word of a reply, Eli tapped on the driver's back, and whisper something in his ear. The geldings began to run faster. Thank God.

In a matter of minutes, they entered the main gates of the estate. And not a moment too soon. Not waiting for the carriage to stop fully, Nika jumped down, and, as fast as the bulk of her stomach allowed, scrambled toward the front steps.

She probably looked as graceful as an elephant in a tutu, but who cares? At the open doors, Nika almost plowed into the stout body of Mrs. Smith. Without pausing to apologize, she zoomed across the foyer, and lifting two fistfuls of her long skirt, skipped upstairs. Belle's delighted barking, and joyous sounds of welcoming commotion followed her all the way to the bathroom.

The master was home.

An hour later they gathered in the dining room for a celebratory brunch. Even though Nika had no appetite, she sat at the table, waiting for the right moment to start her conversation with both Abby and JC. Convincing them to leave right away was imperative. But Mrs. Smith, bless her heart, accompanied by the kitchen stuff, ran in circles around them, piling food and drinks onto the table. Nika barely prevented herself from biting her nails. Or cursing a blue streak.

Dammit, how much longer? She was running out of patience, but for the life of her, she had no heart to bark an order for the housekeeper to leave them alone. The older woman, a surrogate mother to both Coleman siblings, was all but dancing from happiness at having both of her charges home. Nika sighed. Mrs. Smith's exhilaration was short lived. So, why not to let her enjoy a little longer?

Patience, Nika-Daisy. Patience.

Someone else besides her was restless and frustrated. Nika followed her sister-in law with her eyes. Poor Abby. Agitation all but swirled around her like a cloak, as she paced the room. After her mission of saving her brother was accomplished, Abby began to fret and fidget. No need to be a clairvoyant to figure out the main object of her concern. *Alex.* Nika too worried about him, but deep down she was convinced that he was okay. It would take more than a hard knock on the head to harm her favorite cousin. But still.

As much as Nika commiserated with her sister-in-law, she was glad that Abby all but chomped at the bit to get back. She didn't need to do much to convince her, but JC? Her gut feeling predicted more trouble in that direction. *Dammit.*

Why was *he* allowed through the curtain of time, but not Alex?

Moot point, Nika-Daisy. Take a deep breath, and think of the best way to proceed.

The easiest way was rendering JC unconscious, and bodily throwing him through the portal. Sure, as the last resort, but she very much preferred to avoid the violence.

You have a better idea?

Nope, but maybe Eli will.

Fat chance. He'd yet to climb down from the high horse of his ostentatious aloofness. From the moment he stepped foot inside the Coleman house, Eli went out of his way to ignore everybody, except

Mrs. Smith and Belle that is. Like their housekeeper or the dog were the main reason he was free and unharmed.

The jerk.

As soon as they were home, he excused himself, and went upstairs. For almost an hour there was no peep from him. What was he doing all this time? How long does it take to wash and change clothes? Was he deliberately avoiding them?

More than likely, avoiding her, the moron.

Not for long, buster.

Later. She'll deal with Eli later. Right now, her main and more pressing concern was her brother. Just look at the idiot! The former CLO of the Morris' Investment Bank, clad in the borrowed old-fashioned shirt and suit, sat at the dining table, grinning like he had no care in the world. Never mind that he was a century back in time, in 1910, the notion that was supposed to be incomprehensible to any normal human being, especially to such a conservative guy like her brother. But JC, the stupid jerk, seemed to take this highly unusual circumstances in stride. More than that, he enjoyed every moment of it! Immediately upon arriving from the jailhouse, JC held court in the foyer, recalling to the willing audience of Mrs. Smith and the staff their morning events. His own role, of course, was embellished to ginormous proportions. According to JC, he single-handedly managed to free Eli from his impending disaster. Needless to say, he was immediately exalted to a hero status, and fawned over by everybody. Even Eli's presence didn't merit so much attention, or adoration. JC soaked it all up like a sponge. Nika wouldn't be surprised if by now he believed his own lies, the pompous ass.

The only member of the household who acted hostile toward JC was Belle. For the umpteenth time, Nika wondered about the dog's peculiar behavior. Despite her colossal size, and scary appearance, Belle was as docile as a lamb. She loved everybody, and was loved in return. But as soon as she laid eyes on her brother yesterday, the friendliest of dogs on the planet raised her hackles, and started to growl quite menacingly. Puzzled at first, JC all but bent over backwards to befriend the furry giant, but to no avail.

Currently, Belle followed Abby's every step, but kept swiveling her head toward JC. Time and again, a deep warning growl trembled in her throat.

What's gotten into her? As exceptionally intelligent as she was kind, Belle didn't suffer fools, or was duped by a shiny exterior. Her bullshit-meter was superior to any human, and JC more than likely, didn't pass the test. Brazen, he had schmoozed his way in, deceiving everybody, but not the intuitive, highly perceptive mongrel. Feeling fraud, Belle rejected the intruder, and watched him like a hawk. Her dog's protective nature was on par only with Alex's.

If only her cousin knew that she compared him to a dog, he would box her ears for sure. Nika chuckled, then grew serious. Alex.

Dear God, please keep him safe.

Her silent prayer was interrupted by a sound of a loud rambunctious laughter that set her teeth on edge. Fuming, Nika swiveled her head, and her eyes landed on none other than her older brother.

Why am I not surprised?

The obnoxious baboon, was oozing his considerable charm upon Mrs. Smith. Whatever he said, made the old dear blush to the roots of her grey hair.

Was he telling a joke? Really?

Joking at the time where his life and safety all but hung onto a thin thread?

Unbelievable!

Nika drew in a deep breath, then let it out with a loud *whoosh*.

Damn that fickle bitch fate for saddling her with JC. And damn him for enjoying his 'grand adventure' so much. She must admit,

JC never looked more animated, or carefree since that memorable November day, when he arrived on her doorstep after nine years of separation. He gained weight and lost his pallor along with that shattered expression in his eyes that always tugged at her heart. Since then, her older brother came a long way, from a full-blown, stuck-up jackass to a mere annoying jerk. Or an obnoxious clown. A remarkable transformation, all things considering. A bitter combination of regret, sadness, and remorse swept over her. As always, when reflecting on those lost years, Nika wondered what if...So much time wasted. Resentment, pique, pride. It all seemed so pointless, so...immature. And the blame, unfortunately, was not one sided.

She should've done something to connect with her brother— her both brothers. Andrew, the youngest of their threesome, was almost thirty now. Her memory conjured the image of a skinny and affable boy who trailed after JC like an adoring puppy. Was he still thin as a pole? What did he do for a living? Was he single, or married? Was he happy? She sincerely hopped so.

Did Andrew think about his sister at all, or had he forgotten about the black sheep of the Morris clan? Too late to dwell on it now.

The biggest and most unforgivable mistake she'd ever made was thinking that there was plenty of time. God, was she really that arrogant?

So stupid, Nika-Daisy, so unapologetically selfish.

Because there was no other time except now. Period. End of story. She learned that lesson the hard way.

Useless to berate yourself now. Useless, and pointless.

She was helpless to do anything about Andrew, but she was able to do something for her older brother. Like cutting short his impromptu 'grand adventure,' and making sure he returned home, safe and sound. Even against his will.

Gotta do what you gotta do.

Shaking off her pensive mood, Nika concentrated on the immediate agenda.

Abby. Must talk to her first.

That girl packed more common sense than her baboon of a brother.

Her sister-in-law still paced the room with the precision of a marching solder. Giving up on trailing after her favorite human, Belle, exhausted by all that exercise, lay quietly in the corner. But her liquid eyes followed Abby's every step.

"Abby?" Nika pointed at the chair beside herself. "We need to talk."

Reluctantly, Abby obeyed the order. She shifted her shadowed eyes toward Nika.

"What is it, Daisy?"

"Listen to me, Abs. You—"

Suddenly, Belle emitted a loud bark, and jumped up. Irritated by the interruption, Nika cursed, turned her head, and lost her breath.

Her concentration shattered into a tiny gazillion pieces, as freshly bathed, clean-shaven, and impeccably dressed Eli entered the room.

Oh, my...

CHAPTER THIRTY-NINE

A s always, he rendered her mute and deaf. But not blind, thank God.

Nika's eyes trailed up and down Eli's body. Lithe, with long muscular legs, and powerful torso, he was built like an athlete. Or a panther.

The potent mix of citrus and sandalwood of his cologne ambushed her olfactory glands. All her five senses sprang to life, defenseless under the attack of that glory.

Since the first time she laid eyes on the aloof owner of the Coleman house, Nika had the same reaction. Exhilaration, awe, astonishment.

And yearning. Desperate, terrible, and overwhelming.

The way Eli affected her was almost criminal. Guilty as charged, Nika tried to tamper her reaction, but to no avail. Tall, dark and movie star handsome, with the silver- grey eyes, and a deep clefted chin, her husband was larger than life, and more irresistible than a thousand sins combined.

Damn his aristocratic hide.

Her treacherous heart sighed and melted into a puddle. A hot wave of awareness swept over her, leaving her breathless, and needy. And brutally aroused. Trembling, her body tingled in all the places that made her female. Heat pooled between her thighs. Her enlarged with pregnancy breasts strained against the confinement of her shirtwaist. Carnal, explicit images swam before her eyes. Damn, she was acting like a harlot!

Did he notice? As if answering her unspoken question, Eli curved his lips in a smug, satisfied little smile. Of course, he did, the cad.

And what did you expect? The word 'lust' is blinking on your forehead with huge neon letters. Snap out of it!

But her silent self-order was doomed to perdition. Her unruly glands refused to be reined in. Once unleashed, her desire burned like a blazing inferno.

You are mad, Nika-Daisy. Like certifiable.

Yeah, madly in love. Which was the same thing. A helpless little oath escaped her lips. In a futile effort to mask her reaction, Nika forced a deep frown onto her face. Too little too late.

Eli's deep rumble of a chuckle sent another wave of shivers along her spine.

Shit.

Humiliated, betrayed by her own body, she cast her eyes downward.

"Pray continue, Daisy. You were saying...?"

Yeah, sure, talk to me when I don't remember my own name, why don't you?

But what *was* she talking about before his presence rendered her comatose?

More like violently aroused, but...

Shup the hell up.

Praying that she didn't utter that rebuke aloud, Nika gritted her teeth.

Think, Nika-Daisy, think.

She remembered watching JC, being irritated with Mrs. Smith, because she wouldn't go away, then Abby...

Oh, God Almighty, of course!

She was urging Abby to go home! Or started to, before being so rudely interrupted. Nika tore her eyes from Eli, and turned again to his sister.

"Abs, listen. You must return. Today. Both of you must go back."

"I am in total agreement with you, Daisy." After a vigorous nod, Abby grabbed her hand. "There is no time—"

"Why the rush?" This time the interruption came from her brother. Lips pressed in a stubborn line, JC jutted his chin. "I don't want to go just yet. Maybe never."

What? Oh, God. She never expected *that.* Maybe she should. Having a blast, and excited at being treated like a hero, that idiot decided to prolong his 'grand adventure' by making it permanent. Dammit. Now what?

"Shut up, you moron. Of course, you must go back!" Her voice rang with desperation.

"Forward, you mean." The obnoxious jerk had the balls to smirk.

"Okay, fine, whatever. But you have to return."

"Why?" Oh, how she hated his maddening manner to squint and smirk at the same time!

"What do you mean, why? Because your place is there."

"What if I like this place better?"

"Are you fucking nuts?"

"So, it's okay for you to stay here, but not for me?"

"Yes!"

"Why?" A picture of a bullheaded defiance, JC crossed his arms over his chest, and prepared to argue his case.

"Because...because..."

"Because what?"

Tearing her hair out, or beating her head against the wall? Satisfying, but futile. The milewide stubborn streak was a Morris trademark. Who if not her can relate?

Shit, shit, shit!

At the end of her wits, Nika glared at Eli. "You tell him."

"Tell him what, exactly?"

Cool and calm, her husband cocked his brow in her question.

"Oh, don't play games with me, Coleman. Not now. This isn't a joke!"

"No?" Eli sat, and with maddening concentration, unfolded his linen napkin, draped it over his knees. Nika ground her teeth so hard, it was a pure miracle she didn't reduce them to powder. "And here I thought it was all one big joke to you, *ma petite*. I mean, my sister's and your brother's appearance."

An innocent smile curved his lips, but his eyes gleamed like two hard, cold gems.

Oh, she knew that stare! Still angry at her, and not ready to forgive.

Forgive what?!

"You insensitive dolt! Don't you dare to smirk at me. Their appearance, as you put it, was due to your imprisonment. I had no choice."

"As you are in favor of reminding me constantly, *ma petite,* there's always a choice. But I'm curious, what did you do? Put a key back inside the panel with an urgent note? Was *that* your ingenious choice?"

That does it.

"No, you pig. I took the key, and went to fetch them."

Eli's head jerked sideways, as if she slapped him. The fork he held in his hand cluttered to the table. Pale and wide-eyed, he stared at her in utter shock.

"You...you did *what*?"

"You heard me."

"You... went through the portal, all alone and pregnant?"

"Well, since I couldn't leave the baby behind, she went with me, yes."

"Thunderation, Daisy!" His fists hit the table hard enough to send the glasses dancing. "Don't you understand how dangerous that was? For you and the babe?"

"Oh, I understand, alright. More than you give me a credit for." Mirroring his gesture, Nika brought both fists down with all her strength. The pain from her balled hands radiated all the way to her shoulders. She welcomed it. "But know this, Elijah Benjamin Coleman, there is nothing—absolutely nothing—on this earth, or beyond, that would've stopped me. Because your life depended on it. Not that you appreciate it."

Angry tears hovered on her eyelashes like fat rain drops. Impatient, she rubbed them off. He was not worthy of her tears, damn him.

Do not give him the satisfaction, Nika-Daisy!

He's worthy of everything.

He *was* everything. Without him, her life was pointless. Didn't he understand that? On the verge of complete humiliation, Nika swallowed hard, and averted her eyes. She would have fled from the room if not for Abby and JC. Even more important than her grievance with Eli, was the matter of their departure.

She drew in a deep calming breath, then addressed her husband in as much a cool and impersonal voice as she was able to muster.

"Now, that we established that I am a reckless fool, can we get back to the issue at hand?"

"W-what issue?"

For the first time, Nika failed to read his expression. Was he hurt? Mad? Shocked?

Probably all of the above. No time to dwell on it. Now it was imperative to convince Abby and JC to return immediately. And for that, she needed Eli's help.

"The issue of your sister and my brother returning back to the place they belong."

As fate would have it, Mrs. Smith entered the room at that moment. The fragrant aroma of fried ribs turned Nika's stomach. Fighting a gagging reflex, she pressed her teeth together.

Dammit, not now, Button. Behave.

"Oh, Mrs. Coleman," the old housekeeper, steaming plates held in both hands, planted herself in front of Nika, "but they just arrive a mere day ago! After such a long travel, wouldn't it be nice to extend their visit a bit longer? I'm sure Miss Abigail missed her brother dearly. Why would you want them to leave so soon?"

Fighting her bout of nausea, Nika managed not to squirm under the older woman's accusing stare.

Another one is mad at me. Racking it fast, Nika-Daisy. Who's next?

"Miss Abby?" Giving up on Nika, Mrs. Smith turned her pleading eyes to her former charge. "Must you go back so soon?"

"I'm afraid so, Mrs. Smith. You see, my fiancé—"

"Your what?!"

Abby's slip of tongue had the effect of a detonating bomb.

Shocked, Eli surged to his feet.

The kaleidoscope of emotions—bafflement, surprise, joy—swirled over his face.

In two quick strides he reached his sister, and then pulled her by the hands from the table.

"Alex?"

"Who else?" Laughing, crying, Abby fell into her brother's arms. "Oh, Eli..."

"Happy?"

"Enormously so!"

"Oh, my precious *Papillon.*" Wiping his sister's tears with both thumbs, he kissed her forehead. "Then I will be happy for you. For both of you."

Tenderness, love, and unmistakable sadness in his voice tagged at Nika's heart.

"He is one lucky man, our Alex. Please tell him I said so. And my heartfelt congratulations."

"Thank you, Brother."

"Look at the ring, Master Eli. Isn't it a beauty?"

Obliging Mrs. Smith's request, Eli lifted Abby's left hand.

"It is indeed. A princess for the Princess?"

"Yes." A bit wobbly around the edges, Abby's smile lit her whole face. "That's what Alex called it."

"Clever man."

"And such a generous one, too." Mrs. Smith piped in. "I would love to meet your betrothed, Miss Abby. When do you think will he be able to come for a visit? Oh, goodness, and when is the wedding? And wouldn't it be splendid to celebrate it here, in your childhood home? Master Eli? What do you think?"

To Eli's credit, he didn't flinch, or move a single muscle. The only telltale sign of unease was the absent rubbing of his chin with two fingers.

"Yes, I suppose it would, Mrs. Smith. But it's up to the bride and groom. After all, it's their big day, and the decision of the place to celebrate must be left to them."

"You are right, of course." Deflated, the older woman cast her eyes downward. With a mighty sigh, she shook her head, and left the room.

"Abby?"

"Yes, Eli?"

"I failed to express how very grateful I am to you. And to you, JC."

"Don't mention it." All magnanimous, JC smiled, and negligently waved his hand like a king to a peasant. "It was nothing, really."

Nika's answering snort was loud, short, and rude. If the overbearing dick puffed his chest a bit more, he'll burst from within. Unperturbed by her lack of restrain, Eli inclined his head at her brother.

"Nonetheless. There are no words to describe the depth of my gratitude. Thank you both for coming to my rescue. It was very reckless and risky, but without you I would probably perish. Worse, I would be shunned and disgraced. So, I owe my life and my honor to both of you."

"You don't owe us anything, Brother. You'll do the same for me, or for JC. If anyone you must be grateful to, it is Daisy." A light censure crept into Abby's voice. "She risked her unborn babe to save you, Eli. Compared to that, everything fades into nothing. So, if you do *owe* your life and honor to anyone, it is her."

A shadow of guilt darkened Eli's face. Still holding Abby in a one-armed hug, he finally aimed his focus at Nika.

Dear Lord, have mercy.

Blazing heat slammed into her with the force of an explosion. A combination of love and lust in his smoldering eyes was lethal.

Eli.

Her rock, her destiny, her everything. He drove her crazy, and loved her unconditionally. Every single moment with him was a great challenge, and an even greater adventure. Thrown together by fate, blessed by the Universe, united by time.

Her heart overflowed, then sighed, even as it began to thunder against her left breastbone.

"Daisy."

He didn't have to say anything more.

Apology, regret, remorse, and myriad other feelings rolled into a single word.

She understood.

"Eli."

Acceptance, forgiveness, an overwhelming tenderness. And love, infinite, unbounded.

In the hushed silence of the room, their locked eyes spoke volumes, their hearts beat in unison.

She forgot where she was. Her time? His? Does it matter?

She forgot to breathe. When her lungs screamed in protest, Nika gulped some air, but held his gaze.

Mesmerized. Enraptured. She heard her name, even though he didn't say it aloud.

Daisy.

She answered in her mind: *Eli.*

His silent reply brought tears to her eyes. *Only you.*

She smiled.

Always you, my love. Always.

The intimacy of the moment was almost painful. Almost unbearable. Cathartic.

Spellbound, she hovered above the reality, anchored to it by his smoldering gaze.

Silence stretched, captivating, hypnotizing...

A loud cough shattered the enchantment like a hammer on fragile China.

"I hate to interrupt, guys, but it just dawned on me. We can't leave today."

JC's announcement catapulted Nika back to the moment with all the finesse of a dump truck.

"W-what?" Still not in a full control of all her faculties, Nika turned to her brother. "Why?"

"Because we have an appointment with the sheriff tomorrow. Remember? Ten o'clock, at the station? What would happen if we don't show up? Especially Abby."

Sweeping all ten fingers through his hair, Eli uttered, "Thunderation."

"You can say that again, brother."

As commiseration went, however, it was as fake as their neighbor's toupee.

Despite his efforts to look contrite, JC's demeanor was that of a cat who had just swallowed a plump canary.

"I guess, your departure must be postponed, then," Eli stated with a sigh.

"*Merde.*"

"Yippee-Ki-yay."

Two simultaneous exclamations burst free, as three faces turned in her direction for a final verdict. So, the last word belonged to her.

Nika gritted her teeth, wracked her brain, but common sense prevailed.

Exasperating as it was, her annoying brother was right. Again. It was crazy to jeopardize Eli's fate now, after all they've been though. Sheriff Johnson trusted them to keep the appointment. Skipping town was definitely not an option, especially for Abby.

Shit.

Disappointed, disheartened, Nika grudgingly capitulated. "Tomorrow, then. But only for a day, mind you, and not a minute longer."

While Abby's drawn face reflected her helpless defeat, JC didn't even try to mask his joy.

Idiot.

His eager nod didn't fool Nika for a moment. The moron was plotting something, she felt it deep in her bones. But what?

Must keep an eye on him.

Not for long, just until tomorrow.

A sudden *bong* of the grandfather clock knifed the silence like a serrated blade.

Ruthless, unrelenting, its chant echoed through the room like a heralding call of doom.

CHAPTER FORTY

L ater that night, snuggled in Eli's arms after an extremely satisfying and passionate reunion, Nika struggled to settle down to no avail. A heavy and dark foreboding cruised through her blood like a deadly poison. Damn that blasted grandfather clock. It spooked her to the core with its angry irate chiming. Displeased, was it? Well, so was she. No need to remind her of time ticking away, or spreading all that gloom and doom. But obviously, the clock disagreed. That old clunker issued its warning loud and clear.

Time is awasting.

Even though Nika wholeheartedly agreed with it, she was unable to do anything differently. Abby and JC must stay for another day. Eli's fate depended on it. A single day won't drastically change the course of history.

Or will it?

Shivering, Nika pressed her back tighter against Eli's body. They were spooning, her favorite sleeping position, with his hands gently caressing her enlarged stomach. The baby, too, was restless, her little limbs flaying, straining against the cocoon of Nika's womb.

"She kicked me!" Eli's chuckle tickled her nape.

"It's her way to welcome you home."

Eli scooted closer, nuzzled her nape. Naked as the day he was born, glorious in his nudity, and totally uninhibited, Eli lay behind her back, as his busy hands worked their magic. Distracted by her husband's ministrations, she shivered in pure delight. But her unease refused to fade. Like a dark, shapeless shadow, it was sneaking around her subconsciousness, elusive and terrifying.

The baby felt it too. Her daughter's nocturnal exercises were more intense than ever, like she was desperate to escape. Or alert her. Painfully attuned to the baby inside of her, Nika grew more anxious by the moment.

What's wrong, Button?

"Fierce little tyke, just like her mother." Oblivious of Nika's turmoil, Eli trailed his lips along her shoulder blade, as his left hand resting on her stomach, slid up, and cupped her beast. Why were men so fascinated with mammary glands was a constant mystery to Nika. Eli was no exception. To tease him, she arched forward, and pressed her mound into his palm. His hum of approval was almost orgasmic.

"Fearless and strong, just like her father." Placing her hands above Eli's, she brought them to her stomach, linking all three of them. She needed that connection, that tight circle of love and life and unity. Her family.

"Am I? I'm not so sure, not anymore." Coated in doubt, Eli's voice trailed into silence.

"Well, I am. You, my darling, are the strongest man I've ever known. And the bravest." She lifted his hand, kissed his open palm, inhaled his familiar sent. "But more important, you are the most wonderful human being that ever graced this earth. Decent, loyal, honest, and more beautiful than any man has a right to be, and—"

"Daisy, you're making me blush."

She didn't need to see his face to know that two patches of red bloomed on Eli's cheekbones. He was always uncomfortable when his looks were praised.

"...and you are all mine," she finished with a smile in her voice.

"I am indeed." He planted a chaste, almost reverend kiss on top of her head.

"As you are all mine."

"Yep, you got that right, Coleman." Smiling, she closed her eyes. She was so warm, so comfortable. Finally at ease. Like a cozy blanket, sleep crept slowly over her body, tucking her under its protective folds.

"Daisy?"

"Hmm?" Drowsy, buoyant, Nika kept floating toward oblivion, but Eli obviously had another idea.

"I am sorry, *ma petite.*"

"For?" She roused herself enough for an absentminded question.

"For acting the way I did earlier."

"Oh, you mean like an overbearing moron, a stupid ingrate, and a total jerk?" Nika yawned, patted his hand. "Don't mention it."

"I'm trying to apologize, Daisy." Faint irritation crept into his voice.

"You did that already. In many different ways."

"God, woman, I'm not talking about sex!"

Oh-uh. Now he was pissed. Dragging herself from the edge of a slumber, Nika drew a deep breath. "Neither was I."

"What *were* you talking about, then?"

How to explain the unexplainable? How to transfer her feelings into words?

"The way you looked at me. The way you treated Abby and JC. The way you made love to me tonight, which is, by the way, a far cry from having sex."

Tender and slow, careful because of the baby, that lovemaking was more erotic and intense than all their previous encounters put together. Nika shivered in recollection.

"You never fail to surprise me, *ma petite.* And humble me."

"Well, as long as I'm not embarrassing you, that works for me."

"Never, my wild little flower. You can never embarrass me."

"Not even when I call you beautiful?"

"Well, now that you mention it…" He chuckled, then suddenly sucked on his breath.

"What? What is it?" An instant alarm prompted her to turn around. She expected anything but the expression of utter wonderment on his face. Wide-eyed, with his mouth half open, Eli gazed at her as if awestruck. What on earth?

"The babe. She's quieted."

The breath she didn't realize she was holding whooshed out. God, he scared her. Enormously relived, Nika squinted at her protruding tummy. What do you know? The little stinker has indeed settled down. Thank God.

"Finally! I thought she was playing soccer in there."

"Is it painful? I mean, when she trashes her limbs so?"

"No, not painful, just…uncomfortable. A little."

"Poor Daisy." Eli dropped another kiss onto her shoulder, then gathered her close.

"Just a little longer, *ma petite*. Three more months."

Nika didn't have to be clairvoyant to read his mind. *August 10th, 1910.*

Their daughter's day of birth. Margaret Vera will enter this world on a sunny summer morning, delivered by the old family doctor right here, in the Coleman house. The baby conceived in 2020, and born hundred and ten years *before.*

Talk about weird.

Talk about miracles.

For a long time they lay in each other arms, both consumed by their thoughts.

"She'll have your curls, and your eyes. And, God help us, your temper."

Eli's hushed statement held a note of rueful amusement. She'd laugh, if she wouldn't be so overwhelmed. The nature of her daughter's more than unorthodox beginning never bothered her before. Until tonight.

Yes, their daughter will be the image of Nika, with her sunny-yellow ringlets, unusual violet eyes, and quick temper. At twenty-five, she'll fall in love and marry a prominent attorney, then three years later, produce a single offspring, a daughter. And in 1959, that girl will give birth to a son, who later will become a state representative from Massachusetts. Senator Lauder, their great-grandson, who found Nika in 2019, and hired her to restore his family mansion, the Coleman house...

Mindboggling.

Nika crossed her arms around her belly in an attempt to protect and shelter the precious tiny bundle inside. Three more months. Enough time to come to terms with all those bizarre circumstances. Pushing her memories deeper into her subconsciousness, she shut an imaginary lid.

The atmosphere became increasingly unnerving. Time to lighten up. Forcing humor into her voice, she lifted her face. "If she inherits your stubbornness, and controlling streak, Coleman, she'll be a holly terror."

Eli's lips curved into a faint smile. A heavy sigh later, he plopped onto his back. Missing his warmth, Nika scooted closer to his side. A deep frown marred his forehead. Her antennae unfurled all the way up. Something was bothering Eli. His anxiety was all but palpable. Gently she prodded, "What is it?"

At first he didn't answer. Seconds ticked by while her fears intensified.

Finally, Eli drew a broken breath. "If something happened to you..." Smoldering, tortured, his eyes bore into her. "Just promise me never take any chances, Daisy. Without you my life is not worth living."

A helpless plea. An urgent order. A simple truth.

Nika went with her heart, framed his beloved face in her hands.

"That goes both ways, my darling. When those deputes took you away, in handcuffs, I almost died. The only thing that kept me going was the knowledge that I can prove your innocence. And for that, I needed Abby. So, I took the key, and went to fetch her."

Nika decided to omit the awful details of that trip, resulting in her fainting, and a long, painful recovery after that. What purpose would it serve? Eli didn't need to hear about her fear of being too late, or doubts of being lost in time. Or the excruciating agony of being sucked through the tunnel of time. He was familiar with that experience firsthand when he traveled through the portal last year.

A thunderous expression crossed Eli's face. No, she didn't fool him for a moment. He swallowed his anger, cursed under his breath. To calm them both, she laid her head on his chest, listened to the strong beat of his heart, and sent a silent prayer to all the saints above. Safe, unharmed, free.

For that, she was ready to jump through that blasted time tunnel as many times as needed, and the risk will be damned.

"What about JC?" That question took her by surprise. Engrossed in her thoughts, Nika failed to switch gears fast enough to grab the meaning of Eli's question.

"What about him?"

"Why did you decide to fetch him too?"

"Oh, that. It was an accident, really, but now I'm glad it happened. You should have seen and heard him at the jail today. The clown was so convincing that for a moment there I believed his spiel, too." But her attempt at levity failed.

"What if he was discovered as a fraud? What if he was detained? What if—"

"But he wasn't. Relax, Eli. Tomorrow he'll play his role of your snooty, esteemed attorney one last time, and then get back to where he belongs. No harm no foul."

"Dear God, Daisy, *no harm?* Really?" Shaking his head, seemingly at a loss for words, Eli stared at her. After a long moment, he managed to find his voice, "And what of Alex? Truth be told, I'm surprised that he agreed to let Abby and you go without him."

"He didn't. He had every intention to come with us, but the grandfather clock prevented it."

"What? How?"

"I'm not sure, but that old cantankerous thing blasted Alex all the way across the room. Knocked him far away, and dropped him like a sack of potatoes. That's why Abby is so frantic."

"Poor Alex. I hope he is okay, and not badly hurt."

"I do, too."

Nika almost choked on her guilt. Alex, her friend, her sidekick in all her childhood shenanigans, her business partner. Her staunched supporter, her wonderful protector. He managed to save her hide more times than she cared to count. And last year, he saved her life. If not for his discovery of the two graves at the *Bosque Bello* cemetery, Nika wouldn't have made it. She was barely functioning when Alex dragged her from bed, and then straight to that historic cemetery to show her the glaring proof of her own grave with a heartbreaking inscription.

Daisy Coleman, Beloved Wife and Mother, The timeless miracle.

She remembered her confusion like it was yesterday.

"I don't understand. What does this mean?"

And Alex's cheerful reply, *"It means, you got back. Somehow, you got back to your Eli. Look at the date. Yours is the only one, without a date of birth. Because, hey, they couldn't put your real birthday, May 27, 1990, now, could they? And besides, how many Daisies were running around Fernandina in 1909 who qualified for the role? On top of it, being the 'timeless' miracle? Get it?"*

Yes, she owed her life, not to mention her sanity, to Alex. And how did she repay him? By separating him from the woman he loved, and jeopardizing his own life in the process. Selfish bitch. Blinded by a single goal to save her husband, Nika inadvertently put her cousin at risk. And for that, she'll never forgive herself.

"So, Alex and Abby, huh?" Eli's rumble of a chuckle put a stop to her self-flagellation.

"Yeah, Alex and Abby. Are you're okay with that?"

"Okay? My dear, I'm ecstatic! There is no better man than our Alex. I'm proud to be related to him. That reminds me." Eli cleared his throat, then, swinging his legs, sat on the end of the bed with his back to her. "You know, the most peculiar thing happened when I was in that cell. I'm afraid you might think I've lost my mind."

"Let me be the judge of that. Tell me. What happened." But she already knew.

"One night, when I was at my lowest, I decided to write a farewell later to you. And suddenly..." he got up, and unmindful of his nakedness, went to stand by the window. "I felt the presence of...someone. And I saw..."

"Let me guess. You saw Alex."

"Yes!" He turned to her, his expression a mix of wonder and disbelief, "Like he was just there, standing in front of me. But... how do you know?"

"How do you think? Alex really was there."

"But you just told me that the clock—"

"It has nothing to do with it, or the portal. As crazy as it sounds, my cousin traveled in his mind."

"Thunderation! How is it even possible?"

"I don't know, but it seems like Alex has finally come to his gift."

"And what gift is that?"

"The Violet Eyes Gift I told you about. Remember? My great-grandfather, the clairvoyant?"

"How can I ever forget that memorable revelation."

"Well, Alex, like *Verochka,* and yours truly, also inherited the violet eyes of our ancestor. *Verochka* has an amazing intuition. I can manipulate time. So, it was only natural to suspect that he has some kind of a hidden talent, too."

"Quite natural, I suppose. And still, it boggles the mind."

"Stick with Morrises, Coleman, and soon you'll believe in fairies."

Eli chuckled. "No doubt, *ma petite.* I already believe in time travels, and all the miraculous things such as Internet, Skype, and television. What are fairies compared to that?" Absently, Eli rubbed his chin with two fingers. "But back to Alex. So, his gift is...?"

"An ability to travel great distances in his mind."

"Even between centuries?"

"So it seems."

"Fascinating. A man of many talents, our Alex."

"You can say that again. But let me tell you, he was not fascinated at the time. Far from it. Those mind travels shook him to the core."

"I can only imagine."

"I highly doubt it. Apparently, all his senses go with him, even if his body stays behind. When he saw you, he smelled the stench of that dingy cell."

"For that, I am sincerely sorry."

Daisy patted the side of the bed in silent demand.

Eli complied, coming back, and sliding between the covers. She scooted closer, placed her head on his chest, and felt immediately better.

"So, after he came back, so to speak, he was shaken. And disgusted with the way you were treated. He was dead set to come to your rescue, but fate, or that stupid clock, interfered."

"Huh. I wonder why is that." Eli mulled it over for a long moment. "Wrong timing? Rotten luck?"

"Beats me. The mystery that we will never solve, I'm afraid."

Spent, Nika settled comfortably against Eli's side, and started to drift.

A faint *bong* of the grandfather clock from downstairs sent shivers along her spine.

Even half-asleep, she couldn't squelch a feeling of dread that slithered through her.

CHAPTER FORTY-ONE

Alex was not a pushover, far from it. Why then did he let *Verochka* browbeat him into resting? Because she was *Verochka*, that's why. Stubborn as a thousand mules, and canny as a vixen, she was the only one who had the power to sway him to do anything she wanted. And dammit, she succeeded again. Laying fully dressed on his bed in semidarkness, Alex played the events of the evening in his mind.

"If you refuse to sleep, I will keep you company."

Obstinate and strong she might be, but Verochka *was pushing toward the octogenarian line, the fact he, as a smart man, chose not to voice aloud. Instead, he opted for a safer argument.*

"Gorgeous, you're probably jetlagged after that long flight around the world."

"Nope. I'm fit as a fiddle."

Dammit, now what?

"Verochka, this is ridiculous. You must get some sleep. It's almost midnight."

But all his reasonings fell flat onto her tiny, delicate ears.

"I might be old, my dear, but far from feeble. I can keep up with you youngsters in more ways than one."

"In a drinking marathon? Absolutely. In a card game? No question. Your titanium stomach and renowned poker face are truly legendary. But your exquisite body needs to rest, and recharge its batteries."

"Huh. So does yours."

"I can't sleep. Honestly, I can't."

"Fine, don't. Just lay in bed, then. Give that busy brain of yours some quiet time."

"Verochka."

"Alex."

A high arch of the single brow was arrogant, and as familiar as his own name.

Damn, his grandmother won't give an inch. Headstrong as she was beautiful, Verochka *had the ability to try the patience of a saint. Far from being a saint, Alex still prided himself on being a very patient man. But, darn, his grandmother made it difficult, if not impossible, to keep his self-restrain. On the verge of exploding, he rubbed his head hard enough to scrape some skin, then let out a string of very rude and inventive curses. Now both brows flew up, disappearing under her bangs.*

"Very impressive, my boy. You make your Russian ancestors proud. But."

And his blue-blooded, socialite grandmother executed a few sentences that demonstrated who was the real master in cursing.

Game: Counter-Strike. Level: God. Or Goddess.

A whisper of her native French made those extremely foul words ridiculously sexy.

In a staggering contrast, a truly serene smile curved her lovely lips. A picture of pure innocence, she gazed at him, all sunny and unruffled. Alex blinked. For a brief moment he doubted his own ears. Did she really said what he heard? Then she winked at him, and the mischief all but danced a jig in her violet eyes.

Yep, she sure did.

"Wow, Verochka. I bow to your superior skill." Alex inclined his head in mock surrender.

"Thank you, my dear." Pleased, she nodded regally. "So, are we done with this ridiculous challenge of wills?"

"Seems like."

"*Good. As an indisputable winner, I declare my prize: a few hours of rest for both of us. Or, I'll stay awake, and stick to your side like white on rice. And make you miserable— not to mention, guilty as hell. Denying your old grandmother her beauty sleep?* C'est dommage!"

"*Old grandmother, my ass.*"

Despite his mood, Alex chuckled. Damn if she didn't make him feel better.

"*Okay, Gorgeous, you wore me down. I'll go to my room, and bunk for a while.*"

"*Wonderful, and I'll take the guest room, and do the same. In the morning, we'll put our heads together, and strategize. Like my* Papa *always said, morning is wiser than evening.*"

The wisdom of that old Russian saying always evaded Alex. Who declared that? And why was morning wiser than evening? On top of that, the point of proposed strategizing seemed moot as hell. What could they do? Abby was there, and they were here, with not the foggiest on how to change that situation. Should they go to the Coleman house, and wait there? Or, stay here, and see what the next day brings? Frankly, facing that blasted grandfather clock was the last thing Alex wanted to do. But the old junker was the only link between him and Abby, between his time and hers. A fragile, almost ephemeral, but link nonetheless.

God, Abby, don't make me wait for much longer. Please.

Running on fumes had finally caught up with him. Suddenly tired to the marrow, Alex shut his eyes, and pressed both thumbs against his eye sockets.

Gotta rest, pal.

Irritating or not, his grandmother was right. He was whipped. As in totally. Going to bed for a few hours of shuteye seemed not such a bad idea after all.

With a helpless oath, he rose to his feet from the sofa, and ambled toward his room.

"Alex?" His grandmother's voice stopped him in midmotion. Coming closer, Verochka framed his face with both hands and looked deep into his eyes. "She'll be back, our Abby. I'm sure of that."

"What if she won't?"

And the deep-seated fear he refused to acknowledged until now, sprang to life.

He hadn't doubted for a second Abby's intention to return. It's that fucking grandfather clock he had reservations about. The blasted junker had a mind of its own. And he hated Alex for a reason that still eluded his comprehension.

"Don't you dare to question that girl!" Suddenly incensed, Verochka slapped him with her words. Like a lasso, her voice lashed out, raising a full octave. "Abby loves you! She'll come back. If not today or tomorrow, then in a few days. It's just a matter of time." More gently, she added, "Have a hope, mon cheri.*"*

Rising on her toes, Verochka kissed his cheek, and completely disarmed him.

Not trusting his voice, Alex nodded, and closed the door behind him.

Okay, so here he was, in his bed, exhausted, but fully awake. Try as he might, he failed to shut his brain off. Tomorrow loomed on the horizon, vague and murky as his thoughts. Alex flung his bended arm across his face. Must rest. Must have a clear head for tomorrow. Must think. A sudden burst of brilliant light jolted him upright. Eerie, otherworldly colors swam lazily across the room, distorting the picture like a swirling of kaleidoscope.

Loud chanting of the clock. Shimmering of air. My God, it was happening again!

Nauseated, lightheaded, Alex shut his eyes.

A wisp of breeze. A strange earthy smell. A chirping of birds.

He was outside, sitting on something hard and wet. Grass? Alex dragged his eyes half open. Sure thing. Grass. Green and dewy.

Gingerly he touched the soft blades, dragged his fingers through it. Yes, he was outside, alright. Squinting, he lifted his eyes upward. A blazing sun, a whisper of a rainbow, a cerulean sky. He recognized that unmistakable shade of Florida blue even in his sleep. So, he was still home. But where? And most important, when?

A soft sound of neighing from somewhere behind...

Neighing? As in horses? More curious than alarmed, Alex turned his head. Sure enough, a gorgeous white horse met his eyes. And what a beauty!

Graceful, unmindful of its surroundings, the horse was grazing lazily in front of a spacious grey structure with open double doors. A barn? A tall fence separated the building from the rolling green sea of lawn. He didn't have to be a hardcore equestrian to recognize a coral. When a couple of bay horses ambled outside, his assumption turned into assurance.

Not a barn, but stables.

Okay, so he was near stables. Yippee ki yay. The question remains: where and when. And why.

The gentle white horse shook its head violently, let out a blood-chilling scream, and danced backward. What on earth?

He had no time to blink, much less think, as a black tornado burst from the stables. Alex sucked on his breath. As magnificent as it was humongous, the stallion galloped around, clearly enraged. Even from a distance Alex had no trouble seeing its eyes rolling, or hear the thundering hooves of that black monster. Then it reared up, froze for a long moment on its hind legs, pawing the air furiously.

The wild, primitive cries it emitted were pure madness. Alex shivered. Where were the people? A stable of that size must have a lot of helping hands. So, where were they? That beast must be calmed down, and pronto, before it hurt itself.

Or someone.

A flurry of movement in his peripheral vision caught his attention. He turned his head, and all the blood froze in his veins.

Abby!

Tall, willowy, dressed in a long skirt, with her gorgeous hair hidden behind the riding hat. It was impossible to mistake her for anyone else. Without a moment's hesitation, she ran toward an enraged horse.

No! Has she lost her mind?

"Abby, get back! Get away from it!"

He was yelling on the top of his lungs, but not a sound broke free. Numb all over, trapped in this nightmare, Alex helplessly watched as Abby approached the huge stallion. The beast started to dance nervously, shaking its enormous head.

"Here, Sultan, here boy. It's okay. Come to me, baby." Her clear voice reached his ears. But the mad creature was having none of it. Billowing steam from its nostrils accompanied the shrill screams that curled Alex's blood. Unerringly, Abby inched forward. Her outstretched hand was butted furiously away by the mighty shake of the stallion's head.

My God, what is she doing?

He started to run. It was like plowing through dense, cold jelly. His arms clawed the air, his legs pumped frantically, but to no avail. The invisible shackles immobilized him, holding him imprisoned to the spot.

"Abby! No, get away!"

His voice thundered in his ears. His deafening cries echoed in his head.

Soundless. Unmoving. Helpless.

Two men ran from the stables. Alex recognized his cousin. Thank God. "JC! Help her!"

But both men stumbled to an abrupt stop, eyeing the picture in front of them in mute fascination. Goddamit!

Alex was too far away. Even if he had control over his limbs, he'd never reach her in time.

"Abby, my God, Abby..."

He watched in a shocked stupor as Abby finally reached the black horse, then put her hand on its shoulder. For a moment the great beast quieted.

Thank God!

A shaggy mongrel ran from the stables, emitting deep vicious barks. That's all it took. The stallion, enraged and spooked anew, flung his huge head, and pushed Abby violently away. Rearing up, it towered over her for a split second, before dropping heavily down. Straight on Abby.

Frozen in the horrific nightmare, Alex watched her fell. Watched like two men finally ran forward, and dragged her away. She lay totally still. Unmoving.

That huge dog crawled closer, and put her head on Abby's chest. Then it lifted its head, and sent a blood-chilling mournful cry.

And the world went black.

From a great distance, he heard a helpless chanting 'No, no, no.'

Something firm and unyielding wound up around him.

Arms. Warm, strong.

An unmistakable fragrance of Chloe.

Verochka.

Alex was shaking so badly his teeth clunked in his mouth.

Must get away. Must help. Abby!

Alex jerked away from the embrace, but *Verochka* tightened her arms.

"Ssh-ssh, sweetheart. You're okay. You're safe."

"A-abby, A-abby..."

"I know, baby, I know. We will figure it out. We'll get her back."

"No!" Fighting in earnest, Alex flung her arms away. "She's...she's hurt. I must...do something. I must..."

"Hurt? Our Abby is hurt?" *Verochka*, unfazed by his harsh treatment, grabbed his hands, stilling him. "How do you know that?"

"I was there. I saw..."

"*Mon Dieu*, that's why you were shouting on top of your lungs. I was afraid that someone has broken in, hurting you."

"No, no, no! It's Abby. She's..."

His voice broke, as the horrific images burned in his brain slowly swam forward.

Harsh sobs rocketed his body, the flood of tears burned his eyelids, but Alex refused to surrender. Shaking violently, he fisted both hands until his knuckles went white. *Verochka's* calm voice cut the silence.

"Tell me what did you see."

Unsteady, fighting for every intake of breath, Alex told her, starting from the time he found himself sitting on the grass, and ending at the hideous moment when Abby fell.

"Oh, God, no!" With both hands, *Verochka* covered her mouth. Her soft moan echoed through his skull like the crack of a bullet. "Is she...?"

"I don't know. But I must believe she's alive. Or I'll go mad."

After a long moment, *Verochka* was silent. Tears that ran down her face were ruthlessly wiped away.

"She's alive. I can feel it. Abby is alive, but hurt." Rising to her feet, she grabbed Alex's hand. "We must bring her home. Now."

"Don't you think I know that? But how?"

"We'll think of something. We must! And fast. Because Abby's time is running out." She was almost at the door. "What are you waiting for, Alexander? Let's go!"

"Go? Where?"

"Where else? The Coleman house, of course."

CHAPTER FORTY-TWO

Eli was not a violent man. But he barely restrained himself from wrapping both hands around JC's neck and squeezing the life out of him. The imbecile! The moron! The miserable jerk!

Wasn't he advised on many occasions that Sultan was dangerous? That no one, absolutely no one, but Eli was able to ride that stallion? That it was crazy to even approach the black beast? Of course, he was! But did he listen? Oh, no! Mr. High and Mighty blithely disregarded all warnings, and took the proverbial bull by the horns. Idiot! He swore out loud, pressed both thumbs to his eye sockets hard enough to see the exploding stars.

Shouldn't allow him and Abby go to the stables alone. Should've accompanied them. If Eli was there, the great black monster wouldn't get spooked. And Abby wouldn't be hurt.

Thunderation.

But, God almighty, how was he to know that JC harbored such an infantile notion? How would any of them know?

Because he was JC. Because he wasn't trustworthy. Because he was a know-it-all stupid clown, who shouldn't be even here.

Eli swoped the paperweight from his desk, then heaved it across the room. The sharp crack was greatly satisfying. For about a second. Damn it all to hell and back!

The morning promenade suggested by JC hadn't sat well with Eli from the beginning. As soon as they returned from the visit with the sheriff, the slimy weasel asked to see the stables before returning to his own time. Eli didn't like it, but he owed the man. And Eli always paid his debts. So, against his better judgement, he agreed. And regretted it ever since.

Should've paid attention to your gut, Coleman.

Should've, would've. What point was it now to beat his head against the wall? Or break more valuables. The deed was done.

Heavy and merciless, Eli's guilt tore him apart.

Why didn't he accompany JC and Abby? Thunderation.

But the business matters he ignored for quite some time, demanded his immediate attention. There were numerous reports sitting on his desk he needed to read, urgent messages to address. The Coleman business enterprises were vast, complex, and quite challenging. Eli couldn't help the unfortunate incident of being locked up in jail, but now that he was free, he was chomping at the bit to delve into the matters at hands. So, instead of going with the pair to the stables, Eli bowed out of horseback riding, and closeted himself in his office. Until the screams ripped through his seclusion and all the hell broke loose.

Abby, his beautiful girl, his baby sister. Broken like a doll. Unconscious. Barely clinging to life. Two dislocated collarbones, shattered leg, broken arm. And God only knew what internal damage Sultan's hooved might have cause. Miraculously, Abby's beautiful face and her head were untouched. Small blessings.

Eli wanted to shoot the blasted horse. Daisy prevented his rash decision. It was not Sultan's fault he felt threatened and acted as the wild creature he was. Reason prevailed, but Eli swore to ship that beast to the slaughter if, God forbid, Abby didn't survive. As daunting as the thought was, his sister's predicament was really grave.

The old family doctor examined Abby, all the while shaking his head. After injecting something into her thigh, he then took Eli by the arm and stepped them into the hallway.

"The damage your sister's body sustained is too extensive, Mr. Coleman. I won't sugarcoat it, it's life threatening. All I can do is administer morphine, to make Miss Abby more comfortable. She'll be sleeping now. I am sorry, sir."

"What can be done, Doctor. Should I call a Concilium of experts? Move Abby to the clinic in Switzerland? What?"

The old doctor sent him a glance full of regret and sympathy.

Eli's heart almost stopped. Powerless, frightened, he barely held himself from coming apart at the seams. Or pounding the poor old man.

"You can call a Concilium, of course. But any doctor worth his salt will tell you the same thing. You need a miracle. As to a clinic in Switzerland, I'm afraid Miss Abby will not weather such a trip. I am truly sorry, sir."

Miracle. They needed a bloody miracle.

Eli raked all ten fingers through his already disheveled hair. He was helpless as a newborn babe, and useless as tits on a boar hog. What good were his money and influence? He was unable to do a blasted thing to help Abby. He failed his sister.

I'm so sorry, my little Papillon.

His shoulders hunched under the horrendous weight of guilt as Eli slowly left his office. Defeated, he felt ancient, like he had aged a decade over the course of last hours.

He walked closer to his sister's bedroom, letting out a string of impotent curses, before stepping inside. Converted to a sickroom, this once beautiful space fit for royalty was now dim and stifling. An offensive odor of something acrid and overpowering saturated every inch of the room.

The stench of desperation.

Swallowing the lump in his throat, Eli quietly approached the bed. Was it his imagination, or the room has shrunk in size? The big canopied bed dominated the space. The prone figure of his sister, pale as marble, swaddled in bandages, reminded him of a small rag doll. Broken. Torn. Lifeless.

No. God, please no! Take me instead, but let Abby live.

Daisy sat beside Abby and held her hand. She didn't move a muscle, but he knew she sensed his presence.

"How is she?"

Without turning, his wife shook her head. "Same."

Daisy's back was ramrod straight, but the small tremor of her hands betrayed her strain. When she finally shifted her dry eyes in his direction, Eli sucked in a breath. Smoldering, angry, her gaze all but scorched him.

"It's all my fault." Hoarse, but firm, her voice held a note of final resignation.

"What are you talking about? If someone is at fault, it is me! I should have been there. I should have handled Sultan. I should—"

"*I* should have been there! Instead of taking a nap, I should have accompanied my brother and Abby to the stables. Then I could have slowed time enough for her to run away. But I decided to take a freaking nap! Dammit."

So, Daisy was blaming herself. Why wasn't he surprised? But, thunderation, she was pregnant. It was only natural for her to become exhausted after their long meeting with the sheriff. As soon as they returned home, Eli insisted she take a short rest, all but pushing her toward the bedroom.

Now his fearless time traveler who didn't lose her head for a second after Abby's accident, who didn't leave his sister's side for a moment since, was all but falling to pieces.

"Daisy, listen to me," Eli walked closer to his wife, then pulled her to her feet. "It is not your fault. Stop blaming yourself, *ma petite.*"

Forlorn, clearly unconvinced, she shook her head. "I should have been there."

Lifeless, matted, her infamous unruly ringlets framed her drawn face. Daisy hugged herself tight, shut her amethyst eyes, in a futile attempt to hold her emotions together. His heart broke to see the woman he loved strained to the breaking point.

With a soft oath, Eli hauled her into his arms. For a moment she stood motionless and erect, and then, as if a switch was turned off, Daisy melted against him.

Tears she held at bay finally won the battle of wills. Vibrating from within, she shook in his embrace so badly, Eli swore he heard the rattle of her bones. Brutal, almost savage, Daisy's grief tore at his heart, breaking him apart.

"Ssh-ssh, *ma petite*. Don't despair so. There is nothing we can do, and blaming ourselves will only make us more miserable. We both must be strong. For Abby."

An eon later, she finally quieted in his arms. The meltdown passed, thank God. Slowly, she pulled back, whipped her wet face, and looked him square in the eye. Whatever Eli expected, was not an expression of fearless determination.

His little warrior was back. Eli held his breath.

"Okay, Coleman. Our pity party is officially over." For emphasis, she chopped her hand down, as if cutting something in two. "And now, we must do the only thing that can help Abby. We must take her back, or forward, to the twenty-first century."

Taken aback, Eli gaped at her. Did she just suggested to transport Abby to another time?

"But...Daisy, you heard the doctor—"

"Screw the doctor! What does he know? She needs medical help. *Real* medical help. She needs a surgery in a modern hospital. And she needs it pronto."

"Are you proposing to move her... now?"

"Yes."

"Maybe we should wait for some other time—"

"There is no other time, Eli. Abby doesn't have much time. She needs help. She needs Alex."

"The doctor said we need a miracle, Daisy. A miracle! As much as I like and respect Alex, he is not the answer. Allowing he's able to breach the curtain of time, that is."

"A miracle, is it?" She plunked both hands akimbo onto her hips. "Well, let's *make* a bloody miracle, Coleman. Let's get Abby to 2021."

Whatever he was about to say, got stuck in his throat, as another voice piped in.

"I agree with Nika."

Missed by both of them, JC hovered on the threshold. Eli glared at the newcomer. The gall of the man! Rage filled him to the brim.

"Do yourself a favor, Morris. Get the hell away, and stay away. And if you have an ounce of self-preservation, or a dollop of common sense in that overblown clump you call a head, you'll stay away from me. As far as you can. Or I won't be responsible for the consequences."

"I understand how you feel, Eli—"

"Oh, do you now?"

"Yes. And if I were in your shoes—"

"My shoes? What about Abby's shoes? Look at her! It's all your fault!"

JC winced, but held his ground. "I know, and I am truly sorry. I cursed myself a thousand times, believe me, but there is nothing I can do, except...", he swallowed, casting his eyes toward Abby, and quickly away, "... going through portal, and fetching help. Fetching Alex."

"Forget about it. I'm not trusting you with Abby's wellbeing. If someone will go, it must be me."

"No! Eli, listen, you cannot go. What will happen if you disappear only a day after your release? And Nika is pregnant. It is dangerous for her to make a trip. So, it has to be me. Please, let me do it. I need to. Please."

Unrelenting, Eli was about to snap back, when Daisy's quiet voice interrupted, "He's right, Eli. It is unwise for you to vanish now.

And as much as I want to, I can't go, either. JC must go, and bring Alex."

"Thunderation."

Swearing was an exercise in utter futility, but Eli indulged nevertheless.

Time was running out, time that Abby didn't have. So, as upsetting as it was, the incorrigible bastard was the only one who must go for help. Eli relented.

"Alright, Morris. But if you fail, don't ever show your face here again."

A rueful half smile tugged at JC's lips. "If I fail, Coleman, I will never be able show my face *anywhere*." Once again serious, he gazed at Eli. A resolute expression on his face left no doubt of his true intention. "But I won't fail. I swear. Give me your key, Eli. Trust me that much. I'll go immediately."

Eli ignored a tiny twitch of guilt in his gut. Yes, the trip was dangerous, and fraught with great risk. But if was nothing compared to the risk to Abby's life.

What did he care if the bastard disappeared between times? It was much less than he deserved. Eli nodded curtly.

"Meet me downstairs in ten minutes. I'll bring the key."

Not allowing himself to dwell on his decision, Eli stomped out of the room.

CHAPTER FORTY-THREE

The trip to the Coleman house passed in a frenzied blur. *Verochka* was driving, the fact Alex appreciated more than he was able to express. He was in no condition to function, much less to operate a car. His grandmother, bless her heart, always drove like a NASCAR champ on steroids. Today she broke her own record. In less time than he could blink, they zipped through the main gates to the estate and flew toward the mansion. A squeal of brakes sent a fountain of small rocks flying upward. The abrupt stop careened the Porsche sideways. Any other time Alex would snap her head off for treating his beloved Baby that way, but not now. Now all that mattered was getting inside the house, and confronting the grandfather clock. What will they do after? Beat the damn thing? Demand a safe passage through time? He shrugged off the annoying thoughts running through his mind. They were sure to think of something.

Like what?

Like any-effing-thing.

As soon as the car stopped, Alex jumped out and started to run. Two steps later, he froze on the spot. A shiny red Corvette sat in the middle of the driveway, with its driver's door hanging open. Nika's Coco. No, Abby's. The convertible belonged to her now. Yesterday, in her hurry, Abby must have forgot to shut the door, and lock the car. True enough, the car fob was laying on the leather mat beneath the driver's seat. Picking it up, Alex inhaled the familiar fragrance of Abby's perfume. She smelled like that all over. Her shoulders, the column of her neck, the valley between her breasts...Shutting his eyes, Alex fought his memories. Dammit, was it only yesterday? Seems like eons ago. Helpless under the assault, suddenly numb, he caressed the small fob. Abby. Unmoving, hurt, fallen down.

He shook his head. Denial sprang forward, infusing his resolve. She was alive. Hurt, but alive. He was dead sure of it. Now all he must do is bring her home.

Hold on, Princess. Just a little longer. I'm coming.

He closed the car door, then pocketed the fob.

"Alex? What are you waiting for?" Clicking heels announced his grandmother's arrival. "Let's get inside of that dungeon, shall we? Time's awasting."

Dungeon. Strange epithet for that beauty of the southern architecture Nika so painstakingly restored. But of all people, *Verochka* was the only one who disliked it from the first. Nika was enchanted with it, Abby loved it to distraction, Alex considered it once in a lifetime business opportunity. But *Verochka?* His scary intuitive grandmother, after taking one look at the white structure, labeled it a dungeon, and claimed it gave her the creeps. He always wondered why that was. Her Violet Eyes Gift at work, or something more? No time to ponder on it now.

Nodding, Alex hurried to the main doors. Thank God he had the keys that Abby dropped onto the antic coffee table. He didn't remember picking them up, but he was sure as hell glad he did, because Alex hated to add breaking and entering to the numerous redlight stop offences his grandmother undoubtedly collected today.

Okay, here goes. Stepping inside, Alex strained his ears for any sound. But there was none. Dead silent, the Coleman house struck him as eerie. Ominous. Or was *Verochka's* mood rubbing off on him?

Alex turned to his grandmother, who was hovering on the threshold. Her unease and reluctance were written all over her expressive face. In an unconscious gesture, she hugged herself as if to ward off evil.

Damn, she was scared, visibly shaking from her tousled blond bangs to the tips of her little toes.

"Maybe you should stay outside, Gorgeous?"

"And leave you alone to face the music? No way."

"I'm not afraid of the house, *Verochka*. It's that blasted clock I have my reservations about."

"Well, then, let's face that clunker together."

Resolutely she stepped inside, then closed the door. Squaring her elegant shoulders, *Verochka* took Alex by the hand, and together they started down the foyer, toward the place where the old guardian of the Coleman house stood proudly throughout centuries.

And here it was, the infamous grandfather clock. That magnificent marvel of English engineering circa 1827, stood six feet tall, in all its golden glory.

Like a mirror, its polished mahogany case gleamed mysteriously in the semi-darkness. If Alex didn't know better, he would never believe that the clock was anything more than a priceless object d'art. But it was much more.

Under its golden surface, hiding in plain view was the portal between times.

Alive. That bastard was alive. And waiting.

Cold shivers ran along Alex's spine. Casting a quick glance at his grandmother to gauge her reaction, he tightened his grip on her small cold hand. A deep frown marred *Verochka's* white as snow face. But her sparkling eyes shone with deep rooted resolve. No doubt about it: his *Valkyrie* of a grandmother was set on the mission. A throbbing theme from Mission Impossible thundered in his mind ear. Dammit, that was not funny. Abby was hurt. She needed help. He must get to her as soon as possible, one way or another. But how? Glaring and cursing at the blasted clock will get him nowhere. While he debated his next move, *Verochka* stepped closer to the clock, faced it square on.

What was she doing?

In mute fascination, Alex watched as his grandmother placed both hands onto the clock's shiny face.

"I know you can hear me." Quiet, soft, her voice reverberated through the hushed silence. "I know *what* you are. I have a great favor to ask. Please allow us passage. Just this one time. We do not have the key, but it is imperative we travel back. Abby is in a bad shape. She's hurt, maybe even dying. We must get her help. We must bring her here. Without you, that girl has no chance. You know her better than anyone. You let her pass through the curtain of time to pursue her dream. Please, don't let that dream perish."

After a charged moment, she stepped back, took a deep breath. "You are the time machine. Magnificent, awesome. Magical. But even that is nothing compared to love. Time is insignificant, but love is eternal. A true timeless miracle. It will endure. It will overcome all obstacles."

Taking Alex's hand, she brought it forward, lay it onto the clock. He expected the jolt of electricity, braced for it. But the mahogany case under his palm was soft as velvet, cool as water. Speechless, Alex gazed at his hand.

I'll be darned!

"I'm asking you to let us through," *Verochka's* voice cut through his confusion. "Just this one time. Please. I know you can do it."

For a second, there was nothing. Alex's hope plummeted. *Verochka's* emotional plea was useless.

And what *did you expect? A bloody miracle?*

Suddenly, the air began to swirl in a slow lazy motion. As if awakened, the face of the clock lit up. Golden bright rays illuminated the room as a deep sonorous *bong* cut the silence. An eerie shimmering pulsed all around, distorting the shapes and contours. My God, was it really happening? Or was he imagining things?

Verochka's sharp intake of breath was all the assurance Alex needed.

Not an illusion. The portal was opening.

Astonishing!

Keeping his left palm firmly on the clock, Alex grabbed his grandmother with his right hand, tugged her closer.

"Hold on to me, Gorgeous. No matter what, don't let go."

CHAPTER FORTY-FOUR

"**T**hunderation!"

"Oh, my god!"

Two simultaneous yelps broke through the incessant ringing in Alex's ears.

Male voices. Familiar.

The silence that followed those exclamations was deafening. Did he imagine it? Still reeling, queasy, Alex dragged his eyes halfway open, and tried to focus. Not an easy task. The residual swirling still remained, even as the eerie shimmering faded. After a long moment, the shapes and forms slowly began to crystallized into the clear picture.

The foyer. The sweeping staircase. The posh furniture.

The Coleman house.

Did they really make it? Did they jump from 2021 to 1910? Afraid to hope, Alex concentrated on the two frozen figures in the room.

Eli and JC.

Wide-eyed, open mouthed, they both gaped at him in horrified stupor. Eli's jaw sawed helplessly back and forth. JC's Adam apple jumped up and down. Stunned, both were blinking furiously as if trying to clear their visions. Amusing under any other circumstance, now this mute scene failed to produce comic relief.

Equally shocked, Alex swallowed audibly, and looked back over his shoulder. And here it was, the infamous grandfather clock, the guardian of the portal.

His nemesis. Abby's savior.

Its golden face shone, its mahogany case gleamed, its pendulum swayed in a lazy rhythm. Softly, it ticked the time as any normal and ordinary clock.

And who are you kidding, you old bastard?

Alive. Waiting. Impatient.

Hurry. Time's awasting.

Alex heard the words as if someone uttered them aloud. What on earth was that? He could swear he heard the urgent warning, loud and clear. Dammit, has he developed some kind of a hearing hallucination?

Yeah, that's all he needed for the full measure right now. Alex glared at the clock.

Bizarre. Astonishing. Unbelievable.

Snap out of it, pal. You are here on borrowed time. Better start moving, and fast. If that portal closes before you find Abby, her chance of survival is nil.

The urgent command of his inner voice yanked him out of his stupor.

What was he waiting for? Properly chastised, Alex was about to spring into action, when the vigorous wringing in his arms halted his progress. Twisting and sputtering, a small woman clasped in his arms fought violently to extricate herself. *Verochka!* God, he all but forgot about her!

"*Merde,* Alex, let me go! You're squeezing the living lights out of me."

Slightly disheveled, out of breath, but no worth for wear, thank God. Physically, she came through like a champ, but what about her emotional state?

Verochka's desperate thrashing was accompanied by the combination of French and Russian words, none of them fit for the general public. Immensely relived, Alex removed his hands from around his grandmother. If *Verochka* was cursing like a sailor, then she was okay.

"Sorry, Gorgeous, sorry."

"That's okay. I didn't need those few last breaths anyway." Quickly orienting herself, *Verochka* let out an exuberant cry.

"Eli! JC! *Mon Dieu!*"

Alex watched as Eli took a tentative step forward. His obvious befuddlement was fading, but not quick enough. Seemingly stunned, he turned, and gazed at the pair of them like they had suddenly sprouted wings.

"Sweet Baby Jesus! *Verochka!* Alex! Is that really you?"

"That's really us, my dear." With a brilliant smile, his grandmother hurried toward Eli, and enfolded him in a bear hug. "Oh, I'm so happy to see you!"

A brief hesitation later, he returned the embrace, but gingerly, like *Verochka* was an apparition he was afraid to shatter.

"My Lord, but... how...?" Then his questing eyes bore into Alex. As truth finally dawned, Eli let out a helpless little oath. "Thunderation."

"You can say that again, brother."

JC found his voice at last. "Grandmother, Cuz, what are you doing here?"

Something snapped inside. A blood red mist obscured his vision.

Shaking from within, Alex strode forward, and grabbed his cousin by the lapels. A violent shake sent JC's head wiggling like a bobble doll. Revved, he repeated the process, jerking his cousin to his toes. "You fucking coward! How could you? Why didn't you help her?"

Bam.

His fist to the bastard's jaw felt extremely rewarding, but not as much as seeing JC cringe in fear. Alex's hand sung with pain. He was beyond reasoning, and unraveling fast. He didn't give a damn.

Stunned, JC stumbled a few steps back. "Are you nuts, Cousin? What the hell was that for?"

"Oh, you mean you don't know? Well, let me enlighten you, *Cousin.*"

His right fist flew up for a repeat performance, but *Verochka's* loud voice halted his intention. "Stop! Alex, stop that immediately. That's not helping!"

For good measure, she jumped in between them, and literally hung onto Alex's uplifted arm.

"That's a matter of opinion, Gorgeous."

Still riding the last wave of his rage, Alex could effortlessly shake her off. But, for goodness' sake, it was *Verochka.* Damn if he let his anger spew its ugly venom onto his grandmother. Shaking from the aftermath, still unsteady, Alex capitulated. "Say thanks to our grandmother, you piece of shit."

"Okay, if it will make you feel better, you can pound on him to your heart's content but later. Now we have more pressing issue at hand." And like a self-appointed commander-in-chief, his grandmother started issuing orders in that no bullshit tone of voice Alex was familiar with. "JC, stay away from your cousin. Eli, take Alex to Abby immediately. And you," she turned her smoldering eyes on him, "go get your fiancée, and let's head back. I'm not sure how long the passage will be open."

God, she was so right. Their allotted time here was limited, and precious. And he wasted half of it by engaging in a stupid brawl with JC.

So, who was the bigger moron?

Mollified, Alex cursed under his breath, before turning to Eli. "Where is Abby?"

"Upstairs, in her room. I'll take you."

"I know where it is. Stay here, and keep an eye on that miserable piece of garbage. And for God's sake, don't let him anywhere near me, or I won't answer for the consequences."

With that, Alex bounded up the grand staircase, taking two steps at the time. Behind him Eli's deep voice cut through the tension, "Forgive me, my dear. I'm so flabbergasted, I forgot my manners. Would you like some refreshments?"

"Thank you, *mon ami*, but there is no time. We must get back as soon as possible."

There is no time.

His grandmother's reminder doubled his speed. Hurrying ahead, Alex swirled around the corner, and on the run approached Abby's bedroom. As soon as he opened the door, a great shaggy dog jumped from the foot of the four-poster bed, and ran toward him. Growling in a menacing manner, the dog shook from its broad head to its enormous paws, with its hackles standing on end.

The creature was huge. And ugly as sin. Alex eyed the hairy mongrel. Dammit, it was the same dog that spooked that black monster. Fuming, Alex held his ground, glaring at the mutt. That Quasimodo of all canines squatted in front of him, then sniffed his feet. Then it sat, and lifted its head. As soon as the pair of sad, oddly human eyes looked up at him, Alex's resentment died. The dog was suffering. Stark pain in those liquid intelligent eyes was heartbreaking. Soft and mournful, its quiet cry disturbed the silence, and raised all the fine hairs on his body.

Was he too late? Dammit, no! No way in hell.

"Belle? What is it, girl?" Nika's voice pulled him out of the clutches of fear.

A moment later, his pregnant cousin ambled forward, and almost jumped out of her skin. "Alex?! My god, Alex!"

He barely had time to brace himself as she hurtled into his arms like a compact missile.

"Thank God, oh thank God you're here!" Nika sprung back, scrunched her forehead. "That was fast! How did JC manage to go forth and back so quickly?"

"He didn't. I came myself. As soon as I learned."

"How did you learn?" She gazed at him, as realization struck home. "Oh, darn it, Alex, you've been there?"

"Yes."

"Hell."

"You may say that again." Pure hell. A horrible nightmare. The cruelest torture. Alex ignored the vivid images bombarding his memory, shut them away.

No time to dwell on it, pal. Abby is in danger. Suck it up.

Afraid of what he might see, Alex turned his eyes to the prone figure on the bed.

Abby.

Sweet Lord, Abby!

His daring, free-spirited, spunky Princess, still as a statue, pale as marble. Amidst the pristine white bedding, swaddled it bandages, she resembled a stiff mummy. Lifeless. Motionless. Utterly colorless.

Even her black hair seemed dull and dingy and faded. He didn't know why that insulted him the most. Averting his gaze, Alex concentrated on breathing that had suddenly became difficult. No time to fall apart. Abby needed him. Her fate depended on him being strong and clearheaded.

So, suck it up, and act.

"How is she?"

"Holding up, but barely. Cuz, you must take her home, the sooner the better."

"That's why I came here."

Nika nodded, took a step forward, then suddenly stopped in her tracks.

"Alex, if not for JC, how did you manage to come through without the key?"

"Beats me. Ask *Verochka*. She swayed that old clock with her words alone."

"*Verochka?* Is she here, too?!"

"Yes. Without her, that old junker refused to let me pass."

"Oh, God! I can't believe it!"

"Nik, there is no time. As much as I'd love to visit, we must get back."

"You're right. Yes. Shit. Of course, you're right." Nika grabbed his hand, and propelled him toward the bed.

One close look at Abby, and he almost lost it. It was worse than he imagined. She resembled a pitiful ragdoll that some careless child had smashed to pieces, then threw away. Tears of outrage sprung to his eyes; his tongue burned from silent curses. With a herculean effort, Alex pushed it away. Slowly he traced the contour of her face with his fingertips.

So beautiful. So pale. So still.

Warm. Alive. That's all that matters.

Gingerly he drew away the antique quilt covering her body. Clad in a long silky nightgown, Abby seemed so fragile, so startlingly small. As gently as possible, Alex gathered his precious cargo into his arms. Insubstantial. Almost weightless.

Barely breathing. That shook him to the core.

Deal with it later.

Carefully, Alex lifted her up, cradled her head against his shoulder.

"Hang on, Princess. Just a little longer."

"Try not to joist anything." Grabbing a light throw from the nearby chair, Nika tucked it around Abby. "Easy, Cuz. Don't squeeze that hard."

He was afraid to ask, but he needed to know. "How...how bad?"

Nika's overflowed miserable eyes confirmed his worst fears.

"Shattered leg, broken collarbones, and right arm. God, Alex, it's her painting arm!"

"We'll worry about that later." He cast a quick glance at Abby, afraid that she might somehow overhear, but his fears were pointless. Placid, unnaturally calm, Abby's expression stayed the same. "What else?"

"The doctor wasn't sure about the internal damage, or her spine." She swallowed hard. "He said we need a miracle."

"Fuck that."

Nika let out a watery laugh. "My sentiments exactly." Wiping away tears with both hands, she squared her shoulders. "Let's go, Cuz. There's no time to waste."

The walk down the hallway to the landing took forever. Holding his breath, Alex deliberately slowed his strides. His impatience was killing him, but fear to hurt Abby even inadvertently, was greater.

The shaggy dog followed in their footsteps, moaning with every step.

I know how you feel, girl.

As soon as they reached their destination, Eli sprinted up the stairs. Keeping one steady hand on Alex's elbow, he guided him gently down.

"Verochka!" As fast as she was able, Nika bolted toward their grandmother.

"Oh, Daisy-girl, oh, my sweet baby, let me look at you!"

Crying and laughing, they both fell into each other arms.

Their happy reunion was more desperate than joyous, since both knew it was the last time they'd see each other. Dammit. He hated to bring it to an end, but the time was ticking away. As it was, the eerie shimmering around the clock became fainter, dimmer. Another moment and it might disappear for good.

Resolutely, Alex walked toward the grandfather clock.

"*Verochka?* I'm sorry, but we must go."

"Yes, yes. Of course." Reluctantly she stepped away from Nika. "Be happy, my precious. I love you."

"I love you, too." With tears rolling down her face, Nika made a valiant effort to smile.

"Cuz? You are the best." Her lips trembled, but her spine was ramrod straight. "Goodbye, Alex. Please, be safe, and take care of Abby."

"I will. And Nik?" Despite his mood, Alex managed to lift the corner of his mouth in a little grin. "I love you, Brat. It'll never be the same without you."

"Oh, hell." Pressing both hands to her face, Nika struggled for control. If not for Eli's supporting arm, she probably would have sunk to the floor.

"We must hurry!" The urgency in *Verochka's* voice snapped him back. "The shimmering is dissipating." She cast a quick glance over her shoulder, zeroed in on the lone figure standing apart from everybody. "JC? What are you waiting for? Come here, and let's go. There is not much time."

"I'm not going."

That bombshell of a statement plunged the room into a deafening silence.

Momentarily frozen, they all gaped at JC in mute shock. *Verochka* was the first to recover. "What...what do you mean, you're not going?"

"Only that I've decided to stay here."

"The hell you are!"

Visibly shaken, she marched toward her eldest grandson, and got in his face. Tilting her head all the way up, *Verochka* still managed to glare at him down her perky little nose.

"Of all the stupid, childish things! *Merde.* Stay here? *Absurdite! Sans espoir!* It's insane! It's irresponsible, and...and dangerous as hell!"

Red in the face, *Verochka* skewed JC's chest with her finger. "Forget about it. Game's over. You had your fun, now you're coming back with us, even if I have to drag you through that blasted portal myself!"

"I'm sorry, *Verochka.*" Gently, JC removed her finger, then kissed her hand.

"And it was never a game for me. Fun? Maybe. At the beginning. But not now." Somber, he held *Verochka's* fumigating gaze. "I've made my decision, Grandmother, and you can't stop me. Only Eli can, if he refuses to let me stay."

All eyes turned to the owner of the Coleman house. Clearly thrown off track by this unexpected turn of events, Eli rubbed his chin, then frowned.

"Are you sure, Morris?"

"Yes, I am."

"Well, then." Eli let out a long sigh of resignation. "You may stay. But please remember that it was solely your decision."

"I will, and thank you." JC flashed a relived smile, then winced, and touched his red, swollen jaw, compliments of Alex's fist. "I swear you won't regret it."

"See that I won't."

"I can't believe it!" Sputtering, *Verochka* threw both hands up in helpless defeat. "Eli? Have you lost your mind? What on earth will he do here?"

Before Eli had a chance to respond, JC beat him to it.

"Live. Just live, *Verochka.*" Taking her both hands in his, JC gently brought it to his lips, kissed each in turn. "Don't worry, Gorgeous. I'll be fine. I've lost many things recently, my purpose and self-respect included. Maybe I find them again," he shrugged, mimicking *Verochka's* famous shoulder gesture, "maybe not, but I have to try. I have to start somewhere."

"But...but why here?"

"Why not? It seems like a nice place and time. It feels right. It feels like home."

Dammit, it was a losing battle. Morris through and through, JC possessed their family's trademark stubborn streak in abundance. Once made, any decision was a *fait accompli*. And who if not Alex should know better?

But he still had to ask, "Are you sure?"

Dickhead or not, JC was family, and for the past couple of months he kind of grew on Alex, the stinker.

"Yes, I am."

"Then I wish you well, Counselor. Stay out of trouble."

JC's lips twitched in a mischievous grin. "I'll do my best. Take care, Alex."

Outnumbered, *Verochka* cursed helplessly under her breath.

God only knew where this shocking, emotional interlude would have led, if not for Nika.

A sharp clap of her hands pulled everybody back to the grave reality of the moment. Obviously, his little cousin managed to pull herself together. Dry-eyed, she took the reins of the situation into her two small hands.

"Okay, people. That's enough. Alex, *Verochka*? Time for you to go. Now."

That's all it took to spur everybody into motion. Eli drew Nika closer to his side; JC put a hand on her shoulder. That picture burned into Alex's memory forever.

His family. Three people he loved. Three best friends he'd never see again.

They'll be living in two different dimensions, two different centuries, drawn apart by time. Bizarre. Astonishing. Depressing as hell.

Before he completely broke down, Alex turned away. Cradling Abby, he moved closer to the clock. Behind him, *Verochka* followed suit.

Already in the middle of the faint shimmering, Alex sought Eli with his eyes. "Farewell, brother. And thanks for everything."

"Safe travels, Alex. Be well, and take care of my baby sister." Saluting with his right hand, Eli curved his lips into a smile, but his eyes were somber and misty. "Until we meet again, my brother."

Not trusting his voice, Alex nodded. Another moment, and he wouldn't be able to hold his own tears at bay.

"Oh, I almost forgot." *Verochka,* bless her heart, shattered the charged atmosphere. "Eli? Don't forget to write that letter, and put the key into the back panel."

"I won't, *Verochka.*"

"Good bye, my dears. I love you. I love you all."

Finally, she turned her misty eyes toward the clock, put one hand on Alex's arm, and another on the gleaming golden surface.

As if on cue, the grandfather clock came alive. The rays of gold shot up in a brilliant blinding rainbow. The air crackled. The familiar eerie shimmering intensified, all but obscuring the picture. The images swirled, slowly at first, then faster, and faster, until it became a frenzy of circular motion.

A carousel from hell.

Disoriented, Alex hunched his shoulders to shield Abby.

Hang on Princess.

A moment later, a thundering *bong* shook the ground.

Explosion of lights.

Symphony of noises.

Hurtling with a dizzying speed.

And finally, the bliss of silence...

CHAPTER FORTY-FIVE

Time lost all meaning. One moment he was spiraling through the portal, the next—he was sitting in the waiting area of the hospital, clutching his grandmother's hand. Somehow, she had enough moxie to explain Abby's accident without really giving away any details.

Everything in between vanished like a morning mist. How did they end up here, in this austere, sterile room, was a mystery to Alex. A scent of something sweet and bitter, with strong undertones of artificial chemicals, saturated the air. The typical hospital smell. The hard chair he was sitting on was doing its best to leave a permanent impression on his butt. And it was cold. Miserably so. Alex shook all over, but whether from the subzero temperature in the room, or the leftovers of shock, was anybody's guess. Didn't matter. Nothing mattered except Abby's fate that was now in surgeon's hands. Snippets of the mad dash toward the OR bombarded his memory. Clipped orders of the doctor, slapping sounds of running feet, squeak of the gurney's wheels...

Alex ran with the team of nurses, holding onto that squealing gurney, until he was stopped at the OR doors. Forcing through the human barricade of a single nurse was an easy task, considering his state of agitation. The slender middle-aged woman in scrubs that blocked his way, didn't stand a chance.

Restraining him physically? Really? Laughable.

Alex would succeed in bulldozing his way in, if not for *Verochka*.

Quiet, but urgent, his grandmother's voice penetrated the haze of his frenzy.

"Stop it, Alex. Let them help her. Every second counts."

Like a splash of cold water, the truth of her words hit him square in a face.

Abruptly, his madness evaporated, leaving him deflated. Turning away from the OR door was one of the hardest things he ever did.

Helpless, hollowed out, Alex cursed under his breath. Abby was now at the mercy of the strangers. Qualified, highly trained team of doctors, but still strangers. Dammit.

Pacing the small confinement of the waiting room was driving him insane.

"Sit, Alex. You're making me dizzy." *Verochka* patted the chair beside her.

Reluctantly, he plopped down. Grabbing her hand, he held on to it like it was a life preserver. How did she manage to stay so calm and steady? Even the grip of her small and delicate hand was as firm and stable as an anchor.

Strong, unyielding, unshakable, *Verochka* was like a rock, like a boulder in the middle of a churning river. Without her he would be swept away, or disintegrated into a gazillion pieces. Grateful, he squeezed her hand.

"We are extremely lucky, my boy. Dr. Miller is regarded as the God of orthopedic surgery. Our Abby's in the best hands. Everything will be fine, you'll see."

That quiet and calm reminder failed to pacify him. Even the best surgeon makes mistakes.

Don't think about that. Fate can't be that cruel.

"This hospital is the state of art, with a brilliant staff, and top-notch technology." *Verochka*, as if sensing his inner turmoil, continued her calm narrative. "And don't forget, it's the hospital that

Eli built, and donated to the city." She turned to Alex, her eyes direct and unwavering. "Have faith, grandson. Fate is on our side."

He sincerely hoped so. Instead of answering, Alex nodded.

And the waiting began. Nerve-wracking, nail-biting, terrifying. Endless.

An hour passed, then another, and another. And still that blasted OR door stayed closed. Glowing red letters "Surgery in progress" were like the drops of blood. Behind those doors, Abby was fighting for her life. Dammit, she was totally helpless, and unconscious, surrounded by strangers. And so frighteningly alone. He should've been there, beside her.

And what can you do, idiot?

Something. Anything. Oh, God, please...

Brightly lit room...

An operating table...

Beeps of the machines...

Gleaming instruments...

The surgeon's hands smeared with blood...

And in the middle of that table Abby, with the plastic tube in her mouth, her beautiful hair covered by a blue net...

"We have a bleeder. Suction. One more. Hold it..."

Before his next heartbeat, everything disappeared. He was sitting in the brutally hard chair in the sterile impersonal waiting room, shaken and bewildered.

What just happened? Was he really allowed a glimpse inside that operating room?

Yes, he was there. For just a moment, he was there, and saw, and heard.

Dammit, why was he yanked back so quickly?

Why?

Alex cursed under his breath. Okay, alright. If he managed it once, he can do it again. But as much as he tried to concentrate, his mind remained firmly in the present. His gift, or curse, refused to let him go back.

Helpless, mad, scared, Alex glued his eyes to the wall clock.

God, how much longer?

Sensing his bubbling panic, *Verochka* leaned sideways, put her head onto his shoulder.

"Be patient, sweetheart. Just a little longer."

"It's been almost four hours!"

"I know, but I'm sure the doctors are doing their best. Have a faith, Alex."

For apparent reasons, Alex decided to omit his mental trip to the OR. *Verochka* didn't need to know all the details of what took place in that room.

Bleeder. They had a blasted bleeder! Even unfamiliar with medical jargon, Alex knew what that meant.

Damn it all to hell and back!

Shaken to the core, he let out a long stream of curses.

Clueless, *Verochka* interpreted it the only way she knew, and patted his knee. "That's okay, baby. Swear to your heart content if it helps you."

"I'm so scared, *Verochka*. I'm so fucking scared."

Bleeder. Oh, God!

"I know, Alex. Me, too. But our Abby is young, healthy, and strong. We must concentrate on that."

"What if there is some... internal damage?" God help him, he dreaded to force the daunting word 'bleeder' past his lips.

"Then the doctors will fix it. Don't think about 'what ifs.' Think positive, and send the healing vibes into the Universe."

"Yeah, like that will help."

"More than you know, Alex." Dark bruises shadowed under her violet eyes, but the resolve in them shone through. "Our girl will be fine, you'll see."

"Your famous intuition?"

"That, and my unshakable faith in cosmic justice. Despite every inconceivable obstacle, that girl managed to cross the barrier of time, and find her dream. Find you. Do you think it was all for naught?"

"And a lot of good that did her." Disgusted, he turned away, but not before glimpsing the angry flashes in *Verochka's* eyes.

Cold and brutal like a whip, her voice lashed out, "Stop feeling sorry for yourself, Alexander. Abby needs you now more than ever. Your strength, your support, and yes, your love. So, snap out of your funk, and man up, for goodness' sake!"

He must admit, it irked, that verbal slap in the face.

Man up? Really?

Hurt to his core and at a loss for words, Alex glared at her.

A heartbeat of silence, after which *Verochka* continued more gently, "Do not despair, my dear. It's useless and pointless and demeaning. Here, I think you should hold on to this."

She reached into her pocket, pulled out some object, and placed it onto his palm. As soon as he realized what it was, Alex sucked in a breath.

"The ring. Abby's ring. But...how?"

"The nurse removed it from her finger before taking Abby to the OR. She gave it to me."

The lump in his throat made swallowing almost impossible. Shaken, Alex closed his hand into a tight fist. Abby's engagement ring. Warm to the touch, it pulsed like a beating heart in his palm. Alive. Happy. Full of hope and joy and love.

Just like Abby.

That small ring managed what all *Verochka's* efforts failed to accomplish: it gave him peace, and eliminated all his doubts. Abby will be fine. He was as sure of it as the fact the sun will shine and the ocean will churn. She'll be healthy, and strong, and happy. Damn if he let his fears cloud his mind.

They loved each other. They were meant for each other. Born centuries apart, they still managed to meet, and fall in love. And they will live happily ever after.

Drawing the first free breath of the day, Alex let himself relax.

A brief glance at the clock. Five and a half hours. No, he wouldn't think of time, or of what was happening behind those doors. He'll wait as long as necessary, patiently, calmly, and hold on to Abby's ring. And to *Verochka's* hand.

"By the way, Gorgeous, how did we manage the back trip through that portal?"

"You don't remember?"

"Totally blank."

"Maybe, that's for the best. Well, the trip back was more...uncomfortable. Longer, for one, and much louder, with all the bells and whistles. Guess, that old bastard was showing off. But it got us back. You almost passed out, but held Abby in a death grip. As soon as I came to my senses, I rushed to the car, poured you and Abby in—and I mean that literally—and drove to the hospital as fast as your little Porsche allowed."

"In other words, you flew like all the bats from hell were chasing you."

A familiar shrug of the shoulders that only a true Parisian could pull off with such negligent panache was his answer. In spite of everything, Alex gave a short bark of laughter. "*Verochka*, you're something else." Sobering, he brought her hand to his lips, kissed it. "Thank you. For everything. If not for you..."

He failed to suppress the shiver that ran down his spine. *Verochka* truly performed a series of miracles. She managed to sway that infamous Coleman grandfather clock with her verbal plea, get them through the portal and back, and single-handedly delivered them all to the hospital. Astonishing. Mindboggling. She was one of a kind. She was his very own true miracle.

Overwhelmed, he pressed their joined hands to his face. "Abby is so lucky to have you."

"Abby is extremely lucky to have *you*, Alex." *Verochka* brought their intertwined fingers to her own cheek. "You both are lucky."

As they both were getting watery-eyes, Alex opted to lighten the mood. "By the way, what's that you're wearing?"

"Huh?" A quick glance at herself, and *Verochka* let out a sequence of Russian and French cussing words. Like well-executed pirouettes, they swirled around the waiting room. Alex swallowed his laughter.

There was very little that managed to put a look of such utter befuddlement onto his grandmother's face. Dazed, she blinked at him, as a stunning disbelief slowly faded into a helpless embarrassment.

"You...you mean, I traipsed through two centuries, wearing my...pajamas?"

"Not just any pajamas, but the pure silk Hermes ones."

"But...but it's pink!"

"Shockingly so." With a tongue in his cheek, he added, "It's so you, Gorgeous."

"*Merde,* Alex, why didn't you pointed it out sooner?"

"Because I just noticed it a moment ago. Sorry."

A brief pause later, *Verochka* shrugged, and with an innate aplomb delivered her verdict, "The hell with it."

"That's the spirit."

On a whoosh the door to the OR flew open. Their banter forgotten, Alex and *Verochka* jumped to their feet, their hands still linked in a tight clasp.

Equally famous for his brusque manners and his magical hands, Dr. Miller emerged, glaring at them both. His blue surgical scrubs were wrinkled, but clean, missing the offensive blood splatters Alex glimpsed earlier. Thank God.

A wilted mask dangled from his left ear. In comical contrast with Dr. Miller's scowling face and exhausted eyes, it failed to produce a relief.

"Doctor...?"

Verochka's breathless voice pulled those glowering eyes in her direction. Without a preamble, his shockingly high tenor cut the silence, "That young lady is fortunate in more ways that I can count on both hands. It's a wonder she escaped without broken spine, or more severe injuries."

His accusing eyes landed on Alex, as if he was a reason for all Abby's grievances. Absurd as it was, Alex nevertheless barely suppressed a wince. "Horse accident, my ass. More like a brutal attack. Her spleen is a history, her leg's a mess, both clavicles shattered, as to her arms—"

Clearly incensed, *Verochka* interrupted his angry litany, "*Merde*, Doctor, just tell us if she's okay!"

"After I operated on her for nine hours?" A snort as belligerent as Dr. Miller's glare burst free. "She is more than okay. She's fantastic! With all that titanium hardware in her bones, she'll be up and dancing in no time. And spleen? She didn't need it much, anyway."

"Thank you, oh, thank you so much! You are a godsent!"

"Correction, my good woman, I am the God."

Talk of the overblown ego. Unperturbed, *Verochka* let go of Alex's hand, marched toward the doctor, and grabbed his surgical gown by two fistfuls. A smacking hard kiss onto his scowling mouth whipped that irritating egocentric smirk, rendering Dr. Miller mute. Shocked, he gazed at *Verochka* with open panic.

"Thank you, Doc. You are the best. I owe you a case of the most excellent French champagne."

"Y-you d-don't have to..." Stammering, the surgeon gazed helplessly at the elegant pj clad tornado in front of him. His grandmother, God bless her heart, managed to do the unthinkable: reduce the uppity dictator into a malleable, stuttering putty.

"I insist." *Verochka* let go of his scrubs, patted it in place. "And a generous donation to the hospital."

"That'll be appreciated." Finally shedding his temporary lapse in composure, Dr. Miller squared his shoulders. His perpetual scowl was back in place. "Okay, sorry, folks, but I must be going. You both should go home, too. Our patient will be sleeping for quite some time, so there is no point for you to be here."

"I'm staying." Alex immediate response bore no arguments.

After one quick glance at him, Dr. Miller nodded. "As you wish. But you won't be able to see her."

"Doesn't matter."

With a final furtive look toward *Verochka*, the surgeon quickstepped out of the room.

"But Alex—"

"*Verochka*, save your breath. I'm going to stay here, but you should go home. That pjs, as much as they're fetching, is still kind of... embarrassing. You're practically parading in your negligee, Hermes or not. And lose those silly things." Alex pointed down. The vanity button always worked like a charm. One look at her feet clad in pink sleepers with cheeky satin bows was all it took. With a mighty sigh, *Verochka* finally capitulated.

"Okay, I'll go, change my unseemly attire, and come back. And no," she interrupted before Alex voiced an argument, "I won't leave you here by your lonesome, so don't even try. Anything I should bring you?"

"Yeah, your astonishingly awesome self. And a gallon of coffee."

CHAPTER FORTY-SIX

Floating. The sensation was pleasant, if a bit disconcerting. Comfortable, carefree, happy.

Abby smiled. She was safe. She was home where she belonged. But where was Alex? She heard his voice. Murmurs of love, whispers of encouragement. Gentle and soft, calm and soothing, his words filled her with peace, and joy, and utter contentment.

"Hang on, Princess. Just a little longer. I love you, Abby."

I love you too...

She was not alone in this delightful dreamlike place. Alex was here, too.

She felt him, smelled him, heard him. But why can't she see him?

Like a shadow, faint and elusive, he was always out of reach. Frustrating.

Every time she turned to look for him, something prevented her intent.

Merde.

Beeping... strange noises... voices...

Go away. Leave me alone. Alex. Where was Alex?

"I'm here, Princess. Right here. Calm down. Everything is fine."

Alex. Happy and content, she turned to the sound of his voice.

"That's right, sweetheart, nice and easy. Just breathe."

She drew a deep breath, breathed him in.

Alex. Don't go. Please.

"I'm not going anywhere. I'm here, right here."

Peaceful. Happy. Alex always made her happy.

They were betrothed now. Did she refuse him at first? Silly girl. There was no one else for her. Just Alex. Abby lifted her left hand, jolted. Her ring was gone!

Where was it? Did she lose it? Oh, God. How did she manage to lose her engagement ring? A princess for the Princess.

My ring!

Agitated, she swept her eyes all around to no avail.

Beep...beep...beep...

"Hey, baby, it's okay. Don't worry, your ring is safe. I have it."

Oh, thank God! But why did Alex remove the ring from her finger? Had he changed his mind? No, impossible. Then why?

Confused, so confused...

"You can't have any jewelry in ICU. But as soon as you wake up, I'll return it to you. Calm down, Princess."

Okay. She can't wear any jewelry in ICU. Is that what this wonderful paradise is called? No, that's not it. ICU. She knew what that means. But couldn't remember.

Her memory was hazy, but not unpleasantly so.

I'll remember. Today, or tomorrow...

Soaring, weightless, like a feather on the light breeze... or a beam of sunshine on a gentle wave. She liked the sensation. Buoyant. Was she on water? She loved being afloat. Eli's boat...going places with her brother...visiting the neighboring islands...St. Simons, Jekyll, Cumberland...

No, she didn't want to visit Cumberland. She was cross with Carnegies, but for what? Something...something concerning Eli...

Can't remember.

Why can't she remember? She must! Frowning, Abby tried to concentrate.

Beep...beep...beep

That incessant beeping was the only thing that spoiled this blissful place. That, and the unfamiliar voices. Female mostly. Her maids? No, there was no such things as maids, not in the twenty-first century. Who were they, then?

"Abby, sweetie? It's me." *Verochka.*

Enormously relieved, Abby smiled. Her guardian angel, her honorary grandmother. Love covered her like a comfortable warm blanket. *Verochka.*

She was so beautiful, so kind, so clever. And so feisty. Abby wished to be just like her when she's older.

"How are you today, my girl? Looking much better. Still pale, but stunning as ever."

Abby almost laughed. Stunning she was not, not right now. Somehow, she knew that. But... how? Can't remember. Must remember...*Afraid.*

Strange sensations...images...poked her memory like sharp little needles as if trying to burst through a dense fog.

Neighing...alarm...danger...

Suddenly scared, Abby pushed away those visions.

I don't want to remember. Not yet.

Beep...beep...beep...

"Ssh-ssh. That's okay, sweetheart. You're safe, you're home. Everything is fine. I'm right here."

She wanted Alex. *Where is Alex?*

"Alex will be back shortly. He just went home to take a shower and change clothes. Let me tell you, that boy started to stink to high heaven. If not for that, he would never leave your side. For five days Alex been sitting beside you. And no one, not even your surgeon, was able to pry him away. Don't worry, baby, he'll be back in no time."

Alex will be back. Soon. She can wait for a little while.

Five days. Surgeon. ICU.

Slowly her murky thoughts began to crystallize, only to be shattered by *Verochka's* cheerful voice.

"Don't you think it's time to open your eyes, Abby? I bet you missed sunshine. What do you say, sweetheart?"

Funny. Missed sunshine? But it was always sunny in her little paradise.

And what was it about her eyes? Time to open them? Oh, *Verochka* is just being silly. Abby glanced around. Quiet and warm, pretty as a picture.

Sun, the ocean, sand.

The colors were mostly pastels. She frowned.

That's not right. They supposed to be bright and vivid and bold.

Golden sun, cerulean sky, brilliant grey-green water.

Why is everything muted and pale and soft? Not right. Something is awry.

But wasn't it comforting, all that subdued hues, calm, and peaceful?

She must paint it, this blissful, heavenly spot. What would she use? Aquarelles? Colored chalk? Yes, definitely chalk. As soon as she was able to paint again...

But why can't I paint now?

Where was her favorite palette? Her canvases? Her paints?

Wrong, something was terribly wrong.

Confusion. Fear. Panic.

Where am I?

Beep...beep...beep...

"No, sweetheart! Please, lay still. You can't...Abby, no!"

Flurry of motion...stern voices...loud noises...

Hands, touching her; light shone in her eyes. And that insistent beeping...

"Mrs. Morris, you have to leave."

No, Verochka, please don't leave me!

"I'm not going anywhere, doctor."

"I said, now!"

"And I said, no freaking way! Better start treating your patient. *Now.*"

Rude swearing. More poking.

"Benzodiazepines, two and a half milligrams. Stat."

Warm numbing flow...she was slowly swimming toward oblivion...

No! I don't want to float anymore! I don't want to stay in this place!

Gathering all her strength, Abby fought the web of mist.

"Alex!"

Hoarse, her voice was a mere whisper, barely recognizable.

"Here, Princess. I'm right here. Thank God, oh, thank God..."

Two strong arms enveloped her, as familiar violet eyes gazed at her in shock and wonder. Alex. Hollowed faced, sickly pale, with a dense dark shadow on his cheeks and chin, he looked as if he had barely escaped a horrible wreck. His gaze bore into her, as if searching for answers.

"Alex..."

"Oh, Abs, I've been dying to hear your voice again. Thank God, you woke up."

"Was I...sleeping?"

"For five days straight."

"But...why?"

"You don't remember? Of course, you don't."

"Why don't I remember? And where am I?"

"You're in a hospital. But everything is okay now."

"Hospital? What happened? An... accident?"

"Of sorts." Alex looked over his shoulder at the older robust man in medical garb. Still hovering nearby, he was frowning in a rather austere manner. Was he displeased? Or just angry?

"Who...who is this man?"

"That's the surgeon, Abs. Doctor Miller. He operated on you. If not for his magic hands..."

Confused or not, good manners prevailed. "T-thank you, doctor. I'm v-very grateful."

"I don't need your gratitude, young lady. All I need is for you to obey orders, and try not to mess up all my good work."

"I'll try my best not to waste it."

"See that you don't." With a curt nod to her, and totally ignoring Alex and *Verochka*, the doctor sailed out of the room.

"Geez, was it something I said?" *Verochka's* question hit Abby as hilarious. She wanted to laugh, but the dryness in her mouth prevented it.

"Probably the bad 'f' word you used... when he tried to get rid of you, *Verochka*." Barely a croak, her voice abraded her throat.

Coming closer, *Verochka* leaned over, and gently kissed her forehead. A luminous smile played across her grandmother's striking face, even as a single tear rolled down. "You gave us a great scare, sweetheart."

"A... great scare? But... what did I do?"

"Alex will tell you." She patted her grandson's shoulder, then kissed his bald crown. "I'm proud of you, Alexander Zacharias Morris. You are one remarkable man."

"I didn't do anything, Gorgeous. If someone is truly remarkable, it's you."

"True." *Verochka* fluffed her short blond hair in a coquettish matter. "So true. As a remarkable and *astute* woman, I know when I'm being a third wheel."

Kissing Abby one more time, she drew a deep breath. "I'll leave you two alone. You kids have a lot of catching up to do. And I need to crash for a couple of days, to recoup my depleted strength."

"Depleted, my ass. Who are you kidding, you human dynamo?" Alex's counter seemed to please *Verochka*.

"Even dynamos need to recharge their batteries, smarty-pants," she answered, gathering her purse. "Well, *au revoir* for now. Abby, I'll come for a long visit tomorrow."

Abby managed a smile, as she gazed at the elegant woman she loved to distraction.

"*Verochka?* I love you. And I'm sorry for...whatever I did to scare you so."

"I love you too, sweets. And no apology is necessary. Just get better."

At the door, *Verochka* sent her an air kiss, and a little wink. *Verochka.* There was no one quite like her.

"She's amazing."

"You can say that again."

"Alex? I can't believe I'm seeing you at last. I was searching all over for you."

"Oh, Princess, I was always here, beside you."

"I know. I heard you, even smelled you, but never saw you. Like I was trapped in an eerie place, floating... always floating."

"Might be all the good drugs they pumped into you."

"Was I really sleeping for five days?"

"Yes. Five hellish days. Christ, Abs, I didn't know if I was going to bear it."

"But...why? What happened?"

"You were hurt, badly." Alex sought her eyes, then finished quietly, "In 1910."

"Y-you mean... I went back?" Confusion flowed back like a tidal wave. "Why did I go back? How? When?"

"Calm down, Princess. You went because Eli was in trouble. Nika came for you, and you—"

"I remember! Eli...he was in jail, and Daisy and JC...and you...you were hurt! The clock... it threw you..." And the memories slammed into her, stealing her breath. "My God, Alex. How badly are you hurt?"

Beep...beep...beep...

That irritating beeping started to shrill anew. Placing both hands onto her shoulders, Alex gently pressed her down onto the bed.

"Relax, tigress. Don't freak out. I'm okay. Just knocked the breath out me."

"Are you... s-sure?"

"Dead sure. I'm fit as a fiddle. But you...you were..."

Alex swallowed hard and shut his eyes. Poor Alex. Abby lifted her hand to touch his beloved face, to give him reassurance, but her arm refused to move. She frowned. What was wrong with her arm? Her attempt to shift her body failed miserably. All her movement were severely restricted.

Dear God, was she paralyzed?

Blinking, Abby dragged her eyes over her body. White cast on her elevated right leg, held in some horrible steel contraption. Both arms dressed in a similar manner, but not attached to any mechanism. Bound ribs and shoulders. No wonder she can't move.

My hands!

Cold panic. Frozen. Horrified.

Holding her breath, Abby cast a glance at her hands. Her fingers were free of the cast, thank God. But when she tried to wiggle them, pain shot up her arm, all the way to her shoulders. A shocking cry of desperation broke free. How will she hold a brush? If she won't be able to paint, she might as well be dead.

No, fate cannot be that cruel! Panting, she shook her head in denial.

"Alex! My god, Alex! I'm broken to pieces! My leg, my arms..."

"Ssh-ssh, Princess. You were broken, past tense. But not anymore. Doctor Miller performed a true miracle. Your leg will heal, as will your collarbones, ribs, and arms. And before you ask, both of your hands are okay. So are your internal organs, and your spine. You're really lucky that black monster didn't do any more damage. If he landed a bit to the side, he would have smashed your head and face."

"Black monster?"

"Sultan."

"Oh, Lord, is he okay?"

"He was a few days ago. If Eli didn't shoot him by now."

"He won't! It wasn't Sultan's fault. It was..." swirling images finally resurfaced, "JC's, wasn't it? I remember now. Oh, God have mercy, I remember!"

Cry of the stallion, barking of Belle, and fear that she won't be in time to catch Eli's tempestuous horse. But how did Alex learn about her calamity? They were centuries apart. And then it dawned at her. "You...you were there!"

"Don't remind me." Alex muttered a rude word under his breath. "I was there, alright, trapped in my mind, unable to do anything but watch. It was pure hell. The most horrific experience of my life."

"I'm sorry."

"Not your fault."

She was suddenly too tired to argue, but the need to know the rest wouldn't let go.

"H-how... did I turned up in the hospital... in 2021, w-when I got hurt in 1910?"

"Okay, Princess, I'll tell you, but first..." with that Alex lifted her left hand gingerly, slipped a ring onto her finger.

"My ring! I was so afraid I lost it."

The diamond twinkled, dazzling and familiar and beautiful.

Finally, everything was right with the world. Smiling, she turned her gaze to Alex.

His tale was short, shocking, and terrifyingly amazing. Even in its abbreviated version, it frightened and humbled Abby at the same time. Now she knew who she owed her life to: Alex and *Verochka*.

Dr. Miller might have stitched her up, but the true heroes were those two who, despite all odds and laws of physics, managed to transport her through centuries, and deliver her unconscious, broken body into the hands of doctors.

A true miracle, thy name is love. Even time was defenseless against it.

"Don't cry, Princess. Everything will be okay."

Was she crying? Silly girl.

"I know. Everything will be marvelous."

Overwhelmed, she closed her eyes. That familiar floating sensation...strong, but not scary. Shimmering pastels, warm, welcoming...

"S-sorry, so drowsy..."

"That's alright. You need to rest in order to heal. Go to sleep, Abs."

"Don't go..."

"I won't. I'll be right here when you wake up."

"I love you..." Heavy, her tongue barely rolled inside her mouth. Her words began to slur as she surrendered to that buoyant pull.

"I love you, Princess. Forever and ever. Close your eyes, Beautiful."

Warm, sheltered, safe...

"Alex? Y-you... have a...?"

Why did Alex's scruffy facial hair fascinate her so?

"Yeah, well, I've decided not to shave until you wake up."

"Silly." Her eyelids weighed a ton. Need to sleep. Just for a while.

Like from a great distance, a murmur reached her ears.

"Don't worry, as soon as I get my hands on a razor, I'll be smooth as marble once again."

No, please don't. I like it this way.

"Then I'll leave it. But no complaints about marrying a pirate."

A knight. You are my beautiful knight in shining armor...

Drifting toward the oblivion, she heard Alex's soft chuckle.

"Aww shucks, Princess, a beautiful knight? Really?"

Really...truly...surely...

CHAPTER FORTY-SEVEN

An enchanting September twilight cast its magic, sparkling over the calm waters of the Atlantic. Almost below the horizon, the sun shot its last rays toward the lavender sky. Crisp and clear, an autumn air smelled of promises and secrets.

Such an magical evening worthy of a very special occasion. Her wedding.

Marveling at the intricate paths of fate that brought her here, Abby held her breath.

Her silk wedding dress, teased by the light ocean breeze, murmured in feeble protest. Thank God she opted against the veil, or she'll be forever fighting to keep it from her face. Instead, Abby wove baby breath flowers into her braid, and left it at that. She wiggled her toes as sand dusted across them, but she was happy she chose open toed Jimmy Choo sandals for this special day. Elegant and cheeky, made from satin and lace, they were studded with sparkling crystals, front and back. Her elegant bridal gown had one major flow, compliments of her illustrious grandmother. A gift from *Verochka*, that Chanel dress was rather modest from the front, but completely backless. Held in place by the crisscrossing strings of tiny pearls, it left Abby's spine totally naked. Quite scandalous in Abby's opinion, sensual and adventurous in *Verochka's*. Bless her heart, she was so convincing, that at the end Abby capitulated. The woman has done so much for her, it was impossible to deny her such a small thing. Abby chuckled. If *Verochka* would ask her to strip and parade nude, she'd probably comply. There wasn't anything—absolutely anything—she wouldn't do for *Verochka*. And the adorable tyrant knew it and used it shamelessly to her advantage.

Abby wanted something small and intimate, just the three of them. But her beloved grandmother, bless her heart, has other ideas.

Upset that she was unable to participate in Daisy and Eli's nuptials, *Verochka* badgered and pestered her and Alex, until they both were ready to scream. The manipulating despot, she used every available weapon in her vast arsenal, guilt and tears included. At the end, Abby and Alex surrendered. A pure act of self-preservation on their part. So, instead of a small and intimate gathering, they ended up with a grand ceremony worthy of royals. Oh, well.

Unbeknownst to the bride and groom, *Verochka* invited a throng of people. All the Rostoffs, including the kids, Marie Dubois, Abby's mentor, and her husband, and even Vic, Daisy's and Alex's good friend and former attorney, were happy to attend. Of course, *Verochka* wasn't satisfied with the arrangements until she appointed that peculiar creature Maximillian, Vic's beloved dog, as ring bearer.

Abby had to admit, a furry midget clad in tiny black tuxedo with a red bow, was truly adorable. Maximillian held a miniscule basket with his jaws, quite wilted from his slobbering, that contained the wedding rings.

As to the place and time, Abby and Alex held firm to what they wanted. The ceremony must be on the beach at twilight. Unflustered, their crafty grandmother adjusted accordingly her initial plan for an indoor wedding at Ritz.

Finally, the day arrived. The long-awaited moment was almost upon them.

"You look beautiful, my dear. Positively radiant." Dmitry Rostoff offered his arm in invitation. He was giving her away, the role he embraced with enthusiasm.

"Thank you, sir. I feel beautiful and radiant."

"Well, shall we?"

"By all means." Abby looped her arm through his. A bit strained and wobbly, his answering smile was a dead giveaway. The almighty Rostoff, the famous Jewelry Emperor, feared and regarded throughout the world, was nervous as a green youth. Moved, charmed, Abby patted his hand in reassurance, then kissed his cheek.

"It's okay, sir. Don't fret. I'm ready." And she was. Ready, and calm, and steady. Shouldn't she be even a bit edgy, or anxious?

Then she looked at Alex, who waited for her farther ahead by the flowery wedding arch, and the answer was obvious.

Hell, no.

Two grand dames, *Verochka* and Natasha, Dmitry's wife, flanked Alex from both sides. Both dressed to kill, elegant and exquisite, they watched Abby through their misty eyes. Vic, the best man, stood beside the groom, wearing an enormous smile and an eye-popping magenta tux. Maximillian, the ring bearer was prancing nearby. In long gown the color of burnished gold, her former mentor Marie Dubois shimmered like a beacon of fire. Both Rostoff teenagers tried their best to look indifferent and bored, but failed miserably.

Abby's eyes skimmed through the familiar dear faces of friends and family, but all her attention was on the dashing groom. Alex. Her destiny. Her one and true love.

Barely containing his exuberance, he grinned from ear to ear, awaiting her approach. Poor Alex, he wished for a June wedding, pushing her and *Verochka* both. But even after her grueling physical therapy was finished, and Abby was finally free of the walker, her gait was still uneven. A cane was not that cumbersome, but still. Despite all Alex's arguments, Abby held firm. She was determined to walk down the aisle on her own accord, without any help or hindrances of devices. Grudgingly and quite unenthusiastically, Alex agreed to wait the extra months.

Today his wait was over.

Just look at him. So handsome, so adorable. Her very own beautiful knight, sporting a neat little beard, clad in a formal black tuxedo. A sight from a fairy tale.

Abby's heart melted. Her savior, her hero. Her everything.

His molten violet eyes held her captive all the way to the arch.

"Hi Princess."

Meant for her ears only, his soft greeting sent shivers along her spine. Breathless, Abby couldn't tear her own eyes away from him.

"Hi yourself."

Enthralled. Enchanted. Spellbound.

God knows how long they would just stand there, lost in each other, oblivious to everything, if not for the discreet coughing from Dmitry Rostoff.

"I think we'd better start," he addressed the minister, and placed Abby's hand in Alex's waiting palm. A rueful chuckle later, he added, "As soon as possible."

With a curt node, the minister erased an indulgent smile from his weathered face, and began the ceremony as old as time.

"Dearly beloved, we are gathered today..."

After that, Abby hadn't heard a word. Linked by hands, caught in the wonder of the moment, they both stood absolutely still.

You. Just you, Princess. Always you.

She heard the words as if he said them aloud.

Only you. I jumped through the curtain of time to find you.

He squeezed her hand in a silent response.

A gentle breeze played with her braid, droplets of ocean spray dampened her gown, warm sand tickled her toes. She didn't care.

Drenched in a magic, saturated with love, she had eyes only for Alex.

The enchantment was broken by a light scratch at Abby's ankles that announced the arrival of the tiny Maximilian. Chuckling, Alex bent down, and after a short tug of war with the dog, retrieved the now mangled ring basket from his miniature jaws. Before he slid the platinum band onto Abby's finger, he turned it, and let her see the engraving inside.

Time has no meaning. Love will endure.

Unashamed of the tears streaming down her face, Abby repeated his action.

"I now pronounce you..."

Without waiting until the end of minister's speech, Alex hauled her into his arms, and kissed her until she forgot her own name, let alone her new one.

"...husband and wife. You already kissed the bride, but hey, who's counting? Might as well do it again."

Laughter spilled over, joyous and carefree, as her new husband gave a victorious shout, and lifting Abby, twirled her a few times.

"Hello, Mrs. Morris." And he kissed her again with unbridled passion.

"Gosh, guys, restrain yourself. You are embarrassing the heck out of everybody, especially the poor kids." Vic pulled them apart. "Maximillian is positively shocked." The funny dog at his feet made a yapping sound of agreement. "See? He's scandalized."

If anything, the tiny rascal was grinning, lolling his pink tongue.

"I'm sorry, Maximillian." Abby scratched him between his enormous furry ears. "And thank you for being such an amazing ring bearer."

The dog licked her hand, and yapped again. Vic chuckled.

"Oh, by the way, you forgot to throw the bouquet." His intentionally loud announcement plunged the party into a short silence, after which everybody began to cheer enthusiastically. Amongst the most demanding voices were *Verochka* and Natasha's.

"Crap, Vic. No one would notice, if not for you." But Alex's frown was all for show.

"Tradition, my friend. Can't ignore it. Say thanks that I omit a garter belt removal ceremony."

"Thanks a lot."

"Don't mention it." Vic turned his laughing eyes to Abby. "Go ahead, Mrs. Morris. Do us all proud."

"Well, then."

Abby pivoted, held her breath, and sent her bridal bouquet flying backward.

"I caught it! I caught it!" Jumping up and down, Lana brandished her prize with both arms. "Look, Deda, I caught the bouquet! I'm going to marry next!"

"Over my dead body." Visibly pale, Dmitry Rostoff gazed at his thirteen-year-old granddaughter with something close to a panic on his patrician face.

"Of course, you're going to marry, pumpkin." Chuckling, Natasha enveloped Lana in a hug. "One day." She kissed the girl, and looked at her husband with sparkling eyes. "One day."

"God help us all," he muttered.

CHAPTER FORTY-EIGHT

"I thought they'd never leave."

Alex shut the door, and for a good measure gave the handle a tug, just to make sure that it was really locked and secured. He wouldn't put it past Vic to decide to drop by for a nightcap.

Over my dead body.

At last, all the guests, well-fed but tipsy and overstimulated, poured into the waiting limo, and departed to celebrate the wedding at Salt, the Ritz's posh restaurant.

The newlyweds opted out, heading to the whimsical octagonal house by the ocean. Abby was quite adamant to spend their first night as husband and wife here, where it all began. Frankly, Alex didn't care one way or another. If she decided to consummate their marriage on the freaking moon, he would happily agree.

"Everybody had such a wonderful time, darling. No wonder they didn't want the evening to end." A light censure in Abby's voice was in stark contrast with her blazing eyes. If he wasn't mistaken, she was as impatient as he to see the conclusion of this spectacular evening, and celebrate in private. In the bedroom.

Oh, yes, please, God.

Holding his breath, Alex watched Abby. His princess. His wife now. Dazzling, magnificent, heart-breaking beautiful, she was like an exquisite sculpture from a world-famous museum. The face of a siren, the body of a temptress, the soul of an Amazon. From the moment he laid his eyes on her, she simply stole his breath. He had yet to regain it back.

I almost lost her.

Like an electric current, a violent shiver zipped through him, as the ominous memories tried to break free. With an effort of will, Alex bored down, and pushed the past away. He won't think about it now, won't let anything intrude on this moment.

Tonight was all about happiness and joy, about dreams that become a glorious reality. All about Abby.

And if he doesn't get his hands on her soon, he'll explode.

Patience, Alex. You have waited for this moment for a long time. What's another few minutes?

Are you kidding me?!

He was shaking like a stallion who sensed a filly. And Abby was as aware of him as he of her. Almost pewter, her eyes sparkled with barely restrained passion. Rapid breathing, glowing face, thundering pulse on the hollow of her throat—all the unmistakable signs of an arousal. Damn, talk about pouring gasoline onto the proverbial fire pit. Another moment, and he would rear back like Sultan, Eli's infamous black monster of a horse.

Get a grip, pal. You're losing it.

Grinding his teeth, Alex watched his new wife. As if absently, she took her hands on a slow journey over her body draped in that deceptively modest wedding gown. Demure up front, its back was positively eye-popping. Correction: it does not have any back. The effect was gut twisting, heart-stopping, and unabashedly erotic. One glimpse, and any red-blooded man was doomed to swallow his tongue. Alex was no exception.

What the hell was she doing? Smiling, beaconing, teasing. Damn.

Driving him insane, that's what.

The lump in his throat made swallowing impossible. His lungs constricted; his heart thundered. One particular part of his anatomy jumped to the occasion with a vengeance. Briefly he wondered if his trousers were be able to restrain his rioting appendage. One shake of

Abby's head, and the river of black hair tumbled loose. Alex stopped thinking altogether. Panting. God help him, he was panting, and salivating like a dog at a sight of a treat.

You are pathetic, pal.

I don't give a damn.

"Well, Mr. Morris, what do you say we lose those cumbersome, albeit exquisite garments, and ..." *Oh, yeah, baby, now you're talking.* A lick of a tongue across her luscious lips tied his gut in painful knots. "...get some rest?"

Like a slash of a serrated blade, those words cut through his erotic haze.

"W-what? A... a rest?!" Was she serious? Lord have mercy.

Rich and wicked, the sound of Abby's laughter was as carnal as his abruptly shattered visions. Damn it all to hell and back. Only Abby was able to reduce him to the state of a pathetic amoeba, and then shoot him up to the stratosphere.

"You're playing with fire, Mrs. Morris."

Shit, even his voice was quivering.

"Oh, I sincerely hope so, Mr. Morris."

That does it.

His famous self-control snapped like a dry twig. In two strides, Alex was beside her. Almost ruthlessly, he grabbed her, took her laughing mouth, and poured all his bubbling frustration into a kiss. Like a fist in a solar plexus, Abby's familiar flavor slammed into him, stole his breath. Reeling, Alex plunged deeper, drinking from her lips like a man dying from thirst.

Finally.

From the moment she woke up in the hospital, he was desperate to touch her, but her injuries were too severe for anything more strenuous than a chaste peck on the lips. Later, her brutal physical therapy simply destroyed any sprouts of his libido.

It was a bloody nightmare. Even after she's been cleared by the doctors, Alex was reluctant to touch her. Almost afraid. Because the scars, albeit hidden under her clothes, were still there, as a stark reminder of the horrific accident that almost cost Abby her life.

As God was his witness, he desperately wanted to be careful now. But, dammit, he was just a man. Frustrated as hell, hurting all over.

Seizing a fistful of Abby's hair in one hand, Alex looked deep into her eyes. One telltale sign of uncertainty, a faint whisper of fear, and he swore to stop. Even if it kills him. Holding his breath, praying, he searched her face.

She met his probing gaze head on.

Blazing. Defiant. Triumphant.

More. More!

Her silent demand was unmistakable. Thank you, God.

With a low guttural sound, Alex covered her mouth again.

Bold and daring, her tongue slid past his marauding lips, battling for dominance.

Onslaught of feelings. Frensy of emotions.

Not enough.

He wasn't sure who moved first.

Impatient hands, almost bruising. Rustle of clothes. Thunder of heartbeats.

Abby's laughter.

And finally. Finally! They were skin to skin.

All sounds died. Time stopped.

And then reality crashed back.

Ravenous, they pounced at each other, fell onto the bed in a tangled mass of feverish bodies, greedy hands, demanding mouths. Swiftly, Alex rolled on top, pinned Abby beneath. A sudden warning burst the bubble of his euphoria.

Keep your weight off. Might hurt Abby.

Momentarily contrite, Alex was about to lift onto his elbows, when she snaked her legs around his hips. The last coherent thought evaporated, as pure madness ensued.

Flurry of limbs, broken cries, slaps of flesh. Uninhibited, primitive.

It was mating in a most basic sense of the word, almost brutal, swift, and raw.

What the hell has happened?

Dazed, mute, and deaf, Alex struggled to catch his breath. Try as he might, he was unable to move a muscle. Slowly, inevitably, the reality returned. *Abby.*

Dear God, he all but brutalized her tender flesh with all the finesse of a sledgehammer. The bastard. And he was crushing her. Hell.

Swimming in guilt, Alex managed to lift his head.

"Abs?"

"Hmm?"

"Are you...okay?"

"Hmm..."

"What does that mean?"

"It means...fantastic, amazing, terrific. You?"

"Poleaxed. Blown to pieces."

"Huh." She arched, pressing fully against him. The friction was almost painful. Alex barely swallowed his groan.

"Feels solid enough to me." A light pat on his butt, and his still sheathed shaft began to harden and throb anew.

All bravado aside, Abby wasn't ready for a repeat performance, and frankly, neither was he. With every intention of pulling away, Alex braced on his elbows.

But his wife was having none of it. "Where do you think you're going?"

Shackling both legs around his hips, she pulled him back. "Much better, don't you think?" And the little vixen smirked. Damn, he created a monster.

"Abs, I'm crushing you. You must be sore, and uncomfortable, and—"

His noble protest fell onto dead ears.

"Let me be the judge of that," and bowing her body further, Abby tightened her vice-like grip around his middle. Instinctively, Alex's hips jerked forward, almost fusing their pelvic bones. His eyes crossed.

"Fuck."

Deliberately misinterpreting it like a call to action, Abby batted her eyelashes in a fake demure manner.

"Yes, please."

Alex was laughing before he realized it. "God, Princess, you're something else."

Her answering smile was hot enough to singe a layer of skin.

God, what a woman!

Before his roaring libido revved to max, Alex managed to rolled over, reversing their positions. Momentarily confused, Abby blinked at him from above.

"Ah, Alex?"

"Hmm?"

"What...what am I supposed to do?"

"What you do so well, Princess. Ride."

Abby bit her lip. Still unsure and hesitant, she tentatively moved. Once, twice.

Emboldened by his groan, she resumed her action, increasing the speed.

Dammit, she was killing him. Cursing helplessly, grinding his teeth, Alex had no choice but to bear that carnal assault, and pray to survive.

With more enthusiasm than skill, Abby quickly found her rhythm, as she rode them both toward madness. Head thrown back, eyes closed, body undulating, she was the epitome of passion. Or sin. A witch. A Goddess. A woman.

Mesmerized, enchanted, lost, Alex was unable to tear his eyes off of her. Hovering on the brink, Abby threw both arms up, lifted her face, and cried out. A name. His name.

"Alex!"

Unable to withstand this sweet torture, he surged up, hugged her tight.

"Jump, Princes. Jump. I'm with you."

As they leaped over the edge together, twin cries of surrender and victory slashed the predawn silence.

They dozed for a while, both dazed, drained, and depleted.

Later, when the tender dawn spread its pastel wings over the ocean, they made love again, slow and gentle.

A romance, overshadowed by an explosive passion, refused to be ignored any longer. Every drugging kiss, every soft touch, every quiet murmur was like magic, overwhelming, fascinating. Irresistible.

Drunk on flavors, lightheaded from tenderness, they savored each other in hushed wonder. The path to the ultimate peak was more like a leisurely stroll. And when they finally reached the apex, a gentle wave, light like a breath, slow like a smile, swept them unhurriedly away...

CHAPTER FORTY-NINE

B rilliant sunrays shimmered through the Palladian window, turning the bedroom into a golden paradise. Oblivious to that splendor of light, Abby was lost in a deep slumber, dead to the world.

Disheveled, mouthwateringly naked, glowing in a sheen of sweat, she was a picture from a fantasy. An explicitly and unapologetically erotic one.

Still shuddering in the aftermath of their lovemaking marathon, elated and ecstatic, Alex held her in a loose embrace, unable and unwilling to let go.

His own exhaustion was slowly pulling him under, winning the battle of wills. By their own volition, his eyelids began to droop, heavy with fatigue.

And then Abby wiggled her delectable ass, and murmured something in her sleep.

Instantly awake, Alex winced, as the most sensitive and unruly part of his anatomy sprung up with renewed hope.

The insatiable little tyrant.

Disregarding demands of his overzealous dick was not a willing choice on his part, but a necessity dictated by nature. He was whipped. Most important, Abby was totally drained, almost comatose. No way either of them were ready for an encore. Gingerly, Alex scooted away.

Abby's voice, barely audible and slurry, stopped him in midmotion, "What's that, baby?"

"Eli and Daisy...I wish...they were... here."

"So do I, Princess." Leaning forward, he placed a light kiss onto her shoulder. "So do I."

A delicate shudder preceded her quiet sigh. "The Coleman house..."

"What about it?"

"Decided to... gift it to... city. A... museum. D' you mind?"

"No, Princess. I don't. I think that's a terrific idea. Eli and Nika would approve."

But Abby no longer heard him. Even and relaxed, her breathing resumed its gentle cadence. Alex caressed her hair, then tucked one unruly strand behind her ear. A gleam of the wedding band on her ring finger caught his attention. Enormously pleased, Alex rubbed it with his thumb. A symbol of infinity. A promise, a pledge, and a bond.

Grinning like a fool, he flopped onto his back. He was a husband now. Holy cow!

And Abby was his wife. His princess, his timeless miracle. His everything.

Poor baby, she was totally worn out, dead to the world. Who knew that inside that elegant and proper façade lay a spirit of a true courtesan? Uninhibited, adventurous, ravenous. And wasn't he the luckiest son of a bitch on Earth?

Damn, but he was beat. Drowsy, Alex began to drift.

The Coleman house... A museum... Huh. I wonder what Eli's reaction would be...

A famous 'thunderation'? A sheepish expression? Boy, he wished he could see that...

If the Coleman house will become a public museum, what would happen to the portal? That sudden thought jolted him wide awake. Wracking his brain, Alex tried to find the answer.

Think, Alex, think.

The portal opened with the original key only. They key was in 1910. Without it, the Coleman grandfather clock won't work.

What about Verochka's *coaxing it to open with her verbal plea?*

An exception, a life and death emergency thing only, no doubt.

Dammit, if the clock won't work, then what?

Don't have to have a genius IQ to figure it out: the portal will be sealed.

That means Nika, Eli, and JC...will be forever in the last century. Shit.

Chilled to the bone, Alex let out a helpless little oath.

And then realization struck. They all were where they supposed to be, where each of them belonged, where they found love, and happiness, and purpose.

Fate, that fickle bitch, shuffled her deck of destiny cards, rearranging it according to the precautious game of Universe. And at the end, each of them landed at the right place in time. Nika and Eli, him and Abby, and even JC.

So, the Coleman grandfather clock had served its purpose, and showed them all that time indeed was irrelevant, and true love will endure, and overcome any obstacles.

Time is irrelevant. Love will endure.

An earth-shattering revelation, a universal wisdom that was forever etched onto their wedding rings. Purely subconscious decision on his part, that engraving.

Was he guided by heart, psyche, or fate? Alex shrugged mentally. Who knew?

And the portal? It was no longer needed. End of story.

But before that link between centuries was snapped forever, there was one last thing he wanted to accomplish. So what if his decision to place some pictures inside the back panel of the clock was irrational?

Irrational? How about totally, certifiably nuts?

Maybe, but, hey, if nobody was privy to his folly, there was nothing to be embarrassed about. So, later today he'll make a solo trip to the Coleman house for the last time. His only hope was that the old junker, that infamous grandfather clock, will cooperate without blasting him to hell first.

Chuckling, Alex looped his arm around Abby, drew her closer, and finally shut his eyes.

A faint, familiar *bong-bong* chased him all the way toward oblivion.

CHAPTER FIFTY

E li considered himself a courageous man. Some called him formidable, some—daring and brave. One newspaper article went as far as calling him a pillar of the community, and a fearless leader. If only they saw him now!

Thunderation. Fearless leader, my ass.

Until this morning, Eli was sure that nothing of this side of the grass was able to reduce him to a despicable state of a shaking, pathetic, pitiful coward.

Nothing that is, except a child birth.

As soon as Daisy's first contractions began, he lost his head. Petrified, he watched her, unable to comprehend a single word coming out of her mouth.

Dammit, he was supposed to be calm and supportive. But instead, he stood there in a stupor, mute and deaf, trembling from head to toe. Horrified.

Fully aware that his behavior was highly and unapologetically appalling, Eli was still powerless to rectify it. From a great distance, Daisy's shrilling voice reached his ears.

"What are you waiting for, Coleman? Send for the doctor, for goodness' sake! My water just broke!"

Dear Lord, something broke. Inside of her. What was it? She said water.

What water? Oh, hell, of course! The rapture of membranes of the amniotic sac. He read all about it in preparation for Daisy's labor. A lot of good that did to him now. Or her.

Thunderation.

As far as his feverish mind recalled, it means that the babe was coming.

Soon.

Dammit all to hell and back!

Snap out of it! Don't stand here like a moron!

He must move, he must do something. He was a man, for crying out loud.

And still Eli was unable to drag himself from the stupor that had befallen him.

Obviously disgusted with him, Daisy shouted on top of her lungs for Mrs. Smith.

Despite the early hour, their old housekeep burst into the bedroom in a matter of minutes. Quickly assessing the situation, she took command. The orders flew right and left: dispatch a phaeton for the doctor, fetch clean sheets and blankets, boil lots of water.

Boil water? Oh, God.

"Master Eli, better if you go away." Elbowing him aside, Mrs. Smith glared at him. "You are as pale as a virgin snow. God forbid, you'll pass out, and embarrass yourself."

Embarrassing himself was the last of his concerns. He must stay and help. Somehow. Anyhow.

And what can you do, you imbecile?

Eli sent an imploring look at Daisy, but his wife was absorbed in a task of removing her soiled nightgown, and totally ignored him. Mrs. Smith, bless her heart, calm as a pickled cucumber, murmured quiet encouragements.

Both of them looked resolute and composed, like they were preparing for a major battle. Well, he assumed the labor of a child *was* a battle indeed. *The* battle.

Or a torture.

Definitely for him. The memories of Mary, his first wife that died during childbirth, swarmed at him now like a swarm of buzzing, angry wasps. Suffocating, tormenting, punishing.

Dear God, please have mercy. Please help Daisy. I'm begging you.

And it didn't matter that, thanks to the extraordinary circumstance of fate, he knew that she survived, and the babe will be fine. It was a girl. He even knew his daughter's name, and who and when she will marry. But still.

Nothing mattered at this terrifying moment in time, not even his miraculous knowledge of the future.

"Well, sir? Why are you still here? Go, leave for goodness' sake." Frowning, Mrs. Smith shooed him out.

Eli was only too happy to oblige, even if it shamed him to no end. Without another prompting, he almost ran from the room.

The old family doctor arrived. He immediately hurried upstairs, but not before giving Eli a pitying look. "Don't get so distressed, Mr. Coleman. Your wife is a brave soul, and healthy as a horse. Everything will be alright. You'll meet your child in no time."

Not trusting his voice, Eli nodded.

And so, the torture of waiting began.

After one hour, his stupor finally dissipated, leaving him exasperated and annoyed. Why was it taking that long? What the hell was going on in that bedroom?

As another hour trickled by, Eli grew enraged. Thunderation. How long can it take to bring one tiny babe to life? What was that blasted doctor doing, twiddling his thumbs? Dammit all to hell and back, he should have sent for Doc Smith, Carnegie's trusted physician. Bad blood between them or not, Mister Thomas would never refuse his request, especially where Daisy was concerned.

Too late to dwell on it now.

Oh, hell, how much longer?

Belle, banished from the bedroom, followed his every step, moaning pitifully. God help him, Eli didn't care to pacify the poor dog. Stretched to the breaking point, quivering like an arrow on a bow, he was about to implode. Thunderation.

Another two excruciatingly long hours were spent pacing, cursing, and snarling at any poor soul who was foolish enough to approach Eli. JC got the worst of him. As the poor sap tried to make a joke, Eli silenced him by plowing a fist into his mouth. Dammit, now he turned into a raving violent lunatic!

Get a hold of yourself, Coleman.

His apology to Daisy's brother lack in sincerity, but Eli was beyond caring.

After another two hours passed without any result, he decided enough was enough.

Marching toward the staircase, cursing a blue streak, he was about to run up, as a strange, mewing sound stopped him dead in his tracks.

Petrified anew, Eli helplessly gazed around. A kitten? But they didn't have any cats in the house. What then? That tiny yowling sound increased in volume, and soon the loud, demanding caterwauling echoed all around.

Dear God, was it...?

Eli was running before his brain registered it.

The picture that greeted him inside the bedroom brought him to his knees.

Daisy, in the middle of the huge rumpled bed, pale, disheveled, but positively radiant, was holding a tiny bundle in her arms. Laughing and crying at the same time, she gazed at the squirming creature. His child.

Seemingly angry at the world, his newborn daughter was wailing for all she was worth, flying her tiny fists.

"Dear Lord in heaven..."

Hearing his voice, Daisy lifted her eyes. Dazzling, albeit a bit wobbly, her smile pierced his heart. Tears rolled freely down her face, but the expression on it was pure wonderment. Was it his imagination, or were her features somehow different? Softer, more beautiful, more...everything. Streaming sunrays turned her messy ringlets into a golden halo. Awash with secrets, Daisy's face reminded him of Rafael's Madonna, full of mystery and sacrament and power.

The face of a mother.

"Come meet your daughter, darling."

Even her voice changed. Deeper, mellower.

Shining like two amethysts, misted with tears, her enchanted eyes held him captive.

"Come, Eli, look at her."

At first, his feet refused to move. His throat was so tight, the mere act of swallowing became impossible. As a delayed reaction to his frightful ordeal, a cold sweat broke all over his body and left him trembling. Frozen in place, Eli gazed at mother and infant. His wife. His daughter. Both alive and well.

Thank you, God.

Weak with relief, still stunned by the enormity of the moment, he finally approached the bed, lowered his gaze to the newborn. Half-hidden in Daisy's arms, the babe continued its valiant effort to break free. All he saw was the tuft of pale hair, and a pair of a tiny flaying fists.

"Isn't she the most beautiful thing?"

Red in the face, flushed, and squalling furiously, the little tyke was anything but. To him, it barely resembled a human being. But if he voiced that seditious thought aloud, he undoubtedly will be banished from Daisy's graces forever.

Vastly disappointed, squirming inside from shame, Eli dragged his eyes to his wife.

Please, God, don't let her see my dismay.

No such luck. Chuckling, Daisy shook her head, sending her sunny curls dancing.

"She'll change quickly, Coleman. Do you think you looked any different at first?"

"Daisy, I..."

Suddenly, the babe stopped squealing. The ensued silence was almost shocking.

"See? She sensed her daddy. Didn't you, Button?"

The doctor, forgotten by everybody, cleared his throat.

"More than likely, she's hungry, Mrs. Coleman. You'd better try to feed her."

Eli recoiled. Dear God, she was just born, and already hungry? Thunderation.

Feed her? Does that mean...?

As an answer to his silent question, his wife, unmindful of the audience, quickly bared her breast, and guided the tiny mouth to it.

Oh, for goodness' sake!

Wincing, Eli averted his gaze. Heatwaves flooded his face and neck. Damn, he was blushing. Even his ears burned.

Thunderation.

As the enthusiastic suckling sounds reached his ears, Eli turned around. Despite his acute embarrassment, he let out a chuckle.

Greedy little thing.

Amused, he gazed at the funny creature laboring at her mother's breast. Something huge and warm moved inside of him, capturing his heart in a tight fist. An unfamiliar sensation gushed in, filled him to the brim. Shaking from the enormity of it, overwhelmed, Eli was unable to turn his eyes from the babe.

So tiny, so fragile and helpless, this little human was a vital part of him and Daisy. His legacy, his daughter. His Maggie.

Conceived in the twenty first century, born at the dawn of the twentieth, she was a true miracle. Love, unexpected, unrestricted, unimaginable, lay its ambush when Eli least expected it. It weakened him. It made him feel larger than life.

Unashamed of tears misting his eyes, he quietly approached the bed.

Mesmerized, he watched his child and his wife. His two timeless miracles. His priceless treasures. With a silent painful *ping*, Eli's heart broke in two.

It will never be the same again. *He* never will be the same again.

With the unsteady hands, Eli reached for the precious bundle.

Daisy sent him an uncertain glance, then reluctantly relinquished her hold on the babe. "Careful, darling. Mind her arms and legs."

For such a miniscule thing, she was surprisingly heavy.

Unblinking, his daughter's stare held him captive. Gentle lavender eyes were the exact shape as Daisy's. With a little time, the color will deepen to pure amethyst, just like her mother's. A featherlike mop the color of pale gold already sported a few curling tendrils. Unable to stop himself, Eli touched them with his finger.

So soft and silky, smooth like priceless velvet.

Enthralled, holding his breath, he continued his gentle explorations.

Barely visible, a tiny cleft adorned the center of her tender jawline. Seeing that unmistakable part of himself on his daughter's face, Eli's heart melted.

She might be the image of Daisy, but that dimpled chin was the Coleman family trait, through and through. Ridiculously pleased, he gazed at this amazing little miracle.

"Hello, Maggie. Hello, my precious."

Hearing his voice, the babe stilled completely. The intensity of her gaze was simply astonishing for such a tiny creature. Then his newborn daughter made a cooing noise, grabbed his finger, and stole his heart forever.

A sweet, poignant ache under his left breastbone left him breathless. An explosion of tenderness brought a sheen of tears to his eyes.

Lost. Reborn. Finally whole.

Not trusting his voice, Eli managed a wobbly smile.

"She loves you already." Leaning forward, Daisy touched his hand, linked their fingers over their daughter.

"And I love her right back. So much, that it hurts. Oh, Lord, Daisy, I love you both." With his heart bursting at the seams, Eli looked at Daisy. "Thank you, *ma petite*. For my daughter, for finding me. For everything."

Daisy's answering smile was bright enough to light the darkest night. Then she winked mischievously, and reminded him of a little street urchin he met long ago.

"I did a great job all around, if I say so myself. You helped, too, Coleman. Just a tad, mind you."

Even if his life depended on it, Eli couldn't prevent his laughter. Astonishingly, the deep booming sound of his merriment failed to disturb the babe. As if lulled by it, his daughter closed her tiny eyes, and in the next instant, was down for the count.

A short time later, when both mother and daughter were resting, Eli tiptoed out of the room.

There was one urgent matter he needed to finalize. Leaving the door half-closed, he strolled down the corridor, toward the hidden entrance to his office.

Inside his inner sanctum, Eli went to the fireplace shaped into a lion's mouth, and reached inside. When he drew back his hand, he held the little brass key in his palm. It began to pulse like a living heart. Unsurprised by it any longer, Eli closed his fingers around the small warm object. That done, he went to his desk, unlocked the hidden drawer, and removed two folded pages. All what was left to do was scribble the names onto the envelopes, and drop the letters inside.

One was addressed to Veronica Morris with the explicit order to be delivered on September 2019. He chose to use Daisy's real name so there was no mistake for who the letter was intended. Its cryptic message stated:

Find the key. You know where it is. Hurry, for goodness' sake!

The second was for Abigail Suzanne Coleman.

Be happy, my little Papillon.

That letter included the deed to his family house to be delivered at the completion of its restorations in 2020. And wasn't it amazing, that when his great-grandson, Senator Lauder, accomplished the mission, Eli was a witness to that event?

Talk about miracles.

Gazing at the letters in his hand, Eli marveled at the intricacies of fate. Both missives were penned a while ago, as soon as Daisy and he got back from the future. The deed to the house was executed just recently, drafted by his newly appointed attorney, JC Morris. Eli will give both letters to JC for safekeeping, but it was his daughter who later will execute his will. His Maggie, his confidant and trustee, will follow Eli's orders, and enable Daisy to jump through time. To find him.

But first things first.

Resolutely, Eli shut the desk drawer, locked it, and left his office.

On the first floor, he paused in front of the Coleman house sentry, the old and distinguished grandfather clock. Priceless object d'art, that English masterpiece circa 1827, guarded its miraculous secret for centuries. As the portal between times, it was instrumental in bringing Daisy to this time and place, and into his life.

And for that, Eli was eternally grateful.

"Thanks, old friend. I'm forever in your debt."

The clock's golden face shone enigmatically, as its pendulum swung side to side, lazy and unhurried. Not fooled by its appearance, Eli ran a caressing hand over the clock's mahogany case. Smooth, polished to a mirror gleam, warm to the touch. He'd bet his last cent that the clock was alive and alert.

"You know what I'm about to do, don't you? Please guard this key, until Daisy finds it in 2019. I know I can count on you."

A single melodious *bong* broke the silence. Surprised, Eli briefly looked at the clock's face. Its longer golden hand was poised at the number 3.

Fifteen minutes after the hour. Never happened before. Thunderation.

That meant only one thing: the chime was not an hour mark, but a confirmation.

If he ever needed proof that the old bastard was alive, he just received the ultimate one. Before inserting his hand between the clock's back and a wall, Eli gave it a small hand salutation. Reaching with his fingers, he groped blindly until he felt the little button that opened the hidden panel. As soon as the tiny mechanism sprung open, Eli placed the key inside, and was about to withdrew his hand, as something dry and firm brushed his fingertips.

Was there something inside?

Puzzled, he grabbed the mysterious object, and drew it out carefully.

Two small pieces of paper, solid and sturdy. What on earth...?

As Eli turned them over, his heart squeezed, then lurched, then began to thunder painfully against his ribcage.

Pictures!

The first one was an image of Abby, standing near the ocean, her smile tentative, her eyes a bit guarded. Thunderation, he knew that picture!

That was the very same one that Senator Lauder showed them, before giving Abby the keys and deed to the Coleman house.

Swallowing hard, Eli turned to the other photo. Abby and Alex, clad in the beautiful formal attire, both smiling, joyous and radiant.

The wedding.

In her long and elegant white gown, his sister was a sight from a fairy tale. His new brother-in-law, sporting a trim beard and a loopy grin, was an image of a stupidly happy man. Dear Lord, they were married! Abby was a wife now. His chest constricted with a combination of pleasure and sorrow.

Ah, Abby, my little Papillon. Just look at you, all radiant and joyous.

Healthy, positively glowing, she was gazing straight at the camera. Straight at *him*.

Fighting for composure, Eli traced her lovely image with his fingertip.

Be happy, Abby. I love you.

Then he switched his eyes at her grinning husband. Alex. His friend, his brother, his family. Draped around Abby's shoulder, Alex's hand suddenly drew his attention. Was there something in it? Squinting, Eli brought the small picture closer. Sure enough, dangling from his brother-in-law's fingers was a pocket watch. Made from solid gold, encrusted with gems, he'd recognize it even in his sleep. His father's heirloom timepiece.

A gift he left for Alex under the Christmas tree in 2020.

Eli chuckled. So, the bald devil had found it, alright, and wore it on his wedding day. Not only that, he deliberately demonstrated it for Eli in that photograph.

Pleased and moved and humbled all at once, he smiled through the mist in his eyes.

"Thank you, Alex. Thank you, my brother. Be happy, both of you."

It took him awhile to get a firm control over his emotions. But compose himself Eli did. Wiping the embarrassing moisture from his eyes, he turned to the staircase. He must show those precious images to Daisy. And if he had to wake her, so be it. He was sure Daisy wouldn't mind.

Eager to share his amazing discovery, Eli took two steps at a time, hurrying toward the bedroom. Already anticipating Daisy's reaction, he was about to step inside, as a familiar laughing voice reached his ears.

Farewell, Elijah Benjamin Coleman. Stay out of trouble. Until we meet again.

"Morris, you rascal." And grinning ear to ear, Eli executed a mocking bow.

Deep in his heart, he knew that his foolish gesture was seen, and welcomed.

As brilliant sun finally claimed its victory, a sonorous loud *bong-bong* of the old grandfather clock announced the new hour of the new day.

ACKNOWLEDGEMENTS

To come up with a story and write it down is easy. To make it into a book—now that's entirely different story.

The creative process is a lonely road, sometimes straight and smooth, often like a hike in the hills, but always solitary. And that's how it should be. But every road, no matter how long or hilly, comes to an end, and then...

...you realize that it's not the end— far from it! — but a crossroads, and you need to choose carefully where to turn, or how to proceed and not to get completely disoriented. You need help to choose the right path, a map to orient yourself, a guidance and a gentle nudge (or a mighty push) to start moving again. In short, you need other people. Then, the real adventure begins.

I've been truly blessed. Fate sent me Sloane Taylor, my editor, who very soon became my mentor and my guardian angel. When two years ago I embarked on the *Upon A Time* series adventure, she took me by my hand and dragged me to the right path, showing me the way. And all the time while I stumbled along the thorny path, she was walking behind me, cheering me on, whipping my tears, or kicking my behind. I've never had so much fun, or been so frustrated, in my life, but every second of it was worth it.

Thank you, Sloane Taylor, for sticking up and not giving up on me. Thank you for everything. This book, as the two previous of *Upon A Time* series, is as much yours as it is mine. Without you it wouldn't see the light of a day.

Special thanks to Rhonda K. Outler, Archivist with Amelia Island Museum of History, who graciously answered my questions.

My heartfelt thanks to Justine Alley Dawsett, who created such a beautiful cover.

And as always, my sincere gratitude to the men in my life, my husband Leo and my son George. Thank you for believing in me, guys.

Also by Stella May

Watch for more at www.StellaMayAuthor.com.

About the Author

Stella May is an author of the family saga/ trilogy Once & Forever, and romance-fantasy Rhapsody in Dreams. Love and family are two cornerstones of her stories.

When not writing, she enjoys classical music, reading, and long walks along the ocean.

She lives in Jacksonville, Florida with her husband Leo and son George, her two best friends and partners in family business.

Read more at www.StellaMayAuthor.com.